Married Men

Married Men

Carl Weber

Dafina BOOKS

KENSINGTON PUBLISHING CORP.

DAFINA BOOKS are published by

Kensington Publishing Corp.
850 Third Avenue
New York, NY 10022

Special book excerpts or customized printings can also be created to fit specific needs. For details, write or phone the office of the Kensington Special Sales Manager: Kensington Publishing Corp., 850 Third Avenue, New York, NY 10022. Attn. Special Sales Department. Phone: 1-800-221-2647.

Kensington and the K logo Reg. U.S. Pat. & TM Off.
Dafina Books and the Dafina logo are trademarks of Kensington Publishing Corp.

ISBN   0-7394-2011-9

Printed in the United States of America

*This book is dedicated to
Jeffery Dumpson, Walter Nixon, Albert Butler, Kevin Dwyer,
Bryant Murphy, Harold Gilliam, Travis Hunter,
and Tyrone Thompson—
the best group of friends a man could have.
Oh, and, of course, Martha*

Acknowledgments

First off, let me thank God for all the blessings He's bestowed on me this past year. Although there were some hard times, He alone made life worth living, and for that I give Him praise.

Thanks to all the kind and wonderful people who read *Lookin' for Luv.* Your letters and e-mails have touched my heart and you are the real reason why my book made the Blackboard and *Essence* magazine bestseller lists.

Special thanks to my readers; Ann Murphy, Crystal Burson, Kimberly Carrington, Linda Travis-Isbell, Jerri Lynn, Lauren Dixon, Brenda Cheese, Valerie Skinner, my sisters Maria and Teresa and of course, Antoinette Jorge. Your feedback has been instrumental in making this book what it is today. I'll be taking a bit of each of one of you for the characters in my next book, *Baby Mama Drama,* so don't be mad at me.

Before I thank anyone else I have to thank E. Lynn Harris and Eric Jerome Dickey for paving the way for brothers like myself. In an industry dominated by women authors you two have made it possible for us men to succeed.

Thanks to my fellow authors who came by my stores and encouraged me to write: Timm McCann, Terri Woods, Donna Hill, Marcus Major, Van Whitfield, Kim Roby, Donna Deberry and Virginia Grant, Mary Morrison, Gloria Mallette, Robert Flemming and Chandra Taylor.

Big thanks to my agent Marie Brown for keeping me grounded and focused on what's important.

Thanks to my editor Karen Thomas and the Kensington publishing family. You've made my publishing experience a true joy and I look forward to working with you for years to come.

Thanks to Peggy Hicks for a great job with publicity.

Thanks to Pamela Walker Williams for your patience and a great web site.

And, of course, I'd like to thank all of my customers at the African-

American Bookstore. You've been there from the beginning and your support has been truly appreciated.

If you like to get in touch with me please write or e-mail me at:

Carl Weber

P.O. Box 3045

Farmingdale, NY 11735

E-mail: *cmweb@earthlink.net*

Check my website: *carlweberonline.com*

Married Men

Prologue

It was a warm July day when the white stretch limousine pulled up to St. Mary's church on Fourteenth Street in the West Village of Manhattan. Jay Crawford stepped onto the sidewalk and looked up the steps to the gray stone front of the Roman Catholic church. Placing his designer shades on his head, Jay smiled at two college-aged women who were passing by, making them both blush. At an even six feet, Jay wasn't what most sisters would call good looking. No, he was fine, real fine, and when he walked into a room, everyone took notice. He was tall with smooth baby soft dark-skin and two of the cutest dimples you ever wanna see. He was the kind of man that made women of all races take a second look and it wasn't just his face. Jay's well-chiseled muscular body was by far his finest asset.

Jay turned to his friend Kyle, who was stepping out of the limo.

"Well, we're here. You sure you wanna go through with this?" He motioned toward the two women who were halfway down the block now, the sway of their hips still enticing, even from a distance. "Mmm, mmm, mmm, look at the ass on the one on the right."

Kyle, a short deep-chocolate brother with Caribbean features and a handsome smile, was visibly nervous about getting married. He didn't answer his friend, although he did turn his slim, muscular body in the direction of the woman, trying to appear nonchalant as he checked out her behind. Jay smirked as he busted his friend sneaking a peek. He and Kyle had both been ladies' men for years, and Jay was relieved to see he hadn't lost his friend completely, even on the day of his wedding. Jay was the only one of Kyle's friends who was upset about his upcoming marriage. As far as he was concerned, he was losing his partner in crime.

"Cut that shit out, Jay! You know he's gonna go through with it." Wil Duncan, a thick, light-skinned man with a round, shaved head chastised Jay as he stepped out of the limo. Wil was almost six feet tall himself, and damn near twice the size of Jay. He was Kyle's best man, and clearly in favor of his friend getting married.

Wil smiled as he stood in front of his friend and straightened his tie. "You aw'ight, Kyle?"

"Yeah, I'm cool." Kyle nodded, breaking his nervous trance. He turned to see what was keeping his third friend, Allen, who had yet to step out of the limo. "Al, what the hell are you doin' in there?"

Allen Jackson, a slim, cocoa-colored man with a narrow face and a fade haircut, stepped out of the limo with a bottle of champagne and a glass. He poured himself some champagne as his eyes traveled from Wil, to Jay, to Kyle.

"Why y'all staring at me like that? You didn't think I was gonna let a good bottle of champagne go to waste, did you?" He sipped contentedly. "Ahhhh!"

"Put the damn champagne back in the limo." Kyle slapped Allen in the back of the head. "You can be so stupid sometimes, Al. Can't you see we're going into a church?"

Allen guzzled down what was left in his glass and handed the bottle to the driver. "Yo, chief, keep this cold for me."

The driver nodded his head as he closed the car door.

Turning his attention to the church steps he was about to ascend, Kyle sighed. His insides were churning with nervous energy. Marriage was a big step, and he hadn't slept a wink all night thinking about it. He wondered how anyone ever knew if they were truly making the right choice. He was in love with Lisa, there was no question about that. But would that be enough to make their marriage last?

He was the first of his friends to get married. Maybe it would have been more comforting if one of them had gone before him and shown him that it can work. He glanced at Wil, who was getting married himself in a year, and then at Jay, who had sworn he would never commit to marriage. This was the moment of truth. He had to either climb the stairs to the church, or turn around and get in the limo to ride out of the life of the woman he loved.

"Well, guys," he finally announced with confidence, "let's go get me married."

Jay put his hand in front of Kyle, blocking him on the first step. "You can still back out if you wanna. We could jump in that limo and be in Atlantic City in two hours."

"As tempting as that might be right now Jay, I'm gonna have to pass." Kyle pushed Jay's hand out of his way. "I know you don't understand what Lisa and I have. That's because you've never been in love before. All I can tell you is that I can't see living my life without her."

"Aw'ight, man, I ain't no playa-hater. Hell, I'm a participator. I just hope you know what you doin'."

"So do I. Now get out of my way before I change my mind." Kyle laughed as he walked up the stairs to the church.

"Kyle," Jay called to him.

"Yeah?" Kyle turned toward his friend.

"I'm happy for you, brotha. I don't know why, but I'm happy for you." Jay smiled.

Kyle nodded and headed to the church entrance. When he rang the rectory bell, Father Smith soon greeted him and his friends.

"Well, I see you didn't get cold feet," Father Smith laughed as he led them down a small, narrow hallway into an equally tiny room. "You boys have a seat. We've got some time before we're gonna get started."

Kyle and Allen sat on the only two chairs in the room. Jay and Wil leaned against a table, facing their nearly wedded friend, who still had "nervous" written all over his face.

"Ya know, Kyle, I'm happy for you, bro," Wil said with folded arms. "Lisa's a good woman, and she really loves you, man."

"Thanks, Wil. That means a lot coming from you." Kyle had always respected the advice of Wil, who was usually the most level-headed of the group.

"I feel sorry for your partner in crime over there." Allen joined their conversation, gesturing toward Jay. "You gonna be aw'ight chasin' women by yourself, Jay?"

"Man, I been runnin' solo ever since he met Lisa's ass. The boy's pussy whipped!" Jay sucked his teeth.

"Come on, Jay, we in church, man." Kyle shot him a dirty look.

"So you guys gonna try ta have kids right away or what?" Wil changed the subject.

Kyle grinned. "The minute we get on that cruise, I'm tossing her diaphragm overboard." They all laughed. Even Jay couldn't help but smile at the thought of a Kyle, Junior, running around.

"Ya know the one thing I want when I get married? I want all of our kids to be close like we are," Jay said.

"Amen to that," Kyle agreed.

"I still can't believe you're getting married," Allen said sadly.

"Damn, Al! You act like I'm dying or somethin'."

Jay laughed at that one.

"Nah, it's not like that. I just never imagined you or Jay settling down."

"That's true. I never thought either of you would get married," Wil agreed.

"Hey, man, I'm twenty-seven. I can't be a player all my life," Kyle reasoned.

"Speak for yourself," Jay stepped away from the table and puffed out his chest. "I'ma be a player till I die."

"Truth is, I shoulda been the first one to get married." Allen had a distant look in his eyes. "I shoulda married Cinnamon when I had the chance."

"Yeah, you shoulda," Wil stated matter-of-factly.

"She wasn't gonna marry ya ass, Al." Kyle stood and started pacing.

"Why the hell not?" Allen asked.

"'Cause your ass ain't got no job, that's why." Kyle laughed, stopping in front of Allen. "Who the hell's gonna marry a brotha with no job?"

"I can get a job anytime I want to."

"Yeah, right!" Jay laughed. "Last job you had was two years ago, and you quit two months later."

"That's 'cause school was about to start again," Allen protested.

Wil sat down next to Allen and faced him. "Allen, you been going to school eight years. When the hell you gonna get a degree?"

They all burst out laughing at that one.

Allen lowered his head. He knew his friends were joking, but he wished he had an answer for them.

"Ahem!" Father Smith interrupted them. "The bride's just pulled up to the church."

"Okay, Father Smith," Kyle nodded, "can we just have a minute?"

"Sure, son." The priest walked out, closing the door behind him.

Kyle placed one arm around Allen and the other around Jay. Jay put his arm around Wil, and the four friends pulled together into a tight circle. They were silent for a moment until Kyle spoke to his life-long buddies.

"I want you all to know I love you. We've been best friends since the fifth grade and better friends a man has never had. You three have always been there for me, and I wanna thank you for that. Lisa may have my heart, but it's you guys that built it. I love you."

"We love you too, Kyle," Jay said for the three of them. "Come on. It's time to go get you a wife."

Seven years later

1

Kyle

My wife Lisa pulled our Ford Windstar minivan in front of the Jamaica train station and leaned toward me for a kiss. The scent of her White Diamonds perfume reminded me of the incredible night of passion we'd shared last night. Lisa had started the night by seducing me with a black Victoria's Secret negligee with a matching thong that would have made a gay man straight. She knows how much it turns me on to see her in some lingerie, and last night not only was she wearing the hell out of that see-through number, she was an animal in the bed.

We didn't have that usual don't-make-any-noise-so-the-kids-won't-hear-us sex. Nooo, not by a long shot. Last night was one of those pre-kids nights. The kind of night when neither of us cares about who's listening. Things got so out of hand, round two wasn't a possibility but a necessity. That was the kind of night that reminded me why I fell in love with her in the first place. Not the sex, but the passion and desire we had for each other.

Just remembering the night's passion was starting to make my nature rise as we sat in the minivan with our kids in the back seat. I was supposed to be getting on a train to meet my boys for the first game of the over-thirty basketball league. But I swear, if this game wasn't so important to Jay, I would have had Lisa turn the van around, stop at Blockbuster for a video for the kids, and tried my best to reenact every damn minute of the night before. Of course, I knew I couldn't because the last thing I wanted to do was listen to Jay's mouth about how I let him down. After twenty-five years of friendship, I knew him well enough to know that he would never let me forget it if I missed the game.

I shook the memory of passion out of my mind and turned my attention to the back seat, where my three daughters sat smiling at me.

"Bye, girls, I love you." I smiled.

"Bye, Daddiiee!" they replied in unison, blowing kisses to me.

"I'll call you later, Hun." I kissed my wife again.

"Do you want me to pick you up tonight, Kyle?"

"Naw, it's aw'ight. Allen's going to Rose's tonight. I'll catch a ride with him."

"Okay, babe. I love you." Lisa smiled.

"I love you too." I smiled back, stepping out of the van.

"Kyle!"

"Yeah, hun?" I turned and spoke to her through the open window of the passenger side.

"Last night was wonderful. Let's do it again tonight," she winked.

I smiled as she pulled off. I didn't tell her often enough, but I really loved my wife. It was times like these that reminded me just how much.

As I watched Lisa pull away in the van, I thought about our life together. I'd fallen for her the day we'd met eight years ago, and she'd made me the happiest man in the world when she agreed to marry me a year later. We'd struggled the first few years when I maxed out the credit cards and used all our savings to buy a struggling African-American beauty supply business. The bill collectors were calling on practically a daily basis, harassing her whenever she answered the phone. Lisa had actually packed her bags to leave me, the stress had been so bad at one point. The truth is, if it wasn't for our first daughter, I would have let her go. Our relationship was so strained because of money, there were more than a few nights I didn't want to come home. I didn't want to face the dirty looks and the arguing. She just didn't get it. We were going to have to struggle a little in the beginning if we were going to have a successful business. Lisa didn't seem willing to struggle with me, and at times I resented it. To be honest, I didn't think our marriage was going to last.

But slowly and surely I turned the business into a successful chain, moving us out of our tiny Rochdale Village apartment and into a huge, five-bedroom house in the exclusive Jamaica Estates area of Queens. I'll never forget the look on Lisa's face as we lay together in our Jacuzzi bathtub the first night in our new home. It was the first time she'd looked truly happy in years. Not that my wife was a materialistic person, but a $500,000 house will do that to you after you've lived in fear of not making the rent every month. The day we moved into our own house was the day my life went back to normal and my wife became my wife again.

I checked my watch as I walked up the stairs to the Long Island Railroad. It was only 10 A.M. I had plenty of time before my train, so I took out my basketball from my duffel bag and practiced dribbling on the platform. I was on my way to Chelsea Piers in Manhattan where my friends and I would whup some ass on the basketball court against another team trying to recapture their youth.

I wasn't a great basketball player, like my friends Jay or Wil, or even good like Allen. The truth is, I couldn't shoot worth shit. Jay had threatened to kick my ass if I took a shot this year, but that didn't stop him from wanting me on the team. Especially since I was the most unselfish player in the group. Combine that with the fact that I could dribble and pass with the best of them, and I made the perfect point guard.

As I practiced on the empty platform, someone slammed into me from behind, knocking me to the ground.

"What the fuck!" I yelled as I watched my ball roll off the platform and onto the tracks. As I gathered my senses, I saw this tall, light-skinned teenager scrambling to his feet. That son of bitch didn't say sorry, excuse me, or nothin'. He just took off down the platform.

I was pissed! I'd just bought that damn ball, but there was no way I was going to jump down on those tracks to retrieve it. The train was due any minute. I looked down the platform and saw that the kid was still running. What the hell, I thought, struggling to my feet to give chase. I'd been a track star in high school and college so I caught up to him pretty fast, but before I could get my hands on him, my body reminded me I wasn't a kid anymore. I was thirty-six years old, way past my athletic prime and about to pull a hamstring. I slowed down and watched the kid take off.

"Damn, damn, damn!" I watched him getting away as I hunched over and struggled to catch my breath. It's probably a good thing I didn't catch him. What was I gonna do, make him go get my ball? Besides, these young brotha's are crazy. For all I knew, he was packin' a gun.

Dusting off my sweatsuit, I went to get my bag, hoping it would still be there. I'd been the only person on the platform, but with the way my luck was going, anyone could've walked up and snatched it by now. Plus, I still wanted my damn ball back. I walked to the edge of the platform, and there it was, in plain sight, right by the third rail. I considered jumping down there to get it, but I'd never outrun a train with a pulled hamstring. I stepped back and was startled by a loud voice behind me.

"*Freeze, police!*"

I turned my head quickly. I'd be lying if I didn't say I was shocked to see two police officers pointing their guns at me.

"*I said, freeze!*" one of them screamed.

I didn't move, I didn't blink, and I tried not to breathe. The last thing I wanted was to become another statistic. Amadou Diallo and every other brother who'd been wrongfully shot by cops taught me that lesson. I was just glad I had told my wife and kids that I loved them before they left, because you never know what could go wrong when cops have guns drawn. Especially in New York City. I was scared to death.

"Officer, I'm gonna put my hands in the air. Please, please, don't shoot me! I got a family." I raised my hands slowly over my head.

"Lock your fingers behind your head!"

I did what I was told and thanked God when one of the cops let down his gun. He twisted my hands behind my back and handcuffed me. Even though I was handcuffed, I let out a long sigh of relief. Now I could get things straight and find out what was going on without worrying about a trigger-happy cop.

"What did I do, Officer?" I asked, trying my best to be respectful. I kept telling myself the cops were only doing their job and this must be a big misunderstanding.

"Stop acting stupid," one officer said, slapping me in the back of the head.

"Hey! What the hell'd you do that for?" I protested as I turned toward him.

"Shet-the-fuck-up," the other cop snarled, slapping me in the same place.

"That old lady's gonna be in the hospital a long time," his partner said.

"Hospital? Old lady? What're you talking about?"

The cops obviously didn't wanna hear anything. Maybe cleaning up this misunderstanding would be harder than I thought. A small crowd gathered round as the officers frisked me roughly. And it was just my luck that three women who frequented my Jamaica beauty supply store were among the onlookers. I'd never been so embarrassed in my life.

"What'd he do?" one of the women asked the sergeant, who was pushing his way through the crowd. I was happy to see the sergeant was a brother. Finally someone who would listen to my side of the story. He was an officer, but I figured every black man alive could relate to the whole mistaken identity thing.

"He smashed a lady's head in with a baseball bat over at the ATM on Archer Ave," the sergeant explained to the woman with a look of disgust on his face.

"Oh, my God!" The woman stared at me as her friend dragged her away.

The sergeant stood in front of me. His face was so close I could smell the cigarette he'd been smoking earlier. "Ya know its niggas like you that give our people a bad name," he whispered. So much for my hope. But I pleaded with him anyway.

"Sergeant, I didn't hit no woman with a baseball bat." My voice cracked. "If ya just let me ex—"

"You're full-a-shit," he interrupted, purposely spitting as he talked. "Before she passed out, that woman said it was a black man in a red sweatsuit. Then she pointed toward the train station. You the only one I see wearing a red sweatsuit at this train station." He made a show of gesturing toward the crowd, pretending to search for more red-clothed black men.

"Look, this young boy was runnin' through here about . . ." I tried to explain, hoping somehow to reach this brother through all his super-cop arrogance.

"*Sarge!*" My explanation was interrupted again, this time by one of the officers who had been searching my duffel bag.

"He's got three hundred bucks in his bag, Sarge. Crisp bills, like they came out of a bank machine. Plus, when we cuffed him, he was sweating all over like he'd been running."

"Read this son of a bitch his rights, Mike." The sergeant growled. He didn't even look in my direction as he strutted toward his car. I decided to try one last time to find some human compassion in this cop.

"But, but, I didn't do it. You gotta listen to me!" I practically begged. "I got that money from my account."

The sergeant spun around angrily. "Lemme give you some advice. One of your rights is the right to remain silent. Use it."

I watched the sergeant's eyes get smaller. That's when I realized I was in trouble, real big trouble. I decided to take the sergeant's advice, remembering a time I'd heard Johnnie Cochran speaking to a group of black youth on television. When you're arrested, never talk to the police. Always demand a lawyer.

The officer read me my rights and shoved me into the squad car.

"Now that you know your rights, would like to tell us why you robbed that old lady?" The officer finally asked without even looking at me.

I had tears in my eyes and was struggling to hold them back.

"Look, for the last time, I didn't rob that old lady." Being respectful had gotten me nowhere. "And I ain't sayin' shit till I have a lawyer."

"Suit yourself." The officer shook his head.

The rest of the trip to the station was in silence, save for the occasional squawk of their police radio. The lack of conversation left me with ample opportunity to worry about how the hell I would get myself out of this nightmare.

2

Allen

The look on Jay's face was frightening as he stared Malcolm down on the basketball court, and I kept waiting for one of them to snap and go off on the other one. Don't get me wrong. I knew Jay had a quick temper, but for the most part he kept it under control. But for some reason he and my cousin Malcolm hadn't gotten along since junior high school. They'd had at least five knock-down drag-out fights when we were kids, and a few more as grown men. And Jay looked like he was trying to provoke another one by talking shit as he hit shot after shot on the court.

I'd asked Malcolm to join our team when Jay's older brother Dump told us he wouldn't be able to play after the first game. He was moving to Atlanta. Malcolm had just moved back from San Francisco and I figured that it was time to put this petty squabbling between him and Jay to rest. Besides, I knew Malcolm was a decent player, and we needed all the help we could get.

I knew Jay was gonna have a problem having Malcolm on the team, and he protested the minute I opened my mouth to suggest it. But I'd already talked to Wil and Kyle, hoping to defuse the situation. Jay tried to bully me as usual, saying there was no way he would play on the same court as that uncoordinated fool. But Kyle intervened before the discussion got out of hand. He pulled Jay to the side for a little talk, and when they returned, Jay was cool. Now it looked like Jay had just delayed all of his aggression until they were actually on the court together.

During their one-on-one, Jay played hard, and pretty much dominated the court. Finally, Malcolm got the ball and drove to the basket. He was about to finger-roll the ball like he was George "the Iceman" Gervin when Jay seemed to fly out of nowhere.

"Get that shit outta here!" he screamed, slapping Malcolm's shot away from the basket.

I could hear a chorus of ooo's and ahh's from the small crowd that had gathered around during our warm-up. Malcolm's handsome high yellow face was now a hardened crimson red from the embarrassment.

I felt kinda bad for him, but he was the one who had challenged Jay to the game of one-on-one. I tried to tell him Jay was one of the best players in the league, but he had to prove a point. Jay gave Malcolm a little shove with his hip and ran to the ball. He dribbled between his legs, laughing all the way to the basket, where he slam-dunked the ball.

"Game, mothafucker!" he said confidently, throwing the ball hard at Malcolm, barely missing his face. I wasn't sure if Jay had done it on purpose or not, but the look on Malcolm's face said he took it personally.

"Ay, what the fuck is yer problem?" Malcolm took a few steps closer, clenching both fists.

"What! What! You got a problem? I'll kick your pretty ass." Jay lifted his fist as an invitation to fight.

"Uh-oh," I muttered. I was wondering if their little game was gonna come to this. Keeping the peace between these two was going to be harder than I imagined. I glanced up at the bleachers, hoping Wil would come down to help, but he had his ear glued to his cell phone. He was probably talking to his wife Diane. I loved Wil to death, but since he got married, he'd been one henpecked brother.

"Jay, man, why don't you just chill out? Malcolm's on our team." I stepped in between them and turned my attention to Malcolm. "You need to chill, too. He was just trying to pass you the ball."

"Fuck that punk," Jay grunted, turning to walk away.

"No, fuck you, faggot!" Malcolm returned the insult.

"What'd you call me?" Jay screamed, damn near jumping over me. Thank God his brother Dump grabbed him, 'cause he was out of control.

"You heard me, faggot," Malcolm smirked.

I turned to Malcolm. "If you wanna play with us, you need to chill out. I told you before. This is Jay's team. He's the captain."

"I don't give a shit whose team it is. Next time that faggot hits me with the fucking ball, I'ma smack the shit out 'im," Malcolm threatened, ignoring my warning. I guess he must have felt safe with Dump holding Jay, 'cause on a bad day, Jay'd kick his ass without much effort.

"Lemme go, Dump!" Jay struggled like a madman to get out of his brother's grasp.

"Yeah, let 'im go, Dump," Malcolm demanded taking a few steps closer.

"You sure you want him to do that?" I asked Malcolm. "'Cause I'll tell Dump to let 'im go."

Malcolm looked me in the eyes, probably wondering if I was serious. He must have been considering his options, 'cause he stood silently and glared at us for a few seconds before he finally sucked his teeth and turned to walk away. He knew he didn't wanna mess with Jay. Last time he and Jay got in a fight was five years ago, and poor Malcolm got his ass kicked. He never even threw a punch.

After Malcolm walked away, I pulled Jay to the side, trying to take his mind off the confrontation. I would deal with patching up their latest squabble later, when my friend was a little calmer, and a little less likely to hit anyone. "Jay, man, where the hell is Kyle? The game's gonna start in ten minutes."

"I thought Wil was talkin' to him on the phone. He shoulda been here." Jay was still watching Malcolm walk across the court while he spoke.

We walked up the bleachers to talk to Wil, who was frowning as he hung up his cell phone.

"Yo, Wil, what's up with Kyle?" Jay asked, as we sat beside our friend.

"I don't know," Wil shrugged. "Lisa said she dropped him at the train two hours ago."

"Get that nigga on his cell phone," Jay demanded.

"Already tried. No answer."

"Damn! I'm tellin' y'all, Kyle's up to somethin'. He always answers his cell. He's probably knee deep in some booty right about now."

"Not everybody's like you, Jay," Wil scoffed. "Besides, Kyle wouldn't miss a game."

Jay smiled at me. "Yo, Allen, tell 'im about that fine-ass nurse you and Kyle met last week. Didn't she give Kyle her number?"

"Please! She wasn't all that. Kyle was just tryin' ta be nice 'cause she was buying a whole lot of hair at his shop," I told him.

Like Jay, Kyle always had women trying to hit on him. He didn't have those pretty-boy looks like Jay. He wasn't bad looking, but he definitely wasn't one of those light-skinned pretty boys. You'd be surprised how many fine women would try to seduce that brother. They'd come into his shop, figure out that the friendly brother behind the counter was actually the owner of the business, and they'd practically offer to give him the goods right then and there. It didn't matter if he told them he was married. That little bit of information never even slowed their game. For some of them, it just made them play a little harder. And with the problems he and Lisa went through a few years back, even I'm surprised Kyle remained faithful.

Jay, on the other hand, was a totally different story. He didn't know what faithful was. I can't remember him ever walking out of a bar alone.

"Trust me, Jay, a brother like Kyle doesn't just disappear without a good reason." Wil knew, like I did, that Kyle wasn't one to mess around on his wife. He sounded worried. "Look, after the game I think we better try and track Kyle down. If he is on a booty call, we better get our stories straight before Lisa finds out. 'Cause you know she's gonna ask fifty million questions." Jay and I nodded our agreement.

"Damn! That means we gotta play with Malcolm a week earlier," Jay complained. "Shit! With him playin' we gonna lose for sure." Jay hated losing more than anything.

"Don't worry, bro. If we lose, I got the first round tonight," I told him, patting his back.

"If we lose, I'ma kick Kyle's black ass," Jay responded, " 'cause this is all his fault." The three of us headed toward the game court, a little worried about the game and seriously worried about Kyle.

We'd won the game, with a last-second steal by Malcolm, who passed the ball to Jay for an easy lay-up. Thank God for small favors, 'cause Malcolm had played terribly until then. Jay had been yelling at him all game and they came close to blows during a time-out.

Our excitement over our victory was short-lived, 'cause as soon as we headed out to celebrate, we got some really bad news. Kyle's wife Lisa called Wil on his cell and dropped the news that Kyle had been arrested for attempted murder. Now, you'd have to know Kyle to understand this, but there's no way in the world he'd try to kill someone. That is, unless Jay was there. It's really weird, but the two of them feed off each other. You could be around Kyle, and he'd be the calmest person in the world. But if Jay walked into the room, it wouldn't take much for him to pump Kyle up or vice versa. Without Jay, Kyle was a pussycat, so none of us could believe the charges against him.

Jay took the news pretty hard. He'd even suggested putting up his house in Jersey to bail Kyle out, but Wil told him Kyle wouldn't have bail until he saw the judge Monday morning. Jay flipped out. He literally tore apart the men's room in Penn Station. He and Kyle were always real tight, and he didn't want to hear that his man would be spending the weekend locked up.

As for Kyle and me, we had an interesting relationship. He was my man and the whole nine, but up until recently I hated the fact that I was always on the wrong end of his jokes. Now, he's a funny guy, and always in a good mood. The only problem was, he could take things too far sometimes. He didn't really mean anything by it, but I'm not gonna lie. Sometimes it hurt. Especially when it was in front of my mother or my girl Rose. At one point I'd told Wil if Kyle joked about me being a super-super senior one more time in front of Ma or Rose, I was gonna punch him in the mouth. Now that I've got my degree and a good job, I'm glad I didn't.

About three years ago, I graduated college and started working at Nickelodeon. That's when I noticed the jokes had stopped. Then one day out of the blue, Kyle stopped by my job. I'd just been promoted to assistant department head of one of the Human Resource departments. Kyle walked into my office and sat down with a big grin on his face. Before I could say anything, he handed me a small package and said, "I know I never told you this, but I'm really proud of you. You've come a long way in the last two years, and I didn't want you to think it went unnoticed."

Man, when he left my office I had tears in my eyes. I never realized how important having his approval was 'til then. But that's when I started to understand who he was and why he was joking me about not going to school or having a job. The guy loved me, and he was just showing me tough love. As embarrassing as it was to be on the receiving end of his jokes, it was probably what drove me to finally finish school.

It was pretty late when I stumbled up the steps to my girlfriend Rose's apartment. I was tired and a little tipsy from having a few drinks with Jay and Wil after the game, but I was hoping she'd still be up. We hadn't been intimate in two weeks, and I was definitely in the mood. Maybe a quickie would help me forget that Kyle was in jail. 'Cause the truth is, I was more than a little worried about him.

Unlocking the door to Rose's apartment with my key, I tried to enter quietly but was startled by Rose's loud voice.

"Where the hell have you been?" she shouted, pushing her reddish brown hair out of her beige freckled face. "Do you know what time it is?"

"I, I, was with Jay and Wil," I stammered. "We went out to have a few drinks."

"Well, I hope you got some ass from Jay, 'cause ya damn sure ain't gettin' none from me." She got up with an attitude and walked to her bedroom.

"Damn!" I mumbled, glancing at my watch.

What the hell was she trippin' about? I'd told her I'd be over around eleven, and it was only twelve past. Shaking my head, I placed my gym bag on the sofa, hoping I wasn't going to be sleeping on it. The last thing I wanted was for Rose to be in one of her moods. Her moods always led to arguments, and I hated arguing. For a split second I contemplated walking out before the fireworks started, but leaving wouldn't solve anything. It probably would have caused another argument. Better to just stick around and face the music.

I followed her into her bedroom, where she made a point of taking off her robe as slowly and seductively as she could, all the while refusing to look me in the eyes. Damn, even angry she was fine. Rose was tall with a thin waist and a shapely body, and believe me, she knew how to use it. Her naked flesh made my manhood spring to attention. Sitting on the bed, she cracked a smile when she saw the large lump in my pants. I exhaled softly, relieved. She was only teasing me. She was completely naked under her robe, which meant she was going to give me some tonight. Rose always wore nightgowns to bed unless she was gonna give me some. The only real question was how much was it gonna cost me.

I hated the idea that Rose always asked me for money when we were about to make love and it really pissed me off that she would hold out on me until I gave it to her. But I loved her. She'd been by my side back when I was unemployed and going through some pretty rough times. I planned on marrying her someday so eventually my money was gonna be hers anyway. At least that's what I kept telling myself. I just wished I could get my boys to understand that. I really didn't appreciate how they had labeled her a gold digger. I was sick of hearing them tell me how I was being played. Shit, they were married and kicked out way more loot to their wives than I ever gave to Rose.

"Did you get paid on Friday?" Rose tried to make the question sound innocent.

"Yeah, why?"

"Fifty-eight dollars' worth of long-distance phone calls, that's why. Damn, can't your boy Jay call you sometimes?"

Jay lived in New Jersey, right over the George Washington Bridge. He wasn't far by car, but it was still a long-distance call. So I didn't answer Rose. I just reached in my pocket and pulled out my wallet. She knew that Jay called me as much, if not more, than I called him, but she'd been trying to drive a wedge between my friends and me for years. And although I didn't think my friends took their oath seriously anymore, we had all pledged as kids that no woman would ever come between us.

"Oh, and another thing. Why the hell does your mother keep calling my fucking house collect?" Rose picked up the phone bill from her dresser and read it out loud. "Thirty collect calls last month. I know that's your mother, Allen, but she lives five fucking minutes away. It's a local call, for Christ's sake! You need to talk to her. She's becoming a real pain in the ass."

All I could do was look at her and shrug my shoulders. I knew my mother was a pain in the ass. Hell, so was Rose. But I wasn't about to confront her. No way, not me, not Allen, not in this lifetime. She'd kick my ass. Even though I was thirty-six years old, my mother would still threaten me with a beatin' whenever she felt the need. My problem was that I'd lived in Ma's house so long that I never established an adult relationship with her. So she treated me like a child. For years I'd tried to talk to her about it, but she'd just start screamin' and cussin' every time I brought it up. After a while, I stopped bringing it up. All I wanted was for everyone to be happy and enjoy life like I did. Truth is, I'd do anything to avoid a fight.

"How much did the calls come to?" I asked.

"Sixty-five dollars. This shit is ridiculous!" Rose placed her hand on her hip as I opened my wallet.

"And don't forget the long-distance calls, either."

I handed her three fifty-dollar bills without a word. I was positive she was lying about the amounts, but it wasn't worth the argument.

"See, you could be putting this money down on my ring." She huffed loudly, grabbing hold of my shirt. "Allen, do you love me?"

"You know I do, baby." I wrapped my arms around her waist, looking for a sign that it was all right to kiss her.

"Then how come you haven't asked me to marry you?" She lowered her head and batted her eyelashes. "All your friends are married. What makes their women more deserving than me?"

"No one's more deserving than you, Rose." I stroked her hair gently. "All my life I've been a fuck-up. I'm thirty-six years old now. It took me 'til I was thirty-three to get my shit together and get a real job. I just wanna make sure I can take care of myself before I start tryin' ta take care of someone else. I promise you you're gonna get your ring. I just need a little more time."

"I'm gonna hold you to that." She kissed me softly.

"You do that."

"Can I have some money to get my hair and nails done?" She kissed my neck, running her tongue all the way up to my ear. She slowly unbuttoned my shirt, kissing her way down past my nipples, stopping at my belly button.

"Mmm, that's the spot," I whispered. "Keep going."

If there was one thing Rose knew how to do, it was please a man.

And if there was one thing I wanted at that particular moment, it was for her to please me, and I was willing to pay for her hair and nails to get it done.

"W-Will a hundred do it?" I asked as she massaged my manhood through my pants. Somehow I pulled out two more fifties from my wallet.

"Thank you," she said, slowly unhooking my belt buckle.

Rose shoved my arm off her chest when the phone rang. I could hear her fumbling on the nightstand trying to find the receiver in the dark. I probably should have got up and answered the phone myself. I'd just been lying there with my eyes closed. I hadn't been able to sleep at all. I kept dreaming about Kyle being in prison and some big guy named Bubba chasing him.

"Hello?" Rose answered groggily, but was wide awake within seconds. "Damn it!" she shouted in my ear as she tapped the phone against my head. Pain shot through my skull, and I sprung up like a disoriented jack-in-the-box.

"Your mother's on the phone." She shoved the phone at me angrily.

"Hello," I sighed.

"We have a collect call from Mrs. Audrey Jackson, will you pay?"

"Yes, operator, I'll pay."

"You damn right you're gonna pay." Rose switched on the light and glared at me.

"Ma, what's wrong?"

"I can't find my blood pressure medicine."

"It's in the medicine cabinet," I said automatically. This wasn't the first time this had happened. My mother was looking for attention.

"No it ain't, I just looked in there," Ma insisted.

"What time is it, Ma?"

Rose shoved the digital clock in my face. Shit! I didn't realize it was that late.

"Ma, it's three in the morning. You don't have to take your medicine till nine o'clock."

"You don't think I know that? My feet been swellin' so bad I thought I'd take it early."

"Look, Ma, the blood pressure medicine is in the medicine cabinet, okay?"

"Allen Hershel Jackson, didn't I tell you the damn blood pressure medicine wasn't there?" Ma's voice was so loud Rose could hear each syllable clearly, and let me know it by rolling her eyes.

"Yes, Ma, you did tell me," I mumbled.

"Now you get your black ass out of that damn bed, and come home and help me find it!!"

"Yes, Ma."

"I know you're not going home," Rose huffed as I hung up the phone.

I pulled the covers back and sat on the edge of the bed, rubbing my eyes. I didn't even look at Rose, 'cause I already knew she had her arms folded and her lip poked out. I was in a Catch 22. If I stayed with Rose, Ma would probably call an ambulance and go to the hospital just to make me feel like I'd neglected her. And if I went home to Ma, it would probably cost me another hundred to keep Rose's trap shut. I decided Rose could probably use a new pair of shoes or earrings.

"Allen, I asked you a question. Are you going home?"

I just nodded.

"You know she's just doing this for attention, don't you?"

I nodded again, then stood up and gathered my clothes.

"Let me tell you somethin', Allen! I'm sick of your mother interfering with our quality time. It's bad enough you live with her." Rose sucked her teeth.

"That's my mother, Rose. She needs me to take care of her." I put on my pants calmly.

"You ever think about putting that old lady in a home?"

I spun around, glaring at her with my teeth clenched. "Don't even go there."

Rose jumped back as if I'd scared her. She'd rarely seen this side of me, so I think she figured she better back off a bit. A good thing for me. It probably saved me a hundred bucks.

"I'm sorry, Allen. I was just concerned about where she's gonna live when we get married. She not going to live with us, is she?"

I was sick of all her damn questions, so I didn't answer. I just finished dressing.

"Allen did you hear me?"

"Rose, I gotta go. Let's talk about this after church, okay?" I left the room, trying to avoid the argument that would soon be unavoidable. What would I do with my mother once I was married?

When I walked out the door I could hear Rose yelling, "She's playin' you for a fool, Allen!"

I wanted to yell back, "So are you!" but I just kept on walking.

The ride home was short, and the only thing I could think about was Kyle sitting in that jail. I just wished there was a way to contact him and make sure he was all right. That dream had seemed so real.

I walked into the house to find Ma snoring on the couch. The TV was on. I turned it off and sat down on the sofa next to her. I gently shook her until she woke from her sleep. Ma was a short, heavyset, light-skinned woman in her late sixties. She was never seen anywhere without one of many wigs or hats to hide her gray hair.

"Hey, baby," she said, smiling. Ma had a beautiful smile.

"Hi, Ma. Come on, let's go ta bed."

I helped Ma get up off the sofa and we both walked up the stairs to the bedrooms.

"Lemme go see if I can find your blood pressure medicine, Ma."

"That's okay, baby, I found it right after you hung up."

I threw Ma an I-can't-believe-you look. She'd played me just like Rose had said.

"Where'd you find it?"

"You know, it's the funniest thing. Them pills were right in that medicine cabinet, just like you said. I don't know how I missed 'em."

"Neither do I, Ma. Neither do I." I shook my head.

I made sure Ma got in bed, then walked downstairs to turn off the lights before going to bed myself. I thought about going back over to Rose's, but changed my mind when I looked at the clock.

"Allen? Allen, come up here a minute," Ma called down the stairs.

I knew whatever she wanted was something stupid, but I ran up the stairs anyway.

"What, Ma?"

"You not going back over to Rose's, are you, son?"

"No, Ma."

She smiled.

"How come that girl ain't had no baby by you yet?"

"Ma, I told you ten times. Rose doesn't wanna have a baby 'til we're married and can afford a house."

"Well, what the hell you waitin' for? I'm not gettin' any younger Allen, and you my only child. I would like to leave this here world knowin' my grandchildren."

"You mean that, Ma? You okay with me getting married?"

She was silent for a few seconds before she shook her head. "I guess I ain't got no choice. Rose is a nice girl. I just wish you wouldn't give her all your money."

Both of us were silent as I tried to figure out who told her I was giving Rose money. It had to be Kyle or Jay. Wil wouldn't do that type of thing. Damn, I hated when they got in my business.

"What about you, Ma? Where you gonna stay when I get married?" I asked, changing the subject.

"Same place I always stayed. With you." She laughed as if I should have already known the answer. My stomach got queasy just thinking about it. I'd taken care of my mother since my father's death when I was fourteen. I'd always hoped that when I got married, Ma would cut the apron strings. It wasn't like she couldn't take care of herself. Hell, I was taking care of her, and she would go to her friends' houses and clean like she was getting paid.

"Good night, Ma."

"Good night, son. Sweet dreams." I walked into the bathroom for some antacid. I took the medicine and went to bed, trying to think of a good way to tell Rose that my mother would probably be going on our honeymoon.

3

Wil

I walked into the bedroom of my Rosedale home to find my wife Diane, who was trying to rock our crying eighteen-month-old son Teddy to sleep. She blew a loose strand of hair out of her face, and I could see she was exhausted. Diane worked hard with Teddy, and I loved her for that. I was thinking about getting her a nanny when our second child was born in two months. She would probably need the extra help. I wanted to make sure our children had all the nurturing and love in the world.

I'd met Diane by coincidence a little over eight years ago. At the time, I was working in sales for Johnson and Johnson products, while Diane was the supervisor in the shipping department, which was housed in another building. She had a reputation for being a real pain in the ass, and everyone from my department tried their best to avoid dealing with her. But one day I had this obnoxious client on the line, and he was demanding next-day shipping. The guy was buying almost a quarter of a million dollars' worth of products and was threatening to cancel. I didn't wanna lose my job or my commission, so I called up my usual contact in the shipping department. She told me there was nothing she could do with an order that big without approval from her supervisor. Enter Diane, the tiger lady, who turned out to be a cute little kitten. I explained the situation to her, and without giving it a second thought, she approved the shipping request.

Now, I'm not in the usual habit of sending women I've never met flowers, but Diane had done me a huge favor, which I totally hadn't expected. So to thank her, I sent her a dozen white roses. I figured if I ever needed her help again, she would always remember the flowers. Well, to say she was flattered would have been an understatement. She was overwhelmed. Two days later she sent me some Tommy Boy cologne, which was my favorite. I found out later that she'd been asking the people in Human Resources a lot of questions about me after she received the flowers. I returned the favor by sending her a box of Godiva chocolates. Now this little gift giving went on almost nine weeks without Diane and I ever laying eyes on each other. All we did was talk on the phone. The funny thing is, it would have been easy for one of us to walk over to the other's building and say hello. We'd probably passed each other in the parking lot a thousand times. Finally I asked her to dinner, and the rest is history.

I walked over to the bed and kissed Di on the forehead.

"What's wrong with him?" I asked, looking at our son.

"I think he has gas."

"Here, let me have him." I took Teddy from her gently. "What's up, little man?"

Teddy stopped crying as soon as he heard my voice.

Diane sucked her teeth, "He's such a daddy's boy," she teased.

"No doubt," I laughed, sitting in a wood rocking chair. "Give me a bottle, baby. I'll put him to bed."

She handed me a bottle.

"Dinner's wrapped up in the fridge if you want it."

"Thanks, Di. I had a little somethin' before I came home."

"I kinda figured that. I just wanted to let you know I didn't forget you." She smiled.

I smiled back. "I know, baby. I appreciate everything you do."

"How was the game?" she asked as she rubbed my back.

"We won," I responded absentmindedly.

"What's the matter, Wil? You don't sound right."

"Kyle got arrested today," I whispered

"For what?" Diane was shocked.

"Sssssshhhh." I pointed to the baby, nearly asleep. "Believe it or not, attempted murder."

Diane didn't say a word. She just looked at me. The two of us were caught in a speechless stare.

"You okay, Wil?"

"Yeah, I'm aw'ight," I replied, not believing it myself.

"Who?"

"Whadda ya mean, who?"

"Who did he try to kill?"

"He didn't try to kill anybody, Di. The cops got him on a mistaken identity. I'm gonna take the day off Monday and go down to the court-house to see what's going on."

"Did anyone speak to Lisa yet? She must be going out of her mind." Diane picked up the phone.

"She's aw'ight." I gestured for her to hang up the phone. "Allen and I stopped over there before I came home. She's the only one who's spoken to Kyle, and that was by phone. You should let her get some sleep."

"Okay, but I'm gonna give her a call in the morning."

I nodded my approval, then stood up. Diane looked over my shoulder.

"Is he asleep?"

"Yeah."

"You know he looks just like you." She kissed me.

"Yeah, but he has your eyes." I smiled.

"Why don't you put him to bed then come back and put your other baby to bed?"

"Now that'll work."

I carried Teddy into his room and placed him in his crib, turning on the baby monitor.

"Good night, little man. I love you." I looked down at my son, then up toward the ceiling. "Thank you, God, for Teddy and Diane. And please look out for my boy Kyle."

When I walked back into the bedroom, I was pleasantly surprised. Diane was lying on the bed, wearing a sexy silk nightgown. I had to stop and admire the contrast between her very light skin and the red material that rested softly along her full-figured curves. With her long, soft black hair shimmering in the dim light, she took my breath away. Diane was a big woman, but hell I was big man. So what did I need with a small woman? As I told my boys when we were growing up, "Ain't nothin no small woman can do for me but introduce me to her big friend."

"You know I love you, don't you?" I asked my beautiful wife.

"Yes, I do Wil."

I lay down next to her, wrapping my arms around her waist. She kissed me passionately. I could feel the fullness of her breasts rub up against me, and when she kissed my neck, I let out a soft moan.

"Make love to me, Wil," she whispered. I slid out of my T-shirt, and flexed my muscles with a smile. I'd gained a few pounds over the years, but I was still in pretty good shape for a big man. Sliding my pants off in one motion, I gently crawled onto the bed beside my very pregnant wife.

"You okay?" I asked before entering her.

"Yeah, just put it in," she whispered passionately.

Just as I did what she had asked, the phone rang.

"Don't answer it," Diane said. "Let the machine get it. I just want you to make love to me."

Beep!

"Sorry to call your place so late, guys. This is Kenya."

I rolled over and grabbed up the phone. "Hold on, Kenya."

It took me a few seconds to turn the machine off and think of a good lie. I knew exactly why she was calling. Jay hadn't made it home yet and probably wouldn't be home for quite some time.

"Hey, what's up, Kenya?" I tried to sound natural.

"Have you seen Jay? I been trying to reach him on his cell phone for an hour."

"Uh, yeah . . ." I hesitated for a moment. "We was hangin' out at the Roadhouse earlier. But he left with some brother who was interested in buying his bike."

"Good. I can't stand that damn motorcycle," she said with an attitude.

"Look, Kenya, I'd love to talk, but Di and I were kinda gettin' into somethin', if you know what I mean."

"Oh, I am *soooo* sorry, Wil."

"It's all right."

"Tell me somethin', Wil. Do you think Jay would cheat on me?" There was silence on the line. I think Kenya suspected what I already knew. Jay had been cheating on her for years.

"I don't know, Kenya. Do you have any reason to believe he would?"

"Look, Wil, I'm sorry for bothering you. I'll talk to you later, okay?"

"Bye, Kenya." I sighed, hanging up the phone. I could hear the sorrow in her voice and it didn't make me feel good at all. Times like this, I hated the way Jay treated Kenya. Especially since she just found out she was pregnant.

I dialed Jay's cell phone to let him know he was being hunted down. Jay had two cell phones. One for his wife and family, the other for his lady friends. I'd tried to talk him out of it, but he didn't pay me any mind. The only one who could talk any sense into him these days was Kyle. Di stuck her finger out and hung up the phone before the first ring.

"Please don't start, baby. With Kyle in jail, I really don't wanna fight," I pleaded. We'd had this argument many times before. She hated when I covered for Jay. And she wasn't about to let it go this time.

"Let's get somethin' straight, Wil Duncan. I don't like this little game you and Jay are playing with Kenya. I don't like it at all. If he doesn't wanna be married, tell him to get a divorce."

"Come on, you gonna tell me you never covered for your girls?"

"Hell, no! My girls would never ask me to do shit like this. Now where is Jay anyway?" she demanded, folding her arms.

"I left him in the bar with some woman named Jackie." I lowered my head. "That's between you and me."

"Who'm I gonna tell?"

"Kenya!"

"You don't have to worry about that. I'm not losing my marriage to save someone else's. But I will tell you this, Wil Duncan. Don't make me have to call someone looking for you. 'Cause I don't trust your friends as far as I can throw 'em."

"Never, baby." I meant it. I would never cheat on Diane. But apparently she didn't believe me.

"I'm gonna check on Teddy." She rolled her eyes at me and got off the bed.

"What about . . . you know?" I raised my eyebrows a couple of times.

"We'll talk about that when I come back." She frowned.

When she left the room, I dialed Jay's cell phone again. I never get in trouble for somethin' I do. It's always something they do. All I could do at that point was hope Diane would still be in the mood when she came back. I doubted it.

"What up, Wil?" Jay said, answering on the first ring.

"How'd you know it was me?" I asked.

"I got caller I.D. on this cell phone. Just in case Kenya finds the number."

"What good's that gonna do if you're busted?" I laughed at him.

"I can act like I'm answerin' the phone for business." Jay must have given this plenty of thought.

"Damn, you think of everything, don't ya?"

"Life of a playa, my man. I gotta stay two steps ahead of Kenya or my ass is grass."

"Speaking of Kenya. She just called here lookin' for you."

"Shit! What'd you tell her?"

"That you was showin' your bike to some brother."

"Okay, cool. She wants me to sell that bike anyway."

"Yeah, that's what she told me. Look, Jay, I know it's none of my business, but don't you think you should head on home?" I hoped he would take my advice. I loved him like a brother, but I was getting tired of being in the middle of this.

Jay laughed, "You've seen Jackie. The woman has 44D titties and an ass like Jennifer Lopez. Do you really want me to go home? I don't think so, Wil. Besides Kenya's not home, she's at her mother's. She's just tryin'a make sure I'm not fuckin' around."

"I wonder why. Look, man, call your wife and tell her you're gonna stay at your mom's or somethin'. The woman's worried."

"Okay, Wil, I'll call her."

"Good." I wondered if he was sincere. "You and me gotta talk."

"Talk about what?"

"I can't keep covering for you, Jay."

"Why you trippin', Wil? You used to cover for Kyle all the time."

"Key word, used to. Kyle don't do that shit since he's been married," I reminded him.

"Yeah, right. You really believe that shit, Wil?"

"All I know is, I don't get calls from Lisa every Friday and Saturday night."

"So you gonna sell a brotha out?" Jay asked.

"No, I just said we need to talk. And we're gonna, as soon as Kyle gets outta jail. Now don't forget to call your wife." I hung up the phone without saying goodbye. I wanted him to know I was serious.

4

Jay

I hung the phone up and tried to enjoy the oral pleasure that Jackie was giving me, but as good as it was, it didn't matter. My mind was still preoccupied with my conversation with Wil. I was pretty sure he wouldn't sell me out to Kenya, but he was definitely startin' to get a little pissed off covering for me. I just wish I could find the words to explain to him that what Kenya and I had just wasn't the same as what he and Diane had. I cared about Kenya, but the fact that she didn't wanna have sex anymore had ruined our relationship. God, I shoulda never married her in the first place. I felt so trapped.

I married Kenya four years ago after I found out she was pregnant. She was one fine, brown-skinned honey. We'd been dating off and on for about two years, and she was the first woman I'd ever been able to have a real relationship with. I'd been such a dog before I met her, I honestly didn't know what it was like to have someone to care about me. Would you believe she was actually the only woman I ever felt guilty about cheating on? After a while I even stopped cheating. Things were going so well between us that I felt empty when she wasn't around. That is until about a year and a half into our relationship when she started bringing up the "M" word. Now I cared about Kenya. I cared about her a lot, but marriage was definitely out of the question. Just the thought of it made me revert back to my old, insecure ways of womanizing.

When I made it clear that wedding bells were not in the equation for us, Kenya ended things, only to come back begging six months later. I'm not really sure if I felt sorry for her or just missed the stability she brought into my life, but I took her back. In retrospect, that was a bad move on my part. Six months after we got back together she told me she was pregnant. At first I didn't think it was that big a deal. Three hundred dollars for an abortion and life was back to normal. But when I took her down to the clinic, the doctors said she was too far along. I'd never admit it to my boys, but I'm sure she played me.

I avoided Kenya for almost a month, contemplating my next move. The last thing I wanted was to be a father. I was only thirty at the time, and to be honest, I just wasn't in love with her. But she kept insisting that she didn't care if I loved her, that I'd learn to love her in time. Finally, after talking to my mom, I decided to do the morally right thing. I asked Kenya to marry me. My pops never married my mom, and till this day I love him but I don't have any respect for him. I didn't want that for my child. I decided to try and be the best husband and father I could. Besides, both Wil and Kyle were happily married. How hard could it really be?

At first marriage was fun. Kenya and I did a lot of family things with Wil and Kyle and their wives. I have to admit it took time, but I honestly think I love her. The only problem was that women were still hitting on me even though they knew I was married. The things they were suggesting were hard to turn down. On top of that, Kenya wasn't as sexual as she used to be once the baby was born. At first she really tried to keep up with my sexual appetite, but soon she began using the excuse that she was too tired from taking care of the baby. That got old fast when I took Tiffany to my mom's for the weekend and we still didn't have sex. After two years of being faithful and horny, I couldn't take it anymore. I hooked up with my old stripper girlfriend Keyshawn. I'm sorry, but if I had wanted to be celibate, I would've become a priest instead of a husband.

The only real reason I hadn't asked Kenya for a divorce and moved out was that I loved our daughter more than life itself. I'd decided to stick it out for twelve more years until my daughter was at least sixteen. That way she could have a normal childhood. I'm an honest believer in the theory that children need a complete family. Then out of nowhere Kenya was pregnant again with our second child, which meant another sixteen years shackled to her. I didn't like it, but I had to deal with it. I was just gonna have to lead a double life, one side husband and father and the other side a cheat. I wasn't proud of the fact that I was being unfaithful, but with the sex life I had at home, I didn't feel I had a choice.

I looked down at Jackie, who looked like she could use some encouragement. So I moaned loudly, pretending to be excited. Immediately she started to work harder.

"You like that, Jay?" Jackie asked, lifting her head.

I moaned again. "You know I do."

She smiled and returned to her work.

"Keep doin' what you doin', baby, I just gotta call my old lady."

Reaching for my cell phone, I hit the speed-dial button to my mother-in-law's house.

"Hello?" I recognized my wife's voice right away.

"Hey, baby, I thought you'd be 'sleep. I was gonna leave a message that I'm on my way down there." Kenya was spending the weekend with her parents in Baltimore.

"You're coming down here?" She sounded excited.

"Yeah, I miss you. Plus I was thinking about going fishing with your pops."

"Really?" I could hear the excitement in her voice.

"Yeah, I'll see you in a few hours. Get some sleep, okay?"

"Okay, Jay, I love you."

"Yeah, me too." I hung up the phone certain that any suspicions she had were gone.

Now I could relax and enjoy what Jackie was doing. Looking around to make sure no one was walking around the parking lot, I reached to my side and let my seat recline. I settled back comfortably and closed my eyes. It didn't take long for Jackie to finish what she had started once I was concentrating on her skillful loving.

Jackie sat up and checked herself in the rearview mirror, straightening out her hair. As she put on her lipstick, she glanced in my direction. I knew right away what she was gonna ask.

"Why don't you come on up so we can finish what we started?"

"Sorry, baby, I gotta head outta town. But I'll take care of you Monday, aw'ight?" I lifted my butt and pulled up my pants, buttoning the fly in a hurry.

"Okay," Jackie replied. She looked disappointed, but she'd get over it. She always did. As she opened the car door, Jackie leaned over to me for a kiss. I turned my head and offered her my cheek. No way was I kissing her after what she just did.

Monday morning I walked into the Queens courthouse and paused at the doorway to get myself together. Kyle being in jail had really hit me hard. The bond I shared with him was different than the one I shared with Wil and Allen. Mainly because we'd both played sports and chased women together all our lives. Man, did we have some kind of rep with the ladies back in the days. Kyle was one of the smoothest talkers I've ever met. He could look at a woman, evaluate her, and tell her exactly what she wanted to hear within seconds. And the ones he couldn't charm the drawers off would be mesmerized by my dimples. We were one hell of a team back then, until Lisa came into the picture and fucked it all up.

After he met her, he became a different guy. He didn't go anywhere without her, and fooling around was out of the question. Things just got even worse after they got married. The damn guy started acting like he was Bill Cosby. I wanted the old Kyle back so bad I tried to set him up one time by leaving some old panties and a used condom in his car. I don't know what I was thinkin' about. I guess I just wanted them to break up so Kyle and I could go back to doing our thing like we did in the old days. But I made one major mistake and got myself busted.

I knew Lisa used Kyle's car on Saturdays, so I purposely made him drive one Friday night when we were hanging out. I stashed the condom and panties in the back seat without his knowledge. The next morning, Lisa found the condom and the panties just like I had planned, but she didn't get mad at Kyle at all. She got mad at me. You see, Kyle didn't use latex condoms. He was allergic to the latex. Well, it didn't take a brain surgeon to figure out who left the condom behind. I thought I had ruined my friendship with him for good. It took him almost five months to forgive me for my stupidity, and Lisa still holds a grudge.

When I saw Wil, Diane, Allen, and Lisa standing by a courtroom entrance, I froze. I was afraid that Wil might be mad about covering for me the other night. Not to mention the fact that both Diane and Lisa didn't care for me at all. Lisa I understood. She would probably never get over the fact that I tried to break up her marriage. Diane . . . well that was all Wil's doing. Wil had this theory that once a man and woman were married, they should have no secrets between them. So I was sure he'd told Diane all about my marital infidelities. That's why the only person I was really confiding in these days was Kyle.

Wil spotted me and waved me over. I felt a hell of a lot better when I saw him smile. I really didn't feel like dealing with his shit on the day Kyle was going to be arraigned for attempted murder. I walked over and Allen greeted me with a brotherly hug. Wil came over to greet me the same way. I kissed Diane on the cheek, and for some reason I got a chill. But I couldn't worry about that then. I walked over to Lisa, who'd obviously been crying.

She wrapped her arms around me and gave me a tight hug. I felt her tears fall on my neck, and her sobs had me choked up. We both loved Kyle in our own ways. I just wish I could have thought of a way to tell her I was sorry for all the heartache I had caused in the past.

"Any word?" I asked sadly.

"Kyle's lawyer said he was gonna see him in a few," Wil answered.

I loosened my embrace with Lisa but still rubbed her shoulder as Wil gave me the details.

"Well, what'd he say? Did he tell ya how much bail was gonna be?" I asked. I'd brought the deed to my house just in case they decided to give Kyle a high bail. I didn't wanna take any chances.

"All he told me was that Kyle would be out today. Then he was interrupted by some guy with a folder," Lisa told me.

"Who's his lawyer?"

"His frat brother, Greg Thomas. You remember the guy with the panties on his head at Kyle's bachelor party?" Allen said.

Both Wil and I shot Allen a look. Allen was always saying the wrong thing at the wrong damn time. Lisa didn't even know Kyle had a bachelor party.

"He's supposed to be a real good lawyer," I said quickly, hoping the girls would forget Allen's slip.

"Yeah, he seemed pretty confident after he got that folder." Lisa tried to sound upbeat.

"What the hell was in the folder?" I asked.

"I don't know. But it must have been important, 'cause Greg ran down the hall as soon as he got it," Wil added.

"So, Jay, how's Kenya?" Diane asked.

I could feel the hairs on the back of my neck stand up. "She's fine."

"I know she's excited about the baby."

"Yeah, both of us are. I just hope she has a boy."

"All you guys want boys."

"Gotta keep the Crawford name goin'. But the truth is, I just want a healthy baby."

"I know the feeling." Diane rubbed her baby-filled belly

"Well, why don't you bring her out to the house? Since y'all moved to Jersey, I never see her. We used to be so close."

Something in her eyes told me she knew what had happened the other night. I was kinda glad my cell phone went off so I could slip away. The last thing I wanted was Diane and Kenya getting together alone in a house. They might get bored and start talkin' about me.

"Hello." I walked away from the group.

"Hey, big daddy. I miss you." It was Tracy, a sexy young thing I met a few weeks ago at Kyle's Long Island store. We'd been talkin' pretty regularly, but hadn't hooked up yet.

"Whazz up, baby?" I couldn't help but smile.

"You. I just needed to hear your voice."

"I'm glad you did."

"Is your friend outta jail yet?"

"Naw, hopefully within the next hour."

"When he does, why don't we get together and celebrate?"

I hesitated. Tracy was a junior in college. Not that it mattered. I loved younger women. But she'd been skipped a grade and was only nineteen years old. I was practically old enough to be her father.

"Look, Tracy I'm not sure what these guys are gonna do. Why don't I call you later?"

I could see Wil waving at me, so I cut the call short.

"Tracy, they're opening the courtroom. I gotta go."

"Who the hell is Tracy?" Allen startled me.

"Just a friend." I couldn't look him in the eye.

"I'ma tell you the same thing you told me when I started dating Rose. Be careful."

"Come on, dawg. This is Jay, the number one hound."

"Aw'ight number one hound. Just remember it's not just Wil and me. Diane and Lisa are watching you too," Allen warned as I followed him to the doors of the courtroom.

"I hear ya, brotha. I hear ya." Allen was right. I loved to live life on the edge. I was going to have to be more careful.

5

Kyle

It was hot as hell, and I was sweating like I'd been playing ball all day. I was sitting in a cramped cell in the basement of the criminal court-house on Queens Boulevard, waiting to see the judge. I swear I felt like I was gonna pass out from the stench of the other inmates. The COs had moved me early in the morning from central booking, with about fifty other brothers arrested over the weekend. All of us were waiting to see the judge and hopefully be bailed out. The word was I was lucky. I had a private lawyer. But private lawyer or not, I would have felt a hell of a lot better if I'd been arrested for DWI or drunken disorderly like the rest of my fellow inmates, instead of assault, robbery, and at-tempted murder.

"Richmond, Kyle!" a deputy shouted.

I exhaled and walked nervously to the cell door.

"You Richmond?" the deputy asked.

"Yeah."

"Your lawyer's here to see you."

"It's about time," I muttered.

The deputy opened the door, and I followed him to a small room with a table, two chairs, and a single lightbulb hanging from the ceil-ing. I was so emotional I couldn't decide if I should burst into tears or shout with joy when I saw the small, balding, light-skinned man at the table. Greg was my lawyer and a good friend. We'd gone to college and pledged Alpha Phi Alpha Fraternity together. He'd been my personal attorney since he passed the bar ten years ago.

"You all right, Kyle?" Greg stood and extended his hand.

"Yeah, I could use a shower, but I'm aw'ight." We hugged and gave each other the secret fraternity handshake. Greg backed away pretty fast. Three days in the same clothes will make a man smell pretty funky.

Greg sat down and motioned for me to do the same. He took a small folder out of his briefcase. When I saw that folder, all kinds of stuff went through my head. Why would he have a folder on me al-ready? I glanced over at him. He hadn't made eye contact since our frat handshake. He hadn't even asked me if I was guilty. Damn, he probably thought I did it! I had to make sure he understood I didn't do it. The last thing I wanted was an attorney that felt his client was guilty.

"Greg, before we start, I want you to understand something. I didn't do it. I swear on my children I didn't hit that lady with no bat."

Greg smiled for the first time. "It's okay, Kyle. I know that. Now just tell me everything that happened, and don't leave out a thing."

I explained Saturday's events to Greg. He didn't say much or ask any questions like I expected. He just took a lot of notes until I was finished. Then he patted my hand.

"Don't worry, bro. I'll have you outta here in about an hour," he promised.

"Really? Damn, thanks, Greg." I was smiling from ear to ear.

"Don't thank me until after the lawsuit."

"Lawsuit?"

"Damn right, lawsuit." He opened the folder he'd been holding. "The cops had enough probable cause to detain you. But without a positive ID or your fingerprints on the bat the assailant left behind, they couldn't legally hold you. They didn't have enough evidence."

"Then how come I spent the fucking weekend in jail?" I was angry now.

"They figured you were black, and to them that usually means guilty. They were probably gonna try and hide you in the system until the woman came out of her coma," Greg said matter-of-factly.

"They can do that shit?"

"They're not supposed to. But when you're dealing with blacks and Latinos, many of whom don't know the law, they do whatever they want. I guarantee they never expected you to have your own lawyer. Legal Aid would have tried to talk you into a plea."

"Shit, that's fucked up."

"Is this the guy who ran into you?" Greg opened the folder and threw three black-and-white pictures across the table. They were fuzzy, but I could make out the faces.

"That's him! That's the kid who knocked me over." I grabbed the pictures.

"See the old lady in front of him?" Greg pointed out.

I nodded.

"That's the victim."

"What?" I looked at Greg in disbelief. "Where'd you get these pictures from?"

"The bank's security office. It took all of five minutes to call the bank and get pictures of the ATM transaction. I didn't get them till this morning, but the cops could have had them Saturday."

"Why the hell didn't they do it? I been sitting in this hell hole all weekend and all they had to do was make a call to get a few pictures?" I demanded an answer.

"The police assumed you were guilty. They never followed up."

"This is bullshit, Greg! This is fucking bullshit. Those racist mother-fuckers do shit like this on purpose. Do you know I haven't seen one white person other than COs since I was arrested Saturday?"

"I can believe that."

"What? White people don't do anything wrong?"

"It's their system, Kyle. Even as a lawyer I have to work within their system."

"You've gotta be fuckin' kidding me! Nobody should have to spend the weekend in jail because the cops were too lazy to do their jobs."

I guess Greg could see how furious his news had made me, because he reassured me.

"Don't worry, Kyle, we're gonna make them pay."

"I just wanna get out of this place. We'll deal with the other shit later." I'd seen enough of the inside of a jail to last the rest of my life.

"I'm gonna have you outta here within the hour, Kyle. I'm going to talk to the DA, and then we'll go before the judge. Hopefully we can have your record sealed."

Greg picked up the pictures and folder, placing them in his brief-case, and knocked on the door for the corrections officer to let him out.

"Oh, by the way your wife and buddies are waiting for you out-side," he smiled.

"Hey, Greg," I stopped him before he stepped out.

He turned around.

"Thanks, frat." I hoped he understood how grateful I was.

"Don't thank me. Just pay your bill."

We both laughed.

I sat on my daughter Willow's bed and watched her and her younger sister Jade sleep. Their older sister Jewel snuggled under the covers, watching me. I sighed happily. It was good to be home. The judge dis-missed my case just like Greg had promised. Then she apologized for the police's mistake and had my records sealed. She told the DA, "These pictures show that the police have made a grave mistake in tak-ing away Mr. Richmond's freedom. Now there's a man out there that committed this crime, and I suggest you find him."

I turned around and looked at the two cops and that pain-in-the-ass sergeant who had arrested me. It wasn't very hot in that courtroom, but all three were sweating. I planned on having Greg make them sweat a hell of a lot more when we filed my false arrest lawsuit in a few weeks.

"Daddy," my oldest daughter interrupted my thoughts.

"Yes, Jewel," I replied.

"I'm glad you're home."

"I'm glad too." I walked over to her bed and sat beside her.

"Promise me you'll never go away again, Daddy. My mommy was crying."

"She told me. I'll tell you what. I can't promise I'll never go away again. You know I make business trips sometimes. But no matter where I go, I promise to always call and say good night to you and your mommy. Okay?"

"Okay Daddy," she cuddled against me.

"Look, you need to get some sleep."

"Awww right. Good night, Daddy." She yawned.

"Good night, my little Jewel."

I stroked Jewel's hair until she was fast asleep. The whole time I was in jail, all I could think of was my wife and kids. I'd never been so scared in my entire life. Not of the other inmates. Not even of doing time. I was scared that they would convict me of a crime I didn't commit and keep me away from my girls. I'd only been in jail three days and I'd already been thinking of ways to escape and run away with my family. You never know how good you have it until it's taken away.

But now that I was safe at home and the fear was gone, I was mad. Mad as hell! And somebody was gonna pay for that anger.

"Kyle," my wife called softly, standing in the doorway. She was wearing a pair of black panties and a white cutoff T-shirt that was so thin I could see everything I wanted to see under there.

"Yeah, babe."

"Come to bed, honey." She smiled.

I kissed each of my daughters as they slept then followed my wife into our bedroom, where I watched her strip off her garments. Lisa was a strikingly beautiful woman. Her ancestry was Italian, which gave her an olive complexion. Her hair was jet black and hung almost to her perfectly shaped butt. Unlike me, she was a fitness fiend, so there wasn't an ounce of fat on her body.

"Com'ere," she ordered.

I took a few steps closer and we embraced. The kissing and the touching were so intense that we made love right on the floor. I had no idea what time it was when we finished, but both of us were exhausted from our passion. I'd pulled a sheet off the bed and wrapped it around us. Lisa laid her head on my chest and softly ran her hand across it.

"I was so scared you were never coming home, Kyle," she said quietly.

"I know, hun. I was scared too. I thought I was gonna lose you and the girls."

"You could never lose us, Kyle. But I am glad this is over."

"It's not over," I said sternly. "Matter of fact, it's far from over. I'm gonna sue the fucking police department and each of those cops for everything they got. When I'm finished, we're gonna own this city."

"Why? Why do you have to sue them? It doesn't make any sense. We don't need the money." Her voice was pleading.

"For the fucking principle, that's why." I sat up, pushing her off me. " 'Cause those fucking assholes took me away from you and my girls. And even more importantly, because they might do it again and the next brother might not be as lucky as me." I couldn't believe she was asking me to explain.

"Kyle, this is stupid. The cops were just doing their jobs. They made a mistake. You told me yourself that their case looked good until you spoke to Greg."

"Those mothafuckers were racist, Lisa." I got up off the floor.

"They weren't racist. I was in that courtroom today. That black sergeant tried to apologize to you." She really didn't get it.

"He was just tryin' to save his ass. You don't have to be white to be racist anyway. Racism is a state of mind. You could be the blackest nigga on the block and still hate black people." I was really getting heated.

"How come everything has to come down to race with you? Every time something goes wrong, it's because the white man is trying to hold back poor Kyle. You ever think you might be at fault?"

"What did you say?" I said, trying to control myself. My wife, the woman I had been so worried about, thought it was my fault that a woman got her head bashed in.

"What I was trying to say is that sometimes you have to take responsibility for things that happen. Not necessarily this time, but other things that happen in your life. You do have a habit of reacting before you think." She sounded like she was talking to a child.

"No, you didn't just say that, did you? You said it was my fault." I walked across the room and put on my pants. "Who the fuck are you? You're damn sure not my wife."

"Kyle, will you please calm down? You're gonna wake the girls."

"Hell no, I'm not gonna calm down! This is my goddamn house! I pay the bills here!"

"You know, Kyle, you can be such a—"

"Such a what?" I screamed, cutting her off.

She hesitated, then finished. "Such an asshole!"

That was the first time I ever looked at my wife and saw a white woman, not just a woman. She just didn't get it. She'd been married to a black man for seven years and she still didn't understand. Black people are treated differently than white people. You would have thought that by now she would come to understand that. But she was still living her life through rose-colored glasses.

"You know what, Lisa? Maybe it's time you wake up and look at the real world. There is racism out there that directly affects your own family. I'm gonna sue this damn city and the police department whether you stand by my side or not."

"Well, you're gonna be standing out there by yourself."

I was so mad my stomach was doing flips. I finished dressing in a flash.

"You know what, Lisa? Maybe we should reevaluate this relationship. 'Cause for a woman that has three black kids, you sure don't understand black folks." I could tell she was stunned by my comments, because I saw tears. I turned around and walked down the stairs. I was putting on a sweater when she called after me.

"Kyle, where are you going?"

"Out!"

"When are you coming back?" she asked sadly. She was at the bottom of the stairs now.

"I'm not." I opened the front door.

"Kyle, I love you." She had pleading in her voice.

"You know what, Lisa? Maybe love isn't good enough anymore."

I pulled my Range Rover into Wil's driveway and was glad to see the lights were still on. I sat in the truck for a while, getting my thoughts straight. Had I done the right thing, leaving the way I did? I wasn't sure, but I definitely needed to get away from Lisa at that moment.

I got out of the car and rang Wil's bell. Diane answered, carrying little Teddy on her shoulder.

"Hey, Kyle. Come on in."

"Hi, Di. How you doin'?" I kissed her cheek before walking by.

"I'm fine. A little morning sickness here and there, but I'm doing good. How 'bout you? You look a lot better than you did when I saw you at the courthouse this afternoon."

"I feel a lot better," I lied.

"Good. Wil's in the den watching the Mets game. I'm gonna feed Teddy and go to bed. Good night."

"Hey, Di, can I ask you a question?"

"Sure."

"I'm thinking about suing the police for false arrest. What do you think?"

"If I was you, Kyle, I'd sue the hell outta those bastards." Her eyes flashed anger. "What they did to you was dead wrong."

"Thanks, Di. You're an aw'ight sistah." I wished my own wife could have shown me such unconditional support.

"Good night, Kyle." She smiled gently and held her baby closer.

"Good night Di." I walked down the hall to Wil's den. He was engrossed in the baseball game.

"Bang! If I was really a killer, you'd be dead." I laughed.

"What's up, Kyle?" He got up and gave me a brotherly hug, then turned his attention right back to the game.

"Who's winning?"

"Five-two Cincinnati. Bottom of the ninth. Edgardo Alfonzo is up with the bases loaded, two outs." I sat down and stared at the screen. I wasn't as big a baseball fan as Wil, but I did like the Mets.

"*Yes!*" Wil screamed as Alfonzo hit a long fly ball. Wil was jumping up and down like a school child. But the smile disappeared in a flash when Ken Griffey, Jr., stopped the ball in flight and prevented a home run. "Damn, damn, damn! How the hell did he catch that?"

I didn't say a word as Wil had his tantrum. As cool, calm, and collected as he always was, Wil got crazy when it came to baseball, especially the Mets. Even Diane gave him a wide berth when he was watching a Mets game. It was her one concession to the game, since she had made him give up his season tickets when they got married.

"So what brings you over here, anyway?" Wil asked when he finally stopped ranting about Griffey's catch.

"I need a place to spend the night." I lowered my head.

"You need what?" Wil raised an eyebrow and sat back in his recliner.

"I need a place to stay. Lisa and I got into a fight."

"A fight or an argument? A fight to me means somebody got hit."

"An argument. You know I'd never hit her."

"I never thought you'd be in jail, but you were," Wil said a little sarcastically.

I shot him an evil look.

"I'm sorry, man. What I was trying to say is, I have no idea what goes on in your house, and I really don't wanna know. I just wanted to make sure you're not doing anything stupid."

"I don't hit women, Wil!"

"Aw'ight, so what happened? Why'd she kick you out?"

"She didn't kick me out. I left."

"Why?"

"It's this whole interracial thing, man," I stated simply. "I don't know if I can handle it anymore."

Wil picked up his remote control and turned the television off. He turned to face me, and the expression on his face was serious.

"It's a little late for that, isn't it? You got three kids with that woman."

His words were like a slap in the face. In my confused rage, I hadn't thought about my kids. My anger and hurt were directed entirely at Lisa, but my girls would definitely be affected if I left.

"Now what's going on, Kyle? You never had a problem with this interracial shit before." Wil looked worried.

"Yeah, I did. I just never said anything." I didn't look him in the face.

Wil sat up in his chair. I think he was more than a little surprised.

"Do you remember me asking you way before you got married if you were going to be able to handle an interracial marriage?"

"Yeah, I remember."

"So what happened in seven years?"

"I don't know. It's hard being married to a white woman, Wil."

"It's hard being married, period," he reminded me.

"I know." I sat back in my chair. "But it's different with a white woman. When you walk down the street with Di, people don't stare at you. The other day a sister threw a cup of coffee on me. I'm sure it was because I kissed Lisa before I stepped out of the van."

Wil's eyes got bigger, but he didn't say a word. He just sat back and listened.

"It's not always that serious. Sometimes it's just dirty looks from strangers on the street, but shit like that is always goin' on, Wil. And Lisa acts like she just can't see it." I sighed heavily. "After today, I just can't take it anymore." I was angry again.

"What happened tonight?"

I explained to Wil everything that had happened, and even added a few things that that had happened in the past year. I needed him to understand how so many little incidents had added up to this huge blowout.

"Kyle, I don't agree with Lisa, but maybe she's afraid of what might happen. Cops can be pretty vicious when they're crossed. You wanna subject your family to that?"

"If that was really her problem, why didn't she say that? She said I always make everything into race. But this time, somebody's gotta make a stand, Wil."

"Okay, Al Sharpton." He moved up in his chair and sat at the edge. "Do you wanna get a divorce, Kyle? 'Cause that's where this is leading."

I thought about it a second. I was mad, I was real mad. But three hours ago I was making love to Lisa. I couldn't just remove that from the equation. There were parts of our marriage that I really loved.

"Answer me, man. Do you wanna get a divorce?"

"Nah, I just want her to see things my way."

"You said it yourself, she's never gonna see things your way. So there's gonna be times you gotta stand on your own, and other times she'll be by your side."

"Easy for you to say, Wil. Your wife's a sister. She always stands by you."

"Who, my wife? Are you fucking crazy? Just 'cause we act like the Huxtables don't mean we are."

"Really?"

"Yeah." Wil yawned. "Look, man, it's getting late. I gotta get up early in the morning. I want you to go home to your wife and kids, bro. Talk to Lisa. You may not agree on everything, but you guys are a family."

"Aw'right, man. But if you hear a tap on the window, it's me."

I didn't get home until after one in the morning. I'd gone over to the Roadhouse Bar for a drink to calm my nerves. When I walked through the door, Lisa was waiting for me. Her hair was a mess and her eyes were red. She'd obviously been crying ever since I left. I walked over to her and wrapped my arms around her, hugging her tightly.

"I'm sorry, Kyle," she sobbed. Her body went limp, and I had to hold her to keep her from falling.

"It's all right. We just have a difference of opinion." I repeated what Wil said to me. I wasn't sure if I believed it, but it was the right thing to say at the time.

"Ohhh, Kyle, I was so scared you were going to leave me. I was more scared of that than I was of you going to prison." She squeezed me tighter. "If you want to sue them, go ahead. I won't stand in your way. Just please, please don't leave me."

"It's not about you standing in my way. It's about you standing by my side," I told her, trying to keep my voice calm.

She lifted her head, looking into my eyes. "I promise I'll stand by you."

I nodded my head, and neither of us spoke another word. We walked up the stairs, arm in arm. When we got to our room, she kissed me passionately from my neck to my ears and back to my lips. Smiling a sad, exhausted smile, she guided me to the bed and straddled me, rubbing her hands across my chest. She slid off the oversized T-shirt she was wearing. Everything seemed to be moving in slow motion as she moved seductively, trailing her tongue down my stomach, closer to her final destination. Once she reached it, she sat up with a confused look on her face.

"Kyle, are you still mad at me?" That's when I realized I was barely erect.

"No, baby, I'm just tired. Do you mind if I just hold you?" She lay down on my chest and I wrapped my arms around her. Within minutes we were both asleep.

6

Allen

It was around seven when I sat down at the dinner table with Ma. She'd fried up a few porgies and made some collard greens and corn bread for dinner. Mmm, mmm, mmm, that fish was some kinda good. If there was one thing I loved about living with my mother, it was her cooking. She could take a can of Spam, an onion, and a few potatoes and make your taste buds sing.

We'd been sitting at the dinner table about twenty minutes, and Ma hadn't said one word. I'd just started my second plate when she got up and walked into the living room. When she returned, she had tears in her eyes.

"What's wrong, Ma?" I wasn't used to seeing my mother so silent and weepy.

"Allen, baby, you know how much I want a grandbaby, don't ya?"

I nodded my head though I was a little confused. Ma placed her hand on mine when she sat down and handed me a small jewelry box. I looked at it, then looked at her. I had no idea what she was up to.

"What's this for?" I asked.

"Just open it, baby." Ma's voice sounded so tiny all of a sudden.

I opened the box and had to do a double take when I saw what looked like at least a two-carat diamond.

"Where'd you get this from, Ma?"

"That's my mama's ring." She took the ring out of the box. "It's the only thing in the world I have to remind me of her. I want you to give it to Rose, son." She handed me the ring.

My eyes got watery when I realized what Ma was doing. The sentiment alone made tears come to my eyes. Even with all her eccentric ways, I always knew Ma loved me. She'd tried hard to restrict me to the confines of her world. Giving me this ring was way out of character for her. This was as if she was setting me free. It was as close to blessing my marriage as she was ever gonna come, and I was truly touched.

"Ma, I can't take this ring. This is Granny's ring. Rose will never understand the sentiment it has. Why don't you give it to your first granddaughter?"

"No, Allen. I want you to give it to Rose, if you really love her. This way both of us will be sure you're getting married for the right reason." Ma put her hand on my shoulder and kissed my cheek.

"Okay Ma, I'll give Granny's ring to Rose." I wrapped my arms around my mother and both of us began to cry. "We're gonna have a whole house full of grandkids for you."

I took the following day off from work and drove over to Rose's job at North Shore Hospital in Manhassett, Long Island. I'd spent most of the day trying to come up with a romantic and unique way to propose. I decided to take her to dinner at Louie's Seafood Restaurant before proposing to her on a midnight jazz cruise.

When I showed up at the hospital, Rose was leaving the building with two other nurses. She didn't spot me at first, so I whistled to get her attention. She said goodbye to her two friends and headed toward me, greeting me with a warm, happy kiss.

"Well, what brings you here all dressed up, handsome?" I was wearing my best suit and had just gotten my hair cut. "Mmmmm, lookin' good and smellin' good too." She smiled.

"Thought I might take you out to dinner. You always said you wanted to go to Louie's in Port Washington. We have an eight o'clock reservation."

"Ohhh, Allen, really?" I nodded and she smiled from ear to ear, kissing me again. Then she stepped back abruptly.

"Allen, I can't go to Louie's lookin' like this. Look at me."

I glanced at her nurse's whites and smiled. I liked the way she looked in her uniform. She looked pure, conservative, and untouched, which was a huge difference from the tight-fitting mini dresses and revealing, low-cut outfits she usually wore.

"You look aw'ight, baby," I reassured her.

"*Pleasssse,* you got to be kidding. You think I'm goin' to Louie's dressed like this? Not on your life. Take me home so I can get dressed." What had happened to the sweet woman who was so happy to see me a minute before?

I looked at my watch. "Hold up, Rose. I ain't driving all the way back to Queens. Do you know how hard it was to get eight o'clock reservations at Louie's?"

"*Ohhhh,* that makes sense. Take me to a five-star restaurant dressed like I'm going to dinner at McDonald's." She folded her arms defiantly.

"I'll tell you what. Let's go buy you something to wear. There has to be a mall or boutique around here." A huge smile cropped up on Rose's face and her eyes turned into dollar signs. There was no doubt in my mind she knew exactly where a store was.

"There's a Macy's right down the block. They got this bad DKNY dress I was lookin' at and I saw the perfect shoes to match it. Don't worry, baby, this ain't gonna take long at all. Matter of fact we probably got time ta get my nails done." Rose looked more excited than a kid in a candy store.

I knew this little shopping spree was gonna cost me three, four hundred but it didn't upset me. I'd saved almost three gee's when Ma gave me Granny's ring.

"We ain't got time ta get your nails done, Rose," I told her.

"Okay, baby." She smiled. "Let's go."

Rose was right. It didn't take long at all for her to pick out a dress. Especially since she had the dress and shoes on layaway. I don't know why, but somehow I felt like I was being set up. The whole outfit cost me close to five hundred bucks after Rose insisted on a matching handbag. Despite the money I had dropped on it, I had to admit she looked stunning as we walked out of Macy's.

"Allen, can I get a pair of earrings?" She pointed at a small jewelry store by the entrance to Macy's.

"Sure, why not?" I smiled, tapping my suit pocket to make sure Granny's ring was still there. What was another hundred bucks, when I wouldn't be spending a couple thousand on a ring?

When we walked into the jewelry store, Rose walked right over to the counter and greeted the jeweler.

"Hey, Henry. You still got those earrings I was looking at the other day?" she asked sweetly.

"Sure, Rose," Henry answered like she was an old friend, or at least a very valued customer. He opened the glass case and handed her a pair of emerald studs.

While Rose was trying on the earrings, I took a look at a showcase filled with engagement rings. None of them even compared to the size of Granny's, but I wanted to a get an idea of what they cost.

"This is what you're looking for, sir," Henry said, startling me. He handed me a small box with an engagement ring. He pointed toward Rose, who was now checking out some more earrings in the display case. "She likes this one."

"Does she." I looked at the pear-shaped diamond ring that he'd handed me.

"Yes, sir. It's three-quarters of a carat, with a good color and quality," he assured me in his best salesman's voice.

"How much?"

"Rose is a good customer. For you, eighteen hundred, regularly twenty-three."

If I didn't already have a ring, I would have brought that one on the spot. The price was right, and more importantly, I already knew Rose would like it. I was surprised, though, at the ring's size. I had no idea she would settle for anything less than a carat. The ring I had originally planned on buying her was a carat and a half and almost three grand. Granny's ring was at least two carats, so I figured Rose would be thrilled by the rock when I gave it to her.

"Oh, Allen, isn't it beautiful?" Rose approached from behind.

I looked over my shoulder and smiled. "Yeah, it's real nice."

"I'm gonna take these earrings, Henry." Rose handed him the empty earring box. The gems were still in her ears.

"Well, sir, what about that ring?" Henry smiled at me, then at Rose. He was trying to put me on the spot for the sale, and I sure didn't appreciate it too much.

"I'll be back to talk to you real soon. When I'm alone, okay?" Both Henry and Rose smiled as I slapped down my MasterCard to pay for the earrings.

Dinner was fantastic, and the atmosphere at Louie's set the perfect romantic mood. We shared our gourmet dinners, feeding each other across the candlelit table between sips of champagne. Every once in a while I would rest my hand over my jacket to feel the box that held Granny's ring. I was full of anticipation. The night was young and would only get better when I got down on my knees in front of the woman I loved.

After dinner we strolled over to the town dock and boarded the Sound of Music, a three-story cruise ship that was going to take us around the island of Manhattan. The cruise was great, and so was the band. We were the only blacks on board, but that didn't matter. Most of the people on board were our age, and let me tell you, they could party.

We were having a great time on the top deck, inhaling the fresh night air as we listened to the sax player blow a romantic solo. Rose sipped a glass of wine, holding on to the rail as she watched the full moon creep in behind the Statue of Liberty.

"Pretty, isn't it?" I asked, wrapping my arms around her waist as we admired the statue glowing against the nighttime sky.

"Perfect," she whispered.

"Are you having a good time?"

"Everything's perfect, Allen." She turned around to kiss me.

"What about this? Do you think this is perfect?" I opened up the box and showed her Granny's ring.

"Is that what I think it is?" She was beaming with excitement.

I bent down on one knee and smiled. "Rose, will you marry me?"

Tears streamed down her face as she answered, "Yes, Allen. Oh God, yes, I'll marry you."

I took out Granny's ring and placed it on her finger. It looked magnificent. Rose looked at her finger and then at me.

"Allen?" she said as I stood up.

"Yes, babe." I kissed her forehead.

"Oh, nothing." She just wrapped her arms around me and I held her close.

The next morning I found out what that "Oh, nothing" really was, and it sure was something. Rose didn't want Granny's ring. She wanted the ring from Henry's jewelry store. She tried to be polite about it, but there was no way of being polite when you've told someone that a family heirloom wasn't good enough for you. I was hurt, but I kept it to myself because I didn't want an argument after such a perfect evening. Plus I was more worried about what Ma was gonna say about Rose rejecting Granny's ring than anything.

I sat in the Macy's parking lot for almost an hour, staring at my grandmother's ring. I just couldn't figure it out. Why would Rose want a diamond half the size of Granny's? It just didn't make sense. Finally, I decided not to worry about it. If that's what she wanted, that's what she was gonna get.

I got out of my car and walked toward the jewelry store, sighing as I entered. There was old Henry, engrossed in some work at his jeweler's table. He recognized me right away.

"Ahh, Ms. Rose's friend." He offered his hand. "You've come for the ring, I take it."

I nodded with a frown.

"What's wrong, young man? Afraid to make that commitment?" He gave a reassuring look.

"No, that's not it. I proposed last night." I still couldn't shake the sadness from my voice.

"She did not accept?" Henry sounded surprised.

"Oh, she accepted. It's this she didn't accept." I handed him Granny's ring.

His eyes widened as he carefully removed the ring from the box. He walked over to his table and picked up his eyepiece, and he must have stared at that ring for five minutes without a word. The way he scrutinized it, you would think he was looking at a piece that had been stolen from his family.

"Do you realize what you have here?" he finally said. "This piece might be a hundred years old, and the diamond is a little over three carats. I'll give you twenty grand cash for it, right now."

"Sorry, Henry. This is a family heirloom. It belonged to my grandmother, and maybe even to her mother. I need to give it back to my mother."

"I understand. Ms. Rose made a big mistake." Henry shook his head.

"Yeah, she makes a lot of those, Henry." I pulled out my credit card and handed it to Henry. "I'll take that other ring now if you don't mind, Henry."

"No problem," he said as he ran the card through his machine. "I'm sorry, your card has come up 'declined.'" He tried to say it gently. I think the guy genuinely felt bad for me.

"That's impossible! Run it again." He did, and it came up "declined" again.

I was pissed. I'd been cleaning that card for months just to buy Rose a ring. There had to be room on it. That's when I remembered the dress, earrings, shoes, and handbag I had bought the day before. Not to mention the hundred and fifty dollars I spent on dinner and then the cruise. I'd spent almost a thousand dollars in one night, on a Visa card that only had a twenty-five-hundred-dollar limit. I looked at Henry, and he looked at me, wordlessly. Both of us knew I couldn't go home to Rose without that ring.

The Roadhouse Bar in Hollis had been our meeting place and hangout on Saturday nights since we'd been old enough to drink. The Roadhouse wasn't anything special, just a small local bar. But to us it was a sanctuary. A place we could go and be away from our better halves. We'd shared drinks there over good times and bad, and Jay, Wil, and Kyle had all announced their plans to marry there. That's why I'd waited all day to tell them about Rose's and my engagement. I thought it would be nice telling them in our old haunt. But by the time we arrived, it didn't seem like the greatest idea.

Our basketball team had its first loss of the year, and Jay was overreacting to it. He'd started drinking the minute we walked in. Wil was on his cell phone, getting comfort from his wife Diane. And Kyle was driving me crazy talking about this damn lawsuit he was filing against the police. He wouldn't let me get in a word.

"So, Allen, I'm probably gonna need you to be a character witness if we go to trial." Kyle waited for an answer. "Allen, Allen, you listenin' to me, man?"

"Yeah, I hear ya," I told him distractedly. "Look, can we talk 'bout the lawsuit later? I got somethin' important I need to tell y'all."

"You better not have quit your job again, Allen," Jay slurred.

"Nah, I got some good news," I assured them.

I gestured to Wil to hang up his phone so I could share my news.

"Look, hun, I'll call you back in a few minutes. Allen's got some mystery he's about to reveal." Wil said goodbye to his wife and gave me his attention.

"I'm about to join the club," I told them with a big grin.

"What club?" Jay asked.

I reached into my pocket and pulled out the box that contained Granny's ring.

"Oh, shit!" Kyle shouted. There wasn't any reaction from Jay and Wil until I opened the box to display the three-carat engagement ring.

"Look at the size of that rock," Wil said, his eyes bulging.

"Don't tell me you're getting engaged?" Kyle's voice sounded a little disappointed.

"That' right." I said, trying to figure out Kyle's reaction. "It's about time I made Rose an honest woman, don't you think?"

Kyle gave Jay a look, then shook his head. A look that told me that both of them thought I was crazy. Both Kyle and Jay had been telling me for years how hard marriage was. They said it was worth it, but both of them had days they wished they were single.

"Congratulations, Al." Wil grabbed my hand and pulled me into an embrace.

"Yeah, congratulations." Kyle shook my hand, but his heart was obviously not in it. "You sure you wanna do this? Rose is a nice girl, but why buy the cow when you gettin' the milk for free? Marriage ain't easy, bro."

"I know. But she's waited five years for this," I reasoned, giving them the same argument Rose had given me countless times before.

"I hope you know what you're doin', man." Kyle spoke like someone had just died.

I glanced at Jay, who was still staring at the ring. He hadn't said a word, which was probably a good thing. When Jay was drunk, he spoke his mind, and somebody usually ended up pissed off.

"Is this shit real?" Jay slurred. "I know your cheap ass didn't buy no rock this big."

"Yeah, that is a pretty big rock, Allen. How many carats is it?" Wil took the ring from Jay.

"Three carats, and the color and clarity are almost perfect. It was my grandmother's ring."

"See, Kyle, that's what I mean. Brothers like Allen always fuck up shit for the rest of us," Wil said with an attitude.

"What did I do?" I was expecting a little bit more support from Wil.

Wil's stern face softened.

"Why couldn't you be like the rest of us and get a half-carat? When Diane hears Rose got a rock like this, I won't be able to go home." Wil laughed. We all laughed.

"You would think Rose would like it, wouldn't you?" I asked.

"No doubt," Wil replied.

"She hated it. She told me if I was gonna marry her, I need to buy her a new ring. 'Cause she wasn't gonna wear no secondhand shit."

"Ohhh shit!" Kyle was shocked.

"So what you gonna do?" Wil asked.

"I went and got her another ring," I said flatly. "She's the one who has to wear it. Not me."

"You really gonna marry her after that?" Kyle looked puzzled, and he sounded mad.

"Ha! Ha! Ha! Ha! Ha!" Jay laughed. It was a sarcastic laugh, like he was laughing at me, not with me.

"What's so funny?" I turned my head toward him.

"You are," Jay replied, sitting forward about a foot from my face. I could smell the beer he was drinking.

"Why am I funny?"

" 'Cause you're the only fool I know who'd marry that freckle-faced bitch." Jay sat back in his chair and started laughing again.

"Jay!" Wil said sternly.

"Nah, Wil, let him get whatever's on his chest off. His jealous bull-shit don't mean shit." For once I was gonna stand up to Jay and his BS.

"Jealous?" Jay sat up and was in my face again. "Look, Allen, you know I love you, but I'ma be straight up with you . . ."

"Yo, Jay, let me talk to you a sec." Kyle frantically grabbed Jay's arm, trying to pull him away from the table. Jay shoved him off and continued his drunken speech.

"Fuck that shit, Kyle. You and Wil know Rose ain't nothin' but some pussy."

"That's right. My pussy, Jay. Remember that," I said with attitude.

"If you only knew." His vicious laugh was back.

"Jay, what you and Rose had was a long time ago. Why don't you get over it? She's my girl now, and I'm gonna marry her, whether you like it or not." I was pissed.

I knew this day would come, but I hadn't looked forward to it at all. Jay and Rose had dated a little during college. Both of them said it wasn't really a big deal, but I still hated the way Jay flirted whenever she was around. And to be honest, I think Rose encouraged it. I wasn't worried about them sleeping with each other. Jay would never do that to me. At least I didn't think he would. But the idea that my best friend had slept with my girl wasn't a pleasant one.

"I'm sorry, Al, but you can't marry Rose 'til you know the whole truth." Jay never took his eyes off me.

"What? The truth according to Jay?" I demanded.

"I know you wanna get married and have a few crumb snatchers, Allen, but Rose ain't the one. Brotha, you can do ten times better than her." I couldn't tell if Jay was attacking me or trying to protect me.

Jay looked at Wil, then at Kyle. "Can I tell him?"

Wil nodded. Kyle sat there with a blank expression before he spoke.

"I don't know, Jay. I thought we was gonna go to the grave with this shit." Kyle lowered his head.

"The mothafucker's gonna marry her, Kyle. We're damn near at his funeral now."

"Fuck that! Y'all supposed to be my boys. Tell me what the fuck's goin' on," I demanded.

"Aw'ight," Kyle shrugged, "But Jay, man, let me be the one to tell him. It might sound a little better than comin' from your drunk ass."

"That's cool with me." Jay sat back and crossed his arms across his chest.

"Allen, do you really wanna marry a woman who has slept with all three of us?" Kyle asked me without even blinking.

"What the hell you talkin' about, Kyle?" I sat back in my chair trying to grasp what I had just heard.

"We all fucked her!" Jay screamed, making everyone in the bar turn to look at us. "Shit, me and Kyle had a threesome with her."

I was in shock. I'd known about Jay, but Wil and Kyle? That was another story. I could feel my stomach start to churn like I was gonna throw up. I turned to Wil. I wanted to hear him say it.

"That true, Wil?"

"Yeah, Al, it is." He couldn't even make eye contact with me.

I slumped down in my chair. I couldn't believe my girl was doing *all* three of my boys.

"Look, Allen, it's better you find out now than later." Jay sounded like he was trying to be gentle all of a sudden.

"Fuck you, Jay." I stood up, ready to punch him in the mouth. I knew I would get my ass kicked, but it would've been worth it. If I could just get one good shot in. I took a step closer, but Kyle grabbed me from behind.

"Come on, Allen, let's take a walk." Kyle led me out the door.

When we got outside, Kyle let go of me and I spun around, fists clenched. "How could you do this to me, man? How could you sleep with Rose? What kinda fucking friend are you?" I had tears in my eyes.

"Hold up, Allen. That shit was a long time ago, man. You seem to forget I was the one who introduced her to you." Kyle was pleading with me to understand, but there was just no way. My whole world had just been turned upside down.

"I didn't forget shit. But you musta forgot to tell me you was bonin' her." I threw a punch that landed right on the side of his face, knocking him down. I regretted it right after it happened.

"What the fuck you hit me for?" He scrambled to his feet, rubbing his jaw where the punch had connected. He threw a verbal blow back at me. "Shit, everyone was fuckin' her ass back then! She was a ho!"

"So that's why you introduced her to me?" I asked in disbelief.

"Look, man, you was all depressed when Cinnamon left town. I figured you needed to loosen up, have a little fun. So I talked to Rose about giving you some. How the fuck was I supposed to know you was gonna fall in love with her?" Kyle had stopped breathing hard, and genuinely sounded sorry for the whole mess.

At that point I broke down. I couldn't take it anymore. Tears were running down my face like a river. I slumped down against a car and sat on the cold ground.

I looked up at Kyle. I felt as if I was shrinking right in front of him. The things he was saying were incredible. I'd always thought I had seduced Rose, not vice versa. Suddenly I understood why she never wanted to go out with my friends as a couple.

"I'm sorry, Al. I shoulda told you a long time ago, but you were so happy. And Rose has honestly changed for the better since." Kyle sat down next to me.

"We're supposed to be boys, Kyle." I bit my lip.

"I know, man. I fucked up."

"Yeah, you did, but that doesn't change the fact that I still love her." I had no idea what I was supposed to do with the news my boys had just given me.

"If it helps, I'm sure she loves you too," Kyle told me.

"I know," I said quietly.

"You still wanna marry her?"

I thought about what Kyle was asking me for a second. I had just found out Rose was a slut before we met, and I already knew she was materialistic. But none of that change the fact that I loved her. After my high school sweetheart Cinnamon left town, I was so depressed that I just couldn't get my shit together. I had about fifty grand saved from a life insurance policy from my pop's death, so money wasn't a problem. Plus I lived with my ma, so I didn't have to pay rent. For almost a year I just kinda drifted, living off that inheritance. I didn't put any effort into finding a job or finishing my degree. That is, until I met Rose. She made me feel so good about myself again and sexually she just blew my mind. The only problem was Rose was high maintenance and my little savings were only gonna last so long. By the time I realized I was in love with her, I had spent almost half of it. I didn't wanna lose her, so I did what I had to do to finish my degree as fast as possible. I worked two jobs to buy her the things she wanted. Until she helped me land my present job. She might have been looking out for her own interests, but she did help me get back on my feet during a pretty rough time.

"Yeah, Kyle, I still wanna marry her."

He looked at me in disbelief.

"So you gonna tell her you know about us sleeping with her?" Kyle asked a question I didn't want to think about, but I knew it would have to be dealt with sooner or later.

I shook my head. "Not yet, anyway. It's not gonna help anything. We'd just end up in a fight, and I don't wanna fight with her now."

"Yeah, I guess you're right," Kyle sighed. "Okay, if that's what you want. I'm with you."

He wrapped his arm around my shoulder as we sat there on the cold ground. "I just hope you know what your doin'," he sighed.

"So do I, Kyle. So do I."

7

Jay

I pulled in front of Thomasina's catering hall on Linden Boulevard in St. Alban's, wishing I didn't have to be there. I didn't wanna go to Allen and Rose's engagement party, because I didn't approve of the engagement. But Kenya had forced me to go.

I handed the valet my keys as I stepped out of the car, walking around to open the door for my wife. Kenya was looking good as shit in her tight-fitting red cocktail dress. If you passed her on the street, you'd never know she was five months pregnant.

I chuckled to myself when I caught the valet nonchalantly checking out her perfectly round behind and shapely legs. I gave him a wink and smiled, letting him know it was all right. Hell, if I were him, I'd check her out too. Kenya had a gorgeous figure and it made me feel good when another brother checked out my woman. Kyle and Wil always got mad when they caught guys staring at Lisa and Diane, but when brothers looked at Kenya, I took it as a compliment. I patted her on the ass and gave the valet another wink.

"You're looking good tonight, baby." I stared into her beautiful, light brown eyes and kissed her full, soft lips.

"You look pretty good yourself. Good enough to eat." She returned the compliment. She gave me a deep kiss and brushed her hand against my groin.

I couldn't believe how fast her statement got me aroused. The thought of her, giving me some was almost foreign to me. We hadn't made love in over five months, since she got pregnant. I led my wife into the catering hall with a wide grin plastered on my face. Maybe this wasn't gonna be such a bad night after all.

Thomasina's was a small catering hall, but there was enough room to comfortably hold the hundred or so people Rose and Allen had invited. When we walked in, the DJ was playing Barry White and the dance floor was crowded with couples slow dancing. I spotted Rose's cousin Debra, a cute, dark chocolate sister I'd been sexing a few months back. She stared me down as I walked by. Her husband was sitting next to her, and I gave him a nod as I winked at his wife. You shoulda seen the way she blushed.

Kenya spotted Kyle and Lisa and dragged me over to their table. I hugged and kissed Lisa, hoping that the truce we had come to at the courthouse a few weeks ago was still on. She hugged me tightly, letting me know it was.

"Hey, Kyle!" Kenya opened her arms for a hug.

"What's up, sister-in-law?" Kyle smiled. "Damn, I thought they said you was pregnant. You look like you should be on the cover of *Essence.*"

"Let me tell you something, flattery will get you everywhere." She turned to Lisa. "Hey, Lisa, you wanna switch husbands? I could use this kinda ego boost every day." She laughed.

"Sorry, Kenya, I found him first." Grabbing at Kyle's arm, Lisa pretended like she was jealous.

I watched Kyle and Kenya hug, and I shook my head. They were both so full of shit it made me sick to my stomach. Kenya couldn't stand Kyle. She didn't like him 'cause he married a white woman and moved her into Jamaica Estates, something I hadn't been able to afford as a social worker. Kenya wasn't prejudiced; she actually liked Lisa. She just couldn't stand Kyle because he was a brother with money who had sold out. It didn't matter that he didn't have a dime when he met Lisa or that I dated more white women than Kyle ever had. Nope, none of that was important. Once Kyle had made his money, she said he had an obligation to share it with his black sisters.

Kyle was fronting just as bad, 'cause he knew Kenya didn't like him and still played this nicey-nice game with her every time we got together. If she was any other sistah passing judgment on his life and his woman, he'd be all up in her face. I know he only tried to keep the peace because Kenya was my wife. But that polite shit was for the birds. When Lisa and I didn't get along, everyone knew it.

After a few minutes of pleasantries about whose child had a cold and which private school we were going to send our kids to, the girls excused themselves to find Rose and check out her new engagement ring.

"Y'know, Kyle, I still can't believe he's gonna marry her." I shook my head in disgust as we headed to the bar.

"I know," Kyle agreed. "But what you gonna do? The boy's in love."

"Yeah, but is she in love with him? If I wanted to, I bet I could still bone her, man. You should see the way she looks at me." As sad as it was, I was serious. Rose had always had a thing for me. On more than one occasion in the last few months, I'd gotten the impression that she wanted to give me some of what I'd already sampled. The only reason I hadn't hit it was 'cause Al's my boy.

"Don't even go there, Jay. Last time you decided that you knew what was best for one of our relationships, it nearly cost me my marriage." Kyle glared at me, probably still mad at the day Lisa found the panties in his car.

"We're not gonna go there, are we? You know I'm sorry about that shit," I told him for the millionth time.

"Nah, I'm not gonna go there, but you stay away from Rose." He pointed his finger at me. "Al can handle himself, Jay. Trust me on that."

"You sound awfully sure of yourself." I gave him an inquisitive look.

He smiled at the bartender. "Let me have a Dewars on the rocks, and give him a Heineken."

"What do you know, Kyle?"

He smiled and laughed. His laughter was kinda contagious and I started to laugh myself, even though I didn't know what was so funny.

"Come on, man, tell me what's up," I asked him.

"Aw'ight, but don't tell anyone about this. Not even Wil." He leaned in close and spoke in a conspiratorial whisper.

"Okay, man. Tell me what's up?"

"First off, Rose ain't as slick as she thinks. Remember that first ring Allen gave her, the one that belonged to his grandma?"

I nodded.

"Yeah. Well, that ring's worth at least twenty grand."

"Twenty grand?" My jaw dropped. If anyone should have known about the value of diamonds, it would be Rose and her materialistic ass. But it served that stupid gold digger right, passing up a family heirloom like she did.

"*Sssssshhh!* Why don't you just go over there and tell Rose? Damn!"

"Oh, sorry." I started laughing.

"That's not all." He gestured in the direction where Rose was still displaying her ring for our wives. "See that rock she's flashing?"

"Mmm-hmm."

"Allen couldn't afford the ring she wanted. So he had the jeweler substitute the real stone for a fake. That shit's a cubic zirconia." Kyle busted out laughing.

So did I. I couldn't help myself. I was laughing so hard my stomach hurt.

"I couldn't believe it when he told me that shit," Kyle said when he finally stopped laughing. "He's sure got some balls on him lately, don't he?"

"Yep. And here's to 'em." I raised up my Heineken and handed Kyle his drink for a toast. We headed back to our table.

"Ahem!" We both turned to see the bartender glaring at us.

"Oh, shit. We forgot to leave a tip. Sorry, chief." Kyle reached into his pocket and pulled out two dollars, placing them on the bar.

"Excuse me, sir. This is a cash bar," the bartender informed us with much attitude.

I almost spit out my beer when I heard that.

"Are you serious?" Kyle asked.

The bartender nodded and folded his arms across his chest, waiting for his cash. Kyle reached in his pocket angrily and put a ten on the bar.

"Come on, Jay. I don't believe these cheap-ass people." We walked back to the table where Wil was sitting with Diane.

"Did you know they had a cash bar?" Kyle asked before he even took a seat.

"Get the fuck outta here," Wil replied.

"Who gives themselves an engagement party and then can't even buy their guests a few drinks?" Diane asked, even though I could tell she wasn't trying to judge.

"Cheap-ass Rose, that's who. The same woman who wrote, *We would prefer cash for gifts,* on the engagement party invitation," I said in disbelief.

"How cheesy can you get?" Kyle put down his drink. "I hope Lisa didn't give Rose that envelope yet. I need to take out a couple of bucks for these drinks."

"I wonder if we're gonna get a bill for dinner at the end of the night?" I asked sarcastically as we all had a good laugh at the expense of the happy couple.

"Ya know, Rose and Allen are gonna get paid," Wil added.

"No, Rose's gonna get paid. I bet stupid-ass Allen doesn't even know what's going on." That woman was pissing me off more and more every day.

"Shit, somebody's gettin' paid. They're gonna get presents from the engagement party, the wedding shower, and the wedding. That bitch ain't getting' married for love, she's in it for the loot." Kyle looked sick. "Man, I'm going outside to smoke a cigarette."

"Hold up, Kyle, I'll come with you." I followed him outside.

In front of the catering hall, Kyle lit a cigarette and took a long drag. I hadn't seen him with a cigarette in almost ten years.

"When did you start smoking again?"

"When I got arrested. There wasn't shit to do in that cell but smoke." He exhaled the smoke.

"Damn, that's fucked up."

"Tell me about it. These things cost four-fifty a pack now," he chuckled, then got kinda quiet all of a sudden. His tone turned real serious. "Jay, can I ask you a personal question?"

"Sure, man, what's up?"

"You ever have any problem getting it up?" He couldn't look me in the eye when he asked.

"Hell, no!" I said loudly, so he'd know how much I meant it. "Have you?"

"Come on now. I got three kids. Do I look like I have a problem getting it up?"

"No, but you never can tell." He had me going. I knew if he was asking, then somebody we knew was having a problem, and I wanted to know who it was.

"If it's not you, who is it?" I faced him.

"I can't tell you that." He still wouldn't look me in the eye.

"Come on, man. Who'm I gonna tell?"

Kyle looked at the doors to the catering hall as if he was looking through them at someone inside. I peeked through them myself and saw Allen addressing the crowd.

"Ohhh shit. You mean Allen can't get it up?" My eyes got wide.

"Will you keep quiet? And no it's not Allen. You think Rose would be marryin' his ass if they were havin' that problem?"

"Depends. She might if the money situation was still tight." I tried to lighten Kyle's mood, but he didn't even smile. "Seriously, Kyle. If it ain't Allen, then who?" In the silence that followed, my mind went through every friend that we both knew. Kyle was so serious about this, I knew it had to be someone he was close to. "Nawww," I said slowly. "You mean ta tell me it's Wil?"

Kyle looked around. "You didn't get it from me."

"What happened?" I couldn't believe what I was hearing.

"He woke up one morning and the elevator wouldn't go to the top floor."

"Damn." The two of us were silent. I tried to imagine what it would be like not being able to have sex. A fate worse than death. Even so, I think Kyle was taking it harder than me. He looked like he was gonna cry.

Wil startled us. "You guys gonna join us? Allen wants us all to make a toast."

"Yeah, we're comin," Kyle answered.

"What's wrong with y'all? You look as if you lost your best friend."

"You would know," I said, about to spill the beans, until Kyle smacked me in the back of my neck.

On the drive home from the party, Kenya actually took her seat belt off and snuggled up against me. I wrapped my right arm around her as I drove. For the first time in recent memory, I didn't think about anyone but her. I glanced over at her smooth, cocoa brown face and smiled. It was just like old times when we were dating, me and her against the world.

"Have I told you I love you lately?" I was almost a little surprised I had actually said it. It had been a long time since I'd felt like saying anything romantic to my wife.

"No, you haven't." She snuggled a little closer.

"Well, I do, and I wish every night could be like this." I pulled her a little closer.

"I love you too, Jay." She looked up at me, her eyes all misty, then turned her face toward the window.

"Jay?" She spoke quietly.

"Yeah, babe."

"I'm sorry." She had real sincerity in her voice, and a tear slid down her cheek.

"Sorry about what?" I prayed she wasn't going to tell me about an affair. I'd cheated on Kenya hundreds of times, but I don't think I could deal with it if she'd been cheating on me too. Call me selfish and self-serving all you want, but I would kill the guy who slept with my wife. I braced myself for my wife's bad news.

"You're a good man and I haven't done right by you," she told me.

"What?" I turned, glaring at her as the car swerved into another lane, just missing a tractor-trailer. "What the hell do you mean? What are you trying to tell me?" I was pissed the fuck off.

"Oh my God, Jay. Watch where you're going!" Her eyes were wide with terror, and her hands went instinctively to her belly, protecting our unborn child.

I almost hit another car before I calmed down and got the car under control. "You been cheatin' on me Kenya? Who the fuck is he?"

"I haven't cheated on you!" She looked offended.

"Then what are you sorry about?" I relaxed my grip on the steering wheel slightly.

"I'm sorry I haven't been taking care of you in the bedroom the way

I should." She was apologizing, but her voice told me she was hurt by what I had just accused her of.

"Oh." To say I felt stupid is an understatement.

"From now on, I'm gonna take care of you at least two times a week." It sounded like she was giving a pledge. One I could happily accept. "And remember all the freaky stuff we did when we first met?"

I smiled and nodded.

"I wanna do that too." She reached over and rested her hand between my legs. Slowly and gently she undid my pants and released my johnson, which had wasted no time standing at attention. In the blink of an eye, her head was in my lap.

I moaned, trying to keep the car under control. Her sweet kisses were about to send me into frenzy. This surprise from my wife reminded me all at once of the Kenya I had fallen in love with.

8

Kyle

I'd been sitting in the reception area of the office of Dr. Jerome Stanley for half an hour. This wasn't my first visit, but I still felt like a nervous child waiting to get his shots. Dr. Stanley was the psychiatrist who I had been seeing ever since the false arrest and the fight with my wife. Normally I wouldn't even consider going to see a shrink, but things had gotten pretty bad for me. I'd reluctantly gone to see the shrink on the recommendation of my personal physician, Dr. Rayburn, who had been treating me because I was having major problems keeping an erection since my arrest.

Lisa had tried to understand in the beginning, but after a while she started taking the whole thing personally. Needless to say, she wasn't the least bit pleased with my performances. I guess one night she just decided she'd had enough. The woman had gone all out, with a new negligee, a bottle of French wine, and candles everywhere. I had to give her an A for effort, but I still couldn't make it work. She lost it in a fit of tears, wanting to know what was wrong with her that I couldn't get it up. She insisted I go see Dr. Rayburn and have him prescribe me some Viagra. At first I resisted, but was embarrassed into agreeing when she reminded me how long it had really been since she'd seen my little man standing at attention. That's when I realized I had a serious problem and needed to seek help.

That first visit to Dr. Rayburn's office was like my worst nightmare. My knees went weak when the receptionist asked me what my visit was for. I had this image of her putting my voice on her little intercom, so the whole office could laugh at the poor guy who couldn't get it up. Add to that the fact that Dr. Rayburn happened to be Jay's first cousin, and I thought I'd never make it out of there with a shred of dignity left. But I have to admit, Dr. Rayburn and his staff made me feel real comfortable. I guess I wasn't the only guy in the world with this problem. He told me that impotence was very common among men thirty-five years and older, and that Viagra would probably help things out. He gave me a few routine tests and explained what the drug was supposed to do. Then he made it very clear that Viagra could help any physical problems that I might be having with impotence, but if my problem was psychological, I would probably need to see a shrink. He wrote me a prescription and I left his office feeling pretty good. I was sure the stuff was gonna work just fine for me. I planned to make that night special. Lisa and I hadn't had good sex since my arrest.

On my way home I filled my prescription and stopped off at the florist to pick up a dozen roses. When I got to the house, I went straight to the kitchen, where Lisa was making dinner. My daughters were at the kitchen table, so I signaled for them to keep quiet as I snuck up behind Lisa and covered her eyes.

"Guess who?"

"Oh my God, Phil, I told you my husband was on his way home," she joked.

"That's not Phil, Mommy. That's Daddy!" my youngest yelled.

We all laughed. I took my hand off Lisa's eyes and presented her with the roses. She smiled, kissing me lightly.

"What'd the doctor say?" she asked seriously.

I looked away from her, biting my lip so I wouldn't smile. Then I reached into my suit coat and handed her a small jewelry box. She opened the box with a puzzled look on her face.

"What's this?" She picked up the small blue pill that rested inside the box.

I grabbed her tightly and whispered into her ear, "Baby, that's Viagra. And that means it's on tonight."

At seven-thirty we finished dinner and Lisa followed the girls into their room to get them ready for bed. She'd given me that "I'll meet you in the bedroom" wink before she left the table, so I started to mentally prepare. Making love to Lisa was important. During hard times when we were struggling, the intimacy of making love was the only thing that kept us together. Now with our disagreement about my lawsuit, we were slipping apart again. Without sex and the kids, we might not have any real reason to be in the same room.

The doc had told me to take my Viagra an hour before sex, so that's what I did. I poured myself a glass of ice cold water and swallowed that little magic blue bullet. Then I headed to the bedroom for a quick shower. I slipped into my silk robe and splashed on some cologne. Then I went to the girls' room to say good night. Lisa was just about to turn the lights out.

"Everyone's bathed and had their story," she smiled.

"I'll get the lights, babe. I wanna say good night to the girls." Lisa looked me up and down and winked. I smiled, watching her purposely sway her ass as she walked to our bedroom. I kissed each of my daughters and said good night, turning out the light.

By the time I was back in my bedroom, the Viagra should have been ready to take effect, and with a little encouragement I'd be ready for action. Slipping out of my robe and under the covers, I waited for Lisa to come out of the bathroom, hoping she'd be wearing something sexy.

I wasn't disappointed when she walked out. Lisa was wearing an all-white teddy with a white garter and stockings. She also had on a pair of white high heels and bright red lipstick. She looked like a Playboy playmate, and I felt like the luckiest man alive when she climbed on top of me. When she kissed me, her tongue slid into my mouth, reminding me how skilled she could be. I imagined all the other places she'd be using it that night. Finally she had worked her way down to my chest, nibbling on my nipples. I wasn't positive, because she was lying on top of me, but I knew I must have been rock hard. That Viagra was doing its stuff. Lisa pulled back the covers slowly and began to trail her tongue down my stomach. I opened my eyes and lifted my head, looking down eagerly. I hadn't seen my poor penis hard in almost two months. I wanted to see it and let out a sigh of relief.

"Kyle, are you concentrating?" Lisa sounded disappointed.

She'd seen it before me. I was limp as an egg noodle. God, what was I gonna do? I knew I couldn't live my life like this. Lisa tried her best to awaken my manhood, but everything she tried just didn't work.

Finally in frustration she shouted. "This is fucking ridiculous! I spent a hundred dollars on this outfit. I should have spent it on a good gigolo." She stomped out of the room.

Lisa slept in the guest room that night. I tried, but couldn't sleep at all. I didn't stick around for breakfast, but drove straight to Dr. Rayburn's office. I had to wait until nine o'clock for him to get in, but when I finally spoke to him he said, "Kyle, I'm sorry to hear that the Viagra didn't work. But I did tell you that this could be a psychological disorder and not a physical problem. Why don't I give you the number to Dr. Jerome Stanley? He's a top-notch psychiatrist, and he's also a brother."

I called Dr. Stanley right away for an appointment. After the first visit, I felt comfortable enough to make a second, and before I knew it, I had seen the shrink five times. He hadn't made any strong conclusions yet, but promised me this would be the visit he would give me his full evaluation of my situation. That's why I was sitting in his office, sweating like I'd run a marathon.

"Mr. Richmond," the receptionist called out, "the doctor will see you now."

I sighed heavily as I entered the doctor's office. I'd be lying if I said I wasn't nervous. I had this terrible image of the doc telling me my problem was permanent. Things were already bad enough at home. I'd been avoiding Lisa and hadn't slept in our room since the night of the failed Viagra. Not only that, but the girls were starting to sense the problem between us and it was obviously affecting them. My oldest, Jewel, a perfectly behaved kid, was really starting to act up in class.

I shook the doc's hand when I entered, and he gestured for me to have a seat by his desk. The doc was a brown-skinned man, probably in his fifties. While I sat down, he rummaged through a few of his desk drawers. I couldn't tell if he was stalling or really trying to find something, but his lack of eye contact made me very uncomfortable.

When he looked up, I tried to lighten my mood by asking, "So, Doc, do you think you can cure me?"

He shuffled the papers on his desk and looked at me with a tiny smirk. "Yes, Kyle, I think I can cure you." Then he returned to his paper search until he found a folder.

"Sorry about that. I'm a little disorganized today."

I laughed. "Don't worry, Doc. I'm disorganized every day."

"Mr. Richmond, I think we can be certain your problem originated around the time you were falsely arrested. But I don't think it was entirely your arrest that caused your impotence. I think it was stress-related."

"Stress?" I was confused.

"Yes, stress-related. I think you need to take a vacation. Preferably just you and your wife. The normal strains of your everyday life had been intensifying, and this fiasco with the police just sent you over the edge."

I stroked my mustache as I listened intently to the doctor. What he was saying made a lot of sense. I'd been working sixty-plus hours a week for almost five years, and the only time I had to relax was playing ball with the fellas and making love to Lisa. I hadn't been on a vacation in three years.

"Okay, Doc. I think that's a good idea."

"I'd also like you and your wife to come in together for an hour session each week, in addition to the time we spend one-on-one." He reached into his drawer and handed me a business card. "I know this is going to be hard, but I'd also like the two of you to see Beverly Jenkins. She's one of the best sex therapists in the business."

"Sex therapist? I'm not going to a sex therapist. Why do I need a sex therapist?" Just the sound of it made me feel that even if I could get it up, this so-called professional didn't believe I would know what to do with it.

"Doc, you said it was stress. Why can't I just take a vacation and cut back my hours at work? I'm gonna be seeing you twice a week."

"I said your problem was stress-related. I didn't say it had anything to do with work. In fact, work is probably the place you're least stressed."

I looked at the doc strangely. He was really confusing me now.

"Kyle, your stress derives from your marriage."

"Hold on. I have to disagree with you. The only thing stressful about my marriage is that I can't get it up," I explained, like I was the one with the medical degree.

Dr. Stanley sat back in his chair and folded his hands. He didn't say a word, just watched me until I calmed down.

"Let me ask you something, Kyle."

"Go ahead."

"Why'd you marry your wife in the first place? Do you have a problem with black women?"

"Hell no. What kind of a question is that?" I was offended.

"Then how come in every session we've had you've admitted to avoiding affection with your wife when black women are around?"

"That's because sisters be trippin', they get all jealous and start talkin' shit about you."

"Why should that bother you? You're married." I didn't know how to answer him.

"Didn't you also say that you don't let your wife come to your stores because you didn't want your customers to know you were married to a white woman?"

"Yeah, but that's just business. Some sisters get offended when they find out I sold out, and they take their business elsewhere."

"Oh, so you think you sold out by marrying a white woman?"

"Yes. Uh, I mean no. It's just that sisters don't wanna do business with a brother who's married to a white woman." He was confusing me, and I was getting angry because it seemed so easy for him to do.

"I don't understand. What's more important? Your wife, or a few prejudiced women that won't buy their hair care products from you because you married outside your race?"

"Doc, you're black. You know how it is." I shrugged my shoulders, hoping for some sympathy.

"No, Kyle. I don't know how it is. And whether I'm black or not has nothing to do with it. Especially since my wife happens to be white, too. You have a problem with your wife being white, Kyle. And I think we need to come up with a plan to deal with it."

"Doc, that can't be right. I love my wife." Everything he was saying about me was scaring me.

"Well, Kyle, you can always get a second opinion. But you said yourself that you no longer see your wife as a woman, but as a white woman." He was killing me with my own words.

"I didn't mean that, Doc."

He looked at me with a doubtful expression.

"At least I didn't mean it that way. Did I?" I must have looked stupid.

He looked at his watch, then at me. "You've gotta make a decision. Either you're going to get some help or you're not. Go home and talk to your wife. Give me a call in a few days."

"Okay, Doc." I walked out of that office feeling much worse than when I walked in. Could this man really be right about me?

I didn't go home after seeing Dr. Stanley. I couldn't. I was just too embarrassed to tell Lisa that the doc diagnosed my impotence as race-related. So I went to the Roadhouse Bar to have a couple of drinks and play some chess. I wasn't there five minutes when this fine dark-skinned sister, probably about twenty, walked over.

"Hey, baby, the bartender said you're drinkin' Dewars on the rocks. If I buy this one, think you can buy the next?" She sat down next to me, handing me a drink. "My name's Sheika, what's yours?"

"Just call me married." I lifted my left hand and showed her my wedding ring.

"What?" She laughed, sitting back in her chair. "You gotta be kidding. Is that supposed to mean something?"

"Look, baby, you look good, real good. But I'm not interested, okay?"

"Is that so?" Would you believe this bold young sister reached under the table, slid her hands between my legs, and took hold of my penis. Instantly making it hard. "That's not what your friend's saying." She kept massaging me, and I was getting harder and harder.

I knew I should have stopped her, but I couldn't. It just felt too damn good.

"Come on, baby. Let's get outta here," she offered. "I'm horny as hell, and I only live two blocks away."

"Aw'ight, let's go," I agreed with barely another thought.

You know, in seven years of marriage I never once cheated on my wife. I'd had opportunities. Plenty of them. And I came damn close more than once. But I always found the willpower to stop myself. That wasn't gonna happen this time. My stuff hadn't had any action in so long, I was powerless against the desire this fine young thing had awakened in me with just one touch.

We both got up, and I followed her to the bar.

"Maria, I'm going home, baby. I found what I was looking for." She high-fived a gorgeous Latino sister with long black hair.

"Aw'ight, girl. I'll see you at home in a while," her friend replied with a devilish laugh.

It didn't take any time to walk the two blocks to Sheika's apartment. She lived above a real estate office on Jamaica Avenue. When we entered the apartment, she immediately walked over to the stereo and turned on some slow, romantic music. It was dark in the room and I couldn't see a thing, so I just stood and waited for her lead.

"Come on, baby, my room's back here." She took my hand and guided me down the narrow hall to her room. The lights were still out, and I couldn't really see how her room was decorated, but I could see the silhouette of the bed, so I sat down.

"You know, you still haven't told me your name."

"Kyle. Just call me Kyle."

"Kyle, I like that."

A street lamp outside cast a subtle golden light in the room. I watched her slip out of her tank top and jeans, and the light made her spectacular body appear to glow. She had large breasts, and a butt shaped like a Georgia peach. She swayed like an exotic dancer, and I swear I've never been so turned on in my life. I gently took hold of her waist and let my fingers do the walking. She was so soft. I pulled her in close, sucking on her breasts until both her nipples were fully erect. Then I laid back on the bed, pulling her up until her womanhood was right over my face.

I performed oral sex on her for what seemed like an eternity. Every time she had an orgasm, I would pull her down to give her another one. Finally she gasped. "Okay, baby, that's enough. It's just too sensitive down there."

I let go of her, and she slowly removed my pants, sliding her head down to return the favor. I was rock hard, and it felt so good when she licked me. I let out a long moan.

"Ohhh, you think that's somethin'?" She climbed on top of me, mounting me like a horse. "That ain't nothin'."

I let out another moan, this one even louder. For twenty minutes I watched her ride me like an expert. Then, out of nowhere, I saw someone standing in the shadows of the doorway. It had to be her roommate Maria. She was taking off her clothes, and I watched her silhouette in amazement, thinking of the possibilities.

"Mind if my friend joins in?" Sheika asked.

"Hell no." I closed my eyes and savored the moment. I hadn't done anything like this in ten years.

Sheika slid off me, and immediately a pair of warm hands took hold of my penis. Her friend was stroking me so good I had to open my eyes to watch. That's when I saw my wife Lisa with my penis in one hand and a twelve-inch butcher knife in the other.

"Hi, honey," was all she said as she raised the knife above her head, preparing to whack off my best friend.

"*Nooooooooooo!!!!!!!!*" I screamed, sitting up in the bed. Lisa was still standing in front of me, but she wasn't holding a knife and I wasn't in Sheika's apartment. I was in the guest room of my house.

"Kyle, are you all right?" Lisa asked frantically. "You were screaming so loud I thought you were going to wake the girls."

I reached down between my legs and held on to my penis for dear life. "It was only a dream," I muttered, rocking back and forth. "It was only a dream."

"Kyle, are you all right?" Lisa reached to touch me and I scampered to the other side of the bed. I'd never been so afraid of anyone in my entire life.

"Look, I'm going back to bed. This is bullshit." I was trembling as I watched Lisa walk out of the room.

I hadn't been able to sleep for two weeks. Every time I laid my head down, I had that same damn dream. I swear, there are a lot of bad things you can dream about, but your wife cutting off your penis has to be the worst. I'd basically isolated myself from Lisa and the kids. I was so paranoid and sleep deprived that I was at the point where I would snap at anyone and everyone for no good reason. Finally, perhaps out of desperation, I decided to confront my problem. I sat at the breakfast table with my family for the first time in over two weeks.

"We're having omelets and sausage, Daddy," my daughter Jade told me.

"He can see that, Jade. You're so stupid," Jewel told her.

"I'm not stupid." Jade began to cry.

"Jewel, stop making your sister cry," I ordered.

"Why should I, Daddy? You make Mommy cry every night." I turned to look at Lisa, who had her back to me, preparing something at the counter.

"What have you been telling her?"

"Kyle, she's seven years old. She doesn't need me to tell her anything. She sees things." She turned to look at me, and that's when I saw the knife she was holding. I swear it was pointed right at my penis. I broke into a cold sweat and nearly had a heart attack on the spot.

"Kyle, are you all right? Maybe you should go see Dr. Stanley again." Lisa placed the knife on the counter and walked toward me. It took me a second to recover from the nightmare image I had just seen.

"I'm aw'right." I got up from my seat, trying to put some distance between Lisa and me.

"What is wrong with you? You're acting so strange lately." Lisa had an attitude.

"Nothing's wrong," I insisted, though I still had flashes of her wielding the knife.

"Look, I gotta get outta here. I gotta go to work." I walked toward the foyer leading to the front door and picked up my briefcase and coat.

"Kyle." I turned, and there was Lisa, standing behind my three daughters.

"You forgot to kiss them goodbye." She looked down at the girls.

My mind was in another world. I had never forgotten to kiss my girls goodbye. Even when I was mad at Lisa, I always kissed them goodbye.

"Daddy's sorry, girls." I bent over and gave my two youngest a big kiss on the lips. Jewel resisted, turning her head so that I could only kiss her cheek. I didn't even look at Lisa. I just turned and walked out the door.

"Excuse me, sir?" the woman said in a soft Jamaican accent.

I opened my eyes and smiled at the beautiful, golden brown stewardess as she politely placed the delicious smelling tray of food in front of me. I was glad I decided to spend the extra money on first class instead of coach. The service was excellent.

"You said you couldn't make up your mind between the filet mignon and the lobster, so I brought you both." She smiled.

"Thanks."

"No problem at all. Just call me if you need anything else."

As I placed my napkin on my lap and started my meal, I thought about Lisa. She'd probably gotten my note by now.

When I left the house that morning, I drove straight to the nearest real estate office. Two hours later I was back home, packing my stuff to move into my new apartment. Thank God Lisa wasn't home. I don't think I could have faced her. But I also couldn't take living with her anymore. The dreams were driving me crazy, and being around her was making me constantly paranoid. On my way out the door, I wrote her a ten-thousand-dollar check, and a note that said:

Dear Lisa,
   I'm going on vacation alone. I don't know when I'll be back, so don't wait up. Trust me, it won't be anytime soon.
                                                          Kyle

It was a cruel way to leave things, and it would probably come back to haunt me, but I just didn't want to face her. Not until I cleared my head and got rid of those damn dreams. I finished my dinner and leaned my head back to try to sleep. If things turned out right, I would have a dreamless sleep, and wouldn't wake up until the plane had already landed in Africa.

9

Wil

It was almost midnight when the phone rang, and I was feeling pretty good. Diane was lying on her back, half-asleep, and I was giving her one of my patented foot massages. We'd just made love for the second time that night, which was pretty amazing, considering the baby was due in less than ten days. I reached for the phone, trying not to disturb her.

"Hello."

"Wil, it's Jay. You alone?"

I hesitated for a few seconds, looking at my wife. She looked real comfortable. Heck, I was real comfortable. Whatever Jay had to say couldn't be that important. I figured I'd just let him get it off his chest and get him off the phone fast.

"Yeah, Jay, I'm alone." Diane sat up straight and glared at me. I put my hand to my lips, trying to keep her quiet.

"I just got a call from Kyle."

"He called you?" I couldn't believe Kyle called Jay instead of me. None of us had heard from him in so long, but I always figured he'd contact me first.

"Yeah, he's flying home in the morning. He wants us to pick him up."

Kyle had been missing for four weeks, and he hadn't even called his kids. I knew he was having a few problems with Lisa, but I never dreamed he'd up and leave his family. To make matters worse, there were fifty million rumors circulating around the Roadhouse Bar about his disappearance. The rumors ran the gamut from he was hiding out from the Mafia because of debt, to he'd met some young woman and run away to Europe with her. And even his closest friends didn't know the truth about where he was and why he'd left. I was glad to hear that he was coming home, though. Despite whatever he had done or not done, he was my man, and I missed him.

"Flyin' in from where, Jay?" I demanded. Diane tugged on my arm insistently, so I interrupted Jay before he could even answer. "Hold on a minute." I covered the phone.

"Has he been talking to Kyle?" Diane whispered.

I nodded. Diane got up angrily and walked out of the room. I guess it was a good thing I'd gotten some earlier, 'cause now she was in one of her moods. There would be no more passion in our bedroom tonight.

"So where's Kyle?" I returned to my phone call.

"It's a long story. I'll let him tell you himself."

"No, you tell me now," I demanded.

"Aw'ight. But don't yell at me. I'm not the one who screwed up this time."

Just then I heard Diane pick up the other extension in the living room. At that point, I knew it was gonna be a long night.

"Jay Crawford, where the hell is Kyle? Lisa and those kids are going crazy over there," she said sternly.

"This is none of your business, Diane," Jay stated flatly. "Let me and Wil handle this, aw'ight?"

"Nigga, please! I'm the one who's been goin' over there watchin' them kids and dryin' up Lisa's tears. I ain't seen your ass over there once since Kyle left. You're probably the one who talked him into leaving. So don't you tell me what's not my business."

"You better check your wife, Wil, 'fore I hurt her feelings." I could feel the anger in Jay's words.

"Check me for what? Ain't nothin' your sorry ass can do to hurt me. Only one you know how to hurt is Kenya. Fuckin' around with all those nasty-ass women. One day somebody's gonna call Kenya and open her eyes," Diane threatened.

"And who's gonna do that, Diane? You?" Jay was trying to stay calm, but I could tell Diane's threats had him worried.

"Maybe I will, Jay. Maybe I'll tell her about your friend Jackie, or about what you did with her cousin Wendy. Or maybe I'll—"

"Diane, will you please hang up," I interrupted her attack. I really didn't want her to go on. When she was mad, Di had a habit of repeating things I'd told her in confidence. And I really didn't want all the things I'd told her about Jay to come back and haunt me.

"No, Wil!" She was heated.

"Diane! Hang up the fucking phone!" Now I'd had it.

"Don't you talk to me that way, Wil Duncan! I'm not one of your friends." I could hear Jay laughing in the background.

"Then hang up the phone!"

"Nah, Wil. I'll hang up," Jay offered. "I don't need to be discussin' anything on your phone no more. Obviously there's no secrets in your house, with you bein' married to the town busybody and all."

"No, Jay, hold up. What about Kyle?"

"What about him? Isn't it obvious he needs our help? He'd never leave his kids if he didn't have real problems. That's why he wants to see his *best friends* before seeing Lisa. But best friends know how to keep confidences, unlike you." He hung up.

I tried to call him back on both his cell phones, but he didn't answer. I even called his house, but Kenya said she thought he was with me. About five minutes later, Diane walked into the bedroom with her head down. I don't think I'd ever been as upset with her as I was at that moment.

"Wil?" Her voice was barely a whisper.

I didn't say anything, I just looked at her. She knew she had fucked up.

"Wil, honey, say something." Tears ran down her face.

"I think you said enough for the both of us, Diane. Now Jay's gonna tell Kyle and Allen that I can't be trusted. How many times do I have to tell you to stay out of our business?"

"It was Jay's fault. He just makes me so mad." She took a few steps closer.

"Don't blame this on Jay. You're the one who picked up the damn phone." I exhaled loudly. "Why can't you ever leave well enough alone? You knew I was gonna tell you whatever he told me."

She didn't say anything. She just kept staring at me, holding her stomach.

"Why are you holding your damn stomach? You're not gonna have the baby now."

"I'm sorry, Wil. Please don't be mad."

I got out of bed and put on my robe, ignoring her. "I'm gonna go check on Teddy." I could hear her call after me as I walked out of the room, but I never turned around, and she didn't follow.

I'd been half-asleep in a rocking chair in Teddy's room for almost an hour when I heard her call my name again. I didn't answer, but when I opened my eyes, she was standing in the doorway holding her stomach again.

"Wil," she whimpered.

"What?" I snapped.

"It's time."

"Time for you to leave me alone," I mumbled.

"Wil, really, it's time. I'm gonna have the baby." I could tell from the way her voice shook that she was serious. I jumped out of the chair and ran to her.

"Okay, try to breathe like we practiced," I coached as I guided her down the stairs. All my anger had subsided as I gazed at her. How could I be mad at a woman getting ready to give birth to my child?

"You okay, honey?" I helped her into a chair.

"Yes, I'm . . . Ahhhh!" she screamed.

"Was that a contraction?" When Diane nodded, I checked my watch to see how far apart they were coming. "I'll be right back. I'm going to call Mom and get Teddy. I handed her my watch. "I want you to keep track of the contractions, okay?"

It didn't take long at all for me to get Teddy dressed and help him and Diane into the car. Before I stepped into the driver seat, I looked into the night sky. It was cloudy, but I could see one star, bright and clear. Three months before we'd seen an ultrasound, and knew we were having a girl. "Just make her healthy, God," I prayed out loud. I swear that star twinkled.

The drive to my mother's took less than ten minutes. We left Teddy with her, and within twenty minutes we were in Jamaica Hospital's labor and evaluation room, which was the biggest pain in the ass in the world. All I can remember thinking was, *We should have taken Rose's advice and had our child at a Long Island Hospital.* Would you believe they separated Diane and me until she was ready to go into delivery? They had me waiting in the damn emergency room lobby for almost two hours while the nurses in labor and evaluation probed Diane. I ranted and raved to every person who looked like a hospital employee, right on down to the janitor. Finally a nurse came out and told me I could join my wife for the delivery.

Thank God, when we did finally get into the delivery room things went a lot smoother than I had expected. Diane's doctor, Jill Lowenstein, was great. She knew just what to say to make Diane comfortable during the delivery process. I held on to Diane's hand, trying to help her with her breathing the best I could. We'd skipped the Lamaze classes when Teddy was born and Diane had a real painful delivery. The second time around she made me promise to take the classes with her. From what Kyle had told us, Lamaze really helps if the couple works on it together.

"Come on, honey. Breathe," I told her as the pain of another contraction hit her.

"How the hell can I breathe when this baby is trying to rip me open?" she screamed, staring at me with bugged eyes.

"Just calm down. Try to *breatttthhhhee,*" I murmured, exhaling like I wanted her to.

"I can't calm down. It hurts! You did this to me, Wil. And when this is over, I ain't ever lettin' you near me again." The look Diane gave me as she tried to push our second child out was deadly serious. I was pretty sure she would change her mind after she had the baby, but at that moment I knew she meant every word. So much for Lamaze.

I looked down at the doctor, who was in between the stirrups like a baseball catcher. "Dr. Lowenstein, can't you give her something for the pain?" The doctor ignored me and told my wife to push again, which she did with one huge scream.

"Wil, please make them give me something for the pain," she pleaded.

"Doctor, can't you give her another epidural?"

"Come on, Diane, push," the doctor told her, still ignoring me.

"Doctor, can't you please give her another epidural?" I shouted this time.

The doctor popped her head up from between my wife's legs and turned her attention to me for a split second. "Mr. Duncan, why don't you step down here so I can show you something." She was asking, but it sure felt like an order.

I took my place beside the doctor and looked between my wife's legs. Let me tell you, as soon as I saw my daughter's thick black hair, I yelled right along with the doctor, "Come on, Diane, I can see her hair. *Puusssshhhh! Puusssshhhh! Puusssshhhh!*" The nurses in the delivery room were all laughing at my sudden personality change.

My excitement gave Diane renewed energy, and she strained through a long push. I watched the doctor grab hold of my child's head, helping the birth process. Thirty seconds later my daughter was born. I cried like a child as I watched the nurses clean up my daughter and wrap her in a blanket. They placed our beautiful baby on Diane's chest and I watched in awe as mother and daughter laid eyes on each other for the first time.

"We did it, Wil. We did it." Diane was crying as she handed me our daughter.

"No, baby. You did it." I kissed my wife, then our child. "Well, what's her name?"

"Katherine, after your mother." Diane looked at me and smiled.

"Katherine, I've got a feeling you're gonna be your grandmother's favorite grandchild." I bent over and kissed Diane again. It's unbelievable how things turn out. Six hours ago I was as mad as hell at her, but as I held my infant daughter, Diane could do no wrong in my eyes.

10

Allen

It was quarter to nine, and I'd been sitting in my car outside the Parsons Boulevard stop of the E train for forty-five minutes. Jay was supposed to meet me at eight so we could pick up Kyle at the airport, but he was his usual late self. I was just about to call to find out what was taking him so long when my cell phone rang.

"This you, Jay?" I answered.

"No, it's Wil."

"Wil, what's up, man?" I hadn't spoken to him in about a week, and it was good to hear from the big man. Although I did think it was strange that he wasn't going with us to meet Kyle.

"Diane had the baby last night. A six-pound–three-ounce baby girl." His voice was full of fatherly pride. God, I couldn't wait until Rose and I had kids.

"Congratulations, Wil," I said happily. "What's her name?"

"Katherine Nicole, after my mom."

"After Aunt Kathy, huh? Man, that's beautiful. I'm real happy for you, Wil."

"Well, I hope you're gonna be happy for yourself too, 'cause we'd like you to be the godfather."

"Really, Wil, you serious?" I liked that idea.

"Yeah, I'm serious."

I have to admit I was more than a little choked up. I'd never been a godfather before. Jay, Wil, and Kyle had all passed me by with their other kids, probably because I didn't have my shit together. But now that I had a good job and was getting married, Wil and Diane must have thought it was time to bless me with the honor of being a god-parent.

Tap, tap, tap

"Hold on Wil," I said when I heard tapping at my passenger window. There was Jay, standing outside the car. I hit the button to unlock the door and watched him get in the car. He actually gave me this funky look, as if he couldn't imagine what the hell I would be doing on the phone.

"Come on, Allen. Let's get goin'. We're runnin' late," he ordered.

"Aw'ight, hold on a sec, I'm talkin' to Wil." Jay rolled his eyes. "Wil—look, man, Jay and I are about to head on over to Kennedy to pick up Kyle. I'll stop by the hospital after we drop him off, okay?"

"Damn, y'all going to get Kyle now?"

"Yeah, can you believe it? I can't wait ta see that brotha."

"Me, either." Wil sounded as if he wanted to go.

"Want me to swing by and pick you up?" Jay started gesturing and shaking his head in disapproval. I don't know how, but I think Wil sensed that something was wrong because he immediately turned me down.

"Nah. I gotta go over to my mom's and get Teddy," he answered. I wasn't sure if I believed him.

"You sure?" I asked, ignoring Jay.

He hesitated before speaking, "Yeah, I'm sure."

Jay was starting to look impatient so I figured I better go. "Look, I gotta go. We shoulda been there a half an hour ago."

"Before you go, lemme ask you a question. Did Jay tell you why Kyle left?" Something was strange about the way Wil was questioning me, but I couldn't figure out what it was.

"Nope, I don't think he knows."

"That's what I thought. Look, Allen, tell Kyle to call me."

"Aw'ight, later."

"Later, Al."

I clicked off my phone and pulled the car onto Archer Avenue, headed toward the Van Wyck Expressway and Kennedy Airport.

"He wasn't talkin' about me, was he?" Jay sounded a little paranoid.

"No." I shook my head. "He was tellin' me that Diane had the baby."

"You sure he wasn't talkin' 'bout me?"

"I said he was tellin' me about his baby." I turned and looked at Jay seriously. "Yo, what's up with you two lately, why y'all always arguin'?"

" 'Cause Wil's got a big mouth! He's always tellin' Diane my business. You know she threatened to tell Kenya I was fucking around?"

"Get the fuck outta here."

"Hell yeah. She told me that shit to my face. So watch your back, 'cause you could be next."

"I'm not worried about Diane, 'cause I don't fuck around," I told him confidently.

"Not yet anyway," Jay said sarcastically. "Not yet."

"Not ever," I said, hitting the accelerator.

We pulled up to the TWA terminal at Kennedy Airport, and Kyle was standing out front next to three large suitcases. He was wearing a traditional African dashiki with a matching kuffee. His arms were folded across his chest, and a frown darkened his face. I was not about to take the blame for making him wait like this.

"You know he's pissed we're late." If there was one thing that had always bugged Kyle, it was people who were not on time. Unfortunately that was Jay's trademark.

"Man, what was I supposed to do? Kenya wouldn't let me leave without givin' her some." Jay opened his door and smiled. "What up, dawg?"

Kyle tried to hold back a smile, but he couldn't. "What's up, Jay?" The two of them embraced as I walked around the car.

"Sorry were late, Kyle." I smiled at him.

"Don't worry about it, bro, I know it wasn't your fault." Kyle gave a sideways glance to Jay. "I bet if I was some woman you wouldn't be late, would you?"

"Well, you damn sure ain't no woman." Jay lifted the bags and placed them in the trunk.

"Hey, where's Wil?" Kyle asked as he slipped into the front passenger seat.

"He's at the hospital. Diane had a baby girl last night," I told him.

"I guess I'm gonna have to go to check him out after I see the girls."

"Yeah, he told me to tell you to call him."

As we drove out of the maze they call Kennedy Airport, we were all silent until Kyle finally spoke.

"Man, I can't tell you how good it is to be home."

"It's good to have you home," Jay said.

"So are you gonna tell us where the hell you've been, or what?" I glanced over at him.

"Yeah, I guess I owe you guys that much," Kyle answered. "I was in Africa."

Jay burst out laughing, "What the fuck was you doin' there? Tryin' to find yourself?"

Kyle turned to Jay, expressionless. "Yeah, Jay, that's exactly what I was tryin' to do. Why, you got a problem with that?"

"Nah, man, I was just askin'." Kyle always did have a knack for putting Jay in his place.

"Look, I'm not tryin' to start no shit, but I do got a problem with it," I announced. Kyle looked at me in disbelief as I explained. "We're supposed to be your boys. You could've told us you were leaving. Obviously you got some kinda problem. Maybe we coulda helped."

"You're right, Al. I should have told you." Kyle lowered his head. "But there are some things a man has to do on his own."

"So what's up? Did you find what you was lookin' for or what?" Jay asked.

"To be honest with you, Jay, the only thing I found was that everything I was looking for is right here in New York."

At that point, the ride became silent. I think all of us, including Kyle, were trying to figure out exactly what he meant by his last statement.

11

Kyle

Allen pulled his Maxima into my driveway and turned to me with a solemn look. After he and Jay picked me up at the airport, we made a quick stop at my apartment to drop off my bags, then headed over to the house so I could see my kids. Allen had been more than a little upset to find out I'd rented my own place. And believe me, for a guy that hates to argue, he sure let me know how he felt.

"You want us to go in with you?" Jay asked from the back seat.

"Yeah, bro, why don't we go in with you?" Allen had already taken off his seatbelt. Although he was probably sincere, I wasn't sure if he wanted to go in to support me or to find out why I left Lisa.

"No, this is something I have to do by myself," I told them.

I sighed heavily as I opened the car door. It had been over four weeks since I'd seen my family, and I missed my girls terribly. Truth is, I started missing Lisa too, once those horrible dreams stopped. I just didn't miss her as a husband misses his wife, but more as one friend would miss another. To use an old cliché, I loved Lisa, but I wasn't *in love* with her anymore. As I stepped out of the car, I said goodbye to Allen. I really appreciated that he was there to support me.

"Hey, Kyle. Sorry about the way I acted back at your new place. It's just that if you and Lisa can't make it, what chance do me and Rose have?" Allen asked sincerely.

I didn't answer him, 'cause I didn't have an answer. For his sake, I hoped Allen and Rose worked out, but in the back of my mind I gave them a year, tops.

"I know you're not ready to talk yet, but whenever you are, I'm here for you." Jay stepped out of the car and gave me a one-arm hug.

"Yeah, I know," I replied, watching him get into the front seat.

As they pulled off, I walked to the front door of my house. I had butterflies in my stomach, and perspiration was forming on my forehead. I was more than a little nervous about what kind of reaction Lisa would have to my sudden reappearance. I was about to coward out and go back to my apartment, but Allen had pulled off and was headed down the street.

At that point I had no choice but to face the music. I pulled out my cigarettes and lit one to calm my nerves. I smiled, releasing the smoke as I listened to my girls playing on the other side of the door. Hearing their laughter made me put all concern for their mother's reaction behind me. I dropped the cigarette, crushing it with my foot as I rang the bell. I was greeted by Lisa's best friend, Karen.

"Oh, my God. What are you doin' here?" She rolled her eyes.

"I'm here to see my family," I said humbly. I could tell she was about to say something smart, but my two youngest daughters interrupted.

"Daddy!" They ran over to me, and I scooped them up in one huge bear hug. I kissed both of them, trying my best to hold back the tears. There is no way to describe how good it felt to hold them again.

"I missed you guys."

"We missed you too, Daddy," they said in unison.

"Where's Jewel?" I asked, carrying them past Karen.

"She's in the family room with Mommy," Jade told me.

I walked down the hall to the family room, nervous but eager to see my oldest daughter Jewel. I found her in front of the TV playing with her Barbies. Lisa sat in a chair nearby.

"Jewel," I called out softly, still standing in the doorway.

She turned toward me and smiled, then looked to her mother. Suddenly her smile became a frown and she ran to Lisa, grabbing her tight. I felt so empty at that moment I just wanted to burst into tears. Out of all my kids, I had been closest to Jewel. Ever since she was born, she was the one who always wanted to go with Daddy or sit on Daddy's lap. We'd developed a bond that I thought would never be broken. Until now.

"Jewel," I called again, this time a little sterner. My heart sank when she gripped her mother tighter. It took everything I had to stop myself from screaming at Lisa, who silently glared at me from her seat on the couch. This had to be all her doing. Why else would Jewel run from me?

"Get down for a minute, girls." I let my two little ones down and walked into the family room toward Lisa and Jewel. "Come'ere, Jewel. Daddy wants to talk to you." I stretched my arms out, and Jewel buried her head into Lisa's breast.

"Can't you see she doesn't wanna talk to you, Kyle?" Lisa's voice was hard, almost threatening. Some kind of strange mixture between anger at me and concern for her child. But whatever it was, she knew better than to speak to me that way in front of my children.

"What have you been telling her to make her hate me?" I shouted.

Lisa's eyes became small and she gave me a look that made me take a step back. In one fluid motion, she moved Jewel from her lap and was in my face.

"I didn't tell her shit, Kyle, because I didn't know shit. But what I shoulda told her was that her poor excuse for a father walked out on us 'cause he ain't worth shit."

If she had punched me in the face, Lisa couldn't have hit me with a harder blow. Not that I had a right to be, but I felt so disrespected that I almost struck her. I guess the thing I hated most was that everything she had said was the truth.

"Get out of my face, Lisa," I demanded, my eyes never leaving hers.

"Hey, girls." Karen took hold of Jade and Willow's hands. "Why don't we go in the kitchen and get some cookies?"

"That's a good idea," Lisa told them, still staring angrily at me.

"I don't want any cookies," Jewel pouted.

"Go get some cookies while I talk to your father, Jewel," Lisa told her in a no-nonsense tone.

"Come on, Jewel." Karen called.

Jewel got up and reluctantly walked to the kitchen.

"You gonna be all right, Lisa?" Karen asked.

"Yeah, I'll be all right." Lisa gave her friend a reassuring look. "He's already been to jail once. He didn't like it."

"Okay." Karen turned, closing the family room door behind her.

Lisa and I stared at each other silently for a good two or three minutes, neither of us saying a word. I didn't speak mostly 'cause I didn't know what to say, and because I didn't wanna say the wrong thing. Finally Lisa broke our silence with a question I was totally unprepared for.

"Who is she, Kyle?"

"Who is who?"

"Who the fuck did you leave me for? And please don't tell me it's a man," she said sarcastically.

I don't know why, but I cracked a smile. Something I regretted as soon as I felt Lisa's hand connect with my face. The blow hadn't really hurt, but the fact that she'd done it was painful.

"What the hell was that for?" I asked, touching my face in disbelief.

"That's to remind you that I'm not a fuckin' fool!" She'd taken a step back for safety, but her attitude was definitely still there. "Now who the fuck is she, and don't insult my intelligence."

"There is nobody else, Lisa. I swear to God." I took a step backward myself just in case she decided to swing again. But her hands stayed by her side.

"Then why, Kyle? What did I do that was so bad that you had to leave us?"

"It's not you, Lisa. It's me. I've got issues." She sat down, unable to control her tears.

I thought about telling her the whole truth. About the dreams and what Dr. Stanley had told me. But I couldn't. In seven years of marriage, Lisa and I had always been able to talk, but for some reason I just couldn't bring myself to admit these things to her.

"What kind of issues, Kyle? Are we in trouble financially again? Diane told me that the Mafia was after you."

"Oh, God. Please don't tell me you've been talkin' to Diane about our problems?" I shook my head in disgust.

"You damn right I talked to Diane. You've been gone a month. After a week I was ready to talk to anyone who might make some sense out of this shit." I sat down next to her.

"No, it's not money, and it's not the mob." I wrapped my arm around her shoulder. As awkward as this whole reunion was, I hated to see her so upset. She shrugged me off, reaching for a box of tissues on the coffee table.

"Well, if it's not money and it's not another woman, then what is it?"

"I'm just not happy with my life," I answered weakly.

"What do you mean you're not happy with your life? Aren't you coming back home?"

I thought about the question, then lowered my head. I could see by the look of disappointment on her face that she knew my answer.

"No," I replied quietly. "I just came by to see the girls."

"My God. This has got to be a nightmare." She buried her face in her hands. "Do you want a divorce?" She turned her head toward me.

"Yes. No. I don't know. I haven't made up my mind yet." I stood up and walked to the window, looking outside in a daze.

"Kyle, look at me." She gazed across the room. "Do you still love me?"

"I don't know that either, Lisa." I felt like shit as the words escaped my mouth.

"Then what the fuck *do* you know?" she yelled. "I've given you seven fucking years of my life and you don't know if you love me. You don't know if you're ever coming home. You don't know if you want to stay married. You fucking bastard!" She picked up an ashtray and threw it at me wildly, then collapsed in hysterics on the couch. When she finally composed herself enough to speak, she stared at me through her tears and asked, "It's the black-white thing, isn't it?"

I let out a slight gasp, amazed that she was so close to the truth.

"Isn't it!" she demanded.

"How'd you know?" My eyes began to tear as I felt the shame in that truth.

"When you disappeared, Wil mentioned it to Diane. She didn't believe it, but now that I think about it, it's the only thing that makes sense. Your impotence, the way you avoided me before you left. It all adds up. When you said you're not happy with your life, you didn't really mean your whole life. You're not happy with me."

At that minute, I wanted to kill Wil for having such a big mouth.

"I always thought it would end up being some glamorous black woman who'd take you away from me. I never thought it would be my skin."

"Lisa . . ." I tried to explain, but she stopped me.

"When, Kyle? When did all this happen? When did you decide that I wasn't good enough for you? I thought we were happy together."

"We were, but—"

"But what? You woke up and realized I was white?" Now she was getting angry. "You know what? This is ridiculous. Just forget it. I can't apologize for who I am. So if you're not happy with the choice you made seven years ago, then maybe we do need to end this marriage."

Lisa stood up, wiped her eyes, and looked down at me. She wasn't crying anymore, and her voice was more serious now than it had been during the entire conversation.

"Do you love your children?"

"Yes, I do love them. More than life itself."

"Then go in the kitchen and spend some time with them. Before I kill you," she said flatly. "They need you Kyle, especially Jewel."

"I know." I stood up and looked at Lisa. "I'm sorry, I'm really sorry."

"Save it, okay." She turned her back on me, so I headed for the kitchen. She stopped me before I left the room.

"Kyle."

"Yeah?"

"I was a good wife to you."

"I know that, Lisa."

"How could you hurt me like this?"

I didn't have any answer, so I walked to the kitchen without another word.

12

Jay

It was a warm Saturday afternoon when I strolled up the steps to Allen AME Church on Merrick Boulevard. I was holding the hands of my daughter Tiffany and my wife as I entered. The three of us really looked like a family in our matching navy blue and white. Kenya had bought some fabric that coordinated with my Sunday suit and made dresses for her and Tiffany. For me she made a tie. I wasn't really a church-going guy, but this was Wil's daughter's christening, and there was no way I was gonna miss that. Wil and Diane had been Tiffany's godparents. Besides, I was really into anything that had to do with our kids.

Speaking of kids, our second child was practically due. Things had been going really well between Kenya and me, and I hadn't fooled around in over three months. She'd really busted her ass to keep me satisfied after the pledge she made. But now that she was almost due, she'd cut me off again. Don't get me wrong I understood why. Shit, she was gonna have the baby soon. But that didn't stop me from being horny as hell. I wished I had as much self-control as Kyle or Wil, 'cause I was going damn near crazy. I really didn't want to have to resort to my old ways to get some satisfaction, but she was leaving me no choice.

When we entered the building, Kyle greeted us. He was handing out programs as he kept an eye on his three girls playing in the back row. As soon as Tiffany saw them, she let go of my hand and ran to the girls. Our kids loved each other like cousins. I looked at Kyle, and his smile was as wide as mine. We were both thinking the same thing. We'd always envisioned our kids would be this close.

I looked around to see if Lisa had come. It was Kyle's weekend with the girls, but Diane had made it clear that Lisa was her friend, and as far as she was concerned, Lisa was more welcomed than Kyle. I have to admit it was still weird seeing Kyle without Lisa. I'd become so used to seeing them together he looked like an unfinished painting without her.

"Hey, Kyle!" Kenya opened her arms for a hug.

"What's up, sister-in-law?" Kyle smiled. "Now look, I don't want you havin' that baby in here, aw'ight?"

"If I do, you gonna deliver it," she joked.

"Now I *really* don't want you ta have that baby in here." Kyle gave her a bug-eyed look.

"What's up there, bro?" He hugged me.

"Nothin' much, dawg."

"Jay, keep an eye on Tiffany. I'm gonna go say hello to everyone," Kenya told me.

"Aw'ight, baby." I grabbed her by the hand and kissed her passionately. "I love you, Kenya."

"I love you, too." She walked away smiling.

"Damn, I haven't seen you two like this since before you were married." Kyle looked happy.

"I know, but I'm not gonna lie. I've been fiendin' for some booty. Kenya ain't gave me none in two weeks."

"You need to stop. The girl's gonna have a baby in a few weeks. Give her a break." Kyle looked disappointed. "Two weeks. You know how long it's been for me?"

"No, and I don't really care. If you really wanted some ass, you'd go home to your wife and stop actin' like a little bitch." Kyle looked at me with disbelief. He probably was trying to figure out how I could be such a hypocrite. So was I.

"Who the fuck are you to be givin' me advice on marriage?" I had definitely hit a nerve. "You been faithful for three months, and now you're a fucking expert?"

"Nope, I'm no expert, but I am your best friend. I was there when you got married. I tried to talk you out of it, remember? But you were in love, and you still are."

"That's what you think."

"No, that's what I know. You might be fooling everyone else, Kyle, but you're not fooling me. You're hurting inside, man. You're hurting real bad. I just haven't figured out why."

"Oh, so you're a psychic now? You can read my mind?" He was real sarcastic.

"Nope, I can read your face. You might be smiling, but your face tells it all. You've got the same look you had when you got cut from the basketball team in eighth grade. The same look you had when Kelly Wright dumped you for Bubba Richardson in college. So don't be bullshitting with me. I know you too well for that." I could see his eyes starting to water.

"Jay, man, this whole thing's a lot more complicated than you think."

"Yeah, well, I got some time." I folded my arms and stared into Kyle's face.

Kyle started a story that I never would have expected to hear. This was no ordinary I-left-my-wife-'cause-I-was-bored scenario. He explained everything about his impotence, his shrink's evaluation, and the dreams he'd been having. I was pretty much blown away. I had some serious problems in my marriage, but nothing compared to his. He was honestly scared of Lisa.

"Look, Kyle, I don't know what to say, man. If there's anything I can do . . ."

"I know you wanna help, Jay, but this is something I have to work out myself."

I nodded. I understood what he was saying, but I felt helpless. Here was my best friend who really needed me, and there wasn't a damn thing I could do to help him.

"Yo, Jay, don't sweat it, man," Kyle reassured me. "I made an appointment to go see my shrink on Tuesday. I've been away from my family for three months. It's about time I got myself together and went back home."

"I'm glad to hear it, man," I told him as I turned to watch our daughters playing. "Those kids really need you at home and so does Lisa."

After the baptism we all went over to Wil and Diane's place. Al's mom had cooked most of the food, and Mama Jackson could cook her ass off. There were over thirty-five people in Wil's little house, and five minutes after they served the food, you couldn't hear a sound other than black folks sucking ribs and shoving collard greens in their mouths. I'd gotten up to get Kenya another plate of ribs when Allen's cousin Malcolm bumped into me. That fool spilled his whole plate of ribs all over my suit.

"What the hell is wrong with you?" I screamed. Every head in the room turned. I could see Wil, Allen, and Kyle all heading toward us from different directions in the room. They must have thought I was gonna knock Malcolm's sorry ass out. And if my daughter hadn't been in that room, I probably would have.

"Jay, man, what's the problem?" Wil stepped between Malcolm and me.

"This fool's the problem. He threw a plate of food on me." I pointed at the floor. "And look what he did to your carpet."

Wil turned to Malcolm angrily.

"I'm sorry, Wil. It was an accident. I'll pay for your carpet to be cleaned." Malcolm reached into his pocket and handed Wil a hundred-dollar bill.

"It's aw'ight, man," Wil replied.

"What about my suit?" I asked.

"I'll get it cleaned. But I'm buyin' you a new tie. Where the hell did you get that thing from, Kmart?"

I looked across the room and saw the embarrassed expression on Kenya's face. I couldn't help myself. I broke free from Wil's grasp and slapped the shit outta Malcolm. "My wife made this tie!"

Malcolm charged at me, but before he could swing, I hit him right between the eyes, knocking his dumb ass out. The next thing I knew they were dragging me outta the house.

"Jay, man, calm the fuck down. It's us." Kyle tried to snap me out of my rage.

"Where's Kenya and Tiffany, Kyle?" I didn't want Malcolm's family going after my pregnant wife.

"I'm right here, Jay." Her tone was full of attitude.

I turned around. Both Kenya and Tiffany were standing behind me.

"What is wrong with you, Jay?" Kenya shoved me.

"What're you talkin' 'bout?"

"I'm talking about this macho man shit. Why did you hit that man?"

"I was protecting you. Didn't you hear what he said?"

"You weren't protecting me. You were embarrassing me. I don't even know that man. Why would I care what he had to say?"

I looked around at all the people standing there. If she wasn't pregnant, I might have slapped her for embarrassing me like that in front of my boys.

"Is it all right if she spends the weekend here, Wil? 'Cause I'm sick of her shit." I cut my eyes at my wife.

"If she wants to," Wil replied, obviously uncomfortable with the whole scene.

"That all right with you?" I asked Kenya, though I really didn't care if it was.

"Just pick me up tomorrow night." She grabbed Tiffany's hand and walked back in the house.

"I'm outta here," I told my boys as I headed to my car.

"Jay!" Wil called.

When I turned, he was standing between Allen and Kyle.

"Stay outta trouble."

"I don't think so, Wil."

When I got home from the baptism, I stayed in my house for about two hours before I headed for the New Jersey Transit train station. On the way to the station, my cell phone was ringing, but I didn't have to check the Caller ID. I knew it would be Tracy. She'd taken two buses and two trains from Brookville, Long Island, to come see me in Jersey. She was waiting for me at the train station.

"Hello?"

"Jay, I'm here." Tracy's voice was sweet and sexy and I couldn't wait to get in her pants.

"Okay, baby, I'll be right there. I'm about two blocks away."

I'd broken down to temptation. When I got home and checked my cell phone messages, I had two messages from the nineteen-year-old college coed. Her first message was the usual just-checking-in message. She wanted to know if I was interested in hanging out since she had just finished finals and hadn't seen me for a while. Of course she didn't know the real reason we hadn't hooked up was that I'd decided to be faithful to my very pregnant wife. When she didn't get a call after her first message, I guess she decided to turn up the heat a little, 'cause her second message was off the hook.

"Hi, this is Tracy. I fell asleep waiting for your call and had the wildest dream. The two of us were together, and I was your personal sex slave. I did everything and anything you wanted without question. You had me wear a thick black dog collar with a chain, and anytime I misbehaved, you would spank my bare bottom with your hand. God, Jay, that dream was so hot." She sighed heavily into the phone. "If I told you I wanted you to make my dream come true, would you do it? Just the thought of calling you master as I sit naked at your feet, ready to do whatever you ask, is getting me moist. I bet I can make it the kinkiest time you've ever had. Gimme a call tonight. I'm leaving to go back home to DC for the Christmas break tomorrow night."

I must have listened to that message eight times before I called her to find out if she was serious. My own personal sex slave. Damn, that shit had me turned on like a mothafucker. And after what had just happened with my wife, I was through with this faithful husband charade.

When I pulled into the terminal, I spotted Tracy right away. She was one fine young sistah. About five-ten, Tracy had a smooth honey brown complexion with a short, nappy bleached blond hairstyle. Her makeup was flawless. I swear she looked like a supermodel standing there in her stylish black trench coat and high heels. My nature began to rise when I remembered she'd promised to be completely naked under her coat. Grinning from ear to ear, she jumped in the car and gently kissed me on the lips. Her lips were so soft my heart skipped a beat.

Tracy didn't have any idea that I was married. I'd lied when we met and told her I lived with my sister and her two kids. So I felt more than a little uneasy taking her back to my house instead of a hotel. But money was real tight with Kenya out on maternity leave. I'd planned on asking Kyle for a little loan after the baptism, but never got around to it after the bullshit fight with Malcolm. Not that I was worried about Kenya popping up. With her being pregnant and without a car, she wasn't going anywhere until I was good and ready to pick her up from Wil's house.

The ride home was short and uneventful for the most part. Tracy and I talked about her studies and when she was coming back from Christmas break. The subject of her sex-slave dream never even came up during the ten-minute ride to my house. When we pulled in the driveway, I made a quick mental check to be sure I had hidden all my wedding pictures. I'd spent almost an hour making sure all the evidence of my marriage was stowed away. I also made a diagram of where everything belonged so I wouldn't get myself busted putting things back in the wrong place. The last thing I needed was for Kenya to find something out of place and start asking a whole bunch of dumb questions.

When we entered the house, Tracy didn't even look around. She just turned to me with a sexy smile.

"Where's the bedroom?"

"Upstairs, second door to the right." I pointed to the staircase and she gently took my hand to lead me up the stairs. Standing outside the spare bedroom, she wrapped her arms around me. Her hazel eyes seemed to sparkle as she seduced me with her gaze.

"I'm about to make this a night you'll never forget." She pulled me down for a kiss.

To tell the truth, I was disappointed. I'd heard that same line from a few dozen women over the years, and most of them I couldn't even remember their names. For some reason I'd hoped Tracy would be different. Luckily, not long after her overused line, she proved herself to be anything but common. That girl gave me the French kiss of a lifetime. Enough to make me weak in the knees. The way she moved her lips and tongue against mine made me feel like I was in some type of erotic trance, floating on air. I'd never had a kiss like that in my entire life, and every time she broke the kiss, I would pull her in close for another. We must have stood in the hallway kissing like that for twenty minutes before she guided me into the bedroom. I was still mesmerized by her mouth and eagerly accepted more when she pushed me back on the bed and straddled me. She hadn't even taken off her trench coat, yet I was more excited than I'd ever been in my life.

"I really like you, Jay Crawford." She kissed me on the bottom lip. "And I want you bad, real bad."

She stepped back, reaching into her coat pocket to pull out a black dog collar. My eyes bugged out of my head as she buckled it around her neck. When the collar was secure, she reached into her other pocket and pulled out a long chain that she hooked to the collar. She took a step forward and placed the chain's leather handle in my palm. In one fluid motion she let her trench coat hit the floor. All I could do was gulp and stare. Words can't describe what my eyes were seeing. Tracy had the finest body I'd ever seen. She was so perfect I was afraid to touch her.

I'd had sex with over a hundred different women in my lifetime, but with Tracy standing there in front of me, I felt as if I'd never been with a real woman before. I remember thinking to myself that this had to be a dream. No woman could make me feel the way I was feeling. We hadn't made love yet, but I could feel myself getting choked up with emotion. I wasn't sure if I was about to experience true love, but I sure as hell wanted to. I felt like the woman who had never had a real orgasm. She always heard her friends talk about it, but just once she wanted to experience one for herself, to see what the fuss was all about.

"Well, master, what's your first command?" she asked humbly.

I held that chain in my hand and was honestly speechless for the first time in my entire life. What she was offering was so enticing and overwhelming, but so not what I wanted.

"I don't wanna command you. I don't wanna fuck you. I just wanna make love to you, Tracy." I couldn't believe those words had come out of my mouth, but they did. God, I sounded like a soap opera, and the crazy thing is I meant every word. I can't ever remember wanting someone the way I wanted her. I didn't just want her physically. I wanted her emotionally too. Honest to God, I wanted to make love to her, to make her body sing in a chorus of my love.

"Okay." She nodded. "I know exactly what you want. I want that too. I just didn't think I would get it." She unhooked the dog collar and stepped closer to me, placing both hands on the side of my face. Gently, she eased me down on the bed and kissed me. We made love so passionately that I swear I was crying the entire time. I can't remember when we stopped, but when we did, she fell right asleep in my arms. I didn't wanna let her go for anything in the world.

Sometime before sunrise I woke up and she was still in my arms. I'd never been so happy and so confused at the same time. My body was still tingling from our passion. Her body was curled up against me and she was still sleeping like an angel. If I didn't know any better, I would have sworn I was in love. But I was too old to confuse good sex with love. Or was I? She rolled over and kissed me, then closed her eyes to fall back to sleep. She was so beautiful. Even after sweating off her makeup she looked like an angel. When the sun came up, I went downstairs to make breakfast for my young sweetheart. I wasn't Allen's mom, but I could cook some mean pancakes.

While I was cooking, I picked up the phone and called Wil's house.

"Good morning." Wil sounded wide awake. I could hear Teddy and Tiffany playing in the background.

"What up, dawg?"

"What's up, Jay?"

"Nothin'. I just woke up and wanted to check on the family."

I considered telling Wil about the woman in my bed and how I felt, but he would never understand. Shit, I didn't fully understand what I was feeling. All I know is that Tracy was the first woman I'd ever met to totally satisfy me. And it wasn't just physical.

"Kenya wasn't feeling too good, so I'm watchin' Tiffany and Teddy. I think she's lying down. Want me to wake her?"

"Naw, just tell her I'll pick her up around eight tonight."

"Aw'ight, bro. I'll see you then."

"Hey, Wil. She ain't still mad, is she?"

"Man, let me tell you. Ten minutes after you left she was talkin' about how sorry she was."

"Get the fuck outta here."

"For real."

"That's good to hear. Tell Diane not to cook. I'll pick up some Chinese on my way over."

"Bet. Make sure to get some shrimp fried rice."

"Okay, bro, I'll talk to you later. My pancakes is burning."

I hung the phone up and finished making breakfast. When I came in the room, Tracy was just waking up. I watched her stretch and admired her fine, young body.

"Good morning," I smiled.

"Mornin'," she replied, trying to see what was on the tray I was carrying.

I placed the tray over her lap and kissed her passionately. I wanted to throw the tray on the floor and make love again, but she resisted.

"I'm so hungry. The food in the dorm is horrible."

"Can I feed you?" I felt like a kid in a candy store.

"I'd like that." I took the linen napkin out of the holder and placed it on her lap in front of the tray. I fed my little princess. I'd never been so excited to be with a woman in my life. After we ate, Tracy and I made love for most of what was left of the morning and into the afternoon. She was by far the most incredible lover I'd ever been with. When we finished making love, she laid on my chest.

"Jay?" she whispered.

"Yes?" I whispered back.

"I don't want to complicate things, but I could fall in love with you."

"Yeah, I know the feeling." I stroked her hair.

"What are we going to do?"

"I don't know. Maybe we should try to take it one day at a time."

"I'll do whatever you want. I just don't wanna get hurt."

"Tracy, if you knew what I was feeling inside, you'd know the last thing in the world I wanna do is hurt you."

"I hope so, Jay, 'cause I can be a real bitch when someone hurts me." With that she laid her head on my chest and we both fell asleep.

I had no idea what time it was when I woke up, but I could see it was dark outside and the street lights were on, so I suspected it was early evening. I turned over to kiss Tracy and panicked when I realized she wasn't in bed. She'd mentioned something about catching a train back to Long Island before it got too late, but I didn't think she would do it without saying goodbye. I'd wanted to drive her back myself. That way I'd be able to spend a little more time with her before she left for DC. I was so relieved when I heard the shower running in the bathroom that I jumped up to join her. I poked my head into the steamfilled bathroom and called to her.

"You aw'ight? You need shampoo or a towel or somethin'?"

"Baby, the only thing I really need in here is you."

I couldn't help but smile. Everything she said made me feel good. I was about to grab a towel from the linen closet when I heard what sounded like a car door slamming in my driveway. That's when I got this chill, and intuition told me to take a look out the window. I was glad I did. In my driveway, parked behind my car, was Diane's car. My heart completely stopped beating when I saw two women walking toward the front door. One of them was Diane, and the other was my unmistakable pregnant wife.

Now I'd been in quite a few sticky situations in my life, but this had to be the stickiest. Tracy was in the shower waiting for me to join her, and Kenya was about to walk through the front door. I had to think quick. I knew I had to stop Kenya from coming in that front door. So I leaped down the stairs in three tremendous strides, trying my best to put on a sweatsuit as I went. By the time I hit the door, Diane was standing in the foyer.

"Hey, what're you doing home?" I startled Diane, who dropped Kenya's keys.

"Jay, you scared the hell outta me." Diane picked up the keys. "Your wife's about to have this baby."

"Why didn't you take her straight to the hospital?" I gave Diane a nasty look as I approached Kenya, who was leaning against the entry, holding her stomach. "You okay, honey?"

Kenya nodded with a grimace.

"She wouldn't go to the hospital without you," Diane stated flatly.

"Have you ever heard of a telephone? I could have met you there." My mind was spinning. I didn't know what to do. I looked down at Kenya, who looked like she was gonna pass out. Shit, I was so nervous I felt like I was gonna pass out too.

"We tried to call, Jay, but the line was busy and your cell phone was turned off."

"Oh, yeah, I was on the Internet most of the afternoon," I lied. I'd taken the phone off the hook right after I made breakfast. The truth is, I wanted an excuse just in case my wife did try to call. At least if she got a busy signal, she couldn't accuse me of being out of the house with another woman. I guess this time I was too damn smart for my own good.

Thud!

Something fell upstairs and Diane immediately looked up the stairs then glanced at me suspiciously. My knees almost gave out, I was so scared I was gonna get busted.

"I'm gonna kill that damn cat of yours, Kenya," I stated more for Diane's benefit than Kenya's. I don't think Diane believed me, though, 'cause she looked up the stairs again with a smirk. Thank God Kenya had another contraction and yelled out in pain.

"Ahhh, the contractions are getting closer," Kenya moaned.

"Girl, we need to get you to the hospital," Diane demanded. "Come on, Jay."

"Look, Diane, you get Kenya over to the hospital. I'm gonna lock up here and put some sneakers on." Kenya grabbed my wrist.

"Jay, I want you to take me. You missed Tiffany's birth, I don't want you to miss this baby's birth too."

"Don't worry, honey. I just have to put my shoes on and I'll be right behind you."

"No, Jay. I want you to take me." I looked up the stairs, terrified that any second Tracy would call my name or stroll out of the bathroom naked.

"Okay, honey, I'll take you. Diane, put Kenya in your car while I get some shoes and lock up. We'll all drive over together in your car, okay?"

Kenya let go of my wrist and nodded. I looked up the stairs again as I helped them back outside. Once I got them both in the car, I came into the house and closed the door behind me nervously. I heard Tracy call my name and ran up the stairs as fast as possible. She was standing in the hallway, naked.

"Who was that?" She followed me into the bedroom, where I was putting on my shoes.

I didn't know what to say. At that point my mouth just wouldn't allow me to tell her a lie, but at the same time I wasn't about to tell her I was married and take a chance on losing her. So I just avoided the question.

"Look, I gotta go out for a little bit. I want you to stay here 'til I get back, okay? I'll explain everything when I get back." I think she was fine with that answer till Diane leaned on the horn outside.

"What's going on, Jay? Who were those women I heard downstairs?"

"Trust me, Tracy. It's much too complicated to talk about now. Like I said, I'll explain everything when I get back." I kissed her forehead and ran down the stairs before she could protest.

She looked so innocent standing at the top of those stairs, watching me with those big, beautiful eyes. I felt like shit walking out the door, but I had no choice. I left before she could ask any more questions. I jumped into Diane's car and she immediately pulled out of the driveway. I could see Tracy peeking through the blinds. Thank God Diane was too preoccupied watching Kenya in the rearview mirror to look back at the house.

All I could think about on the way to the hospital was how the hell I was gonna get Tracy out of that house. I had to tell her to wait there or she woulda tried to follow me out of the house right then. But there was no way I could risk her really waiting there for me. What if Kenya sent Diane to the house to get clothes or something? If that happened before I could get back there and get rid of Tracy, I was gonna be one dead brotha. It was times like these I was glad I had good friends, 'cause the minute they got Kenya settled in a birthing room, I ducked into the john to make some very important phone calls.

13

Allen

Rose scooped up some dip with a chip and offered it to me as I watched the game. I closed my lips around it, softly kissing her fingertips. We'd made love all morning and she'd been real sweet all day. Almost too sweet. So in the back of my mind I was prepared for her to ask for something. I only had about sixty bucks in my pocket and had purposely left my ATM card at my ma's house just to avoid this type of situation. So whatever Rose wanted it had better be cheap.

"Another chip, baby?" She scooped up some more dip.

"Sure." I opened my mouth.

"Are you comfy?" She tried her best to fluff up my pillow before laying her head on my shoulder.

"Yeah, honey, I'm comfy. Thanks." I tried to get into the game, but just when it was getting good, she called my name.

"Allen, can I talk to you about something?" She was using a soft baby voice so I knew she was getting ready to make her request.

"Is it important, Rose? 'Cause if it's not important, why don't we talk about it after the game?" She reached over and picked up the remote control, clicking off the TV.

"Yes, I think it's important." She sat up and held my hand.

"Oh, all right, what is it?"

"I think we need to go down to the bank tomorrow morning and have my name added to your bank accounts."

It took a second for her comment to register, and it didn't register well.

"What'd you say?" I stared at her, hoping I'd heard wrong.

"I think it's time you added my name to your bank accounts."

"I don't get it. What's the rush? We have three months till the wedding."

"Don't you think there are certain things that need to be taken care of ahead of time?" She didn't give me a chance to answer. "I mean, we are engaged. I'm not wishing this on you, but what if you walk out that door and get hit by a bus? Who's gonna take care of the arrangements? Shit, who's gonna take care of me?"

"I told Ma—"

"Ma! Your mother's not gonna do shit for me. That old lady hates me. If something happens to you before we're married, she might not let me in your funeral."

I sighed, because she was right. Ma wasn't exactly her best friend, especially after she rejected Granny's ring.

"Okay, why don't I take the entire day off tomorrow? That way we can go to both your bank and mine."

"My bank? Why we going to my bank?" She gave me a strange look.

"So you can add my name to your accounts. What'd ya think?" I couldn't believe the look she gave me.

"I'm not putting your name on my accounts." She had the nerve to have an attitude. "What if you decide to leave me?"

"Why would I leave you? I love you," I insisted. "Besides, you could just as easily leave me."

"Allen, I'm a woman. I need security. Men don't need security."

"That's stupid, Rose."

"It's not stupid." She sucked her teeth.

"Look, I don't wanna talk about this no more. If you're not gonna put me on your accounts, then we can just have separate accounts." I clicked on the TV.

"That's not fair, Allen." Rose walked over to the TV and stood in front of it. Thank God the phone rang, 'cause I could tell she was gearing up for one of those all-day arguments.

I reached over to the coffee table and hit the Caller ID. It was Kyle. "What's up, Kyle?"

"Listen, we've got an emergency." He sounded agitated. "I'm coming to pick you up as soon as I drop off the girls."

"What's going on? Everybody aw'ight?" His tone scared me.

"Hell, no. We gotta go save Jay's ass again."

"Uh-oh, what'd he do now?"

"I'll explain everything when I get there. Come on out when I beep."

"Damn it!" Wil slammed his fist into the dashboard. "How could he be so stupid?"

We'd just crossed the George Washington Bridge heading for Jay's house in Jersey. Kyle had just finished explaining what he knew about Jay's dilemma, which was actually pretty comical if you could get past how pathetic it was. Jay had had some woman named Tracy at his house when Kenya and Diane showed up unexpectedly. He'd managed to hide the woman, but had to leave when Kenya went into labor. Now Wil, Kyle, and I were racing against time to his house before his in-laws showed.

"Would someone please tell me how he could be so damn stupid?" Wil repeated.

"I don't know, Wil," Kyle replied as he hit the speaker on his ringing car phone.

"Yeah?"

"Yo, y'all ain't got there yet?" Jay's voice blared out of the speakers.

"Jay, chill the fuck out. I'm drivin' as fast as I can."

"I keep tellin' you my in-laws are on their way to the house. That old man thinks he's Speed Racer, Kyle. Hurry the fuck up!"

"Will you relax? It's gonna take them at least three hours to get up here from Baltimore."

"Earth to Kyle. Did you listen to me when I called you earlier? Kenya called her mom's before she left Wil and Diane's house, two and a half hours ago. I swear if y'all fuck this up—"

"Y'all?" Wil interrupted. "Hold up, Jay. You actin' like this is our fault. We're not the stupid ass who left some chickenhead at his house while his wife's about to deliver a baby."

"She's not a chickenhead, Wil, so don't go there. Her name is Tracy. And whatever you do, don't tell her I'm married."

From the look on Wil's face, he was about to explode. He and Jay hadn't been getting along too well since Kyle had returned from Africa. Wil was still upset that Jay had cut him out of the loop. I decided it might be best to change the subject before someone said something they'd regret.

"Kenya have the baby yet, Jay?" I leaned over the back seat.

"Nah, she's only dilated five centimeters." Not that I knew what that meant. "Look, I better get back. They're thinking about giving her a C-section."

"Aw'ight, man, go handle your business." Kyle hung up the phone.

"Can you believe this guy?" Wil shook his head as he stared out the window.

"Of course I can," Kyle chuckled. "It's Jay. He's been doin' this kinda shit since we were kids. You expected him to change?"

"No, but I did expect him to grow up a little."

Kyle laughed, then I laughed. Wil just sat there shaking his head. We all knew Jay was never gonna grow up. He was having too much fun being a kid.

It didn't take long to get to Jay's house from the GW Bridge. We were all pretty relieved when we pulled into the driveway and there was no sign of Jay's in-laws. That is, until we heard the beep of a horn and Kenya's mother and father pulled in right behind us.

"Now what do we do?' I asked.

"Give me a second ta think." Kyle rubbed his temples then smoothed out his mustache as we all sat in scared silence. "Okay, I got it," Kyle finally announced. "Allen, I want you to go inside and find the girl. If she's in the guest room, I want you to get her the hell outta there, 'cause that's where Kenya's people sleep." He handed me the keys.

"What're you and Wil gonna do?"

"We're gonna buy you some time. If there's one thing Kenya's old man can't resist, it's a good stock tip." I had to grin. Kyle was right. Kenya's old man was greedy as hell. "Allen, whatever you do, don't let that chick come out of the house."

Kyle stepped out of the car and greeted Kenya's parents like he was a politician standing in front of the polls. If there was one thing he and Wil could do it was talk, and while they were doing that, I slipped out of the car and into the house. As I closed the front door behind me, I called the girl's name. "Tracy? Tracy?" I ran up the stairs and searched the guest room. The bed was made, and there was no sign that anyone had been there.

"Tracy?" I called again. "My name's Allen. Jay asked me to come get you." I searched every room upstairs twice and couldn't find her. When I came downstairs, Wil was standing in the foyer holding a bassinet, minus Kyle and Kenya's parents.

"What's up, Kyle still outside?" I asked in a whisper.

"Naw, he talked Kenya's parents into going straight to the hospital. He's with them." Wil looked relieved. "You find the girl?"

"Nope. If she's here, she ain't upstairs."

"Shit." He placed the bassinet on the floor. "You check the kitchen and basement. I'm gonna check the living room and dining room."

"Wil, what if she's not here?"

"We thank God she had enough sense to get the hell outta here, then we head over to the hospital and tell Jay. That's all we can do."

We musta searched that house five times from top to bottom before we gave up and drove Kyle's car to the hospital. When we arrived, Kyle informed us that Jay, Diane, and his in-laws were in with Kenya, who had an eight-pound–three-ounce baby girl. It didn't take long for Jay to come find us, and when he did, he immediately gestured for us to follow him.

"You find her?" He whispered, leading us into the men's room.

I shook my head. "If she's in that house, she's the invisible woman."
Jay exhaled a sigh of relief.

"She musta caught a cab to the train." Jay smiled like he'd just gotten away with murder. "Man, I thought I was gonna get busted for sure. You shoulda seen me. I almost pissed on myself when Kenya and Diane walked in the door."

"That was a little too close for comfort, don't you think?" I asked. I noticed Wil was whispering something to Kyle. He had an agitated look, and I knew he wasn't pleased.

"I'll be straight up with y'all. It woulda been worth it if I'd gotten busted. I swear, I ain't never been with a woman like Tracy before in my entire life." Jay turned to Wil, who was leaning against a sink with a solemn look. "What's wrong with you, big man?"

Wil took a few steps and got in Jay's face.

"What d'you think is wrong with me? What the hell is wrong with you bringing some damn woman to your fucking house? Your daughter sleeps in that house, man. And why didn't you tell me you had a girl there when you called? I woulda never let Diane and Kenya come to your place."

" 'Cause I was afraid you'd open your big-ass mouth and tell Diane, that's why." Jay had an attitude and I had no idea why. We had just saved his cheatin' ass for the millionth time.

"Ya know what, Jay? I'm sick of you and these damn bitches." Wil pointed his finger in Jay's chest.

"I told you before, don't call out her name, Wil. She ain't a bitch. Her name is Tracy, and you gonna give her some respect." Jay's voice was serious, and Wil was obviously shocked. So was I. I can't ever remember Jay defending a woman other than Kenya, especially not to Wil. Whoever this Tracy was, she had to be awfully special. But Wil didn't seem to care.

"I don't give a shit what her name is. And I'm gonna give her about as much respect as she gave your wife when she fucked you in her house. You tryin' ta tell me some *bitch* is more important than Kenya?" Wil pushed Jay. "Well, is she?"

"Look, I gotta go check on Kenya." Jay tried to step around Wil, but he wouldn't let him.

"Let me pass, Wil." Jay's tone made it clear he'd had enough.

"Answer me, Jay. Is some *ho* off the street worth losing your family? Losing Tiffany? Or your new baby? Damn! I don't even know what the baby's name is yet." Wil pushed him again. "You know what, Jay. You're acting just like your father."

"Fuck you, Wil. I am not my father!" Jay pushed him back and clenched his fists.

"What, you gonna fight me over some *bitch?*" Wil threw both his hands in the air, daring Jay to take a free shot.

"I told you not to call her a bitch!" Jay threw a punch that landed directly in Wil's eye. I could tell he regretted the blow as soon as it landed. "Oh, shit! Wil, I'm sorry, man."

Wil's first reaction was to grab his eye in disbelief, but then he lunged for Jay, grabbing him by the shirt and slamming him against the ceramic tile of the rest room wall. Kyle and I both ran to split them apart before any more blows were thrown.

"Wil, man, chill out. He didn't mean it!" Kyle yelled, struggling to keep Wil under control.

"Fuck that shit! He meant it." Wil lunged at Jay again.

"Wil, I'm sorry, man. It was an accident." Jay wasn't scared, but he meant his apology. I could hear it in his voice. "You was aggravating me."

It took a few minutes for us to calm Wil down.

"You know what, Jay? Next time you get in trouble, don't call me to help your sorry ass." Wil was obviously still angry, and it was a good thing he didn't look in the mirror, 'cause his eye was swelling by the second.

"Wil, man, I'm sorry." Jay offered Wil his hand, but Wil ignored it.

"I'm outta here, I'm going to find my wife." Wil walked toward the door. "But I promise you, Jay, you're gonna need me one day. And I ain't gonna be there for you." Wil left the rest room without another word. Kyle and I looked at each other in shock. Was it possible that twenty-five years of friendship were truly over?

14

Wil

It was early Tuesday morning and I was jammin' to the sounds of the Doug Banks Show on WBLS. I'd taken a few days off work to give my eye a chance to heal after my little scrape with Jay. He'd hit me a lot harder than I thought and my eye was so swollen it was damn near shut. After all I'd done for that guy, I still couldn't believe he actually hit me over some woman. I heard the doorbell ring, so I slipped on a pair of shades before I went to the door. You'd never believe how embarrassing it was for a guy my size to be seen with a black eye.

Matter of fact, yesterday when Diane sent me to the supermarket to pick up some groceries, some guy stopped me and said, "Damn, brother, if you look like that, what the hell's the other guy look like?" He thought he was being funny. I didn't.

I smiled when I saw Lisa standing in the doorway with my goddaughter, Willow.

"Hey, Willow." I picked up my goddaughter and gave her a kiss.

"Ay, Uncle Wil." She hugged me.

"Hey, Lisa, how you doing?" I kissed her on the cheek.

"Fine, Wil, how are you?"

"I'm aw'ight, but if you're looking for Di, she's not home."

"I know. She told me you were taking the day off, so I stopped by to talk to you. How's your eye?" I gestured for her to come in.

"It looks like hell, but it doesn't hurt anymore." I took off the shades to show her my shiner.

Lisa grimaced at the sight of my poor eye. "That Jay is crazy," she stated.

"Tell me about it." I put the shades back on. "So what brings you here?"

"I came to talk to you about Kyle." She walked over to the living room sofa and sat down. I sat across from her on the love seat.

"Willow, why don't you go play with Teddy's toys in the family room?" I watched her scamper away before I spoke. "What about Kyle?"

I knew Lisa wanted information. The truth is, I didn't have much to give her and what I did have I wasn't really sure if I should share with her.

"Wil, I need you to be straight with me, for the kids' sake. I promise nothing we talk about will ever get back to Kyle."

"Lisa, I don't know if this is such a good idea. If you wanna know something about Kyle, maybe you should ask him."

"I would if he'd talk to me. I tried to sit down and talk to him Sunday when he dropped off the kids, but all he did was hand me a check. He wouldn't even come in the house." Her eyes were brimming with tears. "Wil, you've got to help me. I don't know where else to turn."

"Why don't you guys go see a marriage counselor or something?"

Lisa laughed cynically. "I tried that. I even tried to get him to go see Father Smith, the priest who married us, but he won't go."

"What do you want me to do, Lisa? Since Katie's been born, I barely see the guys."

"I just wanna know if he's planning on getting back with me or not. So I can get on with my life."

I didn't like the sound of that. I didn't believe her at the time, but Diane had told me Lisa was dating this guy named Mike. Mike was the brother of Lisa's best friend.

"What do you mean 'get on with your life'?" I tilted my head and made sure my voice was serious. "Have you been seeing Mike?"

"Please, Wil, Mike is engaged." She waved me off. "And your wife has entirely too much time on her hands to be speculating on me."

"How'd you know it was Diane who told me?"

Lisa chuckled. "When I told Diane that I had a really nice dinner with Mike Friday night, the first thing she asked me was if I was sleeping with him. She didn't even wanna hear that Mike's fiancée and his sister were at the dinner too."

"Yeah, Di does have a tendency to hear what she wants to hear." I'd been putting up with that for years. "Lisa, do you really wanna file for divorce?"

"Of course I don't wanna file for divorce, Wil. I love Kyle, but I've been sitting in that house for three going on four months waiting for him to get over his little problem and come home." Tears began to stream down her face so I handed her a box of tissues. "And I'm willing to do whatever it takes to make things work, but I'm not gonna sit in that house and wait anymore. Now he's your best friend, and you know I've been a good wife to him, but I need to know something. I need to know if he's planning on working on this together. Otherwise I'm filing for divorce."

"Aw'ight, I'll talk to him today. I promise." I'd planned on talking to him about Jay, but this seemed a little more pressing.

"Thank you, Wil."

"I'll do what I can, Lisa."

Lisa stood up and called Willow. "I'm going to Jersey City to see Kenya's baby, then I'm gonna ride down to Philly and spend the night with my mom. Why don't I call you tomorrow?"

"That's fine, but who's watching Jade and Jewel tonight?"

"Mike and his fiancée Jenny are going to pick them up from school."

"You know we coulda watched the kids for you, Lisa."

"I know, Wil. Truth is, Kyle would have probably watched them. But Mike and Jenny both live with their parents, so they jumped at the chance to stay at my house for the night."

"Say no more. It wasn't that long ago Diane and I were living at home." Both of us laughed as Lisa and Willow walked out of the house. "Call me tomorrow."

I closed the door then walked up the stairs to change out of my sweats and go pay a visit to Kyle.

I walked into Kyle's Jamaica Avenue store and smiled at Sharon, the store manager, as she helped a customer.

"Hey, Sharon. Kyle in?"

"He's in the office, Wil." She did a double take, probably wondering why I was wearing sunglasses on a rainy winter day.

"Thanks." I walked to the back of the store and knocked on the door to Kyle's office, which was marked PRIVATE.

"Come in."

I walked in and Kyle smiled, taking his feet off the desk.

"Big Wil, what's up?" He leaned over his desk clenching his fist so that we could knock knuckles.

"Same ol', same ol', bro." I sat down in a chair in front of his desk, admiring his office. Kyle's office was a shrine to his family and friends. Not only did he have pictures of his family all over the place, but he also had pictures of his friends, including Jay's family and mine too. He even had quite a few pictures of Allen and Rose.

"Hey, what's up with the shades, man?" He sat back in his leather chair.

I took off my sunglasses to show him my eye.

"God damn! Did Jay do that?" He scrunched up his face in disbelief. "Ya know, what he did to you the other night didn't make no damn sense."

"Yeah, well I got somethin' for your boy Jay next time I see him."

"Oh, so he ain't your boy no more?" Kyle frowned.

"You got that right. I can't fuck with him no more."

"Wil, man, I know you're pissed at him, but Jay didn't mean to hit you."

"You can defend him all you want, Kyle. I'm still not fuckin' with him no more." I folded my arms across my chest.

"Look, I know he plays by his own rules sometimes. Hell, that condom stunt he pulled a few years back almost cost me my marriage. But Wil, I know he didn't mean to hit you," Kyle repeated.

"Even if he didn't, Kyle, Jay's out of control. He don't care about nobody but himself. Look at that shit he pulled this weekend. Would you ever dream of fucking some woman in your wife's house?"

"No, but. . . ."

"There ain't no buts, Kyle. The man's thirty-six years old. That shit was all right when we was teenagers, but we ain't teenagers no more."

Kyle sat back in his chair and rocked a few seconds. "I hear what you're saying Wil, but I've got too much love for Jay to give up on him." Kyle pointed to a picture of Jay and his family on the wall. "Plus, I know he loves his family."

"You actually believe that shit, don't you?" He nodded at me. "Do you think he and Kenya would still be together if it weren't for us? Hell no!" I said, answering my own question. "And that's because we're his conscience. Do you know how many times I've saved his ass from losing Kenya over the years?"

"Probably about as many times as Allen or I have, but that's what being a friend is all about. We're his conscience, Wil, and it's our job to remind him he's married."

"Yeah, well, I'm sick of being his conscience, especially when this is what I get for it." I pointed to my eye. "From now on, he can fuck up his marriage for all I care."

"You don't mean that, Wil." Kyle leaned toward me.

"Oh, yeah I do. I'm starting to think that Jay and Kenya would be better off divorced."

"Well, I'm sorry, I don't subscribe to that theory. I think a family should stay together."

"No, you didn't . . . No, you didn't just go there. You got some fucking nerve," I muttered, sitting back in my chair.

"What'd you say?"

"I said you got some fucking nerve!" I really didn't wanna go there this way with Kyle. I'd hoped to discuss his situation over lunch, but he'd opened the door, and I was still upset about Jay.

"What's that supposed to mean?" I picked up a picture off his desk and stared at it before placing it back down, facing him. It was a family portrait of him, Lisa, and the girls.

"It means you're tryin' to fix someone else's shit when your shit is twice as fucked up. I guess I gotta give Jay some credit. At least he still lives at home."

Kyle shook his head. "Ohhh, that's fucked up, Wil."

"I call 'em as I see 'em, bro."

"So that's how you see it?"

"Ya know what, Kyle? I never really gave it much thought 'til today. I figured it was your business, and that you and Lisa were working on things and eventually you'd get back together. But Lisa and Willow stopped by the house this morning, and Lisa and I had a nice little conversation."

"Conversation about what?"

"About you."

"What about me?" Kyle asked suspiciously.

"Let's put it this way, Kyle. If you don't get your shit together and go home soon, you ain't gonna have a home to go to. Aw'ight?" I stared him down after I dropped that bomb.

"What're you tryin' to say? She wants a divorce?"

"She did mention filing for divorce, but it's a little more personal than that. She's seeing someone, Kyle. Which means she's probably giving up—"

"*The booty!*" Kyle finished my sentence for me, and I could see the concern on his face. I'd lied about Lisa seeing someone, but it was for Kyle's own good. He really needed a wakeup call. He was probably the most jealous guy I knew next to myself, so I figured the thought of Lisa with another guy would drive him crazy enough to get him home.

"You bein' straight with me, Wil?" Kyle's eyes were wide.

"Kyle, I swear on both my children that my wife told me Lisa was dating Karen's brother Mike." I wasn't lying this time. Diane did tell me that. I just left out the part where Lisa swore it wasn't true.

Kyle stared at the picture of his family on his desk. I was expecting him to cry, but not a tear fell.

"Well, she's a grown woman. She can do whatever she wants as long as she doesn't bring a man into that house with my kids." To say I was bowled over by his response is an understatement.

"You serious?" I couldn't believe it. This was definitely not what I was trying to do.

"Yeah, I'm serious." He nodded his head as if everything was okay. "I've been with Lisa almost eight years, Wil. She's been a great mother and wife, and she doesn't deserve this. Shit, this whole thing's my fault anyway. If she's found somebody who can make her happy, then I'm happy for her. I owe her that much."

Well, you could have knocked my big ass over with a feather. I couldn't believe it. I mean this was his wife we were talking about and he was cool as a cucumber. He musta given this whole thing a lot of thought before I even showed up, 'cause I actually believed he meant every word. But I had to be sure.

"Kyle, you're talking about breaking up your family, man."

"No, Wil, my family's already broken up. That happened the day I walked out on them. It's about time you and I realize that."

Buzzzzz . . . Buzzzzzzz.

Kyle leaned over his desk and hit the intercom button. "Yes."

"Kyle, Mr. Webster's here from Weaves-Are-Us." Sharon's voice echoed from the speaker.

"Give me a minute then send him in, Sharon." Kyle glanced at me. "Wil, I've gotta meet with this guy over lunch. Why don't I give you a call tonight."

"Okay, man, but think about what we talked about. You don't wanna lose your family." I didn't wanna leave. I felt the need to some-how fix what I might have fucked up. As I got out of my chair to walk out, I looked back at Kyle, who was staring at one of his wedding pictures. God, I hoped he had already been thinking they were through before I walked in the door. I didn't think I could live with the fact that I was the final blow that ended his marriage for good.

15

Kyle

Wil walked out of the office looking confused, but convinced that I was okay with the idea of Lisa divorcing me. That couldn't have been farther from the truth. I was devastated, and the minute he walked out the door, I started to sob. It hadn't been easy holding back those tears in front of Wil, but the little bit of pride I had left made me do it. I didn't really wanna lose my marriage or my family. The whole idea had me hurting inside, hurting so bad my stomach ached.

"Dammit!" I slammed my hand down on my desk in anger. "How could she do this to me when I was just about to come home?"

As I started to calm down, reason took over for anger and I realized I wasn't angry with Lisa for starting to date. I was mad at myself for screwing up and not going home a long time ago. Stupid thing is, I'd made an appointment with Dr. Stanley for that afternoon and had planned on taking Lisa and the kids to dinner Friday for her birthday. I was going to ask her if I could come home then, but that was dead now. Besides, she was probably going out with Mike on Friday night.

I picked up the phone and dialed Dr. Stanley's office.

"Dr. Stanley's office," the receptionist said.

"Hi, my name's Kyle Richmond. I have a three o'clock appointment with Dr. Stanley."

"Yes, Mr. Richmond, I have it right here."

"I'd like to cancel that appointment."

"Okay, Mr. Richmond. Would you like to reschedule now?"

"Nope."

"Okay, well I'll let Dr. Stanley know you're not coming in." She hung up.

Knock, knock.

Shit, I completely forgot Webster was waiting to see me. "Just a minute!" I sat up at my desk trying to get myself together. I wiped the tears from my face. "Come in."

Richard Webster walked into my office, smiling like he always did. I'd lied to Wil about going to lunch with him. I needed a convenient excuse to get him out of the office before my emotions got the best of me.

"What's up, Brother Kyle?" Webster was a short, heavyset light-skinned man with a balding head. He looked and acted more like a preacher than a salesman.

"How you doing, Webster?"

"Woke up this morning, checked to see if I had ten fingers and ten toes, realized I had a little air in my lungs, had to thank God for a good start to the day." Webster chuckled, and so did I. I always liked his analogies.

"I take it you've come for your check?" I was back to business right away. My mind still heavily clouded with grief.

"Yes sir, praise God, but I've also got some new products that I'd love to show you." He smiled like a Cheshire cat.

"Nope, not today, Webster. I had a death in the family. But you can leave some brochures with Sharon up front." I reached in my desk and handed him his check.

"Thank you," he said, taking the check. "I'm sorry to hear about your loss. I'll keep them in my prayers. Was it someone you were close to?"

I shook my head. "It wasn't a someone, Webster, it was my marriage. I'm getting divorced."

Webster bit down on his lip. "Oh Lord, I'm sorry to hear that, Brother Kyle. Were you married long?"

"Seven years."

"Any children?"

"Three beautiful girls." I took the picture of my family off my desk and handed it to him.

"Yeah, they are beautiful." Webster smiled, handing me the picture back. "Sure you wanna give them up?"

"Not my call anymore, Webster. I had a chance but I blew it." My eyes were being to tear again.

"Brother Kyle, I don't know if you knew this, but I'm a minister. And as a minister, there is one thing I know for certain. If you have a problem, the best thing to do is pray on it. God always seems to give me a sign when I pray. It's not always what I wanna hear, but he always gives me a sign."

"You know what, Webster? I might just do that. It's been a long time since I prayed."

"Well, Brother Kyle, there's no better time than the present. Why don't we pray together now?" I don't know why but I agreed. I'd been to a shrink, went to Africa to find myself, and none of that had worked. Maybe a little prayer would give the answers I'd been looking for.

Webster stretched his hands across my desk and I grasped his hands. We prayed together for a good ten, fifteen minutes, and in truth I honestly felt good about it until Sharon interrupted us.

Buzzzzz. . . . Buzzzzzz.

I reached down and pressed the intercom button. "Yeah?"

"Kyle, you have a call from your attorney, Greg Thomas, on line one."

I didn't know why Greg was calling, but I couldn't help but look at Webster with a frown. "I guess God decided to send me that sign a lot sooner than either of us thought, huh?"

It was almost 2 A.M. when I stumbled up to my Highland Avenue apartment. It turned out that my lawyer wasn't calling me about divorce, but about the lawsuit I was filing against the police department. After I talked to him, the memories of what happened combined with news that Lisa was divorcing me had me so full of anger I had to leave my office before I said the wrong thing to my employees or a customer. So I headed to my apartment to take a nap and hopefully forget what was slowly turning into the worst day of my life. When I woke up, the pain of Lisa divorcing me was still there so I went to the Roadhouse Bar and spent the rest of the evening drinking one drink after another. I did order some food in between drinks to keep myself from getting too high, but I was still drunk enough that Val, one of the bartenders, took away my keys and drove me home.

"Hey, Val. I can't get in without my keys," I slurred, staring at the cleavage her low-cut blouse revealed. Val had one of those bodies that could get a brother in trouble, a whole bunch of trouble. She had large round hips, a thin waist, and a pair of perfect titties, all highlighted by a beautiful cocoa brown face that woulda made Whitney Houston jealous.

"Here," she said, handing me the keys. I don't know how, but I fumbled with the lock and opened the door.

"Where's your bathroom?" she asked, following me in. "I gotta pee."

"Down the hall, second door on your right," I pointed, then plopped down on the sofa watching her hips sway as she disappeared down the hall. Next thing I remember she was shaking me.

"Get up, Kyle," she scolded me.

"I'm up. I was just resting my eyes." I rubbed my eyes till she came into focus.

"Well, you been resting your eyes for twenty minutes."

"Sorry about that." I tried to get up, but my knees reminded me I was drunk.

"You better sit your drunk ass down," Val laughed, grabbing me before I fell.

I smiled as our eyes met, thinking thoughts I shouldn't have thought. Val and I had been friends for about three years and had always flirted and talked shit back and forth about what we'd do to each other if we were single. It was just talk back then but now things had changed. She'd broken up with her longtime beau, and Lisa and I were on the verge of divorce.

"You thinkin' what I'm thinkin'?" I smirked, raising my eyebrows.

Val pushed me back onto the couch sucking her teeth. "Don't get slapped. You know it ain't that kinda party."

"Sorry, I thought with T out of the picture and me getting divorced—" Val cut me off right there.

"Look, Kyle, I like you but I don't wanna give you the wrong idea. I'm not a ho."

"Have I treated you like one?"

"No."

"Aw'ight then."

"Look, we need to make a decision. Either you're gonna give me money for a cab or I'm spending the night. Which means you buying me breakfast and driving me home in the morning."

"Why I gotta pay for your cab?" It's not that I wouldn't have paid for the cab in the first place, but she made it seem like she was tellin' me, not askin' me.

"You gotta pay 'cause if it wasn't for your drunk ass, I wouldn't have missed my ride, that's why." She had a hint of attitude.

"You don't have to get nasty. I was just asking."

"So, what's up? You gonna give me the money for a cab or drive me home in the morning?" She folded her arms, waiting for an answer.

"It's up to you," I threw the ball back in her court. Just in case we did end up in bed and at that point I was pretty sure we would, I didn't want her blaming it on not being able to get home.

"I don't feel like riding all the way to Brooklyn in no cab. I'm tired." Yep, it was just a matter of time before we got busy tonight.

"Aw'ight, so spend the night. But I'm not gonna lie. I snore."

"Please, that don't matter to me. You sleeping on the couch, anyway."

"I am?" I couldn't hide my disappointment.

"Now I know you didn't think you was sleeping with me." She

placed her hand on her hip and tilted her head. "And I damn sure know you ain't think I was sleeping on no couch."

"Oh, it's like that, huh?"

"You got that right." She sucked her teeth. "Just 'cause me and Terrance broke up don't mean you getting some ass." She waved her hands in the air for effect. "Now where do you keep your towels and face cloths? I smell just like that smoky bar."

"Linen closet, first door before the bathroom. You'll find a tooth-brush in there too." Val walked down the hall, and a few minutes later I heard the shower running. I sniffed my clothes. I smelled like smoke too.

The alcohol in me told me I should walk down there and jump in the shower with her; after all, that's what she really wanted. Why else would she come to my place at two in the morning and spend the night if she didn't really wanna get busy? But the common sense side of me, that side we all have when we're drunk but never want to admit to said, *Don't be a fool. This is the kind of woman you could start a new family with. Maybe even have another kid with. Don't fuck up.* I lis-tened to the common sense side but I have to admit the alcohol side had made some good points too. It wasn't an easy thing to keep myself on that sofa knowing a beautiful woman was down the hall with no clothes on, dripping wet.

While Val was in the shower, I picked up the phone and dialed the house. I knew it was late but I wanted to clear the air between Lisa and me before I did something stupid. If she wanted a divorce, I wanted to hear her say it. I had no reason to distrust what Wil had told me earlier in the day, but like he said, this was my family we were talking about, and I had to be sure. Plus if something did happen between Val and me, I wanted to have a clear conscience and no regrets.

"Hello," a groggy male voice answered. I hung the phone up think-ing I'd dialed the wrong number in my drunkenness. Then to be sure I dialed the right number, I hit #83, the speed-dial number to the house.

"Hello," the same groggy male voice replied again, damn near causing me to have a heart attack.

"Can I speak to Lisa?" I know I had an attitude. But shit, I couldn't believe she had some man in bed with her while my kids were in the house. I don't even wanna get into the fact that he was answering the phone, for cryin' out loud.

"May I ask who's calling?" he replied, still groggy.

Who the hell was he to ask me who's calling? He was in my damn house in my damn bed on my damn phone.

"Can I speak to Lisa?" Now I had even more attitude.

"Who's calling," he replied with a little attitude himself.

"Who the fuck is this?"

"Look you called here, who the fuck is this?"

"If you don't put Lisa on the phone, I swear to God I'll be over there in five minutes to put my foot so far up your ass you'll be feeding my toes when you eat."

The line went silent. He was probably telling Lisa it was me on the phone and I was threatening to come over. Just thinking about her lying in a bed with another man was making me wanna jump in my truck and kick both their asses.

"Is this Kyle?" He'd lost his attitude and sounded humble. Not that it mattered to me. I wasn't about to lose my attitude.

"Yeah, this is Kyle. Put Lisa on the phone."

"Uh, she's not here right now, but . . ."

"But what? You know what, forget it. Just tell Lisa to call me. And if I were you, I'd think twice about sleeping in another man's bed." I slammed the phone down in anger.

It took me a minute to calm down, and while I was doing that, I took the pillows off the sofa and pulled out the sofa bed. That's when the phone rang. I sat on the edge of the bed and answered it.

"Hello?"

"Kyle?" It was Lisa, and she didn't sound happy.

"What?"

"What the hell are you playing games on the phone for? And why are you threatening my guests?"

"I wasn't playin' on the phone. I was calling for you."

"At three in the morning?"

"Yeah." I hesitated for a few seconds. "I wanted to tell you I'm filing for divorce in the morning."

The line was silent for a few seconds, then I heard her start sniffling. Shit. This definitely wasn't what I had wanted to say to her, but I was so heated when she had another man answering my phone. No one should have to put up with that kind of disrespect. And what the hell was she crying about now? She already had another man takin' my place and now she's crying about a divorce?

"Lisa, did you hear me?"

I could hear her sniffle again.

"Lisa?"

"I heard you, Kyle," she said weakly.

"Look, I hope this isn't gonna get ugly."

"It already is ugly, Kyle."

"I know that. I was talking about financially. I'm willing to give you your fair share. I just wanna maintain control of the business and have joint custody of the girls. That's fair, isn't it?"

"I can't talk about this shit right now."

There was silence on the line again, and I thought she'd hung up until I heard her sob quietly.

"Kyle, do you have a T-shirt I can wear?" I covered the phone and turned around. There was Val with only a towel wrapped around her.

"Yeah, look in the bedroom, top left-hand drawer."

"You don't look so good." Val walked over and put her hand on my shoulder. "You okay?"

"Yeah, I'm aw'right." I tried to smile as I pointed to the covered phone. "I'm just trying to straighten out a few things with my wife about our divorce."

"Oh, sorry." Val turned fast and walked toward the bedroom.

"Lisa, you still there?"

"I'm here. Who was that?"

"A friend."

"You have a female friend over there at three in the morning? Asking for a T-shirt? You fucking bastard! No wonder you're filing for divorce!"

"You've got some nerve. Who the hell are you sleeping next to?"

"Your daughter . . . You know what? I'm not even gonna justify that with an answer. You'll be hearing from my lawyer." I heard a click, then a dial tone.

I sat on the sofa bed and wiped away tears until Val walked in the room wearing my Alpha Phi Alpha sweatshirt. She sat cross-legged on the other end of the bed without a word. I looked over at her and could see her dark blue panties clear as day. The effects of the alcohol had worn off after my conversation with Lisa, so I had no problem telling her to close her legs.

"Everything okay?" She looked sad as if she could feel my pain.

"Nothing I can't handle." I grabbed one of the sofa cushions and laid my head on it.

"Yeah, that's the same way I felt when me and Terrance broke up."

"You still love him, don't ya?"

"Yeah, I can't help myself. But I'm not gonna let him play me no more. That nigga's worse than your friend Jay."

"I doubt it. You don't know Jay." I laughed. So did she. I think we both needed to laugh. "What's up, Val?"

"What's up with what?"

"Why'd you volunteer to drive me home? You could have just as easily put me in a cab."

She looked sad as she spoke. "I don't know. I just didn't wanna go home to an empty apartment."

"So you decided to come over here to push up on me?"

"Don't flatter yourself, Kyle. If I wasn't on my period, I would never have come over here." Oh, now that was a slap in the face. No woman would say that to a man she was tryin' to get with.

"So why me? Why of all people did you pick me to hang out with?"

" 'Cause you've always been my friend. And no matter what, you've always been respectful. For some reason, even drunk I trust you more than I would anyone else."

"So you just wanna be friends?"

"Yep, for now just friends is all I can handle. But who knows what the future holds."

Val was right. Friendship was about all I could probably handle at this point, too. I slept on the couch, hoping that in the morning I would have some clue about what to do with my crumbling marriage.

16

Allen

Beep! Beep! Beep!

I looked down at my beeper and read the numbers. Not that I had to. I already knew who was beeping me before I looked down. *911 69.* That was Rose's code for, *Where the hell are you and how come you didn't call me the first time I beeped you?*

Like an idiot, I'd given Rose *my* cell phone, so there was no way I could have called her back the first time. Now I was standing in front of her house as I got her second page, and of course, that meant as soon as I got inside, I'd have to hear her mouth. The last thing I wanted to do was deal with her bullshit tonight. I'd just finished up a thirteen-hour workday, five of which were tedious, number-crunching overtime. All I wanted was to get in the house, put on my pajamas, cook the steak I'd left marinating in Ma's secret recipe all day, and have a quickie with Rose before I went to sleep.

But the chance of that happening was slim to none, 'cause Rose was probably gonna be ranting and raving the minute I walked in the door. She hadn't let up about me putting her name on my checking and savings account for almost two months. I think the fact that I hadn't given in yet was really getting on her nerves, 'cause she'd stopped having sex with me about two weeks ago. So far I'd been strong. I hadn't given in, though the arguing and my horniness were sure wearing me down.

I cleared my head as I walked up the steps and opened the door, prepared for confrontation. To my total bewilderment, Rose greeted me at the door with a big smile and a kiss. This was definitely not what I had expected. And even more surprising was the fact that she was fully made up and wearing a tight-fitting outfit at eleven-thirty at night. By this hour she was usually ready for bed.

"Where were you?" she asked sweetly. "We've been waiting over three hours."

"We?" I asked, raising an eyebrow. Her nicey-nice attitude was so out of character it was making me nervous.

"Yes, we. Come on in the kitchen. I have someone I want you to meet." I followed her into the kitchen and there, sitting at the table eating what looked like the steak I'd been craving for my dinner, was a very handsome, brown-skinned brother in a suit.

"Allen, this is Ray Johnson. Ray's my cousin." Ray looked reluctant to stand up to shake my hand. I don't think he wanted to leave that steak. Why should he? That steak cost me ten bucks.

"How you doin', Ray? That looks like a good steak you're eatin'." I extended my hand and tried to smile, but I was so hungry I wanted to grab what was left of that steak and eat it caveman-style.

"Man, this is the best steak I've ever had. It's like butter. The damn thing just melts in your mouth." He shoved another piece of steak in his mouth before he extended his hand.

"I thought I'd met all of Rose's family. I didn't know she had any Johnsons in her family." I tightened my grip around Ray's hand.

"Ohhh, ah, Ray's my cousin from marriage. It's kind of complicated," Rose replied with a hint of worry in her voice.

"Yeah, real complicated," Ray smirked.

I let my eyes tell him I didn't trust him. Rose gently touched my hand, reminding me I was still crunching Ray's. I let go of his hand and watched him sit back down to eat my steak. My stomach growled for everyone to hear. I rolled my eyes at Rose then glanced at my watch. It was 11:41 P.M.

"So, Ray, what brings you by at such a late hour?"

"I asked him to come by, Allen," Rose said excitedly. "Ray knows a lot of insurance agents." She said it as if it was supposed to mean something to me.

"I'm happy for him. That still doesn't explain why Ray's here at damn near midnight eating what should be my dinner." I know I was being rude and obnoxious, but the guy was eating my steak. I faked a smile, trying to defuse my last comment. "No offense, cuz."

"None taken, Albert."

"The name's Allen," I corrected him through clenched teeth.

"Oh, sorry," he smiled and made sure I was watching as he shoved the last of my steak in his mouth. "Maybe this wasn't such a good time, Rose."

"Maybe you're right, Ray. Allen's a little hungry. I'm gonna fix him some bacon and eggs then the two of us will talk."

Inside I wanted to scream. She was gonna fix me some bacon and eggs after he just got finished eating my steak. I wasn't one to argue, but she was gonna get a piece of my mind the minute he walked out the door. Ray picked up his briefcase and stood, kissing Rose on the cheek as his free hand brushed against her hip. "You've got a fine woman here, Allen. Don't blow it. There's plenty of brothers who'd love to get with her." He smiled at Rose then winked at me as his hand came dangerously close to copping a feel. I grabbed Rose's arm, pulling her closer to me.

"I know you two have a lot to talk about, so I'll see my way out." I watched Ray walk out of the kitchen. I was prepared to grill her about whatever had just happened, but before I could say a word, Rose was in my face.

"How could you embarrass me like that?" she screamed.

"Embarrass you? I just watched him eat my dinner. No man is supposed to come home to that shit!"

"Well, if you had brought your ass home at eight like you're supposed to, it would have been you eating that steak." She crossed her arms and raised her eyebrows like she thought her reasoning was perfectly logical. So much for treating your man with respect.

"Home like I'm supposed to? Hold up, you're the one who said I should work as much overtime as possible before the wedding."

"I didn't tell you to work overtime tonight. We were supposed to be discussing adding my name to your accounts over dinner tonight. Remember?"

Oh, I remembered all right. That's why I had volunteered to do overtime. I figured by the time I got to her place, Rose would be too tired to argue. I was wrong about that.

"Look, Rose, it's late and I haven't had a thing to eat since lunch." I walked over to the cabinet and pulled out the peanut butter and jelly. "I really don't feel like arguing about adding you to my accounts right now. So I'm gonna tell you this, and it's going to be final or we can call the whole damn wedding off. The day we go to the bank and add my name to your accounts is the day I'll add you to mine."

"Okay, Allen." Her voice was so sweet it scared me. "Why don't we do it tomorrow?"

"Huh?" I couldn't believe it. "Did you say why don't we do it tomorrow?"

"Yes, if that's okay with you."

"Yeah, it's okay." My voice was calm, but I was worried. She'd given in way too easy. I'm not gonna lie—the thought that she might have cleaned out her accounts did cross my mind.

"Why don't you go and watch the game on ESPN in the living room while I fix you something to eat?" Yep, something was up. She never volunteered to cook.

So I settled in front of the TV and waited while my woman cooked. After a few minutes I realized I had not even asked Rose for an explanation of this Ray character and his mysterious presence at my dinner table. Once again, Rose had managed to take control of our *discussion*. She definitely followed the strike-first tactic. She was in my shit so fast about coming home late that I totally forgot to ask her what the hell he was doing here. I think it was pretty obvious he wasn't her cousin. Now I was just too tired to argue about it. It would have to wait.

Fifteen minutes later, Rose placed a tray of cheese eggs, sausage, bacon, and a side of pancakes in front of me. It wasn't my steak, but it quieted down my growling stomach. After I ate, she crawled on top of me, wearing only her bathrobe.

"Allen," she whispered.

"Yes, Rose," I whispered back.

"You think your mother would like me more if I had a baby?" She kissed my neck.

"Would she. She'd probably have you nominated for sainthood. Why?"

"I don't know, I was just thinking maybe we should make a baby tonight."

"Huh?" I raised my eyebrows. "What'd you say?"

"I wanted to know if you'd like to work on making your mother a grandmother tonight."

"Look, don't be playin' around like that. You know how much I wanna have kids. And don't use my mother's name to get to me tonight."

"I'm not playin', Allen." She pointed toward the kitchen. "Go look in the kitchen and see for yourself. I threw all the condoms away."

I got up and walked into the kitchen to look in the trash. To my surprise, she wasn't lying. All the condoms we had were in there. But that wasn't enough proof for me. I walked back in the living room still wary that she might be up to something. As much as I loved Rose, she could be as slick as they come.

"You really wanna get pregnant before we're married?"

"Yes," she nodded.

"What about a house? We're not gonna be able to afford a house right away."

"I know, Allen." She seemed sincere but I was still skeptical.

"Why the sudden change?"

"Jesus Christ, Allen! Why does everything have to be so complicated with you? I'm thirty-three years old and I'm getting married in two months, not to mention the fact that my biological clock is ticking like shit."

"Yeah, but . . ."

"But what?" she asked.

I could tell she was getting frustrated.

"Allen, I'm horny and I wanna have your baby," she sighed heavily. "Now do we have to fight over whether you're gonna make love to me?"

I smiled. She was right. Why the hell was I arguing? Just the thought of having sex with her without a condom was enough to make a believer out of me. In the five years I'd been goin' with Rose, she had never once let me have sex without a condom. I lifted her up and carried her into the bedroom, kissing her the entire way. As I laid her down, I noticed she was holding an envelope.

"What's that for?" I tried to take it from her hand.

"Nothin'. We'll talk about it later." She pulled her hand away and placed the envelope on her nightstand. "Com'ere big boy and make me a mama."

"Ohhh, Allen, that's it, baby! That's the spot. One more time, boo." We'd been at it almost twenty minutes and I was deep inside Rose with her legs wrapped around me tight. She was as close to an orgasm as humanly possible and that was a good thing, 'cause I didn't know how much longer I could last without exploding myself. It had been so long since I'd had sex without a condom that I'd completely forgotten how much better it really felt.

"Ohhh, shit! Yes, yes, yes!" Rose moaned loudly. There was no doubt in my mind she was having an orgasm. Her entire body went rigid, then burst into small convulsions that sent me into my own howling orgasm. When it was all over, I collapsed on top of her, totally exhausted.

"I think you did it, Allen. I think I'm pregnant," she grinned at me, full of excitement.

I looked at her doubtfully. How the hell could she still have all this energy after an orgasm like that? I barely had enough energy to move, but I had to answer her.

"You need to stop, Rose. You couldn't possibly know if you're pregnant."

"Trust me, Allen. A woman knows these things."

"Ya know what, Rose? You're a trip." I struggled to roll off her, onto my back. I was starting to feel like she was up to something again. And by the look she gave me, I think she knew it.

"I'm a nurse, Allen." She rolled on top of me and looked directly in my eyes. "You act as if I don't know when I'm ovulating."

I had to think about that a second before answering. I guess she'd made a good point. Maybe she had planned the whole evening around her biological clock after all.

"You're really serious about having this baby, aren't you?"

"Of course I'm serious. Have I ever let you stick your dick in me without a condom?"

"No."

"That's because I had two abortions before we met. I been tellin' you ever since we met that getting pregnant was not gonna be a problem. I'm fertile as a damn bunny rabbit."

"You had two abortions?" I didn't pay attention to anything else she had said.

"Yeah," she replied nonchalantly as if it was no big deal. "And both times I knew I was pregnant the minute I conceived."

"You had two abortions?" I repeated. This time she noticed my tone.

"Yes, Allen, I had two abortions." She sucked her teeth and rolled her eyes. "You wanna call the wedding off because of my past sins or deal with the fact that you're gonna be a daddy?"

I hesitated before I spoke, 'cause she was right. When my boys told me they'd all had a piece of Rose before me, I'd already made the decision that her past wasn't gonna affect our future.

"Am I really gonna be a dad?"

"Allen, I promise you if I'm not pregnant now I'm gonna be before the wedding." Deep down I still felt like she was up to something, but the thought of being a father pushed all that to the side.

"I'm gonna be a dad. God, I can't wait to tell Ma."

"Let's wait 'til the doctor confirms things before we tell the world, huh?" She wrapped her arms around me, laying her head on my chest.

"Okay." I held Rose for almost half an hour before either of us spoke again. The entire time I kept replaying how wonderful it felt to be inside of her with no latex between us. It was like being blind for five years then being able to see again.

"Rose, you awake?" I whispered.

"I'm awake." She snuggled a little closer.

"Was it better for you without the condom?"

"Wassss it." She turned her head so we were face to face. "Allen, that was the best you've ever been." She kissed me and I blushed.

"Wanna do it again?"

"Does a crackhead want ten dollars? Of course I do." She rolled on her stomach, smiling. "But this time let's try it from the back."

17

Kyle

It was a little after noon when I walked into the office of the Saint Anthony's Christian Academy. My daughter Jewel was sitting in a chair outside the principal's office, and she burst into tears as soon as she saw me. The school called me at work after they couldn't get in touch with Lisa. I walked over to the counter, ignoring Jewel. She was the kind of kid that only cried when she'd done something wrong, so I was sure she wasn't sitting there for nothing. I tried my best to hide the disappointment that was building inside me as I spoke to the woman behind the counter.

"Hi, I'm Kyle Richmond. Mrs. Cottman asked me to come down because of my daughter Jewel."

"Yes, Mr. Richmond, she's been waiting for you." She opened the small gate and I followed her into the principal's office, where a brown-skinned woman I recognized as the principal sat behind a desk. "Mrs. Cottman, this is Mr. Richmond, Jewel's father."

"Yes, I know we've met. How are you, Mr. Richmond?" She stood to shake my hand. Then gestured for me to take a seat. "I'm sorry you had to leave work to come down here."

"So am I, Mrs. Cottman." I sat down in front of her desk. "What exactly did Jewel do?"

"Jewel went into the cubby room and smashed all the boys' lunches."

"What?" I sat up straight in my chair. I was about to get up and drag Jewel's narrow ass into Cottman's office but there was a knock on the door.

"Come in," the principal said.

A short light-skinned woman entered.

"Mr. Richmond, this is Miss Bailey, our school social worker. I asked her to join us."

I reached over and shook the social worker's hand, a little apprehensive as I spoke to the principal. "You told me on the phone that Jewel was having a small discipline problem. Why is the school social worker here?"

"Well, Mr. Richmond, in addition to what happened today, we've found that Jewel's been havin' some other problems."

"What kind of problems?" The principal reached for a file. Then with a very serious look, she handed me a picture from the file.

"Oh God" were the only words that escaped my mouth as I stared at my daughter's artwork. The picture was of a man with the word DADDY written underneath it. The word LIAR written at least twenty times surrounding the man.

"Wh-what exactly does this mean?" I turned to the social worker for my answer but found it hard to look her in the face.

"We were hoping you might be able to help us with that, Mr. Richmond," the social worker replied.

I glanced at the principal then the social worker, lowering my head in shame. I knew Jewel was having problems adjusting to the breakup. Shit, so were Willow and Jade, but most of the time they were just vying for my attention. A hug and a promise of a new Barbie or an ice cream cone always seemed to fix that. At least that's what I thought until now. I scratched my head as the social worker stared at me, still waiting for my answer. I didn't know what to say, but before I did, thank God, the principal was talking.

"Mr. Richmond, I'm not going to lie to you. Your wife's told us about your separation." Good ol' Lisa was telling everyone she could that we were separated, probably to get sympathy. "To be quite honest, I was rather relieved when we couldn't reach her and had to call you."

"Oh, why is that?" I lifted my head and stared in her face.

"Well, for starters, I wanted to tell you how much you've been missed. We don't get to know many of the fathers of our children, and ever since Jewel became a student here, both you and your wife have been our most active parents. You alone have probably been to more functions and attended more field trips than any mother other than your wife. But that stopped a few months ago, and that's when we started noticing a change in Jewel's behavior and her schoolwork."

She was right. I never missed one of Jewel's school functions until after the separation. "Yes, I know she's been having a few problems adjusting to me moving out of the house. To tell you the truth, I've had a few problems adjusting myself. I guess that's why I haven't been around as much as I should."

"We understand that these types of things happen in families, Mr. Richmond, and we'd like to help if we can." The social worker reached over and patted my hand. Which made me feel like shit.

"Help how?"

"Well, for starters, I'd like for Jewel to come see me once a week, if that's all right with you."

"I'd have to speak to her mother but I can't see that being a problem."

First I'm seeing a shrink; now Jewel's going to see a low-rent shrink. What the hell have I done to my family? God, this was exactly what I'd been trying to avoid all my life.

"I'd also like for Jewel to join a school club called Banana Splits."

"What exactly is Banana Splits?"

"It's a club for children of divorced and separated marriages that meets once a week during recess. It gives the kids a chance to talk to other children who may be going through the same thing. I've found that it's really helped in cases like Jewel's."

"Okay, if you think it's gonna help." I reached in my suit pocket for a handkerchief and wiped my brow. I'd always fancied myself a good father, someone who'd always be there for my girls no matter what. But as I looked back at the last few months, I realized I hadn't been there for them at all. Sure, I paid child support and I picked them up every other weekend, but I could have done more. I could have been there.

"I do think it's going to help," the social worker said with a smile.

"Well, I guess the only thing to do now is figure out what type of discipline we're going to give Jewel for what she did today. Do you have any suggestions, Mr. Richmond?" the principal asked.

"Whatever you think is fair, Ms. Cottman. I would like to take Jewel home with me today, though. I think the two of us have a lot to discuss. Maybe I can find out why she drew this picture." I looked at the picture again, shaking my head.

"I understand. Why don't we do that, Mr. Richmond, and before Jewel comes back to school, why don't we have her write a letter of apology to her classmates."

I nodded my head with a frown and reached into my pocket.

"Do you think this will cover the lunches she smashed?" I handed her a fifty-dollar bill.

"Oh, I'm sure this will do it." The principal nodded, taking the bill then shaking my hand.

Jewel and I left the school and walked to my truck without a word. I opened the back door and she jumped in, buckling her seat belt. When I got in the truck, I turned my head toward her. I think she must have expected me to slap her by the way she cringed, but all I did was shake my head, letting her know how disappointed I was. The two of us drove around Jamaica in silence for about twenty minutes before I decided to take her back to the house. That ride must have been torture for her, 'cause when we pulled into the driveway, she was sweating like a death-row inmate. I wasn't one to brutalize my kids, but I did believe in good old-fashioned spankings, something I'm sure Jewel hadn't had since I moved out.

The two of us got out of the car and walked to the side door of the house. I still had keys but I let Jewel open the door with the key she wore around her neck. When we got in the house, I pointed at the kitchen table and the two of us sat down across from each other. Jewel was on the verge of tears so I figured I'd try to be gentle in my approach. Just thinking about that picture she drew made me realize this wasn't all her fault.

"Rough day at school today, huh?" I had a serious look but I tried to smile. Hell, I needed to smile—everything I held dear was slipping away from me at the same time.

"Yes," she whispered, avoiding eye contact.

"Don't worry, I had a rough couple of days myself." I reached across the table and touched her hand. I had tears in my eyes and I'm not really sure why. "You wanna talk about it?"

She shook her head no.

"Why?"

She shrugged her shoulders. "I don't know."

"You know what you did today was wrong, don't you?"

"Yes." I could barely hear her.

"So why'd you do it?"

She didn't answer me. She just shrugged her shoulders again as tears began to stream down her cheeks. I handed her a napkin to dry her eyes.

"Are you mad at me for moving out, Jewel?" She shrugged her shoulders and frowned. "You can tell me if you are. Truth is I'm kinda mad at myself."

"Yes," she said, nodding her head fast.

"That's what I figured."

I stared at my daughter, hoping she wouldn't notice the disappointment building inside of me. I wasn't disappointed in her but in myself. I'd hurt her—something I never, ever wanted to do. But the way things were going between her mother and me, I just couldn't think of a way to make things right. Hell, even if I wanted to come home, things were more complicated now than when I left. I was tempted to ask Jewel about this Mike guy Lisa was seeing, but it would have been wrong to bring her deeper into her mother's and my mess.

"Why are you mad at me, Jewel?" I asked in my concerned fatherly tone.

She hesitated, looking up then down. If I had to guess, I would have sworn she was contemplating if she should tell me a lie or not. I decided not to give her that chance so I reached inside my suit jacket and pulled out the picture she'd drawn. Her eyes told me that she was caught completely by surprise when I unfolded it. "Do you think I'm a liar, Jewel? 'Cause I don't remember lying to you."

"Yes, you did," she blurted quickly then stopped herself.

"Excuse me?" I replied, shocked by her response.

Jewel didn't say a word at first. I think she was afraid she was gonna get in trouble, but then out of nowhere she lifted her head with an attitude. "You did lie to me, Daddy. And you lied to my mommy too. You promised you would only go away on business and that you would call us every day. You lied to me, Daddy, and now you don't even come home at all." She burst into tears as she slid out of her chair.

"Jewel," I called after her as she ran out the kitchen toward the stairs. "Damn," I said to myself. Here I am placing a guilt trip on a seven-year-old child when I'm the one who's wrong. I knew better than this. I should have talked to the girls about my leaving a long time ago.

I waited awhile before getting up and following Jewel. Like me, she probably needed to sort things out. As I sat in the kitchen, I thought about the mistakes I'd made over the past few months. I'd never thought about how I would explain to the girls why I left. I guess I took for granted that their mother would do that. I mean, what was I supposed to say, "I'm not coming home 'cause your mother is white"? I might have my problems with Lisa but she was still the mother of my children and I'll love her for that till the day I die. I could never teach my children that their existence was wrong. Shit, I didn't believe that. Each and every one of my girls was a child of love. I guess inside I forgot about that.

"A child of love," I repeated out loud. That's when I made the decision that I was gonna do a better job as a father, no matter what went on between Lisa and me. I was going to have to spend more than just every other weekend with my girls. If it meant picking them up from school or just coming to the house for an hour to read them a story each night, I was going to have to spend more time with my girls. I was also gonna have to find a way to get along with Lisa. This whole separation and divorce wasn't her fault, it was mine, and it was my responsibility to make it work and bury the hatchet between us.

"Jewel," I called, knocking on her bedroom door. When she didn't answer, I opened the door. She was lying on her bed with her face in a pillow. "I'm sorry," I said, softly walking over to her bed where she was sobbing. "I'm really sorry." I sat down beside her and stroked her hair gently. "I didn't mean to lie to you, baby. I swear I didn't. At the time I wasn't lying. I meant every word. It's just that things changed and I had to leave." She lifted her head, looking me in the face.

"That's not true, Daddy! You didn't have to leave. My mommy said you can stay and that you can come home whenever you want. She even said she missed you and so did Willow, Jade, and me too. So why don't you come home, Daddy."

I didn't know what to say. I had come upstairs hoping to explain things to her. In some way make them right, but she wasn't making it easy.

"It's a little complicated, sweetheart. But Daddy had a good reason for not coming home." Jewel buried her face into her pillow. When she lifted her head back up, she said, "Daddy, I'll be a good girl, I promise. If you come home, I'll never do anything bad again."

"Oh, baby, you didn't do anything wrong." I rubbed my hand over my face, hoping my little girl wouldn't see me cry.

"Then why don't you come home? Tommy Brown said that you left because you had bad kids." I took hold of my daughter and hugged her tight.

"Tommy Brown doesn't know what he's talking about. You're not a bad girl. None of you are."

"Then how come you're not coming home?" I let go of her and patted the empty space next me.

"Sit up, Jewel. Do you really wanna know why Daddy's not staying here?"

"Yeah," she nodded, sitting up straight next to me.

"Okay, you're big enough. Let's see if I can explain it to you." I took a deep breath and exhaled it out. "Mommy and Daddy are what they call separated. Do you know what separated is?"

"No," she said, looking confused.

"It's all right. Do you remember when you and Willow kept getting into fights every day?"

"Mmm-hmm. She kept going in my stuff."

"That's right. And what did Mommy and Daddy do to stop you two from fighting?"

"You gave me my own room."

"That's right, we separated you."

"Oh, so that's what 'separated' means."

"Yeah, that's what it means." I hugged her. "Well Mommy and Daddy were fighting too. Not about you girls but about grown-up stuff. So Daddy decided to get a new place to live. That's why I stay in the apartment now. We're separated. You understand?"

"No. Why didn't you just get a new room like I did?"

"Remember when I was staying in the guest room? Well, I was trying that then but I'm pretty big so I needed my own house."

"Daddy, are you ever coming home?"

"I don't know, Jewel. It doesn't look that way. But I'm gonna spend more time with you and your sisters than I have been. That's for sure. Is that okay with you?"

"Yeah, but I'd rather you come home."

"I know, sweetheart, I know."

I held Jewel in my arms for the better part of an hour as we talked. It's incredible how fast children grow up, and all it takes is the blink of an eye to miss it. Since I'd moved out, Jewel had done so many things I didn't know of that it was actually embarrassing. I don't think I'll ever forgive myself for being in Africa during her ballet recital. But now I just found out that I missed her scoring the winning goal in the girls' peewee soccer championship just because it wasn't my weekend.

When we finished talking, Jewel started on her letter of apology and I headed downstairs to the family room to watch some TV. That's when I heard Lisa's van pull up in the driveway. She must have noticed my truck right away, 'cause the minute the door opened, she called my name.

"Kyle, what are you doing here?" I turned my head toward her as she entered the room. I have to admit she was looking good. Lisa had never been the type to wear a lot of makeup but today she had on some blue eyeliner that matched her pantsuit, which she was wearing the hell out of, I might add. The first thing that came to my mind was that she had probably just come back from a date with Mike and that angered me.

"If you had checked your messages or been home, you'd know why I'm here," I told her with attitude. I know I said I was gonna try and work things out with her but it's hard to work things out when jealousy kicks in.

"Look, Kyle, don't play games with me. What's going on? Are the girls all right?" She gave me a concerned look but there was definitely attitude in her voice.

"Yeah, they're all right. But Jewel got suspended from school for the day. She smashed all the boys' lunches." I wanted to laugh but Lisa's cold stare made me keep it in.

"Oh, my God. She is out of control." Lisa sighed heavily, making a face. I could tell she'd had about enough with Jewel.

"She's gonna be all right. We had a talk."

"Well, she's about to get another one." Lisa turned toward the stairs.

"Lisa, don't! I told you I already talked to her." I reached up from the sofa and grabbed her arm. "Give the kid a break."

"Look, Kyle, you're not the one who has to deal with her every day. So don't tell me what to do," she said flatly, pulling her arm free.

"If you were so worried about her, you should have been home instead of out fuckin' around with your new boyfriend!" I snapped back.

I regretted my words the second they left my mouth. This was not how I had planned on handling things at all. I was supposed to be making peace with her but she wasn't making it easy. The thought of her being with another man was still a large obstacle and a major blow to my ego. And to tell you the truth, I wasn't used to her giving me this kind of lip.

"Get the fuck out my house," she screamed, pointing at the door. "You think you can come over here and insult me after all the bullshit you've put me through. You must be crazy! Get the fuck out of my house!"

"Look, Lisa, I'm sorry about what I just said." She gave me a yeah-right look that made me feel as if I had to explain myself. "No, seriously, I'm sorry. I guess I'm just a little jealous that you found someone so quickly."

"I found someone? You're the one who had a woman at your apartment at three in the morning the other night asking for a T-shirt! Not me!" She rolled her eyes, which made me wanna say something smart about this Mike guy spending the night Tuesday, but at a time like this, it wasn't gonna help. So I kept my mouth shut.

"This is not about me, Kyle. Don't you ever make this about me. You left me, remember?" Lisa's face was full of anger, and tears had begun to roll down her face.

"No, you're right. Look, I think we need to talk," I said submissively, pointing to the sofa. I was hoping to work things out. Lisa looked at me and took a deep breath as if she was about to say something very important. Which she did.

"No, Kyle, you're wrong. We don't need to talk. The time to talk is over. I've waited for you to come home for almost four months. And it's taken me this long to realize what we had is over. I hope you have." She reached into her bag and handed me an envelope. "I figured you'd probably be using Greg Thomas so I had my lawyer contact him this afternoon. I filed for divorce this morning."

Have you ever heard the expression, *You could have knocked me over with a feather.* Well, at that moment Lisa's words felt like she had knocked me over with a baseball bat. I was floored. I couldn't believe what she had just said. Hell, I couldn't believe she said it. Yeah, we had talked about divorce, but this was serious. Lisa had actually placed the papers in my hand. And even more importantly, she had initiated the divorce, something I would have never expected in a million years. All I could do was stare at the papers in my hand. I wanted to say something but words just wouldn't come out. A problem she didn't seem to have.

"I think it's best we let the lawyers handle the money issues. Don't you think?" I didn't answer her. "Kyle!" she shouted. "Do you want the lawyers to handle the money issues?"

"I guess," I replied, snapping out of my fog with one very important question. "What about the girls? I'd like to be a bigger part of their lives."

She bit her lip as she thought for a second. "You can have joint custody but the girls are going to live here. You can see them anytime you want. I want you to be a part of their lives but that's all I want. As far as I'm concerned, you and I are over. You don't understand how much this whole thing has hurt me." Again I didn't know what to say. So I walked toward the front door in silence.

"Kyle." I turned to see what she wanted.

"Yeah?"

"Your keys."

"Huh? What about them?"

"Leave them. You had four months to come home. You don't live here anymore." I clenched my teeth as I reached in my pocket and took out my keys. It took me a few seconds to get the keys off my key ring but I did it, reluctantly placing them on the table near the door. Before I left, I turned to Lisa and said, "I'm sorry," hoping she'd respond.

She didn't and I turned and walked out the door, heading for my truck. I sat in the truck for about five minutes contemplating whether I should open the envelope or not. I could see Lisa peeking through the window. She was probably wondering what the hell I was doing. I opened the envelope and looked down at the papers. Without even reading them, I threw them in the passenger seat and reached for my car phone. Punching in 411, I waited for the operator.

"City and state, please."

"Can I have the number to the Roadhouse Bar and Grill on Jamaica Avenue in Queens, New York, please."

"Certainly, sir, we will connect your call."

"Roadhouse Bar, Val speaking."

"Hey, Val, this is Kyle."

"Hey, Kyle, what's up?"

"How'd you like to go to Red Lobster for dinner tonight?"

"Love to," she said without hesitation. " I get off at eight."

"Good, I'll pick you up at eight."

"Eight it is. Bye."

18

Jay

I was sitting in the Roadhouse Bar finishing up my third beer, about to order another. I wasn't drunk, but that's the direction I was headed and I was trying to get there as quickly as possible. It had been six weeks to the day since Kenya had our daughter LaShawn, but even more important to me was that it had been six weeks since I'd seen Tracy. I don't know why, but I couldn't get her outta my head. I'd been calling her dorm almost every day but her roommates kept telling me she hadn't returned from the Christmas break yet. Deep down inside, I knew they were lying. She was trying to avoid me since I'd left her at the house.

"Hey, Val, can I get another Heineken?" I asked the sexy, brown-skinned bartender.

"Why don't you make that coffee, Val? He's gotta drive." I looked up and there was Kyle, dressed cleaner than the board of health in an off-white cashmere coat and an expensive, dark blue suit.

"Mmm, Mmm, Mmm. Don't you look good." Val smiled at Kyle, licking her lips.

"Thanks, Val." He smiled back.

If I didn't know better, I would have thought there was something going on between those two, 'cause she was smiling from ear to ear and his grin was almost as wide. At least 'til he caught me checking him out.

"What's up, bro?" He patted me on the back.

"Nothin' much, dawg."

"You sure?"

"Uh-hun, why?"

"Kenya called my apartment a little while ago. She said you were supposed to be home at five to take her to dinner." Kyle glanced at his watch then shoved his wrist in my face. "It's quarter to nine. You're running a little bit late, aren't you?"

I slapped his hand out of my face. Who the hell did he think he was anyway, my mom?

"Come on. Let's get your coat on." He lifted my coat from the back of the chair.

"What's up with you? You taken over Wil's job as mother hen or somethin'?" I snatched my coat defiantly and put it back on the chair.

"Look, Jay, your wife's waiting and I ain't got time ta be baby-sittin' your ass, okay?"

"Hey, I'm a grown man. Ain't nobody ask you to baby-sit me."

"If you so grown, why don't you act like it, man? Now come on."

"I'm not goin' anywhere, Kyle." I stood up and got in his face with my fists clenched.

"What you gonna do, punch me like you did Wil? Go ahead, you ain't got many friends left anyway."

Kyle always had been good at giving verbal jabs and I'd never had a problem taking them, but that one hurt. Wil still wasn't speaking to me, and it was six weeks since I had punched him. I sat back down silently and turned to the bartender.

"Val, can I please get that beer now?"

She glanced at Kyle for approval. I was about to curse her ass out, but he nodded that it was okay.

"Jay," he said calmly. "What's up, man? Why don't you wanna go home?"

I glanced over at him as Val placed my beer in front of me. I was afraid to tell him the truth.

"My six weeks is up, that's why."

"Six weeks? What the hell are you talkin' 'bout?" Kyle had a bewildered look on his face.

"It's been six weeks since Kenya had LaShawn. Her doctor cleared her this morning to have sex."

"And?" He gave me an odd look. "Why's that a problem?"

Taking hold of my beer, I took a long sip before I looked up at Kyle, who was still standing over me like I was his teenage son.

"Sit down and I'll tell you."

Kyle sat down and ordered a Dewars on the rocks with a frown. "Please don't tell me you've got gonorrhea again?"

I laughed. That woulda made life a lot simpler. At least that I coulda gotten rid of with a shot. You can't get rid of love that easy.

"No, Kyle." I shook my head. "I don't have VD."

"Thank God for small favors," he sighed. "Okay, so what's the problem then? Why don't you wanna go home?"

" I'mmm . . . I'm . . ." It was hard for me to say at first, but when I did say it, the words just flowed out naturally. "I'm thinking about leaving Kenya."

"Uh-oh." He stared at me in disbelief. "You're serious, aren't you?"

"Yep." I bit my bottom lip and nodded.

Kyle picked up his drink and took a sip. "Hey, Val, can I have a cigarette, baby?" Val walked over from the other side of the bar and handed him a cigarette.

"Need a light?" she asked as she leaned over the bar, close enough for a kiss. Yeah, something was definitely going on between those two. Kyle was being a little too friendly and acting too smooth.

"Yeah, thanks," he nodded, placing the cigarette between his lips. "I promised myself I'd stop smoking, but I need this one. This guy over here just dropped a bomb on my head." He pointed in my direction.

Val glanced over at me. I don't think she liked the idea that I'd upset him. I shot her one of those it's-none-o'-your-business kinda looks. I think she got the picture, 'cause she walked away pretty quick.

"Look, man, I'm the last one who should be asking this question, but why do you wanna leave Kenya?"

" 'Cause I'm in love with another woman," I said seriously.

He grinned, almost chuckled, as he picked up his drink. "Give me a fuckin' break," he laughed into his glass as he drank. "Man, I'm not even sure you know what love is."

I took a moment to think about what he'd said, watched him laugh a little harder as he inhaled his cigarette. He was starting to piss me off.

"No, really, Kyle, I'm in love." I grabbed his arm real tight, making sure I had his attention as I stared him down. "Kyle, I've never felt this way about anyone before in my life."

"Jay," he smirked, "that's the same thing you told me about Jackie and Denise and Susan and—"

"It's not the same, dammit!" Everyone in the bar turned toward me. "Y'all need to mind your fucking business!" I glared at the other patrons until everyone looked away.

"Okay man, relax." Kyle patted me on the back. I think he was finally starting to take me seriously. Either that or he just didn't want to see me go postal on someone in there. "So who is this mystery woman you've supposedly fallen in love with, anyway?"

"Her name is Tracy." I could see he was putting two and two together.

"Noooo." His eyes got wide. "Not the girl you left at the house?"

"That's her."

"I thought you told me you only slept with her once?"

"I did. One time was enough."

"She whipped you like that?" Shock was written all over his face.

"Yep." I still couldn't believe it myself.

"Pussy ain't everything, Jay," he preached.

"I know that, Kyle."

"So what makes you think you're in love with her? Maybe she was just having a good night. Don't you think you should at least sleep with her a few more times before you go declaring yourself in love? I mean, what do you really know about her?"

"I know everything I need to know. Kyle, you don't understand. I can't get her out of my head. She's all I think about." A smile spread across my face as I told him about her. I'd been keeping this inside way too long. "I can't even listen to the radio anymore."

"What? Why?"

"The songs. The love songs. They get to me. The other day I was driving to work and *Missing You* by Atlantic Star came on the radio and I started cryin'. Can you believe it? I started cryin'. I didn't cry at my grandpa's funeral, but I cried over some stupid-ass song and a girl I only slept with once."

Kyle began to smooth out his mustache. He always did that when he was thinking.

"When was the last time you got some, Jay?"

"Six weeks ago when I slept with Tracy."

He sighed as he crushed his cigarette in an ashtray. "You ain't in love, nigga. Your ass is horny," he laughed at his own pronouncement.

"I wish it was that easy, man." I picked up my beer just to have something in my hands. "Do you remember what you said to me on the church steps the day you got married?"

"No, not really. That was seven years ago."

"I'll never forget it, 'cause it showed me how different we really were. You said, 'I know you don't understand what Lisa and I have, Jay. That's because you've never been in love before.' Do you remember saying that?"

"I guess. Why?"

" 'Cause now I understand what you and Lisa had. And I can relate for the first time in my life. Bro, I can't see living my life without Tracy."

Kyle picked up his cigarette. He looked pissed that he'd put it out. "Jay, you don't wanna make the same mistake I made, man. It's not fun. What you think you want one day is not what you want the next. I'll be honest, man, if I had to do it all over, I would never have left Lisa and the girls in the first place." I wasn't sure, but Val seemed to start clinking glasses a little louder and putting bottles down a little harder after Kyle said that, all the while pretending she wasn't eavesdropping. I'd have to remember to ask him what was up with that later.

"Yeah, but you love Lisa. I shoulda never married Kenya in the first place." Kyle didn't say anything, but he did nod his agreement. "I've been trapped, man. Trapped for five years. But now I have a chance to get out and be with a woman I truly love for the first time in my life. Am I supposed to stay married and be miserable for the rest of my life because I made a mistake and married the wrong woman?"

Kyle stayed silent for a while before he replied, "Jay, I'm not sure if you're in love with this Tracy or not . . ." I tried to interrupt but he continued anyway. "But I do believe you think you're in love with her."

"I'm telling you, Kyle. I'm in love with her."

"So then prove it. Give yourself the ultimate test."

"What's that?" At this point, I think Kyle was just saying anything to pacify me. I could see by the doubt in his expression that he didn't believe I could love Tracy as much as I knew I did. But what did I expect? I would have been just as skeptical if he was the one falling in love with a woman he'd only been with one time.

"Go home to Kenya, buy her some flowers, then apologize for not taking her to dinner. After that, make love to her. I mean really make love to her like you did before you were married. Then when you're finished, take her in your arms and hold her for the rest of the night. When you wake up, I want you to walk into your daughters' bedroom and give each of them a kiss. Then walk back in your bedroom and take a good look at the mother of your children. If you're still in love with Tracy after that, then the two of us will talk again. Okay?"

I didn't answer him. I just finished my beer in one gulp and took my coat from behind my chair. "I hope you got room, 'cause I'll be spending the night at your place tomorrow night," I promised.

"I guess we'll see in the morning, won't we?" he answered as I walked by, patting him on the back.

I could see the brake lights and the flashing police lights a few miles ahead when I crossed the George Washington Bridge. I jumped off the highway at the first exit and started driving the back roads home. This wasn't the first time I traveled back roads home so I wasn't concerned about it. That is, until I entered Jersey City and passed a woman I could have sworn was Tracy. I was so sure it was her I almost had an accident trying to make a right turn to circle around the block for a better look. As I made my turn, I realized I was on Tonnelle Avenue, right smack in the middle of what people in Jersey City called "the track," a small strip of blocks with cheap hotels and alleys used by prostitutes to pick up johns.

Following the slow-moving cars, I went around the block three times before I spotted the woman again. At this point I was praying it was a case of mistaken identity, because the thought of Tracy being a prostitute was making my stomach turn. When I spotted the woman again, I pulled alongside her and rolled down my window. That's when I was happy to see it wasn't my lover, but damn near a twin.

"Hey, baby, you going out?" She stepped closer to the car and leaned her head in so far that her breasts practically fell out of her top. She definitely wasn't Tracy, but I have to admit the resemblance was a real turn-on.

"How much?" I asked out of curiosity more than anything else. The last thing I was going to do was screw a prostitute.

"How much you got?" she asked.

She was holding a lollipop and licked it with her tongue as she waited for my answer. My johnson jumped to life as I watched the lollipop disappear into her mouth, stick and all. Having intercourse with her was out of the question, but the thought of her lips wrapped around my johnson was getting more and more enticing.

"How 'bout twenty-five for some head?"

She laughed, pulling her head out of the car. "*Shiiit*, nigga, twenty-five won't even get me in your car." She turned to walk away. One look at her fat ass in those tight, hot-pink satin pants made me say something I knew I'd probably regret.

"How 'bout fifty?"

She turned around and flashed a smile. "Just for a blow job?"

"Yeah?" I said, unlocking the car door.

She got in the car and pointed. "There's an alley about three blocks down."

As I drove the three blocks to the alley, I couldn't help staring at this woman. It was incredible how much she really did resemble Tracy. Maybe if I tried while she went down on me, I could imagine I was back in bed with Tracy. Now that I would pay a thousand bucks for.

"What's your name?" I asked.

"Blondie," she replied. I knew it was probably just a street name. Who the hell would name their kid Blondie?

"Well, Blondie, you don't mind if I call you Tracy, do you?"

"I don't care what you call me as long as I get paid."

As we approached the alley, my conscience finally kicked in and I realized what I was doing was wrong. I was supposed to be heading home to apologize to Kenya and then make love to her. Somehow I'd got sidetracked and was about to pay fifty dollars to a prostitute who was a dead ringer for Tracy.

"Pull in that alley right there," she told me.

I ignored her and passed it. I was about to tell her I'd changed my mind when I heard the whoop-whoop of a police siren behind me. I glanced in my rearview mirror and saw flashing police lights.

"Oh shit!" I tried to think as I turned toward Blondie. "If they ask you, my name is Jay Crawford. You've known me for years. You need to tell me your real name."

"Jay," she said softly.

"What?" I was in a panic, watching the cops get out of their car.

"You're under arrest for soliciting a prostitute." I turned and she flashed her badge.

"Ahhh, man. I can't believe you fucked me like this!"

"I didn't fuck you at all," she laughed as the other officers opened my door.

19

Allen

It was late and I was tired from all the running around Rose and I had done. Not to mention the fact that we'd made love for about an hour when we got home. It had taken three days, but Rose and I had finally gone to the bank and added our names to each other's accounts. Surprisingly she hadn't taken a dime of her money out of any of her accounts. This gave me a renewed sense of trust in my future wife. Oh, I was still concerned about her so-called cousin Ray and her almost obsession with getting pregnant all of a sudden, but I had to admit things were really going well. After going to the banks, Rose and I had finished what was left of our wedding arrangements and headed home.

As was the custom the last few days, we made love until we couldn't make love anymore. Both of us were so exhausted that we collapsed into each other's arms and probably would have stayed that way 'til noon if the phone hadn't rung about 4 A.M. I picked up the phone, expecting it to be Ma.

"Hello," I answered, half-asleep.

"This is the AT&T operator. We have a collect call from Jay Crawford. Will you accept?" The first thing that came to my mind was, *Uh-oh Jay's in trouble again.*

"Yes, operator, I'll accept."

"Allen, that you, man?" I could hear other voices echoing in the background.

"Yeah, it's me," I was starting to wake up. "Where the hell are you, Jay, in a cave?"

"Nah, man, I'm in jail." I could hear the embarrassment in his voice.

"Ahhhh, shit!" I untangled myself from Rose's arms and sat up in the bed. This was worse than I thought. I knew Jay's call meant trouble, but I never expected he'd be in jail. "What the fuck you doin' there?"

"I don't even wanna talk about that shit right now." He was agitated, and his voice was full of desperation. "I just need you to get me the fuck outta here."

"Aw'ight, man, where you at?"

"I'm in Jersey City at the BCI precinct on Boiling Street."

"Okay, I'm getting dressed now. What's your bail?"

"A grand."

"Shit, my ATM card is only gonna give me five hundred."

"Can't you borrow some money from Rose?"

"Yeah, right, that's funny, Jay." I glanced over at Rose, who was still asleep, and almost laughed. I can't ever remember her loaning me money. Not even five dollars. "Don't worry, Jay. I'll get the money. I'll get it from Kyle and Wil."

"Thanks, man. Listen, do me a favor and call Kenya and tell her I'm with you."

I hung up the phone and got dressed, then called Kenya to leave a message on their machine. I was just about to walk out the bedroom door when Rose called me groggily. "You leaving, Allen?" She lifted her head to see the time.

"Yeah, I gotta go take care of something for Ma." I walked over to the bed and kissed her forehead. "I'll be back in a few hours. Okay?"

"All right, just make sure you come back. I need to talk to you about something important."

I kissed her again. "Okay baby. Get some sleep."

I pulled into Wil's driveway and looked up at his house. There wasn't one light on and I was sure everyone was asleep. Shit, it wasn't even five in the morning. I shoulda been asleep myself, but my boy Jay needed me. And even though Wil and Jay were having problems, once Wil knew what was up, he wouldn't mind being woken at this hour either. At least that's what I was hoping as I nervously knocked on the door. When no one answered, I banged a little harder. About two minutes later, Wil opened the door like a wild man, wearing only a pair of boxer shorts and a T-shirt. He was holding a big-ass baseball bat, ready to swing.

"What the hell are you doin' here?" I probably would've reacted the same way if he'd showed up at my door before dawn.

"We've got problems," I told him seriously.

"Let me guess. Jay?" He put down the bat and gestured for me to come in.

"How'd you know?"

"He tried to call me collect half an hour ago."

"He called you too?"

"Yeah, but I didn't accept the call." He chuckled.

"Why?" I glared at him.

I didn't like that. For all he knew, Jay could have been near death. Or worse, he could've been calling to say I was near death.

"I told y'all I'm not fuckin' with him no more." Wil crossed his arms over his chest.

"No one's askin' you to fuck with him. But the least you coulda done was accept his phone call. Someone coulda been hurt."

"Were they?"

"No."

"All right then," he said matter-of-factly. "What he do this time, anyway?"

"He's in jail."

"In jail! For what?" I could hear and see real concern from him for the first time. "What's he in jail for? What happened?"

"Wil, honey, who's that at the door?" Diane called from up the stairs.

"It's Allen, Di."

"Allen? What's he doing here?" Wil's whole demeanor changed as Diane walked down the stairs.

"Is everything all right, Allen?" She walked over and stood next to her husband.

"Yeah, everything's cool. Just a little guy stuff," I told her, hoping Wil would back me up. I liked Diane, but everyone knew she was real nosy, and had the world's biggest mouth.

"At this time of the morning?" She looked at me then Wil suspiciously.

I knew she wasn't gonna budge 'til she knew exactly what we were talking about. Thank God Katie started crying and Diane had to check on her.

"What's he in jail for?" Wil asked as soon as Diane was out of sight.

"I'm not sure. All I know is he's got a thousand dollars bail. I could only get five hundred out of the ATM machine. So I was hoping you'd come up with the other five then ride down there with me."

"Ride down where with you?" Diane asked, catching the tail end of our conversation as she carried Katie down the stairs.

Wil and I made eye contact with blank expressions on our faces. I'm almost positive he was about to agree to go with me, but as soon as he heard Diane's voice, he changed his mind.

"Ride out where with you, Allen?" she repeated, this time sternly. I still didn't answer, so she turned to Wil. "Are you gonna tell me what the hell is going on?"

Wil and I both stood silently.

"This is about that collect call from Jay, isn't it?" She may have been asking the questions, but she already knew the answers. Diane stared Wil in the eyes. "I know you don't think you're leaving here to go save Jay's ass again, Wil Duncan. Not after what he did to your eye. You're not goin' anywhere but back to bed." Diane handed the baby to Wil.

"I'm not going anywhere, Di," he repeated her words weakly.

"You sure you don't wanna go?" I asked.

"He's sure," Diane answered for him, folding her arms as she cast daggers at him with her eyes. I knew the look she was giving him well. It was the same look Rose gave me when she was about to cut the sex off for a week or two. I stared at Wil too, waiting for *him* to give me an answer. But I knew he wasn't gonna say what I wanted to hear. Not if he wanted to sleep in the same bed as his wife.

"I told you before, Allen, I'm not fucking with Jay no more." On that note, I walked over, kissed my goddaughter, and said my good-byes. As I walked to the car, I had to chuckle. Wil and Diane weren't that much different from me and Rose.

I got into my car and put Wil and Diane out of my mind. I had to find Kyle, and I had no idea where the hell he could possibly be. I'd tried to find him before I came to Wil's, but when I stopped by his apartment, he wasn't there. I even drove by his house just in case he might be baby-sitting the girls, but there was no sign of his truck there either. Now that Wil had let me down, I'd have to take another run by his place, and with any luck he'd be home by now.

I started the car and was about to leave when Wil banged on my window, damn near scaring the shit outta me. He was still in his boxers and a T-shirt, barely covered up by what looked like Diane's robe. Let me tell you, that's one time I wished I had a camera, 'cause he looked funny as shit. I was laughing as I rolled down my window.

"What's up?" I was praying he'd changed his mind and wanted me to wait while he changed.

"Here." He handed me an ATM card. "The pin number's my birthday."

I took the card. "You ain't coming?"

"Hell no. If Diane knew I was out here giving you my ATM card, she'd kick my ass."

"I knew you still had love for Jay," I smiled.

"It ain't about love. I just don't wanna see him in jail. And don't tell him I gave you the money."

"Aw'ight, man. Let me go get this brother out."

"Drive safely, Al."

"You got it, Wil."

*   *   *

I'd been waiting almost an hour before Jay walked through the heavy steel doors into the waiting area of the BCI precinct. Once he spotted me, he nonchalantly glanced around the room, probably expecting to see Kyle and Wil too. He looked bad when he walked over to me. I guess what I'd heard in the past was true. No matter how short a stay you have, being in jail was truly a humbling experience.

"Hi, Allen," he said weakly, instead of his customary, "What's up, dawg?"

"You aw'ight?" I asked, hugging him.

"Yeah, let's just get out of here. My car's still over on Tonnelle Avenue." I pointed to the exit, and we walked out to my car without another word. When we got in the car, Jay turned to me humbly and said, "Thanks, Allen."

"Don't mention it, Jay. You woulda done the same thing for me." I started the car. His eyes were watery, and I have to admit I was surprised when tears began to roll down his face. I can't ever remember seeing him cry, and I didn't ever wanna see it again. Tears just didn't fit him. He looked so pitiful I handed him a small pack of tissues.

"Where are the fellas?" he asked.

"Wil refused to come," I frowned, pulling the car out of the police parking lot.

"I figured that would happen," he said sadly. "What about Kyle?"

"I have no idea, I couldn't find him."

"I bet I know where he is."

"Where?"

"I think he and Val got something going."

"Val, the fine-ass bartender?" My eyes got wide.

"Yep, can you believe it? Kyle's fuckin' with that big-thigh cutie pie," he nodded. Jay had always wanted to get with Val.

"Ain't she messin' with that crazy ex–football player, Terrance?"

"That's what I heard. But she was all over Kyle tonight like a condom on a—" Jay cut his sentence short when I turned onto Tonnelle Avenue and we saw the prostitutes waving from in between parked cars. I have to admit, some of them were fine as hell, but I still couldn't understand how Jay could have even considered picking one up.

"They tell you why I was arrested?" Jay asked weakly.

"Yeah," I nodded, hesitating before I repeated his charges. "Soliciting a prostitute."

Jay rubbed his hand over his face. "I fucked up, Allen."

"No, you fucked up again," I reminded him.

"Yeah, you're right." He pointed at his car down the block and I pulled in behind it.

"What the hell were you thinking about?"

"I don't know." He shrugged his shoulders. "I wasn't thinking."

"You damn right you weren't thinking!" I almost slammed my hand into the steering wheel but caught myself. I was starting to act like Wil, and that really wasn't me. "Look, Jay, you got more women every week tryin'a get with you than most brothers have in a lifetime. What the fuck you trying to get with a prostitute for?"

"She reminded me of somebody. Somebody special. Somebody I care about a lot. Somebody I'm probably never gonna see again." He had tears in his eyes again. I wanted to, but I didn't ask him who it was she reminded him of 'cause I didn't wanna see him cry again.

"I've gotta get you to promise me something, Allen," he sniffled. It was so hard for me to watch him like this.

"What's that?"

"That you'll never tell anyone about this. Not even Wil or Kyle. And if it ever comes up, I got arrested for DWI."

"Aw'ight, Jay, but you've got to stop this shit, man." I don't know why I agreed to keep his little secret. If the roles were reversed and I had been the one arrested instead of him, he would've never let me live it down.

"You hungry?" he asked, opening the car door.

"Yeah, I could use a bite." I looked up, and the sun was coming up over the horizon.

"Why don't you follow me over to the house? I'll make you some breakfast." I knew that his real reason for wanting me at his house was to run interference with Kenya. With me there, he had a perfect alibi. She'd never have to know he'd spent the night in jail if he walked in the door with me.

It was nine o'clock when I pulled into Ma's driveway. I figured I'd stop by and check on her before heading back over to Rose's for the rest of the weekend. What I hadn't figured on was that Rose would be at Ma's house waiting for me. In fact, when I walked in, she and Ma were sitting on the living room sofa like they'd been best friends for twenty years. Now that was sure a sight I thought I'd never see in my lifetime. Still, I wasn't too sure I liked this scene. It was a little too sudden for them to be so friendly.

"Hey, baby," Ma smiled. "We was just talkin' 'bout you."

"You were?"

I looked at Ma, then at Rose suspiciously. I didn't know what was going on, but something was definitely up. There hadn't been any love between these two since Rose and I got engaged and she had rejected

Granny's ring. No way was I gonna believe that everything got patched up this quickly without a good reason.

Ma got up with tears in her eyes and wrapped her arms around me tight. "Congratulations, son."

"Thanks, Ma." I hugged her back weakly. I had no idea what she was talking about and that scared me. When she sat back down, she placed her hand on Rose's knee, patting it gently. That scared me even more. A lot more.

"What are you congratulating me for? Don't tell me my numbers came up on Lotto last night?" If that was the case, I was gonna die 'cause I forgot to play Lotto this week.

"You didn't tell him yet?" Ma turned to Rose.

"Tell me what? Damn, my numbers did come up, didn't they?" I stomped my foot in frustration.

Rose looked up and smiled. "I know you wanted to tell your mother yourself, Allen, but I couldn't help myself. When she called this morning, I just had to tell her I was pregnant."

My expression went blank. I'd completely forgotten about Rose's supposed pregnancy. "Ah, hun, I thought we were going to keep that little bit of news to ourselves 'til we had it confirmed." It had only been about two weeks since the first time we had sex without a condom.

Rose grinned. "I took a home pregnancy test this morning. Look for yourself. It's positive." She picked up a three-inch plastic object and handed it to me. She wasn't lying. The damn thing had a pink plus in the middle.

"Oh, Allen, I'm so proud of you." Ma smiled. "Now why don't you come over here and have a seat? I was just about to sign these papers Rose brought over."

"What papers?" I looked over on the coffee table and there was the manila envelope I'd seen at our apartment. I looked at Rose and she wouldn't make eye contact, but she did push the papers closer to Ma. She looked like she wanted Ma to hurry up and sign. Damn, what the hell was she up to? I walked over to the sofa and sat down next to Ma, nonchalantly picking up the pen before she could.

"What exactly does Rose have you signing, Ma?" I gave her a nervous smile. Rose's lack of eye contact gave me that same uneasy feeling I had the night before.

"A life insurance policy. Rose has one for all of us. Isn't that right, Rose?" Ma turned to Rose. "Gotta make sure we look out for my grandbaby's security. Isn't that right, Rose?"

Rose smiled, nodding her head. She still hadn't made eye contact with me. Probably because "security" was a word right out of *her* mouth. And she seemed to have Ma wrapped around her little finger all of a sudden.

Ma picked up a stack of papers that had my name on them and handed them to me. I got a little chill when I saw the policy was for $500,000 and Rose was the beneficiary. I picked up the stack with Ma's name on them. It was a cheaper policy, only $200,000, probably because she was older and would be more expensive to insure but once again Rose was the beneficiary. How the hell could she make herself the beneficiary of my mother's life insurance policy? That was damn sure gonna change.

"Where's your policy, Rose?" I asked with an edge to my voice.

"Why?" she asked, reaching for the stack of papers in front of her. I reached across Ma and grabbed the stack of papers at the same time she did, winning a tug of war. When I looked down at the papers, I couldn't believe what I was seeing. Although I was her beneficiary, Rose's policy was only for $25,000.

"I thought these policies were for the baby's security? Why's your policy so cheap?"

Rose glared at me as if she could will my mouth shut. "Why don't we talk about this at home, Allen?" She tried to sound sweet, but I could tell she was on the verge of screaming.

"No, I wanna know now!"

Rose jumped at my unexpected outburst.

"Allen," Ma said sternly, "don't you upset this girl."

"But Ma . . ." I couldn't believe Rose had brainwashed my own mother so quickly.

"Look, I said leave her alone. She's at an early stage of her pregnancy. Anything could cause her to have a miscarriage. Now you know how much I wanna have a grandbaby. Leave her alone!"

Ma grabbed the pen and signed the papers, then handed the pen to me.

"Sign the papers, Allen," she demanded.

I glared at her in stunned silence.

"Allen, do you remember when your father died?"

"Yes," I nodded.

"You remember what kept us above water?"

I didn't say a word. I knew the answer, I just didn't wanna say it. Neither Ma nor I had to work for almost five years after my dad died 'cause he took out two large life insurance policies. Ma's policy was so large she was able to retire and pay off the house.

"Allen, I asked you a question. Do you remember what kept us above water?" She was sterner this time, talking to me like I was eight years old again.

"Yes, Ma." I hung my head like a scolded kid.

"I don't know about you, but I want the same security for my grandbaby and your new wife that your daddy left us. Don't you?" Ma patted Rose's knee again.

"Of course I do, Ma. But . . ." I stopped myself before finishing that sentence 'cause what I was about to say was cruel. Not to mention the fact that it would probably make Rose call off the wedding and have Ma kick me out of the house for upsetting poor, pregnant Rose. I figured I'd better not tell Ma that the first thing that came to my mind when I thought of Rose and a life insurance policy was her hiring someone to bump the two of us off. I knew it wasn't probable but it was definitely possible.

I looked past Ma into my fiancée's eyes. "I hope you appreciate what Ma and I are doing here, Rose."

"I do, Allen," she said humbly, rubbing her still-flat belly. "I just want what's best for Junior."

"Sure you do," I said, signing the paper without another word. Once again Rose had won and gotten her way, but what she didn't know was that I'd be watching her very closely from now on. She'd crossed a line that no one should ever cross. A bond between a mother and son.

20

Kyle

It had been a long time since I'd kissed someone other than Lisa, and Val's perfume took over my senses as her lips parted from mine. We'd just gone out for a late dinner at the Soul Café in Manhattan, after I'd finally convinced Jay to take his butt home, that is. Val had really surprised me with the sudden kiss when we walked up to her door. I was still savoring the taste of her lip gloss when she pressed her lips against mine again. This time I parted her lips with my tongue and kissed her back passionately. Moving my hands from my side to her hips, I slowly caressed the softness of her curved behind. For the first time in recent memory I felt my manhood spring to life. It had been a long time since I'd felt true desire for a woman and it felt good.

"I thought we were just going to be friends," I whispered as I kissed her neck.

"I was just trying to show you how friendly I could be," she giggled, rolling her neck around so I could kiss the other side. I knew I'd found her spot when her breathing became heavy and she pulled me into her apartment. As we kissed again, my nervousness had disappeared and the only thing I could think of was how wonderful it would be to make love to her.

I'd been hanging with Val for a little over a month now. Nothing romantic, just friendship. At least until now. Truth is, I knew she wanted me. She'd sent me more than enough flirtatious signals the past few weeks to make up for the rejection she'd given me that night in my apartment. I was just afraid to make a move because I didn't wanna embarrass myself if I couldn't get it up. But judging by the lump in my pants, that wasn't going to be a problem tonight.

"I want you, Kyle," she whispered, gently blowing in my ear. If she only knew how much that excited me.

"I want you too, Val," I whispered back.

I kissed her again, slowly undressing her in the middle of her living room. As each piece of clothing fell from her body, I gently ran my fingertips where the clothes belonged until she was standing in front of me wearing only a G-string.

"Now that you've got the package unwrapped, what do you plan on doing with it?" she asked as she slowly removed my suit jacket.

"First I plan on giving you a very delicate, sensual massage. Then I'm going to make your body sing with my tongue. You think you'd like that?"

"Uh-huh," she moaned as if I'd already started. "I'd love for you to make me sing."

I smiled. Things were getting hot, and I could feel perspiration form on my forehead.

"Then after I taste what makes you a woman, I'm going to make love to you in every way imaginable."

"Oh, God that sounds so good," she whispered. "There's just one thing."

"What's that?" I asked. I couldn't imagine a problem the way she was panting by now.

"Condoms."

"Condoms?" I didn't get it.

"Do you have any?"

Now I got it. No condoms, no sex. I'd been married so long I forgot about condoms.

"No, I don't have any."

"Neither do I."

"Damn," I knew this was too good to be true. I was praying she wouldn't change her mind about the whole thing. "Want me to go get some?" I raised my eyebrows, pleading with my eyes.

"I think that would be best." She kissed me. "I promise it'll be worth it."

I took one last appreciative gaze at her naked flesh.

"Of that I have no doubt." I reached down to pick up my coat. She handed me her keys.

"Let yourself in. I'll be waiting." I wanted to get back to her so bad, I almost ran to the door.

It felt like I'd been to every corner store and bodega in Brooklyn before I found a store that sold lambskin condoms. I wanted Val so bad I probably woulda dealt with the rash a latex condom would give me if she had one at her place. But since I had to go to the store, there was no reason to mess around with my allergy to latex.

When I got back to Val's apartment and opened the door, I could smell the incense she was burning and could hear the romantic music in the background. A smile spread across my face when I realized she was playing Montel Jordan, my favorite singer. It was nice to know she was the kinda woman who remembered things like that. As I took off my coat, I couldn't help but notice the large box sitting on the coffee table. I picked up the note on top of it.

Kyle,
Take off your clothes. There's a present in the box for you. There's a bottle of champagne in the fridge and two glasses on the counter. Pour us some. I'll be waiting in the bedroom.
                                                                          Val

I opened the box and there was a powder blue satin robe and a pair of matching boxers. Man, she had really gone all out. I guess she had planned this night all along. I stripped off my clothes and put on the boxers and the robe, checking myself out in the mirror above the sofa. I had to admit I looked pretty damn good. Strolling into the kitchen, I filled the two glasses with champagne and made my way to the bedroom. The door was closed, so I knocked gently.

"Come in," Val purred sweetly.

I opened the door and did a double take. Val looked so damn good I had to pinch myself to make sure I wasn't dreaming. She was wearing a sheer, sexy teddy with a matching thong, the same color as my robe and boxers. But it wasn't just what she was wearing that made her look so awesome. It was the way she was posing. Her pretty brown thighs were fully exposed and crossed over each other as she lay on her stomach, looking up at me.

"*Mmm, mmm, mmm,* don't you look good?" She licked her lips.

I didn't say a word. I just smiled as I walked over to the bed and handed her a glass of champagne.

"Here's to a wonderful night." She raised her glass.

"To a wonderful night," I echoed as our glasses clinked. We kissed between sips of champagne.

"Did you get them?" She was looking at my hands.

"Get what?"

"You know, the condoms."

"Yeah, I got them." I reached into the pocket of the robe and pulled out the box of condoms. You shoulda seen her smile. Val reached up and turned off the light, leaving only the glow of the two candles to illuminate the first lovemaking I'd do in almost six long months. God, what a time I was about to have.

Two wild, sex-filled hours later I was lying on my back, looking up at the ceiling fan as Val snuggled up next to me. She was snoring lightly. The candles had burned down and the champagne was gone, but I had to give her credit. She'd really done her thing. I never thought anyone would be able to match Lisa in the bedroom, but Val had come damn close. Once she got to know my body, the possibilities were going to be truly endless.

If the night was any indicator, Val was about to become a big part of my life. I decided it was time to finally move on. I'd never give up my girls, but it was time for Lisa and I to go our separate ways. The divorce papers had been in my briefcase for almost three weeks waiting to be signed, and for whatever reason I just couldn't get myself to sign them. Well, that was about to change. I got out of the bed, trying my best not to disturb Val. I walked into the living room where I had left my briefcase when I dropped Val off to change after work. I sat down on the sofa and opened it. There it was, the divorce decree, looking up at me. I removed the papers and flipped through them to the final page where my signature would go. With one quick swipe of the pen, I would be throwing away seven years of my life. After all Lisa and I had been through, I never imagined things would come to this. A tear ran down my face as I picked up a pen and signed the papers. Now it was just a matter of time before Lisa and I ended up in front of a judge to finalize child support and alimony to officially end our marriage.

21

Jay

"Oh shit, Jay," she gasped.
   Squeak!
   "Oh, God!"
   Squeak!
   "I'm almost there, Jay!"
   Squeak!
   "Don't stop!"
   Squeak!
   "That's it!"
   Squeak!
The bed was squeakin', Kenya was screamin', but me, I was just goin' through the motions. We'd been doing the nasty for the better part of an hour, and like the rest of my life lately, it wasn't very interesting. Kenya, however, was on a mission. She was trying her best to wear my ass out before I left the house for the night, but she was the one gettin' worn out. It's amazing how easy it is to fool a woman into thinking she's doing the job when you could be thinking about anything but what she's doing to you. All it takes is a few *Ohhhh baby*'s, a couple *Damn, that feels good*'s, and some weird facial expressions and she thinks she's sent you to heaven. Women have always assumed they owned the patent on faking pleasure, but I'd put on a few academy award–winning performances myself over the years.

When I was sure Kenya had gotten hers, I decided to end my little charade by closing my eyes and pretending she was Tracy. Within minutes I had done my thing and it was all over, Kenya none the wiser. Lately, anytime I was with my wife, I had to imagine Tracy to complete the act. Not that it was hard to conjure an image of Tracy. She was all I could think about. It had been six weeks since I'd been arrested and over three months since I'd seen Tracy, but I still couldn't get her out of my head. It was hard even for me to believe how much I loved her, let alone explain it to someone else, but somehow she'd seeped deep inside my soul and taken over my mind.

"Now you can go out," Kenya said with a satisfied smile, startling me out of my momentary fantasy.

If she hadn't been staring me directly in the face, I would have laughed at her. It just seemed incredible to me that she actually thought our little forty-five–minute romp was going to stop me from having a good time at Allen's bachelor party. She had to be fucking crazy. As one of Allen's best men, I was gonna be hosting the bachelor party and it was gonna be *off the hook*. We'd rented the entire Players Club on Sutphin Boulevard, with the help of Kyle's money, of course. And I'd made sure they were going to have thirty of the finest women you ever wanna see performing. I was a club member, so I'd picked these beauties myself. Players was a private strip club that didn't even open up 'til midnight, but that didn't stop it from being the best strip club in Queens. It was owned by two cops and they required either membership or an invitation from a member to get in. The club's exclusive clientele meant the girls inside were fully nude, with no restrictions when it came to sexual acts onstage or off. The club's slogan was "You pay, you play."

I got out of bed and gave Kenya a peck on the cheek, then went to the bathroom to prepare for my male-bonding session with the boys. It was around eleven-thirty and I was supposed to meet Kyle at midnight to head to the party. When I finished taking my shower, I got dressed and headed straight out the door. Kenya didn't even stop me for a good-night kiss, 'cause she was already snoring in the bed. So much for *her* wearing *me* out.

It was half past midnight when I pulled in front of Kyle's apartment and beeped the horn. A few minutes latter he strolled out the door, not looking too pleased at all.

"Think you could be on time for once, my brotha?" He slid into the front seat with an attitude.

"Please, man, them sorry-ass niggas don't know how to party. The real party ain't gonna get started 'til me and you get there and you know it, so stop bitching, dawg."

"I don't give a shit! You know I hate to be late. Fuckin' around with you I'm gonna be late to my own damn funeral."

"Yeah, well, if that's the case, then we always gonna be late 'cause that's one place I don't want you to be on time to, my brotha." I laughed as we pulled off to drive the mile and a half to Sutphin Boulevard.

When we got in the club, contrary to what I had told Kyle, the party had already gotten started. Brothers were gettin' their drink on and some were even gettin' their freak on. The stage was surrounded by brothers watching two fine-ass sisters doing a XXX-rated lesbian show. It musta been a real freak show too 'cause brothers were reaching into their pockets and throwing money on the stage. Off to the right in a corner, Kyle's lawyer Greg Thomas was butt-ass naked with some sister in a cowboy hat riding him like he was a bucking bronco. And there in the middle of everything was my boy Allen sitting on the traditional bachelor party throne wearing only his boxers. He had a beer in one hand and the butt of some fine-ass redbone in the other. Now that's what I call enjoying your bachelor party.

As we walked over to the bar, Kyle and I said our customary *what's up*'s and *how've you been*'s to the brothers we'd invited to the party. Then we sat down at the bar and ordered two drinks, Dewars on the rocks for him and a Heineken for me. We hadn't been sitting there long before Wil stumbled over drunk as hell. He hugged Kyle and ignored me.

"What's up with the camera there, big Wil?" Kyle laughed. Every time Wil went out, he was always carrying that damn camera.

"I figure a party like this, there's gonna be quite a few Kodak moments." Wil grinned and snapped a picture of Kyle.

"Yeah, well, you be careful with that camera. Shit like that could get a brother in some serious trouble. Don't forget what happened to my brother Dwayne." Kyle gave Wil a serious look. His brother had been divorced because his wife found the videotape of his bachelor party.

"Come on, man, don't you think I know that?" Wil slurred.

"Just making sure," Kyle replied. "What you drinkin'?"

Wil held up his empty glass. "The usual."

Kyle turned to the bartender and ordered Wil a rum and Coke. That's when I took the opportunity to clear the air between Wil and me. It had been a few weeks since I tried to speak to him, so I figured this was as good a time as any to see if he was still holding a grudge.

"So what's up, Wil?"

"Nothin'." He cut his eyes at me as if I was annoying him.

"Hey, man, I just wanna apologize . . ."

"Save it, okay? I don't wanna hear it." He turned toward Kyle to continue their conversation.

I put my hand on his shoulder. "Hey, Wil, I'm trying to apologize."

"You better get your hands off of me, Jay."

"What you want from me, man? You wanna hit me? Will that make you feel better?" I raised my hand, giving him the same opportunity he gave me a few months back. I honestly didn't think he had the heart to take a swing at me until I saw Kyle grab his arm.

"Nah, big Wil, you don't wanna do that," Kyle told him as he handed him a drink. Kyle kinda flicked his fingers at me as if to say take a walk while he cools off. I wasn't exactly thrilled with the idea that Wil had attempted to take a swing at me, so I decided he might be right. So I headed over to the stage to watch the show. Not that the show made me feel any better. I mean, you seen one lesbian show, you've seen them all. At least that's how I felt at the time. I was about to order another drink when my phone vibrated. I glanced at the caller ID, but it read unknown.

"Hello?"

"Jay?" I could barely hear whoever it was.

"Can you hold on a minute? I can barely hear you." I walked out the front door into the cool spring air.

"Hello?" I said again.

"Jay, is that you?" a very sexy female voice asked. For a second there I thought I was hearing things 'cause I coulda sworn it sounded like Tracy.

"Yeah, this is Jay. Who's this?"

"Tracy."

The world stopped at that moment, and for a second I honestly didn't know where I was. I dropped the phone, as my entire being flooded with emotion. I'd been waiting for this call for three months, and now that it was here, I didn't know what to do. *Pick up the phone that's what you gotta do, dummy,* a little voice in my head told me. So I bent down and picked up the phone.

"Jay, are you there?" Her voice knocked me out of my fog so that I could finally answer her.

"I don't believe this. Is this really you, Tracy?"

"Yes, it's really me."

"Where have you been? I've been trying to get in touch with you for months."

"I know," she replied.

"Have you gotten my messages. How come you didn't call?"

"Yes, I got your messages. I just wasn't feelin' you at the time." I have to admit that hurt.

"And now you're feelin' me?"

"We'll talk about that when I see you."

"When's that gonna be?" I asked desperately.

"Tonight." She was telling me, not asking, and I didn't care.

"Okay," I replied quickly. "Where you at?"

"I'm at school. You remember how to get to my dorm, don't you?"

"Uh-huh."

"Okay, just call when you get here and I'll come down. Oh, and Jay?"

"Yeah?"

"Why don't we go back to your house?"

"Ahhhh well . . . umm . . . I . . . Ah . . . I . . . ah . . . I don't know if that's a very good idea."

"Why not? I mean, you do share the place with your sister, don't you?" You know it almost sounded like there was sarcasm in her voice.

"Yeah, I do, but my . . . ah . . . ah, my nephews are gonna be home and well . . . ah, that's not, uh . . . the right example I wanna set for them. Yeah, that's not the example I wanna set."

"You know what, Jay? You're full'a shit. And I'm not in the mood to be playing games. So just forget it." She sounded like she was about to hang up.

"I'm not playing games with you, Tracy, I swear to God." I couldn't believe this was happening.

"Yeah, right. Look, I'll call you, aw'ight?" Damn, everything was fine a minute ago. Why did she have an attitude now?

"Oh no. Come on, Tracy, don't do this. I been waiting almost four months to see you. Don't do this to me. Please, I gotta see you." I knew I sounded desperate begging like that but the truth is I *was* desperate. Desperate as hell and I wanted to, no I needed to see her more than anything in world.

"Look, Jay, I changed my mind. I'm going to bed. If you wanna see me, come pick me up Sunday morning at ten."

"Sunday? That's three days from now."

"And?" she snapped. I could hear some laughter in the background.

"Tracy, why can't I just see you now? You don't sound that tired."

"Jay, if you wanna see me, pick me up Sunday or just forget it, okay?" She didn't sound tired but she sure as hell sounded like she was giving me an ultimatum.

"Okay, I'll pick you up at ten." I sighed. "Tracy?"

"Yes?"

"I . . . ah . . . I . . . ah," I wanted to say "I love you" but instead I said, "I missed you."

"I missed you too, Jay." After all the sarcasm she'd just spewed, she finally sounded sincere, but I was suddenly feeling so insecure.

"Really?"

"Yeah, really, Jay. I don't know why, but I missed you." The way she said it I could almost see her smile. "Bye, Jay."

"Bye."

I walked back in the club to let Kyle know I was leaving. I couldn't stay. I needed to be alone to think about why Tracy might have had an attitude. She was probably still mad about me leaving her in the house.

When I got inside, Kyle was nowhere to be found. And for that matter, neither were Allen, Wil, or any of our other close friends. I pulled one of the owners to the side and asked where everyone went. He pointed to the VIP room.

"Knock on the door three times and they'll let you in," he told me.

The VIP room was a medium-size room in the club with sofas and love seats. On most nights it was used as a place the girls could take guys for a little one-on-one, but on nights like tonight it was used for special shows. As I stood outside the door, I could hear the laughter from inside and I knew whatever was happening in there musta been quite a show. I knocked three times.

"Yo, man, your boys are crazy," one of the bouncers laughed as he opened the door to let me in.

I walked in and realized how right he was. Right there in front of twenty witnesses was Wil, sitting on a love seat, butt-ass naked with not one, but two naked dancers on either side of him rubbing their breasts up against his chest. And if that wasn't bad enough, there was a third dancer on her knees with his johnson two inches from her mouth. I swear to God, if I hadn't seen it with my own two eyes, I would never have believed it. Now don't get me wrong, Wil's no angel. He likes to have a good time just as much as the rest of us, but when it comes to touching or being touched by a woman other than Diane, he ain't havin' it. We'd been to at least twenty bachelor parties and a ton of strip clubs over the years and he'd never gone as far as to accidentally rub up against a stripper. I walked over to Kyle and Allen, who were standing in front of him taking pictures.

"What the hell's going on?" I asked Kyle.

"Hold on, let me get this shot and I'll tell you." He snapped two pictures then handed the camera to Allen, who directed the girls into another pose.

"Wil passed out," Kyle slurred as he laughed. He was a little drunk himself.

"What?" He wasn't making sense.

"Wil drank so much he passed out." Kyle laughed even harder when he saw the pose Allen had moved the girls to.

I looked toward Wil. His eyes were closed and he hadn't moved at all. Now things were starting to make sense. Kyle and Allen were having some laughs at Wil's expense.

"So you decided to strip him down in front of all these people and take pictures of him? Yo, man, that shit is wrong." I was about to walk over and snatch the camera from Allen when Kyle jumped in front of me, blocking my way. I didn't care how much the two of us were fighting. There was no way I was gonna allow them to humiliate Wil like that. He might have been acting like an ass lately, but he was still my boy. Plus he would never do this type of thing to one of us.

"Come on, Jay. You have to admit this shit is funny." Kyle pointed at one of the women squatting over Wil's face as Allen took a picture. Wil's mouth was open, and he had slobber running down his chin. If you didn't know the fool had passed out, you would swear he was going down on her.

"Yeah, it is funny," I admitted, but before I could finish, he shut me up.

"So stop bitchin'."

"Yeah, but this shit is wrong, Kyle, and you know it. Especially the pictures." Kyle smiled. Not his regular smile, but a devilish smile. More like something I would do.

"*Pleeeeease*. If Wil didn't want his picture taken, he shouldn'ta brought a camera." Yep, that confirmed it. Kyle was making up excuses. He would never make excuses unless he was up to something.

"What are you up to, man?"

"Nothin'," he insisted, but wouldn't make eye contact.

"Aw'ight. It's your funeral when he sees the flicks." Kyle nodded like it was all good. "Look, I'm outta here. I gotta meet somebody," I told him.

"A woman?"

"Yeah," I lied.

Kyle smiled. I know what he was thinking. He was thinking I was finally over Tracy and things were back to normal. He couldn't have been farther from the truth.

"Look, you think I can borrow a hundred? I need to get a hotel room. I'll pay you back on pay day." He reached into his pocket and pulled out a money clip, peeling off two hundred-dollar bills. I probably shoulda told him about Tracy and that we were going to meet Sunday, but I knew he woulda given me a hard time.

"Have fun, man. I'll see you tomorrow at the rehearsal dinner." We grabbed hands and hugged.

"Kyle, do me a favor."

"What's that?"

"When you're finished having your fun, make sure Wil gets home all right."

"Don't worry, man. We're both gonna catch a cab home in a few." He gave me a reassuring look.

22

Kyle

"Excuse me, miss, can we get another round over here, please?"

The cocktail waitress nodded as I finished up what was left of my iced tea. We'd all decided that we'd been drinking way too much lately and that we probably should hold off on the alcohol until tomorrow afternoon during the wedding reception. I glanced across the table at Wil, who still looked hung over from the night before. Man, was he wasted last night. I'd never seen him that drunk. I checked my watch for the time and was surprised it was almost midnight. I'd only gotten about two hours of sleep after the bachelor party last night, so it was a good thing Allen and Rose had suggested we stay at the Manhattan Marriott where their wedding reception was being held. Truth is, after the rehearsal dinner none of us felt like driving back to Queens.

"Hey, could you bring us some Buffalo wings and some nachos with that?" Wil asked the waitress. "Matter of fact, make that a double order of Buffalo wings." The waitress scribbled down his order and disappeared.

"Damn, Wil, you hungry or what? We just ate an hour ago," Allen laughed.

"No offense, Allen. I know you didn't pick out the restaurant, but I didn't eat any of that sushi they were serving. That shit is nasty."

"Yo dawg, heads up," Jay whispered, tapping my knee. I glanced toward the door to see Diane, Kenya, and Lisa walking in. Lisa was holding the hand of a tall, handsome Hispanic brother. I tried to hide it, but a wave of jealousy tensed every muscle in my body.

"Damn, dawg, she don't give a *fuck*. She just walked up in here with her new man like you ain't shit." Jay shook his head.

Jay was right. She didn't give a fuck. How the hell could Lisa embarrass me like this, showing up the night before my boy's wedding with some Ricky Martin look-alike? I would never do something like that to her. And on top of all that, she was wearing my favorite dress.

"I'm sorry, Kyle. I didn't know she was gonna bring a date." Poor Allen looked as miserable as I felt.

"It's not your fault, Al. You had to invite her if the girls were gonna be in the wedding." I patted him on the back.

"She probably thought you were gonna bring Val," Wil said nonchalantly. It was obvious he was more interested in the plate of nachos the waitress was handing him than in my little problem.

"Shit, I wish I had brought Val now. She cursed my ass out this morning when I told her it would be disrespectful to bring her to the wedding. I should call her up right now and tell her to catch a cab on over here." I picked up my iced tea and took a sip as I watched my soon-to-be ex-wife sit down with her new man on the other side of the room.

"Wait a minute." I turned to Wil angrily. "How the fuck does Lisa know about Val anyway?"

Wil almost choked on a nacho as he looked up from his plate. "Uh, I mighta slipped and told Diane that you was talkin' to Val." I could tell by his expression that there was no "mighta" about it.

I turned to Jay, who leaned back in his chair looking totally satisfied. He'd been trying to tell us for a while that Wil had a big mouth. He'd tried over and over to warn me Wil was telling Diane our business. I just never believed him until now.

"Wil, this is happening way too much." Allen said, surprising me. I'd noticed that he'd been getting a little bolder lately, challenging people he might not necessarily have stood up to in the past. I had to admit I was impressed.

"Look. Y'all makin' way too much out of this. If you're seeing Val, then what's the problem?" Wil shoved a nacho in his mouth.

"The problem is it's not your fucking business to be tellin' anyone who I'm seeing." I was pissed. "Especially not your wife, so she can blab to Lisa. My fucking divorce isn't even final yet. She could try to get me on adultery."

"He's right, Wil," Allen agreed. Jay stayed out of it. He and Wil were having their own problems.

"And what about last night?" I asked.

"What about last night?" Wil replied.

"Before your drunk ass passed out, you couldn't stop apologizing for breaking up my marriage."

Wil's high yellow face became a pasty white and his expression went blank. "I told you about that?"

"You damn right you did! You don't remember?" He wouldn't look me in the eye.

"Told you about what?" Jay spoke up for the first time.

"This fucking guy comes to my office and lies to me about Lisa seeing some guy named Mike. That's why I started messing with Val in the first place. I figured things were over with me and Lisa." I sat back in my chair, fuming.

"Ohhhh, shit." Allen and Jay turned to Wil in unison.

"I was just tryin' to help," Wil mumbled.

"Well, you didn't. I was gonna go home that night until you came by with that stupid-ass lie. Ask Jay!" I pointed to Jay for confirmation as I gulped down what was left of my tea.

"Yeah, he did tell me he was going home at Katie's christening. He even had an appointment with a shrink."

"Kyle, man, I'm sorry. If you want me to tell Lisa what I did, I will." He gestured like he was getting up.

"Nah, man. It's not gonna help now. In the long run it's probably for the best. Val and me are working out pretty good. I just wish I could see my girls more." I scanned the bar for our waitress 'cause now I needed a real drink. I didn't see her anywhere so I got up to get my own drink.

"I'm going to the bar. Anybody want something?"

"Yeah, but I'll go with you." Jay stood up.

We walked to the bar and ordered our usuals. Jay checked to make sure no one was within listening range. Then he leaned toward me in a conspiratorial whisper.

"That lie Wil told you, that's why you let them strip him down in the club last night, isn't it?"

"Yeah." I nodded, looking away from Wil.

"I figured as much. It all makes sense now. That shit musta really pissed you off."

"You can't imagine." I took a sip of my drink.

"You still mad at him?"

"Naw, not anymore. I'm just disappointed."

"Yeah, I can understand that." He looked back at Wil and sighed. "What'd you do with the film, man? You know that shit could get him in a lotta trouble if Diane finds it."

"Don't worry. I left it in the camera." We both glanced at Wil, who had the camera around his neck.

"Aren't you worried about Diane seeing them pictures?"

"Nah, she never goes near that camera. I bet she doesn't even know how to work it."

"Yeah, you're probably right," Jay laughed. "Man, he's gonna be hot with you when he sees those pictures."

"Fuck 'im. He can't get no hotter than I am right now."

"True, true." We picked up our drinks and walked back to the table. When we sat down, I glanced across the bar and made eye contact with Lisa for the first time. She immediately looked away.

I sat and nursed my drink until I just couldn't take it anymore. There was only so much I could bear, watching Lisa play kissy face with her Latin lover across the room and listening to Wil apologize over and over. Finally I said good night to my boys and carried my black ass upstairs to my room to call Val. I was hoping she wouldn't still be pissed about me refusing to take her to the wedding. Maybe if I was lucky, she would still wanna come.

Just as I was about to stick the plastic key in the door, I heard, *"Pssst, pssst."* I turned around to see Rose sticking her head out of her room.

"Kyle, com'ere a minute." I didn't hesitate to go to her. Rose and I had actually been pretty good friends at one time.

"What's up? You ready for the big day tomorrow?" I smiled.

"I guess I am. I'm a little nervous, though." She did look nervous.

"Yeah, well, that's to be expected. Don't worry about it."

"How come you're not downstairs with everyone else?"

"Lisa showed up with some guy."

"Damn, I'm sorry to hear that. Allen told me you were getting divorced. It must be tough." She didn't sound like she was very sorry, though.

"Yeah, well, life goes on." I glanced at my watch. If I was gonna call Val to come over, I needed to do it in a hurry.

"You got somewhere to go?" Rose asked.

"Nah, I just needed to make a phone call."

"Oh, too bad. I was hopin' you might have a drink with me. My girls all abandoned me for some male strip club down the block."

"I'd love to, Rose, but I'm not in the mood to sit in that bar with Lisa and her friend down there." It was too bad, 'cause I coulda used another drink.

"You don't have to go downstairs. I've got everything we need right here." She opened her door and I was amazed. The room looked more like an apartment than a hotel room. "This is the honeymoon suite. It's got a fully stocked bar. You still drink Dewars on the rocks, don't you?"

"Yep, that's my drink," I smiled.

"So come on in. I'll fix you one."

"I don't think so, Rose. What if Allen comes by? We don't wanna give him the wrong impression."

"Oh please, Kyle. No one is coming by. All my girls are tryin' to get their swerve on tonight and I told Allen it's bad luck to see the bride before the wedding. You know how superstitious he is." There was something almost sarcastic in her voice when she mentioned Allen, but I figured I must have imagined it.

My better judgment told me not to, but for whatever reason I accepted Rose's offer and walked in her room. I did promise myself it would only be one drink, though. No reason to tempt fate. All my boys seemed to be at odds these days. All I needed was for Allen to find me having a drink with his girl the night before their wedding, no matter how innocent things were.

"Have a seat." Rose pointed to the sofa as she walked to the bar to make our drinks. I sat down and watched her mix the drinks as she chatted away.

"You know, Kyle, we never hang out anymore. We used to hang out all the time before you got married. How come we don't hang out no more?" She walked around the bar and handed me a drink, then settled next to me on the couch. "I made yours a double. I hope you don't mind."

"Nope, a double is probably just what I need right about now."

"You didn't answer my question. How come we don't hang out no more?" I sat back on the sofa and put my feet up on the coffee table.

"Probably 'cause for the past seven years I've had a wife and kids. Then, of course, you and Allen hooked up, and well, I just didn't wanna give anyone the wrong idea."

"You sure are worried about what other people think, aren't you?"

"Perception is what people judge you on, Rose. You might wanna remember that after you get married tomorrow."

"So you think me and you hanging out would be perceived the wrong way?"

"There is no doubt in my mind it would be taken outta context. And you know it too. Stop tryin'a play dumb."

"Yeah, you're right, but that's not the real reason we stopped hanging out." Rose stretched her legs out on the coffee table. I couldn't help but notice her robe only covered the top half of her thighs.

"Oh no? What's the real reason then?" She leaned over and I could see one of her nipples through her opened robe. I'm embarrassed to say it, but my manhood stiffened a little.

"The real reason is every time we hung out back then we'd end up in bed." She looked at me and smiled wickedly. Everything she had said was true. For some reason back in those days, she and I had always been quick to get naked whenever everyone was gone. Shit, one time we did it in a lifeguard chair on the beach in Far Rockaway.

"Yeah, I guess you're right." I thought about the many times we'd slept together before Lisa and I met. Truth is, Rose was the best lover I'd ever had until I met Lisa.

"Stay right here. I wanna show you something." She ran toward what was probably a bedroom and ran back smiling. "Do you think Allen will like this?" She held out a sheer white teddy.

"Yeah, it's nice." I said, certain he would like it. But I guess my answer wasn't sufficient, 'cause she frowned like I insulted her.

"What you need is a visual." In one fluid motion she let her robe fall to the floor and she was naked. I almost choked on my drink, and before I knew it, my manhood jumped straight to attention like it had a mind of its own.

"Wh-wh-wh-what are you doin'?"

"Please, Kyle, you act like you never seen me naked before." It amazed me how vain she was. "And if you got a problem with it, why you starin' so hard?" She was right. I was staring like this was the first naked body I'd ever seen. I couldn't help it. Rose's body was much nicer than I remembered. She'd definitely put on weight in the right places. Thank God it only took her a few seconds to put on that nighty.

"Now what do you think?" She struck a sexy pose.

"Oh it's nice, real nice." I took a huge gulp of my drink and decided that it was about time for me to go. I stood up, but Rose took exception.

"Where are you goin'?" She took her hand off her hip and frowned.

"I think I'm gonna go to my room."

"Oh, don't do this. The least you can do is finish your drink. Please?" She gave me this sad look.

"Sorry, Rose, I didn't come here to see you take your clothes off."

"Come on, Kyle, I'm sorry. I really didn't mean to offend you. Just stay and finish up your drink. Please?"

I was about to say no, but that's when I heard the unmistakable laughter of Wil and Diane outside the door. They were probably headed for their room, so now was not a good time to be leaving Rose's suite.

"Aw'ight, I'll stay. But after I finish this drink, I'm outta here."

"Okay," Rose smiled.

I sat back down and Rose walked over, sitting down beside me. She laughed out loud before taking a long sip of her drink. "Ya know, it's funny how things work out. Tomorrow I'm getting married to your best friend."

"What's so funny about that?" I was still trying to get over the fact that she was half-naked.

"Eight years ago I woulda done anything to marry you."

"Huh?" I raised my eyebrows and turned so that we were face to face.

"Don't act like you didn't know. You knew I liked you."

"No offense, Rose, but you liked a lot of people back in those days. Especially Jay."

"Jay? Please. The only reason I liked Jay is 'cause everyone else liked Jay. You were the one I wanted to be with. You just never took me serious. Other than in the bedroom, that is." I took a sip of my drink. How the hell could she have expected me to take her seriously when she was banging half of South Jamaica? But she did have me intrigued now that my erection had gone down and I'd gotten past the fact that she was sitting next to me half-naked.

"So why did you want me over Jay? I mean, I'm just a short, ugly, dark-skinned guy."

"You need to stop. You are not ugly and you know it. And as far as picking you over Jay, there was no contest. Everyone knew you were gonna be successful, even back then. You just wanted it more than anyone else did. And then of course there's . . . well, you know." She smiled.

"No, I don't know." I knew what she meant, but it's always good for the ego to hear it out loud.

"Look, I'm not tryin' to give you a big head, but you was the *bomb* in bed." She said it like it was a fact, and I smiled.

"Ohhh, so Jay was a dud in bed?" I looked at her with a smirk.

"No, no, that's not true. Jay could sling some dick. But you had that tongue thing goin' on. I never met anyone who could go down on me like you. I'm surprised that white girl was willing to give you up so easy." She looked down at my glass with a smile. "Another drink?"

I had to think about that a second. She'd behaved herself since dropping her robe so I was sure I had things under control. And if she did try anything stupid, I knew where the door was. So I agreed. Truth is, I was enjoying myself.

Rose and I talked and drank to old times for the better part of two hours before I dozed off on the sofa. I guess the fact that I'd seen her in that teddy, or naked for that matter, was on my mind, because I had a dream about her. It wasn't your ordinary, garden-variety dream either. This was a wet dream, a very wet dream. Rose and I were on a Caribbean beach. I was standing naked with my toes in the water while she was on her knees doing her thing. I mean *damn* was she doing her thing. She was doing her thing so well I woke up moaning, and when I opened my eyes, my shirt was unbuttoned and my fly was down and she was doing her thing for *real*.

"What the hell are you doing?" I jumped up on the sofa, my eyes wide with disbelief and my penis hard as a rock. To say I was confused was an understatement.

"Come back here. I was just gettin' started." She tried to pull me toward her.

"Not with me you're not." I didn't wanna think about how some shit like this would impact on my friendship with Allen. I just wanted to get the hell outta there and as far away from Rose as possible. I rushed to the door with her hot on my heels. I think she finally realized I wasn't with the program when I grabbed the doorknob.

"Kyle, come back. We need to talk." All of a sudden she didn't sound so confident.

"Talkin's what got us into this."

"We need to keep this between you and me." Like I needed to be told that.

"Who the hell did you think I was gonna tell? Allen?" I opened the door and my worst nightmare was right before my eyes. Wil's wife Diane was pushing her daughter Katie in a stroller down the hallway. She hadn't seen me yet, so I tried my best to close the door, but it was too late. She turned her head my way and grinned from ear to ear like she'd just hit Lotto.

"Well, Katie. I guess I can't get mad at you for not wanting to sleep." She turned the stroller toward me. "Say hi to Uncle Kyle and Aunt Rose, Katie."

"This isn't what you think, Di." I turned and looked at Rose wearing that teddy, then down at my unzipped fly. I could only imagine how sleazy this looked to Diane. How the hell was I gonna explain this?

23

Wil

"Wil! Wil! Get up, baby! Get up! You're not gonna believe this!"

Diane's voice was full of excitement as I felt the lights come on, glaring even through my closed eyelids. I was half asleep so I tried my best to ignore my wife. With any luck she'd think I was in a deep slumber and leave me alone, but that idea was shot to hell when my son Teddy started to stir next to me. He's a real light sleeper so I pulled the covers over his head, hoping the commotion wouldn't wake him. I tried to be slick, moving the covers as subtly as I could. Unfortunately I wasn't smooth enough. Diane saw me move and started shaking me. She always did shit like that when I was getting some really good sleep. I opened my eyes and glanced at the clock radio.

"Di, it's three o'clock in the morning. Why aren't you asleep?"

"Katie wouldn't go to sleep so I . . ." She stopped herself in midsentence. "That's not important." She took a breath. "Guess who I just saw coming outta Rose's room?" She sounded just like a little kid getting ready to share a really juicy secret.

"I don't know, Di. Who?" I asked wearily.

"Kyle!"

"So?" I rubbed my eyes.

"So? He was in there messin' with Rose." I was beginning to become annoyed that she had woken me and now she was talkin' some crazy shit.

"No, he wasn't. Now can I go back to sleep?"

I lifted my head and looked at my wife. I was positive she was making something out of nothing. That's what she did. She just couldn't help herself. She loved drama and always had to be in the middle of it. The only problem was when she was in the middle of it, I always seemed to be placed there too. Like earlier tonight, not only did she tell Lisa that Kyle was seeing Val, which I told her not to do, but she had to hook Lisa up with John Hernandez, a Latino brother from work. Can you imagine what Kyle would have done if he'd known it was my wife who had hooked his lady up with her new man? I don't even wanna think about the consequences.

"Yes, he *was* messin' with her." Di folded her arms like that was supposed to mean something.

"Okay, Di, whatever you say." It was late and I wasn't about to argue with her at three in the morning. I laid my head back down.

"Well, are you gonna go tell Allen or am I?" She was not about to let me end this conversation so easily. I sat up and shot her an angry look.

"You're not tellin' Allen anything." I had an attitude now. "I told you about gettin' in my friends' business, so stay out of it. I'm in enough trouble with Kyle 'cause of you and your big mouth."

"But—"

"No buts, Di. I said stay out of it. I'll talk to Allen and Kyle in the morning. Go ta bed!" I turned my back to her and refused to answer any of her protests. Diane went to bed like she was told, but as soon as daylight broke, she was back at it again.

"Wil, are you gonna tell Allen that Kyle and Rose were messin' around last night? I think he needs to know before he walks down that aisle."

"What exactly did go on last night, Di?" I was rested enough to hear her story now.

Diane explained her side of the story, which was basically that she caught Kyle and Rose having wild sex in the hallway. I very seriously doubted her version of events. Even if Kyle and Rose were stupid enough to do the nasty, they'd never be dumb enough to do it in the same hallway where the entire bridal party was staying.

"Well, are you gonna tell Allen or what?" she asked as soon as she finished her story.

"I'll take care of it, Di," I told her with finality. I refused to discuss it anymore until I got a few more hours of sleep.

The wedding wasn't until one that afternoon, but I was supposed to meet Allen, Jay, and Kyle at nine for what would be Allen's last breakfast as a bachelor. When I woke up, I figured I had enough time to see Kyle and get the real story. I doubted there was much truth to my wife's story. I dressed Teddy and told Di I'd be back soon. That way I could visit Kyle's room and find out from him what the hell was really going on. And of course, I could apologize once again for having such a big mouth. I hated the thought of not telling Diane everything, but I had to face reality and stop opening my mouth around my gossiping wife.

Knock, knock.

No answer at Kyle's door.

Knock, knock.

Still no answer. The first thought that came to mind was that he had already gone down to the restaurant, but then I noticed his plastic room key was still in the door.

"Kyle?" I opened his door. His room was pitch black, so I flicked on the lights.

"Turn off the light!" he yelled, pulling the covers over his head.

"Aw'ight, man, calm down." His room smelled like a brewery, which didn't make any sense, 'cause when he left us the night before, he'd only had one drink.

"Get up. It's nine o'clock. We gotta meet Allen and Jay." I turned on a few more lights. To hell with his protests.

"I'm not goin'," he groaned.

"Stop playin', Kyle. Get up." I pulled the covers off the bed.

"Stop it, Wil. I'm not goin'. I'm not going to breakfast and I'm damn sure not going to no wedding."

"Man, you better get up. What the hell is wrong with you?"

"Stop messin' with me, Wil. I know Diane told you what happened last night. She definitely wouldn't pick now to keep her trap shut, would she?"

I didn't move from the spot where I was standing.

"Oh my God. You really did fuck her?" There was a strange silence between Kyle and me. A silence that only two best friends could understand. A silence whose meaning could only be determined by his answer, and Lord help him if it was the wrong answer. He sat up.

"I swear on my kids, Wil, I didn't touch her." His voice was humble. He was begging me to believe him.

"Okay, bro. That's what I thought." I sighed thankfully.

I picked up his pants from the floor and threw them at him. "Get dressed. You still got a lot of explaining to do."

Kyle told me his side of the story as he dressed. A story that actually made sense, although I still shoulda slapped him for going into Rose's room in the first place. And why he stayed after she'd disrobed was beyond explanation and was as asinine as anything even Jay had done in the past.

"You think I should tell Al?" Kyle asked after he finished his explanation.

I took a deep breath. "Probably. But before we make that decision, I think we need to talk to Rose."

"Why? Fuck that bitch."

"Kyle, Allen didn't have a chance to tell you this before you went upstairs last night, but Rose is pregnant. And you know how much he wants to have kids." Kyle's eyes were as wide as silver dollars.

"You serious?"

"Yep." I walked over to the phone. "Why you think Rose and Ma Jackson been so tight lately?"

"I don't know. I never gave it much thought."

"Well, think about this. Rose mighta already told Allen her version of the story to cover her ass. And if I know her, you're the one who's gonna look like the bad guy in the end. We might wanna hold off 'til we know a little more."

"Damn, you're right," he said sadly, scratching his head. "You think he'd believe her over me?"

I didn't answer Kyle 'cause I didn't really know the answer. What I did know was that if it was me and it came down to Diane and my kids or him, well, Kyle would be ass out in the long run. 'Cause I'm sticking with my family, even if Diane is wrong. My kids just mean too much to me. Chances were, on their wedding day, Rose had a good chance of beating Kyle in a game of "guess-who's-telling-the-truth." I picked up the phone and dialed 0 for the hotel operator.

"Can you connect me with room 1611? It's the honeymoon suite."

"Hello?" a female voice answered. It wasn't Rose, but an older woman.

"Can I speak with Rose, please?"

"Rose is getting dressed. She'll have to call you back. Can I ask who's calling?"

"This is Wil. Can you tell her it's important?"

"Hey, Wil, this is Mama Jackson. Everything all right, baby?"

"Yeah, Ma, I just need to speak to Rose. Can you tell her it's about last night?" I never would have expected Allen's mother to be answering the phone in Rose's suite, but things seemed to be getting stranger and stranger. I hoped I hadn't said too much by mentioning the reason for my call. No need to get her suspicious about anything, but I guess it was too late to worry about it. I'd already said it.

Apparently it hadn't meant much to Ma Jackson, because she didn't ask any questions, and a few seconds later Rose was on the line.

"H-hello?" Rose's voice was trembling.

"This is Wil. We need to talk."

"I'm trying to put my wedding dress on before the photographer gets here, Wil. Can't it wait?" I didn't appreciate her evasiveness. She knew damn well it couldn't wait.

"No, it can't wait. Now if you wanna play this little game, you can play it. But if you don't get down here in the next five minutes, you ain't gonna have a wedding to wear that dress to." The line was silent.

"I'll be right there," she finally answered.

"We're in Kyle's room, 1624."

"Okay."

It took longer than I expected, but about ten minutes later there was a knock on the door. I got up and answered it, but to my surprise, it wasn't Rose. It was Allen's mother, and she walked right past me without a word. She sat on the bed next to Kyle.

"Wil, you grab one of them chairs and bring it over here. I wanna talk to you boys."

"Yes, ma'am," I obeyed. Ma Jackson wasn't my mother, but Kyle and I gave her that kinda respect 'cause she damn near raised us.

"Now I heard what happened last night and I hope you boys ain't tryin' to break up this here wedding." Kyle and I both glanced at each other. I'm sure he was thinking the same thing I was. Somehow Rose had gotten to Ma Jackson.

"Ma, I don't know what Rose told you but—" Ma raised her hand and Kyle shut up.

"Rose told me y'all had a friendly drink last night that mighta got misconstrued."

"Well, that's not exactly the truth, Ma. She—" Ma raised her hand again, turning so she was face to face with Kyle.

"It's the truth. Let's leave it at that, okay, baby? Ain't no reason to stir up nothin' on my baby's wedding day."

"But, Ma, she ain't right," Kyle pleaded.

"She's carryin' Allen's baby, Kyle. That makes her all right with me. I know you wouldn't wanna do anything that might keep me from see-ing that baby, would you?" Kyle sat in silence a second.

"Would you?" Ma repeated.

"No, Ma Jackson." He sounded just like a little kid.

"Now that's what I wanna hear." She patted Kyle's knee and stood up. "You boys get downstairs to Allen. Make sure he looks real good. I wanna be proud of him. And don't you worry. I got my eyes on Rose. She's not as slick as she thinks she is." Ma Jackson walked toward the door then turned to me. "Wil, you keep your wife quiet, you hear? I'm countin' on you boys to keep this whole thing between us." She left, and Kyle and I stared at each other in stunned silence.

"Let me ask you something, Wil. Did I miss something or did she not care that her future daughter-in-law is a piece o' shit? I mean, that was scary." Kyle had a look of bewilderment on his face and mine probably didn't look much different.

"I don't know, man, but I'm afraid for Allen."

"Me too, Wil. Me too. If Rose gives Ma Jackson a grandchild, she's gonna let Rose rule over Allen for the rest of his life. Man, he ain't got a snowball's chance in hell of ever being truly happy."

I only wish I could have disagreed.

24

Allen

It was exactly one hour and fifteen minutes from my wedding and I can't ever remember a time when I was more nervous. My stomach was doing flips, and I thought for sure I was gonna throw up at any moment. And if that wasn't bad enough, my hands were shaking so bad I couldn't put my tie on right. Oh, and to top it all off, I just screamed on my boys so bad they decided to go back to their own rooms to get dressed for the wedding. In retrospect I wish I hadn't acted so stupid 'cause I could sure have used some company right about then. I was an emotional wreck and about ready to call off the whole thing.

As I stood in front of the mirror trying to straighten my tie, I thought about Rose and the life we were about to start. Was she really the woman I wanted to marry? Up until breakfast this morning I was positive she was. At least I was until Kyle posed a question that made me doubt the reasons I was getting married.

"Yo, Al, let me ask you a question," Kyle said seriously. He hadn't spoken all morning and had barely touched his breakfast. I hadn't pushed the issue 'cause I figured he'd taken Lisa showing up at the hotel bar last night with her new friend badly.

"Sure, bro. Ask me anything."

Wil cleared his throat and Kyle waved him off saying, "Lemme handle this, Wil. I know what I'm doing." Then he turned to me. "Allen, are you settling?"

"What do you mean, am I settling?" I asked as I crunched on a piece of bacon.

"Are you settling? Are you settling with Rose because the three of us are married and you're not? Or maybe because your mother wants grandchildren? Marriage is not an easy road to travel. Look at me."

I picked up another piece of bacon and smiled as I made eye contact with each of my best friends.

"No, I'm not settling. I love Rose and I'm going to marry her," I said confidently, pointing my bacon at each of them. Kyle dropped it, but all through breakfast and up 'til now I kept thinking about what he had suggested. Now that the seed had been planted, I kept reminding myself that I did get with Rose on the rebound from Cinnamon. Hell, if she hadn't put so much pressure on me and Ma hadn't given me Granny's ring, I might've waited another year before proposing. Throw in the fact that I had gotten sick of Ma constantly asking me when she was gonna get some grandkids. I guess I could've been settling. The ironic thing was now I was feeling pushed into this, not by one, but by two women! Thank God my thoughts were interrupted by a knock on the door. The last thing I needed now was to be left alone to think.

"It's open," I yelled. I smiled when my cousin Malcolm walked in wearing a tailor-made blue suit. I was hoping he wasn't mad at me for not asking him to be in the wedding.

"Somebody told me there was a brother who lost his mind and decided to get married in here. I gotta find that brother and see if I can get him some help, 'cause he's certifiably crazy." Malcolm laughed hard as we embraced. "How you holdin' up there, Al? You nervous?"

"Nah, this is gonna be easy," I lied.

"Sure it is." Malcolm smiled then turned serious. "No, really, Allen. You nervous?"

"Nervous as hell." I took a deep breath, shaking my head. "Nervous as hell!"

"Don't worry. I hear everyone gets nervous a few hours before." Malcolm glanced at my crooked tie and laughed. "Man, you need to get your shit together." He straightened my tie. "Where the hell's that crew of yours anyway? They should be doing this."

"They were getting on my nerves so I kicked 'em out. They'll be back in a few."

When Malcolm finished with my tie, he stood in front of me, checking me out like Ma used to do on Sundays before church.

"You look good," he said, nodding his head in approval.

"Thanks," I replied.

"Congratulations," Malcolm stuck his hand out and pulled me in for another embrace. "Love you, man."

"Yeah, I love you too, cuz. Where the hell you been anyway? I thought you was coming to my bachelor party."

Malcolm sat down in one of the chairs the hotel provided. "Yeah, well, I wanted to but I figured I'd ruin things for you by being there."

"Ruin things, how?"

"By gettin' into a fight with your boy Jay. You know I owe that nigga an ass whuppin' for what he did to me at Wil's house."

"I wish you two would grow up. Y'all too old for this shit."

"Yeah, well, I came to the same conclusion once the swelling in my eyes went down. That boy sure knows how to throw a punch." He rubbed his eyes. "But seriously, I got Jay's number from Kyle so that we could squash things, but every time I call, Jay's never home. I did talk to his wife a few times, though. She's a real nice woman. How the hell did he ever get her?"

"Yeah, Kenya's a good woman." I ignored his last comment. "Look, I want you and Jay to sit down and talk tonight."

Malcolm shot me a look. "You sure you wanna take that kinda chance? You know how we get. He's fire and I'm gasoline."

"On second thought, maybe y'all two should talk when I get back from my honeymoon."

"Aw'ight, man. Lemme get downstairs. My moms and pops are waiting for me to drive them to the church." We hugged again.

"Look, I'm sorry about you not being in the wedding. It's just with Jay—" He cut me off with a wave of his hand.

"Say no more, bro. This is your day. I'm just here to celebrate it with you. By the way, I hear more congratulations are in order." He rubbed his stomach.

"Yeah, I'm gonna be a daddy." I smiled, remembering why there was no turning back.

"It must be a good feeling."

"It is," I smiled. "Hopefully you'll be next."

"You never know. I'm workin' on something as we speak."

"I hope it works out for you, cuz. I really do." We both smiled as he walked out the door.

"Clink, clink, clink, clink, clink, clink, clink, clink!" The entire reception room was filled with the sound of silverware lightly hitting crystal. Rose and I responded by kissing for the millionth time. We'd just been introduced for the first time as Mr. and Mrs. Allen Jackson and were slow-dancing to our wedding song, "Endless Love" by Lionel Richie and Diana Ross.

"I love you, Mrs. Jackson," I whispered in her ear as we danced. All the doubt I felt ended the minute I saw her walk down that aisle. She was so beautiful and I was proud to know she was gonna be all mine.

"That's Mrs. *Brown*-Jackson," she corrected me. "Your mother is Mrs. Jackson."

"Oh yeah." I gave a fake laugh. The last thing I wanted to hear on our wedding day was that she wasn't taking my last name.

When the song ended, we walked over to the reception line to be greeted as man and wife by our friends and family. Standing in the front of the line were Jay and Kenya. Jay had stood in as my best man. Wil and Kyle were my best men also, but Jay stood in front and held on to the rings. I figured it was the least I could do since he had set up my bachelor party.

"Congratulations, dawg." He grabbed my hand tightly and nodded his head with approval before kissing my new bride on the cheek. "Take care of him, Rose."

"I will," she assured him as he and Kenya moved out of the way for Wil and Diane.

"Congrats, my brother." Wil shook my hand.

"Thanks, Wil." I couldn't help but wonder why he didn't smile when he spoke.

"You got a good man here, Rose. *Don't blow it.*" Their eyes were locked on each other. If I didn't know better, I would have sworn Wil had won a staring contest.

"I won't," Rose said as she looked away.

"Congratulations, Allen." Diane wrapped her arms around me tightly then stepped back. "If you ever need a real friend, you know my number."

"Huh?" I gave her a confused look.

"What she means is, you know our number. Right, Di?" Wil elbowed his wife, who gave Rose a wicked smile as they shook hands. I thought it was really odd that Rose and Diane didn't hug or kiss, but that might have had something to do with what happened during the wedding ceremony.

It wasn't funny then, but now that I think about it, Diane did add a little flavor to the wedding. The entire wedding ceremony had been going perfectly. That is, until the preacher announced, "If there is anyone who has reason that this couple should not be married, let them speak now or forever hold their peace." I took a deep breath and glanced at Jay, Wil, and Kyle, and although Kyle and Wil were fidgety, they remained silent. But out of nowhere there was a sudden loud cough that sounded a lot like *She's a slut, she's a slut.* Everyone in the church turned to the culprit, who turned out to be Diane. Just like a child who got caught with their fingers in the cookie jar, she smiled and said, "Oops, sorry. Something got caught in my throat." I don't know if Diane did that on purpose or not, but I was gonna have to ask Rose what she thought when we got to the Bahamas later that night.

When I looked down the reception line, conspicuous by his absence was my man Kyle. "Yo, where's Kyle?" I turned to Wil and Jay, who were congratulating Ma and Rose's parents.

"I don't know, he was here a minute ago," Wil replied. He never even lifted his head.

"I think he took the girls to the bathroom," Jay told me.

I glanced down the reception line again. The girls were with Lisa. She'd really done the right thing by not bringing her friend to the wedding. I'd have to thank her for that one day. But my main concern was where the hell did Kyle disappear to?

"Don't worry about him, Allen, we've got other guests to greet," Rose demanded, tugging on my hand.

It was almost three hours later and my reception was almost over when I finally saw Kyle stroll through the doors followed by my ma and Wil. He'd taken off his tux and was wearing street clothes now as he walked up to me and Rose.

"I'm sorry I missed the reception. I was in my room sick. I think it was something I ate during breakfast." His voice was weak and not once did he make eye contact or even look at Rose. I couldn't help but think he was lying. He had barely touched his breakfast.

"You feeling any better?"

"Nah, I think I'm gonna head on home. I just wanted to say congratulations before I left."

"Aw'ight, then bro, thanks for coming." I grabbed his hand and pulled him in for a hug.

"I hope you're happy, Allen. I swear to God, I hope you're happy," he whispered. When we let go of each other, he stuck his hand out for Rose to shake. "Congratulations, Rose."

"Thank you, Kyle," she said as they quickly shook hands. What I wanted to know was why the hell everyone was shaking hands instead of hugging and kissing. Isn't that what you're supposed to do at weddings? But before I could speak, Kyle had walked toward the doors with Wil in tow. I guess that was a question for another day.

25

Jay

It was eleven-thirty Sunday morning, the day after Allen's wedding, and that empty feeling I'd had for the past four months was finally gone. There I was, like déjà vu, lying on a king-size bed with Tracy's warm breasts pressed against my naked chest as she ran her fingers through my hair. We'd just made love, and I emphasize the word *love,* 'cause nothing I'd ever experienced could compare to the way she made me feel. It was honestly like a dream come true and I didn't wanna wake up.

"Jay?" she whispered, still stroking my hair.

"Yes?" I replied.

"How do you feel?"

I looked up at her and smiled.

"Baby, I feel wonderful." And I did. I lifted my head and kissed her.

"No, I mean how do you feel about me?" Her eyes were filled with concern.

"You're not gonna believe this, but I love you, Tracy." She smiled at my answer, but it quickly became a frown.

"You're right. I don't believe you." She pushed herself off me and walked to the sliding glass door. The early-morning light blinded me when she pulled the shade back to gaze at the Long Island Sound. We'd stayed at the Beach Comber Motel in Bayville, Long Island, a little romantic spot Kyle had discovered about ten years ago. It was right on the water, and considering there was an ocean view from all the rooms, it was incredibly reasonable at a hundred bucks a night. Like the true friend he was, Kyle had shared his secret hideaway with me so I'd have someplace to take a woman as special as the one I was with now.

"I can't believe I'm here." She turned to look at me then turned away. I walked up behind her and wrapped my arms around her waist as I watched a seagull fly by. "I promised myself I'd stay away from you." She sounded so emotional.

"If you were going to stay away from me, what made you change your mind?" I kissed her neck, glad that she had changed it.

"I couldn't stop thinking about you," she replied in a soft voice.

"That's funny," I chuckled, hugging her tightly. "I couldn't stop thinking about you either."

"Yeah, right." She turned around and glared at me, which surprised me.

"You're acting like you don't believe me."

"I don't." She struggled from my grasp and walked back over to the bed, sat at the edge, and stared at the floor.

"Why? Why don't you believe me? I've been calling you every day for the last three months. Why do you think I called?" I wanted her to look at me so she could see how sincere I was.

"I don't know why, Jay. But I know it's not because you love me." When she looked up at me, she had tears in her eyes. I walked over and knelt down in front of her.

"I do love you, Tracy. I swear to *God* I do. I need you to believe that."

Tracy laughed as a tear fell from her eyes.

"You wanna know the real reason I wanted to see you, Jay?"

I nodded.

" 'Cause I wanted to curse your ass out for leaving me in that damn house by myself. That's why."

I gulped hard. We hadn't spoken about that incident since I picked her up this morning, mainly because our passion had taken over the second we saw each other. By the time we made it to the room, half our clothes were off and neither one of us was thinking about having any discussions.

"Look, Tracy, I'm sorry about that, and I'm willing to do whatever it takes to make it up to you." I couldn't have been more sincere if I was standing on a stack of Bibles, but apparently Tracy didn't think that was enough. She asked me for more concrete proof.

"Okay, then, take me to your house and make me breakfast like you did last time." She stared at me seriously and her words sounded like a command. I have to admit I was caught off guard.

"Wh-why? There's a wonderful restaurant right downstairs."

"You said you'd do whatever it takes. Well, that's what it'll take." She folded her arms and waited for my answer. I hated knowing that she was backing me into a corner where my only escape was another lie.

"Like I told you before, I don't wanna make a bad impression. My nephews are at the house."

"What are you tryin'a say, that I'm gonna embarrass you? It's not like I'm spending the night, Jay." I had to think of something quick. I was trying my best to outthink her, but she was on her game.

"No, I don't think you'll embarrass me. It's more like I'm afraid *they'll* embarrass me."

"Is that right?" She sounded suspicious, but I kept trying anyway.

"Yeah, those two boys are real monsters. If—" She cut me off.

"Take me home, Jay." She reached for her clothes. "Take me home. Now!"

"You gotta be kiddin'. We just got here." What the hell was it about going to my house that always set her off?

"I said take me home, and I mean now! I can't stand you!" Her words were sharp and cut like a knife.

"Why are you actin' this way?" I was stunned and my words were defensive. This couldn't be happening after the beautiful love we had just made. It just couldn't be happening. "You really wanna go home just because I won't make you pancakes?"

She stood up with her clothes in her arms and walked over to the bathroom, her face streaked with tears.

"No, Jay, it's not the pancakes." She hesitated, trying to calm her voice before she dropped the bomb. "It's the fact that you're *married.*"

My mind went blank and my eyes went wide. It took me a moment to get over the sudden shock of her words. I had no idea how she knew. I'd been in this situation before at least a dozen times with other women, so I knew the drill, but I couldn't for the life of me think of my next move. There were only two sides to this coin: one was she knew I was married and had some type of proof, the other was she suspected I was married and was on a fishing expedition. With any other woman I might have just gambled and said, "Yeah, I'm married. You gotta problem with it, there's the door," but this was the woman I loved and wanted to be with the rest of my life. I had to tread lightly. I didn't wanna give the wrong answer and lose her again. I searched her face for a clue, but none came up.

"Well, Mr. I-love-you, why didn't you tell me you were married?" She'd stopped crying, but I was pretty sure anything coulda set the water works off again. This was definitely not how I had envisioned our reunion.

"What makes you think I'm married?" Might as well play dumb.

"*Ohhhh!*" She threw her clothes at me and pointed a finger. "Don't you lie to me, Jay! I'm in love with you, motherfucker. Don't you lie to me!" Her teeth were clenched and the tears started again. If looks could kill, I'd be dead twice. But what mattered most was that I'd just heard her say she was in love with me.

At that point I was pretty sure she knew the truth. But rule number one in the players' handbook is don't say shit unless you get caught with your dick in the pussy, and then blame it on her lying eyes. So I kept quiet.

"You know, I was actually gonna sit in that house until you came home," she admitted. "Yep, I was gonna sit there and wait 'til you came back home for me, but my curiosity got the best of me. My mama always told me never snoop around for something unless you're ready to find it. I guess I gotta start listening to my mama." She exhaled before dropping her next bomb on me. "You'll never believe what I found when I looked in your living room closet that day."

"Oh, shit," I mumbled, wanting to kill myself for my stupidity. How could I call myself a player and make such a basic mistake?

"That's right, I found your wedding pictures, your wedding album, and a whole bunch of family portraits. Your daughter is so cute. Can't deny her, can you?" There weren't any tears in her eyes now. Her voice was full of sarcasm. She was enjoying herself. "By the way, are you expecting a new addition? 'Cause that little nursery y'all got hooked up is the bomb."

This was killing me. I wanted to say something but I couldn't. I wanted to tell her yeah, I'm married and I got two kids but I'm willing to give it all up for you, but the words just wouldn't leave my mouth.

"Get outta here, Jay!" she screamed out of nowhere. "I'm gonna take a cab home!"

"Tracy, I—"

"Get the fuck outta here, or I swear I'll be on your doorstep tomorrow morning telling your wife everything from what color panties she wears to where she keeps her Kotex in the linen closet."

I lowered my head and walked over to the other side of the bed. I put my clothes on without another word. When I finished dressing, I looked at Tracy, hoping she might change her mind, but she just pointed to the door. I reached into my pocket and dropped a twenty-dollar bill on the bed.

"For your cab," I told her as a single tear fell from my eye and rolled down my cheek. "I love you, Tracy. More than anything in this world, I love you. You may not believe me, but I'm willing to leave my wife and kids for you. All you have to do is say the word." I was crying now, like I never cried before. It must have been contagious 'cause she was crying again too. I walked out of that hotel room a broken man. By the time I reached my car, I had decided that life just wasn't worth living without her. That's when I heard her call my name.

When I turned, she was on the balcony.

"Jay, wait," she yelled, then disappeared back in the room.

A minute later she ran out of the motel door into my arms, squeezing me tight. "Don't go. I don't think I could take it if you left me again. I hate you for lying to me and being married, but I love you too much to let you go."

"You want me to leave my wife? 'Cause I will." I stared into her eyes to let her know I meant every word. If she said so, Kenya was history.

"No, you've got kids," she answered after she thought about it for a while. "She can have the title for now. You just remember who you're in love with, and who's really in charge."

"I will," I promised as we walked back to the room. "I will."

26

Wil

I made it home from Shea Stadium in record time, and the truth is I'd been sweating all the way. Kyle, Allen, and I had been at the Mets-Yankees interleague baseball game when my neighbor, Mr. Brown, called me on my cell. Mr. Brown wasn't the easiest man in the world to understand with his heavy Jamaican accent but he did make it clear that something was very wrong at my house and that I needed to get home before someone called the cops on my wife. Now that scared me, especially after I called home and I couldn't get Diane. I was even more nervous when the answering machine didn't pick up. Thank God both my kids were at my mom's, or I probably would have had a heart attack from the anxiety.

When I pulled into the driveway, I immediately understood why Mr. Brown had been so alarmed. All I could do was stare in disbelief. Most of my belongings were strewn about my front lawn like something out of a bad horror movie, and when I looked up, the monster of this drama was my wife. She was throwing the rest of my clothes out my bedroom window. I got out of the car and picked up my Willie Mays rookie baseball card that had been ripped in half. Seven hundred bucks right down the damn drain, not to mention the fact that my grandfather gave me the card when I was six years old. My original concern for my wife had passed, and now I was heated. I wasn't sure what was going on, but whatever it was, I thought, Di had better have a damn good reason for it.

"I told ya." Mr. Brown ran up behind me. We both had to jump out of the way when a dresser drawer bounced off the porch roof and onto the lawn.

"Di, what the hell is wrong with you?" I screamed when she popped her head out the window.

"Ask your *whores*, you son of a bitch!" She threw another dresser drawer out the window and the small crowd that had gathered roared with laugher. I'd never been so embarrassed in my entire life.

I didn't know what she was talking about but I chose not to air my dirty laundry in front of the neighborhood. I stormed up to the front door. I felt like a fool when my key wouldn't work. "Dammit!" I slammed my hand against the oak door in a rage. She'd actually changed the fucking lock. I turned around and watched my underwear float down to the ground.

"I'ma kill this woman," I mumbled to myself. That's when I stepped out from under the porch and screamed.

"Diane! Open this fuckin' door!" She answered me by throwing my computer monitor out the window. Pieces shattered all over the drive-way. I ran around back and found the locks had been changed there too. I was so angry by then I decided to break one of the windows to get in, but when I went to get the hammer out of my trunk, two police officers were stepping out of their patrol car. One of them was a sister, and the other a white man.

"Can I help you, officers?" I tried to sound calm, though sweat was dripping down my face and my chest was heaving.

The male officer spoke first. "Yeah, you can start by telling us what's going on."

"My name's Wil Duncan, Officer. This is my house." I pointed to Diane, who was staring down from the window like a deranged ani-mal. "That's my wife, Diane."

"Don't point at me, you motherfucker! I wish I had that cop's gun 'cause I'd shoot your sorry black ass!" she screamed, and of course, the crowd fell out laughing.

"Is she under the influence of any illegal substances, sir?" the fe-male officer asked.

"I don't know what's wrong with her, Officer. When I left this morning, she was fine. My neighbor called and told me there was an emergency and I came home to this."

"What's her name again?"

"Diane. Diane Duncan."

"Mrs. Duncan, come on downstairs and open the door, please. We'd like to talk to you," the male officer shouted. Diane's head disap-peared from the window and a minute later the front door opened.

"I don't want him in my house." She pointed at me.

"Di, what's the matter, baby? What'd I do?" I'd never seen her act this way. *Ever*. The only thing I could imagine was that she was having some type of breakdown.

"I don't want him in my house," she yelled again.

"Mr. Duncan, why don't you wait out here while we talk to your wife?" the female officer asked. It wasn't a suggestion as much as a command.

Reluctantly I agreed and the two officers disappeared into the house. I'd be telling a big-ass lie if I didn't admit I was scared. Not of Di being mad at me. Hell, I hadn't done anything wrong. I'd been the perfect husband. No, I was scared that Di really might be having a nervous breakdown. Maybe the stress of taking care of two kids and going back to work was too much for her.

"Mr. Duncan, you've got a problem," the male officer informed me when he came out of the house ten minutes later. From his tone I was sure he was about to arrest me.

"Did she tell you what this is all about, Officer?"

"Yes, she did." His serious look turned to one of compassion. I was just hoping it was me he was feeling sorry for.

"Mr. Duncan, if I were you, I'd pick up all my stuff, put it in my car, and give my wife a few days to cool off."

"What the hell is that supposed to mean? What'd I do?" I was not in the mood to play a guessing game.

"Maybe this will jog your memory." He handed me a picture that made my knees give out.

"Wh-what the hell is this?"

"It looks like you having a really good time with three women, and none of them is your wife." The officer tried not to laugh, but I don't think he could help himself.

"I'm glad you find something funny, Officer, 'cause that's not me." He took the picture from me and examined it again.

"I don't know, sir, but I see a pretty strong resemblance between you and the man in the photo." I snatched the picture back.

"It looks like me, but it's not me!" I insisted. "It can't be me."

"Look, Mr. Duncan, if you wanna insult my intelligence, that's fine. I'm not married to you. But your wife has a dozen of these pictures in there, and most of them are worse than this."

"From where? Where did she get them from?" I felt like grabbing him and shaking the answer out.

"We didn't get into that, but she is adamant that you're not coming in the house."

"Oh, she's gonna let me in that house." I took a step toward the house but he stepped in my way.

"If I were you, Mr. Duncan, I wouldn't push it."

"Hold up! You mean to tell me I can't go into my own house?"

"Mr. Duncan, I'm not telling you what to do. But if the two of you continue this redecorating plan you have"—he glanced at the lawn—"I'm going to have to arrest one of you for disturbing the peace and possibly domestic violence." There was no smile on his face. He was dead serious, and something told me I was the one who would end up in handcuffs over this.

"Wait a minute. You're gonna arrest me? I haven't done anything. She's the one throwing things out of the house!"

"Look, I'm just doing my job, and my job is to put an end to this." He put his hand on my shoulder. "Now if you're saying your wife's the aggressor, that's fine with me. But I'm telling you from experience if she walks outta here with bracelets on, she's gonna blame her arrest on you, and your marriage seems to already be in a heap of trouble. Take a good look at that picture. If the roles were reversed, how would you act?" It didn't take a brain surgeon to realize he was right. If I couldn't get her to calm down, I was gonna have to go.

"Yeah, I know, Officer. But I need to talk to her for five minutes. After that I'll leave."

"Okay. Lemme talk to my partner. I'm not gonna promise anything but I'll see what I can do." He handed me the picture and walked back inside. I took another look at the picture and tried to imagine when the hell this could have been taken. I felt like I was in the fucking twilight zone. But before I had enough time to really make sense of the whole situation, Diane walked out of the house, followed by the two officers. Her hair was a wreck and mascara was smudged all over her face. She looked like I felt. Like shit.

"What do you want, Wil?" She folded her arms and huffed. I could tell she was trying to control herself from crying again. Hell, so was I.

"Diane, I swear to God I had nothing to do with those pictures." I could see her eyes get small with anger, and the female officer placed her hand on her shoulder to calm her.

"You see this?" She ruffled through the pictures and flicked at me one with a woman's face an inch from the man's penis. "That's your birthmark, motherfucker."

I had nothing to say, so she continued. I hoped it was making her feel better, 'cause it sure wasn't doing much for me.

"And that's your wedding ring!" She threw another picture and I could hear the white cop chuckle. "How could you do this to me, Wil? How could you do this to us? You son of a bitch!" Tears rolled down her face and I swear to God I could feel her pain. I reached out instinctively to hold her but she slapped my hand away. She sobbed on the shoulder of the female cop.

"Di, I swear to you, baby. I don't know anything about these pictures. I love you so much. I would never do anything like this to you. Please, baby, you gotta believe me." I couldn't help myself. Tears began to spring from my eyes too.

"I hate you, motherfucker!" She turned her back to me, and then suddenly she was in my face. A second later I felt the sting of her heavy hand slap my face. The officers tried to stop her but she got off two more blows before they could grab and pull her off me. "I hate you, Wil! I hate you so much! I can't believe you did this to me!" She was kicking and twisting so hard to get at me she almost broke free.

"I didn't do it, Di. I swear to God I didn't do it!" I dropped to my knees and watched them drag my wife into the house. "Baby, please believe me. I didn't do it! I swear to God I don't know anything about these pictures." I could hear one last "I hate you" as the door closed.

A few minutes later the male officer walked out of the house.

"Mr. Duncan, would you like to press charges?"

"No, Officer." I stood up, trying to compose myself.

"I didn't think you would. Look, the law says that one party has to leave during any domestic dispute of this caliber. I think it best that you get your stuff and go. Maybe give your wife a call tomorrow when she's calmed down."

"Yeah, okay, Officer, I'll leave. But I want you to know I'm telling the truth. I don't know where those pictures came from, but I'm gonna find out." I bent over to retrieve my belongings from the lawn. It took me an hour to get all my stuff into my car.

After I packed up all my stuff, I drove over to Baisly Park and sat by the lake. I loved that park, mainly because I'd had so many good times with Di there. We'd shared our first kiss there and that's where she first told me she loved me. I'd even proposed right on the lake in a paddleboat. Whenever she was mad at me or we had problems, I'd go there and think. Most of the time I'd be reminded of the good times we'd shared and how much I loved her, then end up going home with some flowers or candy. A few times she even came down there and apologized to me. But that wasn't gonna happen this time. Not until we straightened out this whole picture deal.

I sat by that old lake and fed the ducks for almost two hours, trying to figure out what the hell had just happened to my life. I'd worked so hard on my marriage over the years that it just seemed impossible that something like this could fuck it all up in one day. And what I hated most was that the whole thing was so out of my control. I studied the two pictures that Diane had thrown at me plus the one the cop had given me.

Damn, that was definitely me in those pictures. I just couldn't figure out how the hell someone could take a picture like that without my knowledge. Then it came to me. The only naked women I'd been around anytime recently were at Allen's bachelor party. And I had definitely been drunk enough that night to have a few holes in my memory. Kyle said that I'd passed out. The only question was how the hell did I end up with these girls doing this to me? Somewhere in the back of my mind it dawned on me that the only person mad enough at me lately to do something like this was Jay. What I couldn't figure out was why he would do it. It was one thing for him to ruin his own marriage, but why ruin mine? Even if I had to drag him to my house to straighten this whole thing out with Diane, he was gonna explain this mess or I was gonna die trying.

27

Kyle

Allen and I came back from the game, welcomed by Val, who was in my kitchen preparing dinner for us. I walked up behind her and wrapped my arms around her waist. She was stirring sausage and meatballs into a pot of sauce, and the whole apartment smelled like an Italian restaurant.

"Mmm, that smells almost as good as you do," I whispered, kissing her neck. She lifted the wooden spoon so that I could taste the sauce. My girl could cook. A tiny bit of sauce fell on her shoulder and I licked it away. "Mmm, tastes good. But not as good as you."

"You so crazy." She laughed, turning her head to kiss my lips. "How was your game?"

"It was okay." I picked up a piece of garlic bread from the counter and took a bite. "I just wish Jay had come with us instead of using the game as an excuse to see some girl."

"You know Jay is not gonna change, Kyle, so stop thinkin' about it."

"Yeah, you're right. It's just that he's getting too old for this shit." Val peeked in the living room at Allen, who had settled in front of the TV.

"Where's Wil? I thought he was having dinner with us," Val asked.

"Wil had to leave the game in the second inning."

"How come? Is everything all right?"

"I'm not sure. It had something to do with his wife Diane. I should try an' call him now." I took a step toward the phone.

"Oh, no you don't." Val turned and held on to me. "You're not going anywhere 'til I get another kiss."

"Do I look like I have a problem with that?" Before I could kiss her, there was a knock on the door. "Yo, Al, will you get that for me? I'm kinda busy." I kissed Val without waiting for an answer. After a few minutes pressed against Val in the kitchen, we headed into the living room to see the back of Wil's unmistakable bald head. He was sitting across from Allen on the sofa.

"Hey, big man, you're right on time to eat. Val's making pasta and the sauce is the bomb. Wil, you hungry?" He didn't answer me. That was a definite indicator of a problem. Wil wasn't the kinda guy to ignore you when you were offering to feed him.

"Hey, Val, why don't you go in the bedroom for a minute?" I gave her a peck on the lips and gestured for her to give us a little privacy. She was not a happy camper at all, but reluctantly did as I asked.

"Hey, Wil, everything aw'ight at home?" I was standing in front of him now. He looked like he was about to cry so I asked him again. "Wil? You aw'ight, man?"

"No, I'm not all right! But everything's gonna be just fine once Jay gets here and I can kick his fuckin' ass. He's still coming over here, isn't he?"

"Yeah, he's coming over." I took a step back and turned to Allen. By Wil's tone, both of us knew he was serious. Hell, I'd known him thirty years, and although he was known for his sudden outbursts, I'd never seen him this upset. Whatever Jay had done must have been pretty damn serious.

"What'd Jay do now?" I sat down next to Wil and couldn't believe what I was seeing. He was actually crying. I don't think I'd ever seen him cry. I snapped my fingers at Allen to hand me the box of tissues on the end table. "Here, big man." I handed him a tissue and he wiped his eyes.

"What's the matter, Wil? What'd Jay do to you?" Allen leaned closer for a response. Wil sniffled a few times then wiped his eyes again before speaking.

"That sneaky son of a bitch set me up. Can you believe it? I don't know why, but he's trying to ruin my marriage." Wil slammed his hand on the coffee table so hard I could hear the wood crack. "I don't fucking believe this! I swear ta god, I'm gonna kill that son of a bitch. I'm gonna kill 'im!"

"Hold on there, big man. First of all, let's put this talk about killing people to rest. You ain't gonna kill nobody. At least not while I'm around you ain't."

"You got that right," Allen added. "I don't plan on going to no funerals and I'm damn sure not visiting anybody in jail."

"Now where in the hell did you come up with the idea that Jay is setting you up? I know you two haven't been getting along but you know he wouldn't do that kinda shit."

Wil rolled his eyes. "What makes you so sure of that, Kyle?"

" 'Cause he ain't that type a guy. That's why. He's an in-your-face kinda guy. Not sneaky."

"Please, Kyle," Wil laughed cynically. "You ain't saying that shit when he set your ass up with that condom and panties a few years back, did you?" He stared at me and waited for an answer, but he knew I didn't have one. "Uh-huh. I guess you forgot about that, didn't you?"

"Yeah, I did forget that. But just because he set me up doesn't mean he was tryin' to set you up."

"Oh, yeah. Then why did he give these to my wife?" He reached into his pocket and handed Allen and me each a picture.

"Oh shit," I muttered under my breath as the seriousness of what was on that picture hit me. I looked toward Allen with disbelief. He lifted his picture for me to see, and his expression matched mine.

It had been almost eight weeks and I'd completely forgotten about the pictures we'd taken at the bachelor party. How the hell did Diane get ahold of them anyway? Damn, maybe Wil was right. Maybe Jay did set him up after all. Fuck, maybe he set us all up. A well-placed phone call could have easily set this whole thing in motion. *No, Jay wouldn't do that,* I told myself over and over again. He'd tried to talk us out of taking the pictures in the first place. Hell, there were twenty guys in that room. Any one of them could have done this.

"How do you know Jay gave them to Di, Wil? Maybe it was somebody else."

"Please, Kyle."

"Come on, man, at least give the guy the benefit of the doubt until you speak to him." I was grasping at straws, hopeful that by then I could straighten things out with Diane.

"Benefit of the doubt, my ass! He did it, Kyle. Who else would do something like this to me?" Wil's eyes never left my face. "Who?"

He'd stopped crying now and his tear-streaked face hardened with anger as he waited for my answer. As much as I wanted to tell him the truth, I couldn't. I was too afraid of how he might react. He wasn't yelling and screaming as I woulda expected. He was simmering like a covered pot, ready to explode, and I did not want him exploding on me.

"Answer me, Kyle. Who else would do something like this?"

"I don't know, Wil." I shrugged my shoulders and tried my best not to look him in the face as I lied.

"All right, then, Jay did it. I know he did," Wil replied with finality. "And when I get through with him, he won't be able to go home either. If he wants to play the I-wanna-mess-up-your-marriage game, then so can I. Now excuse me, I got business to attend to." Wil stood up, picked up a magazine from the coffee table, and stomped his way to the bathroom.

As soon as he closed the bathroom door, Allen was in my face whispering with attitude. "What the hell was that all about? You know sooner or latter he's gonna find out the truth."

"Look, what the fuck do you want from me? He caught me off guard when he showed me them damn pictures. I was trying to buy us some time. Do you want him taking his anger out on us?" I whispered back.

"You shoulda told him the truth, Kyle."

"Hey, I didn't see you jump up to declare your guilt in this. So get out of my face, okay?" Allen slumped down in his chair like a disciplined child. I didn't mean to be so nasty, but he was getting on my nerves. Hell, he was just as guilty as me. "Look, Al, if we can keep Jay away from Wil, I'm sure I can talk some sense into Diane. She ain't gonna like it, but at least she'll know that Wil ain't have anything to do with it."

"I hope so, man, 'cause Wil doesn't deserve this."

"I know, Al. I know. I just wish I knew how the hell she got those pictures in the first place. I sure as hell never meant for this to happen." Someone knocked on the door and Val walked out of the bedroom.

"I'll get it." I think she was sick of being cooped up in that room.

"No, Val, I'll get it." I had a feeling it was Jay anyway. "Why don't you go check on dinner?" She was fine with that as long as I didn't ask her to go back to the bedroom.

I looked out the peephole. It was Jay, just as I had suspected. I turned to make sure Wil was still in the john and slipped out the door. I wasn't ready to tell him the truth, but I still didn't want Jay walking into a fight on account of a lie I told.

"Yo, bro, we got a problem." I stepped into the hallway and closed the door behind me.

"What's up?" he asked.

"Diane found the pictures from the bachelor party." I studied his face to see his reaction. From his bug-eyed expression, I knew Wil was wrong about his involvement.

"Ain't this a mothafucker. I told y'all not to do that shit." He shook his head.

"Yeah, I know, but it's done now. Ain't shit we can do but deal with it."

"Damn, I feel for that brother." Jay shook his head. "So what happened? Did she kick him out or what?"

"I think so. At least that's the impression I got."

"Damn, I know he's ready to kick your ass. And I can't say I blame him either. Y'all mighta ruined that man's life with this bullshit." Jay sighed as he leaned against the hallway wall. "Boy, you couldn't pay me to be in your shoes right now."

I swallowed hard and took a deep breath.

"Yeah, well, I don't know if I'd wanna be in your shoes right now, either."

"What's that supposed to mean?" He cut his eyes at me.

"Wil thinks you're the one who took the pictures."

"What?" He took a step closer. "How the hell did he get that impression?" I eased back a step just in case he flew off the handle. His neck muscles were popping out like he was a mad man. In our twenty-plus-year friendship I'd never once felt threatened by him. Until this moment.

"I don't know. He just assumed it," I answered weakly.

"What you mean he assumed it? Why didn't you straighten him out, Kyle?"

"I was going to but—" He cut me off.

"But what? You were trying to save your own ass. I'm not taking the fall for this, Kyle. I'm not the one who fucked up this—" He never finished his sentence 'cause the door opened behind me.

"I thought I heard your fuckin' voice!" Wil pushed his way past me. "Why'd you do it, Jay?"

"I ain't do nothin', Wil. Ask Kyle." Jay glared in my direction.

"Wil, chill, man." I tried to grab him but he threw me to the floor like I was a rag doll. By the time I realized what was up, he had Jay pinned up against the wall with his forearm pressed against his throat.

"Wil, I didn't . . . have anything . . . to do with it . . . I swear." Jay insisted between gasps. Both his hands were locked around Wil's forearm trying to loosen the big man's grip.

"You fucking liar. You think those pictures were funny, don't you?" Wil's voice sounded demonic as he applied more pressure and weight to his forearm. "Why'd you do it, Jay? Why'd you do it?"

"I didn't do it . . . I swear." Jay gasped. It was obviously getting harder and harder for him to breath. "Kyle . . . help me, man!" His eyes were pleading with me.

"What the hell is going on out here?" Allen burst out of the apartment. "Aww, shit!" He dashed behind Wil in an attempt to stop him but Wil had too much adrenaline flowing by now. He threw Allen to the floor with his free hand. I finally managed to struggle to my feet and grab hold of the arm Wil was using to choke Jay.

"Let go of him, Wil! You're gonna kill him!" I pleaded frantically as

I fought to pry his arm from Jay's neck. "You're gonna kill him!" At this point I was scared to death that he really might kill him.

"Good, he needs to die!" Wil yelled as sweat rolled down his bald head. He was so out of control I could feel his anger.

"Wil, dammit! Let him go! He didn't do it!" My frantic tone made him turn his head. As our eyes met, I pleaded with him. "Let him go, Wil. Please let him go. He didn't do it. He didn't do it." I hesitated for a second. "I did." I lowered my head in shame.

"What did you say?" Wil immediately let go of Jay, who fell against the wall gasping for air. "I hope you said that just to save his sorry ass." Wil turned to face me.

"I wish I had." I couldn't look him in the face. I expected him to grab me, to hit me at least, but he didn't. He just stared at me for a few seconds before speaking in a wounded voice.

"Of all my friends, you were the one I thought I could always trust, Kyle. Why would you ruin my marriage?" Wil didn't have that look of uncontrollable anger like he had just a few seconds before with Jay. Nah, he was still angry, but now he had a look of despair. Like I'd ripped his heart out. He'd expected this type of thing from Jay, I suppose. And to be honest, I believe he wanted Jay to be guilty so he could get even with him for that punch in the eye a few months back. But I could tell he never expected something like this out of me.

"I didn't mean for all this to happen when I took those pictures, Wil. Things just got out of hand," I told him meekly. He took a step forward and I took two steps back.

"You damn right things got out of hand. My marriage is over, Kyle, and it's all your fault." He took another step forward, and this time I took three steps back. "My wife's kicked me out the house and I might lose my kids, and it's all your fault."

"It's not all his fault." Allen came to stand next to me. He was scared. I could tell by the way he kept rocking back and forth, but he was being a man about it. "I took a lot of those pictures too, Wil. I'm sorry. It was supposed to be a joke."

"A joke?" Wil shouted as his eyes got wide. "I don't see a damn thing funny." Wil took another step forward and Allen and I eased back a step.

"Neither do we," I pleaded, praying that he would listen. "Wil, man, I promise I'll fix this. I'll go talk to Diane right now and get this straight."

"You'd better," he threatened. "I still don't understand why you would give her pictures of me like that." He looked as confused as we were about how she managed to get her hands on pictures she was never supposed to see.

"We didn't, Wil. She must have found the film in your camera."

"My camera?" Wil looked even more confused.

"Yeah, why don't we go inside so I can explain what I think went down." A few of my neighbors had peeked out their doors, but luckily no one seemed to have called the cops.

"No, you're going to talk to my wife. Now! I want my family back, Kyle. And I don't feel like talking no more." He pointed toward the elevator.

"We're going. But first I've got to get something off my chest. 'Cause you got some blame in this too, ya know." I wasn't trying to weasel out of doing what's right, but he needed to know how I felt.

"I ain't got shit to do with this," Wil hissed.

"Yes, you do, Wil," Jay said in a raspy voice from the floor. He was rubbing his throat. "If you had minded your own business and stayed outta Kyle's marriage, this woulda never happened in the first place. Shit, if it wasn't for you, we'd probably be over at Kyle's place right now eating steaks and getting ready to take a dip in the pool."

"Oh, so this is my fault?" Wil turned to Jay. "How the hell did I become the villain?"

"Shoot, you act like you don't remember. If you hadn't lied to him about Lisa, he woulda never taken those pictures. You seem to forget you ruined his marriage, too. At least he was only trying to play a joke. You knew what you was doin'." Wil glanced over at me and lowered his head.

"That why you took those pictures?" His eyes were sad when he looked at me.

"Yeah, man," I nodded. "You pissed me off. But I never meant for Diane to see them. I figured you'd get them developed and be embarrassed. Something we could joke on you about. I swear I never wanted Diane to see them."

"How the hell did you take them, anyway?"

"When you passed out at the bachelor party. We took you in the VIP room."

"Damn, it all makes sense now. The pictures, my camera, and Diane flipping out. She must've gotten the film developed. Dammit! Why didn't I take my lazy ass down to the CVS myself and get that film developed?"

"Hey, you mind telling us what you talkin' about?" a confused Jay asked.

"Diane had been on my ass for over a month about getting Allen's wedding pictures developed. I'd taken some really nice shots of Teddy in his ring bearer's tux and she wanted to see 'em bad. I musta been down to CVS a dozen times and kept forgetting to take the film. She probably got impatient and went down there herself."

"It's about time someone made some sense out of this," Jay said sarcastically, still rubbing his throat. "Just wish y'all coulda done it before I showed up."

"For someone who says he had nothing to do with this, you sure are knee deep in it, aren't you?" Wil turned to Jay.

"That's 'cause I was the only one in the room tryin' to stop them from making a fool out of you. If it wasn't for me, it coulda been a lot worse."

"That true?" Wil turned to me.

"Yeah," I nodded. "He did try to talk us out of it. I just wasn't hearing it at the time."

Wil bent down and grabbed Jay's hand, pulling him up. "Thanks."

"What'ya thankin' me for?" Jay gave him a suspicious look.

"For being my boy even though I treated you like shit."

"Yo, it's all good dawg. I'm sorry about that eye jammy I gave you. Come on, y'all. We need to go talk to Diane and get this man's life back in order."

"Hold up, Jay. I think maybe you and Wil should stay here while Allen and I go talk to Di."

"Why can't we come?" Jay whined.

"First of all, Diane can't stand you, Jay," I told him.

"Yeah, I guess you're right about that."

"That's fine for him, but why can't I go? It's my marriage we're trying to fix." Wil waited for an answer with his arms across his chest.

"Look, man. She might not talk to us if you're around. Why don't you stay here and eat? Val just made some slammin' pasta. By the time you finish eating, Al and I should have your shit back in order. With an apology from your wife, okay?"

"Don't worry, dawg. If they can't get her to take you back, I got a plan that can't fail." Jay wrapped his arm around Wil's shoulder with a devilish grin on his face. Wil glanced at me, then at Jay, then back to me. I could see the uneasiness in his eyes.

"Kyle, don't fuck this up. Please, don't fuck this up."

"Hey, don't worry. This is gonna be a piece of cake." I gave him a light jab on the shoulder and headed into the apartment to tell Val I was leaving.

28

Kyle

When we pulled into Wil and Diane's driveway, I couldn't believe the pile of stuff sitting at the curb. Diane had everything from Wil's stereo to his prize golf clubs at the side of the road waiting for the morning trash pickup. It was amazing that the neighbors hadn't carted off half of Wil's things, 'cause laid out there was a gold mine of neat shit. I guess it's true what they say about a woman scorned, 'cause the wrath Diane was trying to rain down on poor Wil was no joke. I turned toward Allen, who was shaking his head in disbelief as he stared at Wil's worldly possessions.

"Did we do this? Did we cause her to do this?" he asked, gesturing to the pile.

"Yeah, I guess we did, Al." I frowned. "I guess we did."

"Kyle, man, she's throwin' all Wil's shit away." Allen turned to me looking so sad you would've thought it was his stuff sitting on that curb. "Do you have any idea how much those golf clubs cost him?"

"Five hundred and eighty-eight dollars. I was there when he bought 'em." I laughed pathetically, remembering how proud he was the day he got them. Damn, I wished I had a cigarette. I was trying to quit, but with all this drama I needed one bad.

"This shit ain't funny, Kyle. It was funny at the time but it ain't funny no more."

"You ain't said nothin' but the truth, Al. I just hope Diane's willing to talk to us, 'cause by the looks of things she pretty much lost her mind." I sighed, reaching over to the glove box to see if I could find a stray cigarette. There were none.

"Hell, yeah. She done lost her mind. Throwing away six-hundred-dollar golf clubs and a brand new stereo. Shit, the least she coulda did was try an' sell 'em."

"Look, why don't you put this stuff in the back of the truck? I'll go talk to Diane alone. Ain't no reason for us both ta get cussed out." Allen didn't object at all. He just opened his door and walked around to open the hatch. It was probably best this way, 'cause Allen usually folded up like a tent whenever the drama got started, and I had a strong suspicion there was about to be a whole lot of drama.

I walked up to the door and rang the bell, still craving a cigarette to calm my nerves. A few seconds later Diane opened the door, looking like a heavier version of the guy from Beetlejuice. Her hair was all over her head, her mascara was smudged, and her eyes were totally bloodshot from crying. She was holding a cigarette, and I wanted to snatch it out of her hand and take a drag. Especially since I knew she didn't smoke.

"Hey, Diane. What's up?" I wanted it to sound like a greeting, but it came out more like an accusation.

"Wil's not here," she said flatly, taking a long drag from the cigarette. This was followed by a cough. "That son of a bitch don't live here no more. He's probably out somewhere with his whores."

"Come on, Di. You know he don't have no woman other than you. This whole thing with the pictures is just one big misunderstanding. You see, he was . . ." She raised her hand and raised her voice.

"Ya know what? I ain't got time for this. And I damn sure ain't got time for you, Kyle." She sucked her teeth as she took another drag of her cigarette, then coughed again. "You're just as bad as Wil. You and Jay probably put him up to this. So I don't wanna hear it, okay." She looked like she was about to cry as she continued. "I woulda done anything in the world for that son of a bitch and he does this shit to me? You motherfucking men ain't shit!"

"Look Di, Wil didn't have anything to do with them pictures. He was drunk and passed out at Allen's bachelor party. He didn't even know the pictures were taken."

"And I'm supposed to believe that?" Diane smirked as she took another drag of the cigarette, then flicked it toward Wil's treasured flowerbeds. "I gotta give y'all credit. You four really stick together, don't you?"

Before I could even reply, she was talking again, shaking her head.

"I can't believe Wil would send you over here with some weak-ass story like that. He must really think I'm stupid. Did he tell you it was his camera I found the film in?" Diane's eyes never left me. "Well, did he?"

I bit my lip and glanced toward the half-smoked cigarette she'd thrown away. For a second I actually thought about picking it up. I sure as hell needed it. Especially since Diane was right. We had been known to cover for one another, and this was definitely one hard-to-believe story. Shit, if I weren't involved, I probably wouldn't have believed it myself.

"Wil didn't have to tell me whose camera they came from, Di. I took the pictures." I think it took a few seconds for what I said to sink in, 'cause it took a while before she replied. But when she did, she was furious.

"Wait a minute. Wait one damn minute! You mean to tell me *you* took those pictures?" I nodded, but couldn't make eye contact. "I don't believe you, Kyle. How the hell could you sit there and watch my husband eat some stinkin' ass whore out and not stop him?" By now tears were rolling down her face. I was already feeling like shit, and the way she looked at me with those tears coming down made me feel even worse.

"I'm not proud of it, Di, but yeah, I took the pictures. I'm tellin' you Wil didn't know it." Diane's eyes got real small and I could see her entire body tense up. I stood back and waited for her to explode.

"You motherfucker! Get the fuck off my property! I'ma make you pay for this shit, Kyle Richmond. I swear to God I'ma make you pay big time!"

"Hold up, Di. Let me explain." I raised both my hands defensively.

"I ain't lettin' you explain shit. Get the fuck outta here and don't come back! And tell that motherfucker Wil I don't ever wanna see his black ass again." She tried to slam the door in my face but I stuck my foot out and stopped her.

"Diane, don't do this. Wil didn't do anything."

"Don't do this! Don't do this? I didn't do shit, Kyle. It was you and Wil who was wrong when you fucked them girls. And don't give me this shit about he passed out, 'cause I don't believe a word you're sayin'. I've seen the pictures. Pictures don't lie." She started crying again.

"Diane, I swear to you Wil didn't have nothing to do with this."

"Yeah, right." She tried to shut the door again, but I wasn't moving my foot until she listened to me. I gritted my teeth as she leaned on the door. It felt like she was crushing every one of my toes, but I couldn't let her shut me out. It was the only chance Wil had at this point. "If you don't get your foot out this door, Kyle, so help me . . ."

"I'm not gonna let you close this door until you let me fully explain. Wil ain't had nothin' to do with this!" Diane stopped pressing on the door and looked past me.

"Is that Allen out there?" I didn't answer, so she took another look. "That is Allen. Does he know you was fucking Rose the night before his wedding, Kyle?" Her voice was like ice and she threw daggers at me with her eyes. I'd completely blocked that night out of my mind until now, mainly 'cause I'd seen Di quite a few times since the incident and she acted as if everything was cool. Now that I think about it, Wil musta made her promise to keep her mouth shut. But this time was different. She was on the warpath, and I was sure she wouldn't hesitate to blow my cool.

"Look, Diane, you're making a big mistake here. We don't need to bring that up."

"No, Kyle, you're the one making a big mistake if you don't get your foot out my damn door." She started yelling, " Hey, Allen!" Then she smirked at me.

"Diane don't do this, Wil loves you and the kids."

"Kyle, I'm not gonna say this again. Get your foot out my door."

"Di—"

"Allen," she called out even louder. Fortunately he was too engrossed in his recovery mission, loading Wil's belongings into the car. But it was still enough to make my heart start pounding. In the midst of all of this drama, all I needed was for her to give Allen some false information about my night in Rose's room.

"Okay, okay," I said as I pulled my aching foot out of the door.

"You ain't shit, Kyle Richmond." She gave me the finger as she closed the door.

Val gently grabbed my waist and pulled me into the bedroom, kissing me tenderly after Jay and Allen walked out the door. I think she felt sorry for me after Wil cussed me then stormed out of the apartment like he was a madman. I really wasn't in the mood to make love but I went through the motions with her hoping she'd find a way to change my mind. I guess my lack of enthusiasm was apparent because in the middle of our lovemaking she stopped.

"You love her, don't you?" she whispered.

I stopped moving my hips and lifted my head so that we made eye contact. I gave her a confused look, then went back to what I was doing until the comment sank in. That's when I stiffened my body, jerking my head away from her breast.

"What did you say?" I gave her that confused look again.

"I said you still love her, don't you?" This time she didn't whisper and I heard every word clearly. It was exactly what I thought I heard the first time.

"Love who?" I was still looking confused. She rolled her eyes.

"Your wife, that's who. You're still in love with her, aren't you?" She gave me a look that demanded an answer, but I wasn't about to give her one until I knew why she had this sudden interest in my feelings for Lisa. Up until now everything had been "Let's take one day at a time."

"Why, did she call or something?" I searched her face for an answer, but all I could see was hurt. I rolled onto my back and stared at the ceiling. Shit, had Val answered my phone while I was gone and her and Lisa gotten into it? I hope not, 'cause it had taken a lot of effort to keep the two of them from bumping into each other the past few months. Plus Val and I had this unwritten rule that we wouldn't answer each other's phones. Not that we didn't trust each other, but her ex-,Terrance, still called, trying get back together and he was one psycho brother. And Val knew Lisa called me whenever something came up with the girls. It just seemed like the best way to avoid stress that we keep off each other's phones.

"No, she didn't call. But I heard you scream at Wil that if it wasn't for him you'd both still be with your wives now." I'd forgotten that she was in the apartment and probably heard every word of the fight Wil and I had when I got back from Diane's. At the time I really didn't appreciate the way Wil was disrespecting me, so I lashed out at him to put him in his place. I wasn't ashamed of what I said because it was the truth, but I damn sure hadn't meant for Val to hear it. The last thing I wanted to do was hurt her. Hell, sometimes I thought I'm falling in love with her.

"Val, I said that because of something that happened a long time ago. It has nothing to do with me and you."

"Oh, yeah? How long ago?" she asked, sitting up and smirking at me like she expected a lie.

"Before you, okay?" I tried to kiss her, but she turned her head.

"You never answered my question, Kyle."

"What question?"

"Do you still love her?" What did she expect me to do, tell her the truth? Of course I still loved Lisa, but I wasn't about to tell her that.

"No, Val, I don't love her," I lied. I think that satisfied her. At least I hoped it did.

"I'm sorry if I sound like I'm tripping, but I care about you and I don't wanna get hurt." Her voice was soft now, almost apologetic.

"Val, the last thing in the world I wanna do is hurt you."

"I hope not, Kyle, 'cause you do not wanna see the bitch in me come out."

29

Wil

My routine hadn't changed since Diane had kicked me out. I'd leave work, go to Carmicheal's Diner on Guy R. Brewer Boulevard for dinner, then ride over to the Roadhouse Bar to drown away my sorrows before carrying my sorry ass over to the Jet Motel to sleep. Not that I was getting much sleep these days. Without fail I'd wake up around 2 A.M. and wouldn't be able to fall back to sleep. For the most part I'd just stare at the ceiling and feel sorry for myself until the clock radio went off around seven-thirty. That's when I'd drag myself into the bathroom to wash up. That ritual was always followed by a call to what used to be my home. A few rings later Diane would answer the phone with a nasty attitude.

"What the fuck do you want, Wil?" she'd ask without hesitation. She wouldn't even bother to ask if it was me first.

"I wanna come home, Di." My plea was the same each morning.

She'd laugh and say something like, "Hell no, motherfucker! What's wrong, your whores ain't washing your dirty drawers?"

So I would plead some more before she'd finally say, "Look, I'm busy," and put my son Teddy on the phone. I'd talk to my little man for a few minutes until he'd start asking when I was coming home. For me there was nothing more painful than not being able to give him a straight answer, so most of the time I'd just say goodbye. My life was so depressing that I'd even go into work on Saturday and Sunday just to keep myself from thinking about Diane. Half the time I didn't even remember to sign the time sheet, so I wasn't getting paid for the extra work.

Yep, that was my routine for the last two weeks and it was pretty damn depressing. So you can imagine how happy I was when I received Diane's e-mail at work this morning inviting me over to the house for dinner. Finally things looked like they were gonna change, and with any luck I was gonna get my life and my family back.

I showed up at the house around five o'clock, my arms filled with a dozen roses, a gold ankle bracelet Diane had been asking for, and a bottle of her favorite wine to go with dinner. She'd always made my favorite seafood gumbo on our anniversary so I couldn't wait to get a whiff of that Cajun aroma when she opened the door. Other than seeing Diane and my kids, that gumbo was all I could think about all day. But my dream of sitting down with my family and eating gumbo was far from reality, 'cause when Diane opened that door, there was no aroma from the kitchen and no sign of my kids. I'd been expecting Teddy to run around the corner and into my arms any second. But nope, nothin'. Just Diane, and she wasn't even dressed for dinner. She was just standing there in her beat-up old housecoat with some big-ass rollers in her hair like she was about to go to bed.

"What the hell is all this shit for?" She pointed to all my gifts with contempt all over her face.

"These are for you, and this is to go with dinner." I held up the roses and jewelry box with one hand, and the wine with the other. "Happy anniversary, Di." I smiled, hoping to lighten the mood.

"Please, ain't shit happy about it." She rolled her eyes and took the jewelry box out of my hand. She turned and walked into the house without even a thank-you. I guess I should've been grateful that she left the door open for me and I was, but it would have been nice to have been invited in. As I followed her into the house, I was hoping she'd open the jewelry box, but she just slipped it into the pocket of her robe and walked into the living room. She sat on the sofa, and I sat down in a chair across from her, placing the flowers and wine on the table.

"Now what's this shit about dinner? I didn't say I was going to dinner with you." She twisted her lips as she sucked her teeth.

"What do you mean?" I frowned. I couldn't believe she was acting like this. "Why you playin' games, Di? You know you invited me to dinner."

"Y'know what, Wil? I think all them damn whores you been fuckin' with done warped your brain, cause the only thing I invited you over here for was to talk about getting a divorce."

"What?" I sat back in my chair. "You mean to tell me you didn't send me an e-mail inviting me to dinner?"

"Oh yeah, I sent you an e-mail. But it damn sure wasn't no invitation to dinner. All I asked you to do was come over here around dinner time so we could get some things straight. I didn't say nothin' about *having* dinner." She laughed. "Please. I wouldn't cook you another meal if you was the last man on earth."

Diane smirked, which really irked me, 'cause that's when I knew she was playin' games. She knew exactly what she was doing. She'd worded that e-mail the way she did to lure me over to the house so she could spring this divorce crap on me. It was something she'd tried to talk to me about on the phone, but I had refused to discuss it. Just like I wasn't gonna discuss it now. So I changed the subject.

"Okay, where are the kids? I've got some toys in the car for them."

"The kids are at Lisa's." She smirked again.

"You know what, Diane? You're getting really petty. You knew I was coming over here. The least you could've done was make sure my kids were here. I haven't seen them in two weeks. After the shit you just pulled, you owe me that much."

"After the shit I just pulled? Don't go there, Wil." She was truly angry. "Don't you dare go there or you won't see those kids at all."

Well, there it was. Diane was taking things to another level, threatening me with my kids. Why the hell do women do that? I looked up at her and stood without another word. If I stuck around, I was sure things would get ugly, so I decided to get out fast. I figured if the kids were at Lisa's, I'd stop by there.

"Where you goin'? Just cause we ain't havin' dinner don't mean we ain't got things to talk about," she shouted from behind me.

"What'd we have to talk about Di, divorce?" I shook my head. "I don't think so. You're my wife and you're always gonna be my wife. I told you a long time ago I didn't get married to get divorced. I can understand you not wanting to believe what I told you about those pictures. Hell, when I look at those pictures, I don't wanna believe me either. But I've told you a hundred times that I'm innocent. I did not have anything to do with it. I'm gonna give you some time and space for a while. To be honest, I think we probably both need it. But believe me when I tell you, we are gonna get back together. It's just gonna take some time and hard work, but it's gonna happen. So all this talk about divorce is just that, all talk. 'Cause I love you too much to let you go." Diane stared at me silently for a few seconds and I thought my words had actually touched her. But if they had, it was only momentarily.

"Good speech, Wil." She clapped weakly. "But you coulda saved that for the judge. It might get your child support and alimony lowered, but I don't believe a word of it."

Diane's words made me snap. I was sick of her calling me a liar, I was sick of her not letting me see my kids, and I was sick of staying in that damn Jet Motel. But more than any of that, I was sick of her telling me she was gonna take me to court. I ran up to her, squeezed her shoulders tightly, and shook her.

"Look, let's get one thing straight. I don't need no white man's court telling me how to take care of my family, okay? If you or the kids need something, you come to me. You don't go to no damn judge. I'm a man, and I take care of my family because it's the right thing to do.

Do you understand me, Di?" I think I scared her, because for once she didn't have something smart to say. She just nodded. That is, until I let go of her and she could put a few feet between us. Then she went off on me.

"Ohhh, so you a man, huh? Well, a man doesn't put his hands on a woman!" she glared at me in a huff.

"I'm sorry," I told her, still angry myself, "but you know I'm gonna take care of my family. I don't need no damn judge to tell me how to do that."

"You gonna take care of your family? Ha!" she laughed. "You can't take care of yourself with your wrinkled-up pants. Have you ever heard of an iron?" I ignored her jabs.

"That's right. I'm gonna take care of my family. Now you gonna tell me the courts are gonna award you the whole mortgage? Con-Edison? And your car note? Plus give you a hundred dollars a week? I don't think so." I tried my best to calm myself. I could feel my blood pressure rising by the second.

Diane stared at me, probably a little surprised that I was willing to do that much. Shit, I wasn't really sure if I could pay that much and still rent a room without being totally broke, but I meant what I said about taking care of my family.

"You mean that, Wil? You're willing to pay all those bills?" I couldn't tell if it was disbelief or admiration in her voice.

"Yeah, I mean it. I might have to ask Kyle for a part-time job to live on, but I don't want no judge telling me what to do for my own kids or my wife."

Finally, she softened. "Okay, we won't go to court."

I tried to hide a smile as I sighed with relief. Finally things were starting to go my way. Once I started coming around to see the kids, things between Diane and me would slowly but surely work themselves out. Unfortunately Diane must have sensed my hopefulness because it didn't take long for the attitude to reemerge and for her to throw another dagger.

"Let me tell you something, motherfucker. This don't mean I still don't want a divorce!"

"Well, I guess I'm just gonna have to change your mind," I told her. Diane rolled her eyes and sucked her teeth.

"Oh, and another thing—I want two hundred and fifty dollars, not a hundred."

"Di, be reasonable. I'm gonna have to move in with my mother if I give you a grand a month with all those other bills I'm gonna be paying."

"Hey, I am being reasonable, I'm not taking you to court. Isn't that what you want? Besides I've gotta pay child care now that you're gone."

"Hold up. You always paid for child care out of your money before."

"That was then, this is now. You think I'm gonna leave you enough money to take out your whores?"

"Di, this ain't fair. You know this ain't fair." I was getting angry again.

"You wanna see your kids, don't you?" Her face was dead serious.

"Come on, Diane, be reasonable. This is blackmail. What does that money have to do with me seeing my kids? I can't believe you'd keep them from me."

"I keep tellin' you, I am being reasonable. Lisa gets four thousand dollars a month plus living expenses from Kyle. I'm just asking for a quarter of that."

"Who told you that? Kyle's not giving Lisa that much money."

"Ya wanna bet?" Diane handed me a stack of stapled papers from the coffee table.

"What's this?"

"That's a copy of your boy Kyle's settlement agreement with Lisa. She gave it to me so I could see how good her lawyer was." I looked down at the paper and my eyes almost popped out of my head. I never dreamed Kyle could afford to give Lisa so much. If this lawyer could do this to him, what the hell was he gonna do to me? I decided maybe I could afford another fifty dollars a week when Diane said, "She's probably gonna get more once the divorce is final."

"Y'know what, Di? I'll give you one hundred-fifty a week but I wanna see my kids every weekend. How about that?"

"Nah, every other weekend. But I'll let you take them to church with me some Sundays."

"Okay, it's a deal." I still didn't know how I would be able to afford it, but I could tell she was serious about keeping the kids away. I stuck out my hand to shake hers, but she never reciprocated.

"I want it written out and notarized when you pick up the kids for church tomorrow. I also want it to say I have full custody."

"Okay." I wasn't concerned about who had custody. We'd done enough bargaining for the moment. I could talk to her about that issue another time, before any official papers were actually drawn up. This arrangement was only going to be temporary anyway. I planned on being home for good within a few weeks.

"Wil, you miss one payment and we're going to court. I mean that." She folded her arms across her chest.

"I'm not gonna miss a payment Di. You'll see." I walked to the door. "You sure you don't wanna have dinner? I'll take you to City Island."

She thought about it for a second and actually answered in a civil tone. "No, Wil." I think she wanted to go, but it was going to take a little more time.

"Okay, good night."

"Good night, Wil."

30

Jay

"Jay? You awake, baby?" Kenya whispered softly as her hand slid around my waist. She tried to be nonchalant, but the way she was rubbing up against my crotch I knew right away that she wanted some. I opened one eye and glanced at the digital clock on the night table. It was a little past 3 A.M. on a Saturday night, but that didn't seem to matter to Kenya. By the way she was tugging on me, it was obvious she didn't have sleep on her agenda. She'd been squirming up next to me for the past half-hour, thinking she could gradually wake me up. Little did she know I was awake the whole time. I just wasn't in the mood to have sex. But damn, she was determined to get me in the mood. It's amazing how people change. A year ago she'd run anytime I mentioned sex, but now that she'd had LaShawn, she'd become quite the sex addict. It kinda made me wonder if she somehow sensed that I'd found someone else.

"Jay, you awake, baby?" she whispered again. I didn't answer. But when she let go of my now erect penis and slid her panties off, I knew my charade couldn't last much longer. Whenever she acted like this, Kenya was the most determined little vixen. She was gonna get some no matter what. And as much as my penis was telling me to give it to her, I just couldn't. In less than seven hours I was supposed to meet Tracy. We were going to head over to the Beach Comber Motel again for a nice romantic day on the beach, which I was sure would end up as a wild night of passionate lovemaking. I needed to rest up for my day with Tracy, and Kenya was messin' me up, crawlin' all over me at three in the morning.

As soon as Kenya's panties were off, her hand slid right back to my crotch. This time she tugged on it so hard I would've had to wake up. "Stop, I'm trying to get some sleep," I grumbled, trying my best to pretend I was half-asleep. I swatted her hand from my penis as if she were a nuisance.

"Come on, Jay. All I want is a quickie." She reached for my manhood again.

"I'll give you some in the morning," I told her in a groggy voice. I knew that my daughter Tiffany would be up way before I'd ever have to make good on that promise. I took hold of her hand, removed it from my lap, and rolled onto my stomach so that she couldn't get ahold of it again. I knew I was gonna have to give in sooner or later, but not tonight if I had any say in the matter. I'd been holding out on her ever since Tracy came back into my life, and that was almost two months ago.

"I can't wait till the morning. I want some now," she whined in frustration. Kenya released a long, aggravated sigh, then tried to reach under my stomach to get to her intended target. When she realized I wasn't gonna budge, she got out of bed and left the room. For a second I thought I heard her on the phone but I quickly dismissed it. Who could she possibly be on the phone with at three in the morning? She must have been talking to the baby. I didn't care. I was just glad I had managed to escape for another night.

I woke up the next morning to the sounds of both my kids' loud voices. My daughter Tiffany was singing "Humpty Dumpty" as she jumped on my bed. My other daughter, four-month-old LaShawn, was howling at the top of her lungs, probably wanting a bottle or a diaper change. I pulled the covers over my head in a vain attempt to ignore them, but it was useless.

"Kenya!" I yelled. "Get the kids!"

When I didn't get any response, I shot my arm from under the covers and playfully pulled Tiffany down to the bed. "Tiffany, do Daddy a favor and go play in your room."

"Okay, Daddy." She jumped off the bed. A few seconds later LaShawn was quiet. Just when I started to relax again, I heard the tap-tap of my wife's shoes approaching the room.

"Jay, get up." There was no warmth in her voice this morning.

"What time is it?" I didn't even budge.

"Seven-thirty. Now get up."

"Seven-thirty? Why you gettin' me up so early?" I poked my head from under the covers. Kenya was all made up, wearing a tight mini-dress, holding LaShawn.

"Where you goin'?"

"Out." She handed me the baby.

"Out where?" Kenya rolled her eyes as if I had no right to ask.

"Out with my girlfriends. And next time I ask you that same question, you better answer it." With that comment I decided to back off a bit.

Kenya walked over to the dresser and put on a pair of earrings.

That's when it dawned on me the kids weren't dressed. "You're not taking the kids?" I sat up in a panic.

"No, I'm not," she turned and smiled.

"B-but I've got somewhere to go."

"So take them with you. That's what I always do. They're your children too, Jay. They need to spend time with their father." She left the room and I followed her downstairs, carrying LaShawn.

"I spend time with them," I protested. It was true. At least it used to be true, until Tracy came back in my life. "Come on, Kenya. I've got something important to do. I can't take them with me."

"Ohhh, well. I guess you're not going." Kenya picked up her keys and pocketbook with a smile as she headed for the door.

"I'll make a deal with you. Why don't you take LaShawn and I'll take Tiffany with me?" I knew Kyle had his kids for the weekend and I was positive he wouldn't mind watching Tiffany. But LaShawn was a different story. Kyle loved her, but he wasn't about to be changing no diapers. He'd made that clear once before.

"No deals, Jay. We're playing a little role reversal today. I'm going out just like you do and you're gonna watch the kids for once." She said it with finality as she took hold of the doorknob.

"When're you coming back?" I jumped up to follow her. God, I did not need this shit today. She was going to ruin all my plans.

"Late," she laughed as if the whole thing were funny to her.

"This is fucked up!" I screamed, which frightened the baby. She started to cry, and Tiffany came running from her room.

Kenya stopped dead in her tracks and turned with an evil glare. "No, you didn't. No, you didn't just say watching your kids was fucked up." Her voice was low and cold.

"I didn't mean it like that."

"Yes, you did." Kenya glanced at Tiffany and ordered, "Go in your room, Tiffany." She didn't have to repeat herself, 'cause Tiffany ran like she'd just seen a ghost. "You know what's fucked up, Jay? What's fucked up is you not making love to me last night. That's what's fucked up."

"Don't start with that shit, Kenya. I can remember a time when I would beg you to give me some. So let's not go there." I could tell that hit a nerve 'cause her eyes got real small like she wanted to smack me.

"Maybe I was afraid I might catch something." She took a step closer.

"What the hell is that supposed to mean?"

"It means I'm not stupid, Jay. I might love you, but I'm not stupid."

She turned and walked out the door, leaving me dumbfounded by her words.

It had taken me half the morning, but by ten o'clock I finally found a baby-sitter for both of my daughters. As I expected, Kyle agreed to watch Tiffany but he immediately passed when it came to watching LaShawn. Man, I musta I called every relative, friend, and ex-girlfriend I ever had trying to find a babysitter for her, but there were no takers. Finally I just decided to take her with me. I wasn't happy about the idea, especially since it would put a stop to my plans to make love to Tracy all afternoon. But spending time with her was what really mattered, and if the only way to do that was to take LaShawn along for the ride, then I would do what I had to.

Thank God, out of nowhere Ma Jackson called the house looking for Allen. I could tell she was lonely and was really just fishing to find out if I'd heard from Allen and Rose, who had taken a little trip to Niagara Falls for the holiday weekend. They made everyone promise not to tell her where they went. After a few minutes of playing along with her weakly concealed interrogation, I decided to ask if she'd watch LaShawn. I fully expected her to say no, but to my surprise she jumped at the chance. She said it would be good practice for her with her new grandbaby on the way. She didn't have to say it twice, 'cause I had those kids bathed, dressed, and in the car in no time flat. A half hour later I'd dropped off both kids and was headed for Tracy's dorm at CW Post University in Long Island.

It didn't take long to get to the university, and after signing in at the front desk of Tracy's dorm, I raced up the stairs to her room. I knocked on the door only to be met by a light-skinned brother, probably around my age, with a beer belly and a bad attitude.

"Can I help you?" He folded his arms across his broad chest and stood in the doorway like one of Puff Daddy's bodyguards. I'm not gonna lie. I had a problem with this brother right away. Especially since Tracy seemed to like older men.

"I'm lookin' for Tracy. Is she in?" He looked me up and down. I figured he was sizing me up. For what I don't know, but if it was a fight, all he had to do was bring it.

"Who are you?" he asked me with a scowl.

I wanted to say, "I'm the motherfucker who's about to kick your ass for being in my girl's room." But I tried to stay cool.

"Look, chief, I don't think that's any of your business. Now where's Tracy?"

"I said, who are you?" His eyes got small and he tilted his head. I think he was tryin' to flex his biceps, too, as if that was gonna scare me. This fool was starting to get on my last nerve. I wasn't sure if he was an ex-boyfriend of Tracy's or a wanna-be, but I was gettin' ready to put my foot in his ass until I heard Tracy's voice.

"Daddy, will you let him in?" Tracy pushed him to the side and smiled at me.

"Daddy? Oh, my God. This is your father? I'm so sorry, sir." I tried to sound respectful as all the blood in my body rushed to my face. I'd never been so embarrassed in my life. "Tracy didn't tell me you were coming up." I could feel perspiration beginning to form on my neck and forehead as I apologized again and again. Not to mention the fact that I felt like I was shrinking right in front of him.

"They didn't tell me they were coming either. They just showed up five minutes ago, but don't worry. He's harmless," Tracy assured me with a sweet smile. Her father wrapped his arm around her shoulder and smiled, too. Not a friendly smile, but one of those this-is-my-daughter-and-if-you-*fuck*-with-her-I'll-kill-*you* smiles. I think Tracy sensed my uneasiness. She reached for my hand to pull me inside her room. I could tell by how moist her hands were that beneath her smile she was just as nervous as I was.

"Come on in, Jay. I want you to meet my mom."

I stepped in the room to greet the strikingly beautiful woman sitting on the bed. She was without question a mature version of her daughter. Tall, thin, and sexy with a touch of class. She even wore her hair in the same short, nappy bleached blond hairstyle as Tracy.

"Mom, Dad, this is my boyfriend, Jay. Jay, these are my parents, Jim and Charlotte Williams." Tracy smiled nervously as she held on to my arm, gazing back and forth between me and her parents. I offered her mother my hand with a smile, then put both hands behind my back to discretely slip off my wedding band.

"It's a pleasure to meet you, Jay. Tracy has told me a lot about you." Her mother stood and put a hand on my shoulder. "Jim, come over here and shake this young man's hand."

Tracy's father didn't budge. He just looked at his watch and declared, "I'm hungry, Charlotte."

"Okay, sweetheart, we're gonna go get something to eat right now. You hungry, Jay?" Tracy's mom turned to me.

"Ah, yes, ma'am. I sure am."

"I like him, Tracy. He's real polite. I like a polite young man." Her mother smiled and took my other arm. I wondered how polite she'd think I was if she knew I was around the same age she was. Or that I had a wife and two kids at home. Thank God I didn't show up with LaShawn. I don't even want to imagine how her father would've reacted.

From the dorm we drove five minutes to Greenvale and had brunch at the Country Cooking Restaurant. Tracy's mother was real nice and chitchatted with me through most of our meal. But her father, he was another story. I was sure he didn't like me, and the way he kept staring at me made me so nervous it was impossible to enjoy my meal.

"So Jay, are you in school, too?" Tracy's mom asked with a big smile between bites of her omelet.

"No, I graduated from Howard a few years ago." *Quite a few years ago,* I thought, feeling out of place. I couldn't remember the last time I dated a woman and had to meet her parents. I loved Tracy, but I would have done anything to get out of that damn restaurant.

"How old are you?" Tracy's father didn't even try to conceal his contempt. I looked up from my plate and he was staring me dead in the face with evil eyes. It was clear he wanted to punch me or something. From the look he gave me, I wasn't sure if I should tell him the truth about my age or not. Especially since I wasn't sure what Tracy had told him. Thank goodness she saved me by quickly answering her father for me. I just wish she had given him a more realistic answer.

"Twenty-three! He's twenty-three, Daddy," she smiled at her father.

Now I look young, maybe twenty-seven, twenty-eight. But twenty-three? Now that was stretching it. I'm pretty sure her old man felt the same way 'cause he rolled his eyes at his wife.

"You got a job, Jay?" he barked, continuing his interrogation.

"Yes, sir. I'm a social worker for child protective services." I was hoping that the fact I worked with kids would impress him, but it didn't. He was still just as sarcastic as ever.

"So, you protect the kids from their parents, huh?" He paused then stared at me seriously. "So who protects the kids from you, pervert?"

"Daddy!" Tracy yelled, obviously stunned by his comment. So was I.

"Don't interrupt me when I'm talking, princess." Tracy's father shot her an evil look and she sat back in her chair with a pout. That look on her face was just one more painful reminder that she was, after all, only nineteen, and still subject to her parents' rules.

"Jim! I thought we discussed this on the way up here." Charlotte sounded like it was a struggle to keep a civil tone.

"I know what we discussed, Charlotte. But my daughter is pregnant and I wanna know what this man's gonna do about it." He pointed his finger at me.

"Pregnant?" I turned to Tracy, who turned to her mother.

"Mother, you promised you wouldn't tell Daddy!"

"What was I supposed to do, Tracy? He's my husband. He knows when something's bothering me. I couldn't keep something like this from him."

"I don't care! You promised!" Tracy turned to me and burst into tears. Two seconds later she was running to the rest room. I stood up to follow her, but her mother patted my hand and told me to sit.

"I'll get her. This is something we need to hash out between us. I hope you understand."

I nodded, but I didn't understand shit. My head was still reeling from the news I had just heard. How the hell could Tracy be pregnant? We'd been so careful to use condoms every time. And now Tracy's mother was insisting I stay at the table with her husband, who was probably ready to murder me now that his daughter was in tears. I didn't want to, but I was just gonna have to sit at the table with him and take it like a man until Tracy and her mom returned.

"Hey, you? Look at me." Tracy's father leaned over the table. He'd been staring at me for over five minutes without a word before breaking our silence. "Give me one good reason why I shouldn't go out to my car, get my gun, and blow your fucking brains out."

"Look, Mr. Williams, I know you're probably upset right now. I don't blame you. But I'm a man, so don't threaten me like I'm some kid." I know I sounded like a smartass, but I was getting tired of this guy's attitude.

"Ohhh, so you feel like a man now that you knocked my daughter up, huh?"

"No, Mr. Williams, that's not how I feel at all. I didn't even know Tracy was pregnant until you said it."

"Yeah, well, you know she's pregnant now, so what you gonna do about it?" He sat back in his chair and folded his arms.

"What do you mean what am I gonna do?"

"Are you gonna marry her or what?" His eyes never left mine and I'm sure he wasn't going to move until I gave him an answer.

I stared at him, trying to figure out what he wanted from me. He couldn't really want me to marry his daughter, could he? I loved Tracy. There was no question about that. Hell, I'd leave Kenya in a New York minute if that's what she wanted, but marriage? I wasn't sure about that one. I'd already married one woman because she was pregnant. I wasn't about to make the same mistake twice.

"What's wrong?" her father pressed. "It's not that hard. It's just a straight-up yes-or-no question. Are you going to marry my daughter? That's not too hard for you to answer, is it?"

He was right. It would have been a simple yes-or-no question had I been younger and single. But for me it was more complicated than doing brain surgery. I didn't give a damn who he was. I wasn't gonna answer a question like that without giving it a lot of thought.

"I don't think I can make that decision until I talk to Tracy, Mr. Williams. I'm not even sure she wants to get married." He smirked, then laughed.

"You're full o' shit, you know that, nigger?" My eyes went wide as I sat back in my chair. He continued. "You think I don't know what you're up to? With your pretty boy looks and your fancy truck. Yeah, you got my wife fooled. And Tracy, she's just a kid. She can't see past your good looks and charm. But me, I know what you're up to. 'Cause I used to be you, motherfucker. I used to be just like you."

"Mr. Williams, I don't know what you're talking about."

He laughed again, "You know exactly what I'm talking about. And don't call me Mr. Williams like you have some respect for my age. You're damn near as old as I am." He sat back in his chair and glared at me while I tried to figure out how the hell he knew how old I was. "I'm not gonna let you dog my daughter. Do you understand me? I'm not gonna let you dog her. I'll spend the rest of my life in prison for murder before I let that happen." He was dead serious, and about to continue his threats when I interrupted.

"Look, Mr. Williams . . . I mean Jim. I love Tracy and I wouldn't do anything to hurt her. I swear to God." He laughed again.

"You know what? I really don't give a shit if you love her or not. You fucked my daughter and now you're gonna take care of her and her baby. You got that?" I didn't reply. I figured it was best to let him think he was making the rules. If Tracy was really pregnant with my kid, I'd do whatever it took to take care of her anyway. He reached in his pocket and slammed a badge on the table. "Did Tracy tell you what I do for a living?"

I shook my head.

"I'm a detective for the DC police department." He leaned in closer. "A very well connected detective, I might add. I have quite a few friends on the NYPD and Nassau County Police Department. You fuck over my daughter and I'll find you. I promise you that. Matter of fact, I'll have your address from your license plate before the evening is over." I swallowed hard. In the fifteen minutes we had been sitting there, this was the first time he said anything that actually put fear in my heart. That's all I needed was for some of his cop buddies to knock on my door and have a little chat with Kenya. You can imagine how relieved I was when Tracy's mother returned to the table. I couldn't take much more of this man.

"Is Tracy okay?" I asked her as she sat down.

"Yeah, she's okay. She's just embarrassed. Tracy wanted to tell you about the baby herself." She shot her husband an evil glance, then patted my hand. "Go talk to her, Jay. She's out by your truck."

When I stood up to walk outside, Tracy's father reached across the table and grabbed hold of my wrist. I tried to pull away, but his grip was a lot stronger than I expected. Staring me in the eyes, he stood and whispered, "You better be prepared to take care of my daughter."

"I'm gonna take care of her. I swear to you," I whispered back, finally able to pull away and walk toward the door. I took a deep breath, trying to gather my composure. My nerves were shot and I hadn't even talked to Tracy about her being pregnant. I spotted her sitting on the hood smoking a cigarette.

"You okay?" I climbed up on the hood next to her.

"No." She turned toward me, her eyes bloodshot and her face lifeless.

"You know you shouldn't be smoking this if you're pregnant," I told her as I removed the cigarette from her fingers and threw it to the ground.

"Yeah," she nodded, her eyes filling with tears. I wanted to ask her if the baby was mine, but that always seemed to be the question that got brothers into trouble.

I wrapped my arm around her and pulled her in close. "How far along are you?"

"I'm five and a half months, but I swear I didn't miss my period until two weeks ago. I haven't even gained five pounds."

"Well, I guess that explains a few things."

"Like what?"

"I couldn't figure out how you got pregnant when we were so careful to use condoms. But now I know it must have happened that night at my house."

"It did," she nodded, looking sadder.

"Damn, what was I thinking about? I knew we should've used condoms."

"It's not your fault. I wanted to feel you inside of me. I'm the one who wasn't thinking. I'm sorry, Jay."

"I can't blame this on you. It's just as much my fault."

"What are we gonna do? I'm too far along for an abortion."

"We handle our business. You wanna get married?" I asked more out of respect than anything else.

"No." she shook her head. "I know how you feel about marriage. Plus you'd have to get divorced. I'm not gonna put you through that. All I want is for you to be there for me and the baby. I'm not trying to trap you, Jay."

"I know that, Tracy. That's why I want you to know that I'm not going anywhere. I love you too much for that." I smiled at her as I wrapped my arms around her. I had no idea what the future would hold for us, but somehow I would make it work. I was gonna have to get the money to get Tracy an apartment. She was the woman I wanted to spend the rest of my life with and that meant I was gonna have to ask Kyle for a loan. I just hated that I was gonna have to lie to him to get it.

31

Kyle

I'd heard stories about things like this happening, but the way life had been going, I never dreamed that Lisa and I would be tonguing each other down only days before we were due in court to finalize our divorce. I know. You're confused, right? Well, you're not half as confused as I was when Lisa pushed me against a wall and parted my lips with her tongue. I was still savoring the taste of her spearmint gum when she kissed me again, this time sliding her hand between my legs.

"Well, well, well, what do we have here?" she whispered, grabbing hold of my fully erect penis. "It's been a long time since I've seen you like this." She kissed me again.

We both jumped back a step when my youngest daughter Willow busted us with a shout. "*Ooooo!* Mommy and daddy are kissin'."

My oldest daughter Jewel ran into the bedroom with a huge smile, but frowned when she saw that we weren't as close as her sister had claimed.

"They're not kissing, Willow." Jewel gave her sister a withering look, probably mad that she had wasted her time. "They can't kiss. They're getting a divorce." Then she stomped back into the living room to watch TV.

"Yes, they were kissing!" Willow looked up at us, waiting for us to back her up. When neither one of us said a word, she followed behind her sister, looking confused.

"So what brought that on?" I was a little confused about that kiss myself.

"I don't know. I just wanted to thank you for taking me and the girls out today." She smiled and took two steps closer. Her lips were less than eight inches from mine, and I have to admit I was expecting her to kiss me at any moment. Hell, I *wanted* her to kiss me again. "The girls and I had a great time, Kyle. Thanks." She brought her lips closer.

"I had a great time too, but I can't take the credit for inviting you. The girls were the ones who wanted you to come," I admitted.

"Yeah, but you could have said no."

I smiled. She was right. I could have said no, but I didn't. I'd promised the girls I would take them to Sesame Place this weekend, but our plans were nearly canceled when Jay begged me to watch Tiffany again. I neglected to remind him that Tiffany needed a bathing suit to go to the park. So I called Lisa and asked if Tiffany could use one of Jade's swimsuits. She told me to come on over and pick it up, 'cuz she wanted to talk to me about something anyway. So we drove over to the house. The second the girls saw their mom, they wanted her to go to Sesame Place too. Thinking it would be a nice gesture, I asked Lisa if she'd like to go, and to my surprise she agreed. I'm really glad she did, too, because we had a terrific time. To be honest, it made me realize what a great marriage we used to have. But of course, that just made the fact that our divorce would be final in five days a little more painful. I cared about Val, but deep down I'll always love my wife.

"Look, Lisa, just because we're getting divorced doesn't mean we can't do family things together. It's good for the girls to see us working together. So why don't we plan some more things to do as a family? What do you think?"

She smiled. "I think that's a great idea. Matter of fact, that's what I wanted to talk to you about. Our family."

"What about our family?"

She smiled at me again, then pressed her lips against mine. We kissed for a few seconds then she spoke.

"Well, I've been doing a lot of thinking and well, I'm not sure if we should get div—" She never had a chance to finish her sentence because the deadbolt on the front door of my apartment was being unlocked and the sound made me step away from her in a panic. I checked my watch.

"Ahhh, shit," I mumbled under my breath when I realized how late it was. A meeting I'd been trying to avoid for almost six months was about to happen. Usually on Sunday nights I'd take the girls home by nine then come back to the apartment and watch TV until Val would come over around ten. But today was different. Jay had fucked me over again and was late picking up Tiffany. He was supposed to pick her up at seven o'clock so that I could take Lisa and the girls home at a reasonable hour, but now thanks to him, it was ten-ten and there was no doubt that it was Val coming through the door. Damn, why does this kinda shit always seem to happen to me?

My daughter Jewel confirmed my suspicions when she yelled. "Hey, Aunt Val, Mommy and Daddy are in the bedroom kissing." If she wasn't a kid, I'd swear she did that shit on purpose.

"Aunt Val?" Lisa glared at me with an attitude, taking a step back herself. "She has a key to your place?"

I didn't say a word. I just nodded. Lisa was about to say something, but Val's entrance interrupted her.

"Kyle!" When I turned toward her voice, Val was standing at the bedroom door with a hand on her hip. She didn't look pleased at all. "Oh, I'm sorry. Did I interrupt something? I didn't realize you had unexpected company. Or maybe I'm the one who's unexpected."

Yeah, right. She didn't act like she was sorry. Matter of fact, by her tone she had probably been expecting to catch us doing the nasty. Thank God we weren't, 'cause with the look she was giving us, she mighta tried to kill us. To her credit, she just walked in, took hold of my arm, and kissed my cheek. I breathed a sigh of relief, happy she was taking the high road in this awkward situation. I think she was waiting for an introduction, but I must not've been moving fast enough for her, 'cause she took matters into her own hands, and I guess she decided not to be as nice as I thought.

"Hi. I don't think we've met. I'm Valerie. I'm Kyle's girlfriend." Val gave Lisa a superior smile as she stuck her free hand out, leaning her head on my shoulder. I think she had sensed the uneasiness in the room and decided to take advantage of a very uncomfortable situation. What she didn't know was that Lisa wasn't the type to let anyone take advantage of her.

"*Ohhh,* so you're his girlfriend, huh?" Lisa smiled sweetly, taking Val's hand before adding some attitude to her voice. "Well, isn't that special? My name's Lisa and I'm his wife, and those three little darlings playing in the living room are *our* children."

"Well," I said abruptly, putting on a fake smile. "Now that we've all been properly introduced, why don't I drive you and the girls home, Lisa? And Val, why don't you watch Tiffany until I get back in case Jay shows up. Okay?" Lisa didn't look pleased, but she was probably about to agree. She'd finish whatever she had to say in the car, probably using a lot of curse words.

Unfortunately Val wouldn't leave well enough alone. She had to go there. The problem is, Lisa wasn't the one to go there with. On the outside she gave the appearance of a shy and quiet white woman that the average sister could walk right over. But in reality, she was a very strong woman who could have a very sharp tongue when it came to protecting what was hers. And right now I think she felt that I was still hers.

"So, Lisa. Isn't your divorce gonna be final soon? I hope you don't mind, but I'm thinking about coming down to the courthouse. It's going to be such a special day for us. Kyle and I have so many plans for the future. Would you believe we're actually talking about getting married?" She smirked at Lisa as she lied, then winked at me. I glared at her to let her know I didn't think she was funny.

"Is that so? You're gonna get married, huh? Well, I hope you've checked with Kyle on that, 'cause we were just discussing whether or not we were even going to get divorced. You know what they say, it's cheaper to keep her, and I'm very expensive. Isn't that right, Kyle?" Lisa turned to me with a grin. I glanced at Val, who looked furious. Not that I cared. I still couldn't believe she'd come out with a lie like she did about us getting married. We never talked about marriage. Shit, we hadn't even said "I love you" to each other yet.

I didn't say a word, but Lisa continued to grin, and that pissed Val off even more. She tightened her grip on my arm and pulled me closer. Believe it or not, Lisa grabbed my other arm and pulled me toward her. Of course, Val automatically pulled me in the other direction. Things were really starting to heat up and I didn't know what I was gonna do.

"Y'know, I really don't appreciate you pulling on my man." Val rolled her eyes at Lisa.

"Hmmph. Your man?" Lisa laughed, pulling me toward her again. "You mean my husband!"

There I was. Torn between two lovers, feeling like a fool. My wife on one side and my girlfriend on the other, both of them pulling on me like I was the last Twinkie at a fat farm. Now at this point they really weren't paying as much attention to me as they were to each other. But I didn't mind that. If one of these two remembered I had a part in all of this before they came to blows, they might ask me to make a decision. And I think I woulda preferred they pull my arms off. The only decision I was ready to make was to get the hell outta there. And that decision had been made as soon as Val had walked in the door.

"*Dammmn!* Y'all got some bonified Jerry Springer shit goin' on up in here! Don't ya?" I don't know when he showed up, but as usual, Jay wasn't helping things at all. In fact, I think his comment incited Val to take things to the next level.

"Look, bitch! I told you to stop pullin' on my man," Val told Lisa with finality. She let go of my arm and reached for her earrings.

"Who you callin' a bitch? And he's not your man." Lisa rolled her head and shoulders around like she was a sister, then stuck her face out toward Val. "He's my husband and I'm not letting him go 'til I'm ready." Lisa didn't let go of my arm, but she was tensing up for what-ever Val was about to bring. I decided it was time to step in between them and put an end to this, but Val had other ideas.

"Yeah? Well, from what I hear, your husband couldn't even get it up when he was with you. That's why y'all getting divorced, isn't it?" Val laughed at Lisa, whose face was crimson with anger.

"He didn't have a problem getting it up ten minutes ago. Did you, Kyle?" Lisa turned to me, but still kept an eye on Val. "Tell her, Kyle," she hissed.

"Yeah, tell me, Kyle. 'Cause I'm about two seconds off both your asses."

"Mommy! Why are you and Aunt Val yelling at each other?" My daughter Jade had come into the room. She, her sisters, and Tiffany were standing behind Jay in the doorway, watching this mess. Now I didn't care who got pissed off. It was time to put an end to this.

"They're not yelling, sweetheart. They were just having a discus-sion. You girls go get your stuff out your room. Daddy's gonna take you guys home."

"Okay, Daddy." The girls ran to the spare bedroom.

"*Ohhh,* hell no! I know you don't think you're taking her ass some-where and leaving me here," Val huffed.

"You know I've got to take the girls home, Val, so stop trippin'."

"Stop trippin'? I walk up in here and you and her are all up close and personal in the bedroom. And now you want me to stop trippin'? Fuck you, Kyle!"

"Hey, dawg. Why don't I take Lisa and the girls home? I gotta go that way to get LaShawn from Ma Jackson's house anyway," Jay of-fered.

Lisa shot Jay one of those looks to tell him to mind his own busi-ness. But Val, she never took her eyes off of me. I could tell our entire relationship was resting on my reply. Once again Jay had put me in a situation I didn't wanna be in. My plan was to take Lisa home so I could talk to her and find out if she was serious about calling off the divorce. Yeah, we'd probably argue a little after what just happened, but at least that way I would know how to handle things with Val. I liked Val a lot, and a few times I had even thought I was falling in love with her. But Lisa was my wife, and I never thought there would be a chance of us getting back together. After tonight, things weren't so clear. If there was a possibility I could get my family back together, I'd be willing to let Val go. But I needed to know for sure, and that meant talking to Lisa.

"You know what, Kyle? You leave this apartment with her and I swear I'm gonna get rid of this baby first thing tomorrow morning," Val said with a growl.

"Baby?" Lisa shouted.

"Yes. Baby." Val said seriously, rubbing both her hands on her stomach. Her eyes never left Lisa's face.

"Damn, not you too, dawg," Jay sputtered in disbelief.

"What baby?" I looked at Val, then immediately broke out in a cold sweat. She couldn't be pregnant, could she?

"Jay, I think you need to give me that ride now." Lisa walked toward the door. I grabbed her arm.

"Lisa, don't go yet. We need to talk. I'm not even sure she's pregnant," I pleaded. After Val's lie about us getting married, I wouldn't put it past her to lie about a pregnancy.

"Kyle, I think Val's the one you need to talk to," Lisa sneered as she pulled her arm away from me. "She's the one having your baby. But don't worry. I'll make sure *your other* babies are taken care of. So make sure your ass is in court in three weeks."

"Lisa . . ." I tried to plead, but she raised her hand to shut me up.

"What, Kyle? What could you possibly say to make this better? You don't know how disappointed I am in you." She turned to Val with a fake smile. "Congratulations on your new addition. Send me an invitation to the wedding. I wouldn't miss it for the world."

"And I wouldn't want you to," Val smirked, rubbing her stomach again.

Lisa shook her head and rolled her eyes at me as she stomped out of the bedroom. She shouted at Jay to hurry and get her out of there.

"Yo, I'll call you after I drop her off, aw'ight?" When I didn't respond, Jay shrugged his shoulders and followed behind my wife. Not too long after that I heard my daughters yelling "Bye, Daddy," then the front door slammed shut.

Val walked over to the dresser and opened what had become her drawer.

"What the *fuck* was that all about, Val?" I had more attitude now than I'd had all night. "I know your ass ain't pregnant. You just had your period last week."

Val reached over to the end of the dresser and picked up her overnight bag. She placed it on the bed and unzipped it.

"Did you hear me?" I yelled. "I wanna know if you're really pregnant."

"Hell no, I'm not fuckin' pregnant. Who the hell would wanna be pregnant by some bastard like you?" She grabbed her clothes out of the dresser drawer.

"Bastard like me? You the one lying your ass off, bitch." Val turned around and gave me a heavy-handed smack.

"Don't you ever call me a bitch after the way you treated me."

"How I treated you? You the one coming in here lying about us getting married and having a baby. I ain't do shit."

"Oh, don't you dare act like this is my fault. You the one who got caught in the bedroom with her, not me."

"Stop exaggerating, Val. We didn't even do anything but talk."

"You know something, Kyle? Even if I believed you didn't do anything, and I don't, you did something all right. You hurt me, Kyle. You used me."

"I didn't use you," I insisted.

"Yes you did, you fuckin' bastard. How many times did I ask you if you still loved her?" I couldn't look her in the face because she had just asked me that question a few days before. "All you had to do was tell me the truth. I could have dealt with the truth. At least then if I got hurt, it would have been my own fault. So let's not talk about some lies I told your wife, 'cause you been lying to me for six months, and payback is a bitch." Val threw the last of her belongings in the suitcase and zipped it.

"Val . . ." I didn't know what to say. She was right. I had been lying to her, and after what she just did to fuck things up with Lisa, payback was a bitch. A bitch named Val. Val picked up her suitcase and walked to the door.

"You know what, Kyle? Lisa was right about one thing."

"What's that?"

"You don't know what a disappointment you are."

32

Allen

I stopped by Ma's house on Thursday evening to check on her since I'd only seen her once since I returned from my weekend at Niagara Falls. With the baby on the way in another three months, Rose had demanded that I help her redecorate our apartment and start painting what would soon be the baby's nursery. I think I finally understood why everyone warned me marriage would be hard work. My back was killing me from all the physical labor she had me doing.

When I walked into the house, I was more than a little surprised that Ma wasn't laid out on the den sofa watching her favorite show, *WWF Smackdown*. Boy, did she love her some wrestling, especially that guy they called *The Rock*.

"Ma?" I called, but there was no answer.

I called again, this time up the stairs. I figured she must have been in her bedroom watching her show. I walked up the stairs and became a little nervous when she didn't answer. Her bedroom door was closed and I didn't hear the TV. I can't ever remember Ma missing *Smackdown*. Before I opened that door, I said a silent prayer that I wouldn't find my ma in there in need of an ambulance. I thanked Him when I opened the door and saw the empty bed. Now I wasn't scared, I was worried. Where the heck could she have gone to? I sat on the bed and reached for the phone, dialing her best friend, Mrs. Wright.

"Hello," a man answered.

"Hello, Mr. Wright? This is Allen. Audrey Jackson's son."

"Hey, how you doin', Allen? I saw your wife the other day with your mama. She's gettin' pretty big."

"Yeah, she sure is," I laughed.

"From the way she's carrying that baby, I bet she's gonna have it any day now."

"Yeah, that's what Ma says, too. But she's only six months pregnant."

"Well, don't pay any attention to me, then. Only thing I know about babies is how to make 'em." He laughed, and so did I.

"You crazy. You know that, Mr. Wright?"

"Yeah, I know," he laughed again. "So what do you want, a girl or a boy?"

"Doesn't matter to me. I just want a healthy child."

"Amen, to that." Mr. Wright used his best minister tone.

"Look, Mr. Wright. I'm at the house and I was wondering if my ma was over there?"

"Nah, her and Sarah went out to Nassau Coliseum to see that rasslin'. They got a whole busload a people goin' out there from the senior citizens center. I don't know what they see in that stuff, though. It ain't nothin' but fake."

"Yeah, well it's good entertainment."

"I guess. I'll tell your mama you called if she comes by here first."

"I'd appreciate that, Mr. Wright. Bye." I hung the phone up and lay down on Ma's bed. It felt good to have a little peace for once. I'd been married to Rose about four months and it already felt like twenty years. I stayed there in that peace and quiet for nearly an hour before I got ready to head back to all of the jobs I knew Rose had waiting for me. I opened Ma's night table drawer to find a pen to write her a note. But it wasn't a pen I found in that drawer. It was an unopened Mail Express envelope addressed to me.

I wondered why Ma would have my mail in her nightstand instead of on the kitchen table where she'd remember to give it to me. It only took a glance at the name on the return address to answer my question. An answer that left me in stunned silence as I ripped open the package. It had been seven years since I'd seen Cinnamon Lindsey. Seven long years since the woman of my dreams walked out of my life and moved to Virginia. Yet it all seemed like it was yesterday.

Cinnamon and Ma had had a huge fight. I mean so huge it actually came down to blows. It was a Saturday night and I hadn't been at Cinnamon's place more than five minutes when Ma called over there demanding that I come straight home and eat dinner. Same shit she always pulled. Cinnamon was heated. She'd slaved in the kitchen making me a lasagna dinner for almost three hours. Unlike Rose, who could be placated with the promise of a new pair of shoes or a piece of jewelry, Cinnamon just wouldn't back down when it came to Ma. It didn't matter what I offered her. She only wanted my attention. And she didn't wanna hear any excuses about my needy mother. As far as she was concerned, my ma had had me for thirty years and now it was her turn.

When Cinnamon and I arrived at the house, Ma hadn't cooked a thing. I mean, she hadn't even defrosted a hot dog. She just wanted me home so she could prove to Cinnamon who was really my boss. That really annoyed me, but Cinnamon? She was fuming and didn't hesitate to let my ma know it. The two of them cussed each other out for the better part of ten minutes. I tried to stop them but Ma pointed her finger at me and told me to mind my business. I did what she said because things were getting too out of hand, and I figured if I got in the middle they'd both be cussin' *me* out anyway. Things got worse when Ma pushed Cinnamon and she fell on her butt. Cinnamon reached out and grabbed Ma by the blouse to break her fall. First chance Ma got she slapped Cinnamon right in her face. I could tell that Cinnamon was about to put a hurtin' on my ma, so I grabbed her. That's when she gave me an ultimatum.

"That's it, Allen! I can't take this shit no more. Either you move out of this house and in with me, or I'm moving to Maryland with my sister." She was screaming at me but glaring at Ma.

I tried to smile, waving her off as if it was nothing. She'd given me ultimatums before, so I didn't think she really meant this one. Plus one look from Ma and I wasn't budging. But true to her word, Cinnamon moved to Maryland a week later. At first I didn't take it seriously. I never expected her to do it at all, but when she did, I just knew she'd be back any day. Any day became six months and six months became a year. I was crushed six months later when I heard she hooked up and married some guy from Fredrick, Maryland. Rumor was she even had a kid with the guy. Not too long after that I hooked up with Rose.

My hand was shaking when I took out the handwritten note and small envelope Cinnamon had placed in the Express envelope.

My dearest Allen,

I hope this letter finds you in good spirit and good health. As for me I'm blessed. You're probably wondering why I'm writing you a letter after all these years. Well believe me, so am I. I heard through the grapevine that you were getting married in a few weeks and wanted to congratulate you. You're a good man, Allen, and I hope you've found the right woman. A woman couldn't ask for a kinder and more warm-hearted man to stand by her side than you. I know, because I've been regretting my decision to leave you for the last six years.

As for me, I've been through quite a few changes since I've seen you last. I've been married and divorced, and that wasn't any fun. But I believe all things have their purpose. My son Evan is my life. It's a full-time job keeping up with him. You'd like him. He's a good boy. A little timid, but he has a good heart. Kinda reminds me of you in that respect. Because of him

*I've been teaching Sunday school, which I love. And although I
wasn't spiritual when I was with you, I've become quite the
churchgoer recently.*

*Well I'm going to cut this letter short. If you ever get the
urge, give me a call. (410) 555-4578. I look forward to hearing
from you. Oh, by the way, say hello to your mother for me
(smile).*

*Good luck in your new life, and God bless you and your
family,*

Cinnamon

*P.S. I've enclosed some pictures. I thought you might want to
see what I've been up to.*

When I finished reading the letter, I checked the postmark. It was almost six months old. Sent almost three weeks before my wedding. My
heart nearly stopped when I realized what Cinnamon was up to. She
was trying to stop me from getting married. That's why it came Mail
Express instead of regular mail. After all these years, could she really
still be in love with me? No, she hadn't said it in so many words, but
I'd been with her from the time I was fifteen to the time I was thirty
and I knew what she was trying to say.

I sighed heavily. I needed this kind of drama in my life like I needed
another hole in my head. But of course, that didn't stop me from looking at what else Cinnamon had sent me.

I set down the letter and picked up the envelope, ripping the right
side open. I had to smile when I saw the first picture. It was Cinnamon
sitting on a beach wearing a bikini. I could tell she'd put on a little
weight in the last five years, but it looked good on her. Damn good.
She'd changed her hair from the short, permed style she used to wear
to long, well-kept dreads that gave her a mature kind of sexiness. The
one thing that had stayed the same were her eyes. Her beautiful, light
brown eyes were as mesmerizing as ever and even in a photo they took
my breath away.

As I flipped through the pictures, I stopped at a picture of her holding a small boy. There was no way she could deny him. He had her
eyes. Seeing the two of them together made me wonder about what
could have been between us so many years before. There was a time I
expected to be having a son of my own with Cinnamon. I looked at a
few more photos until I found what looked like a family portrait of
Cinnamon, her son, and a dark-skinned man. So that was him. That
was the man she got with after me. He wasn't a bad-looking brother at
all, though I couldn't help but notice the kid looked nothing like him.

Maybe he was the new man since the divorce. Nothing was written on the back to explain the picture. Somehow, I just felt I had to know who these people were, so I decided to do something bold. Besides, I wanted to know the real reason she wrote to me. I picked up the phone and dialed the number in the letter.

"Hello?" I recognized her voice right away, and suddenly all the courage I had when I first dialed her number was gone. "Hello?" she said again. I felt like my vocal cords were paralyzed. I was about hang up when she said, "Allen, is that you?"

When I heard her say my name, my entire body froze. I tried not to breathe. How the hell did she know it was me?

"Allen, I know it's you. I can see your mother's number on my Caller ID." Yep, she'd busted me all right and there were two options. Hang up or talk to her. I decided to take the chance.

"Hi, Cinnamon. How you doin'?" I said nervously. I could hear her let out a long sigh.

"I'm fine, Allen. But do me a favor."

"What's that?"

"Don't do that anymore. When you didn't say anything, I started thinking your mother had gotten ahold of my letter and opened it." I had to chuckle. If she only knew how close to the truth she was. "So what brought this call on? I was expecting to get this call a few months ago. I figured by now you just didn't wanna speak to me."

"Well, to be honest, I just found your letter today."

She laughed, "Lemme guess, your mother never gave it to you?"

"Yeah." I gave a fake laugh. Not because I thought it was funny but because it was so damn sad. "I found it in her night table drawer about five minutes ago, unopened."

"Unopened, huh? I'm impressed. I woulda bet she'd opened it."

"Me too."

"So did you see the picture of my little boy?" I could hear the pride in her voice.

"Yeah, I saw it. He's a real handsome young man."

"Isn't he? I guess you're going to be having kids yourself pretty soon?" She didn't wait for an answer. "Congratulations on your marriage. How's things going?"

I hesitated. I don't know why, but I just didn't wanna tell her things were going well.

"Things are all right, I guess. I'm going to be a father in a few months and I'm excited about that."

"Oh, Allen, that is great. I'm so happy for you. You are going to be such a good dad." She sounded sincerely excited.

"You think so?"

"I know so," she said confidently. "So tell me, how are you taking care of this family of yours? Are you still in school?"

"No, I finally graduated. I work at Nickelodeon now as assistant director of one of the human resource departments."

She said she was impressed, then told me about her job at Johns Hopkins University as the hospital head of the social work department, and I was equally impressed. I talked to Cinnamon for the better part of two hours about everything from Rose to the old neighborhood to the failure of her marriage. We probably would have never hung up if it weren't bedtime for her son. I gave her my office number and we promised to keep in touch and talk soon.

After we hung up, I sat there thinking about Cinnamon and what could have been. As much as I loved Rose, I knew in my heart that Cinnamon was my soul mate. I had made a huge mistake six years ago letting her walk out my life. I can't even say I felt guilty about thinking these things, even though I was married to someone else.

My thoughts were interrupted by Ma's loud call. I heard her fiddling with her keys at the bottom of the stairs, so I placed the letter and the pictures in the Express envelope and headed down to see her.

"Hey, baby, you eat?" Ma was smiling until she saw the Express Mail envelope in my hand. "What you doin' with that? That was in my night table drawer. Boy, I know you ain't been going through my things." She pointed a bony finger in my face.

"Ma, how come you never gave this to me?"

" 'Cause you didn't need it." Her answer was matter-of-fact, and she turned her back to let me know she was finished discussing that envelope. "Now, do you want me to fix you something to eat?"

I didn't answer. I just followed her into the kitchen. Ma went into the fridge and pulled out a ham, which she set in the center of the table. Then she grabbed a knife from the counter and started carving.

"Ma, will you answer me? Why didn't you give this to me?"

" 'Cause that damn Cinnamon ain't up to no good, that's why!"

"She was congratulating me on getting married." I reached for the envelope and pulled out her letter. I tried to hand it to her, but she ignored me as she reached into the oven for a frying pan. I was so angry that she wouldn't at least look at the letter that I stood up and headed for the front door.

"Where you goin'?" She yelled from behind me. I didn't answer her. "I'm fixin' you somethin' to eat."

"I'm not hungry."

"Boy, if you don't turn your ass around and march back in this kitchen, I'ma knock you up side your head with this fryin' pan."

I stopped dead in my tracks. Enough was enough. This had to stop right here and now. I turned around and glared at my mother. "You're not gonna do anything to me. I'm a grown damn man. I don't even live in your house anymore. And another thing, I'm sick and tired of you—"

BLAM!!!

"You don't talk to me that way." Ma swung that frying pan, missing my head by only inches. But the vase on the shelf next to me wasn't so lucky. She'd smashed it to smithereens and was about to try to do the same to me again when the phone rang. I raised one hand to protect myself as I picked up the phone with the other.

"Hello," I answered it, watching Ma carefully.

"Allen?" It was Rose and she sounded like she'd been crying.

"Rose, baby, what's wrong?"

"I think you need to come home right away."

"Why, what's the matter?"

"My water just broke. I'm gonna have the baby."

"Oh shit! I'll be right there."

"Okay, but hurry. I'm starting to have contractions." I hung the phone up and rubbed my eyes. I was scared, real scared. Rose was only six months pregnant, and if her water broke, the baby was going to be born premature, which usually meant complications. I'd read enough child-rearing and delivery books in the last few months to know premature babies could have brain damage, cerebral palsy, and a host of other problems. I started praying frantically for the health of my child.

As I sat in a daze, Ma put down the frying pan and came to rub my shoulders. It was like she sensed something was wrong and put aside the little dispute we were having.

"Everything all right, baby?"

"No, Ma. Rose's water broke. She's gonna have the baby," I whispered.

"Oh, lawd have mercy. Come on, boy. We gotta get that girl to the hospital."

It was 1:33 A.M. when the doctor walked into the waiting room and told me that Rose and I had just became the parents of a six-pound, three-ounce baby boy. Rose and I had already decided to name him Jonathan, after her father. Jonathan was a handsome healthy boy with all ten fingers and toes, along with no apparent complications from the premature birth. Actually, the doctor looked at me kinda funny when he walked out of the delivery room and I asked him about any serious complications my son might have. He told me that with modern medicine it's not typical for a baby born three weeks early to have many problems. I was confused when he said three weeks instead of three months, but I figured I'd clear that up later. At the moment, all I wanted was to see my son. I was still a little steamed that I wasn't able to be in the room during the delivery.

After all the Lamaze classes I'd taken and child birthing books I read in preparation for this glorious day, I hadn't even been there to see my son enter this world. After I told her about Rose's water breaking, Ma had insisted on coming to the hospital with us. When we arrived, she also insisted that she be in the delivery room with Rose. The hospital had a policy of only one family member in the room for the birth. Oh, I tried to argue with Ma for what good it would get me, but she just threatened to knock me up side my head with her pocket book. Rose, who appeared to be in a tremendous amount of pain and probably didn't wanna hear us bickering, grabbed my arm and told me she didn't care who was in the room. All she wanted was for somebody to find her a doctor and an epidural. One look at her face and I decided that arguing with Ma wasn't worth it. So I reluctantly watched my wife and mother head into the delivery room without me to deliver my first child. Now that he was born and he was healthy, though, nothing else mattered.

33

Jay

Benny's bar in Hollis, Queens, was smaller but a lot more crowded than the Roadhouse Bar would have been on a Tuesday night. I asked Kyle to meet me there for drinks. He didn't know it, but I needed a favor. A big favor. We'd normally meet at the Roadhouse Bar, but after his breakup with Val, he really wasn't feeling the Roadhouse anymore. I can't say I blame him. From what I heard, Val was trippin'. I spotted Kyle in a booth, talking on his cell. He hung up with a frown on his face just as I sat down.

"What up, dawg?" I reached out and picked up one of his Buffalo wings and took a bite.

"Life sucks, that's what's up." He slid his cell phone into its holster.

"By the look on your face, I guess it does. What the hell's wrong with you anyway?" I finished off the wing in the next bite and ordered a Heineken from a passing waitress.

"That was Lisa on the phone. She still won't believe that Val's not pregnant. Can you believe that shit?"

"Hell, yeah, I can believe it. I ain't never seen her as pissed off as she was the other night. Man, I thought she used to hate me, but I'm her best friend compared to you."

"Fuck it." Kyle slapped the table. "If she don't wanna believe the truth, then the hell with her. Ain't shit I can do about it. She don't have to worry about me no more, 'cause I ain't callin' her ass again."

I know Kyle was serious, but I laughed. I couldn't help myself.

"What the hell you laughing at?"

"You." I continued to laugh. "Didn't you tell me twice yesterday that you weren't gonna call her anymore?"

"Yeah, but I had to get something straight with her before we go to court."

"Something straight like what?" I gave him a sideways look. "Isn't that the lawyer's job?"

"Well, um . . ." He looked at me like I was annoying him. "Why you interrogating me?"

" 'Cause you're full 'o shit, that's why." His face went blank. "How many times you call her today?" He didn't answer me, so I asked again. "How many times you call her today, Kyle?"

"I don't know. Two, maybe three times."

I stared at him and frowned, waiting for the true number.

"Okay, six times. But you don't understand. Lisa doesn't wanna get divorced. It's just that she thinks I disrespected her by getting Val pregnant."

"Yeah, that proves it."

"Proves what?"

"We're getting old, my man."

"Why you say that?"

" 'Cause you sweatin' Lisa like a virgin looking for his first piece o' ass. And me, I'm in love with a nineteen-year-old college student. What the hell's wrong with us? We never woulda done some sorry ass shit like this back in the day." I smiled as I thought of the good old days. Life was a hell of a lot simpler back then. Fuck 'em and leave 'em. That's what we did best.

"Yeah, speaking of that college student, whatever happened to her?" Kyle picked up a wing.

"She's pregnant," I said nonchalantly, taking my beer from the waitress.

"What?" he shouted, spitting out the wing. His eyes were wide with surprise. "Pregnant by who?"

"I fucked up, man. I got her pregnant. But I'm gonna be there to take care of her and the kid."

Kyle sighed. "You really love this chick, don't you?"

"Yep, but I told you that five months ago."

"Yeah, but I didn't believe you 'til now. But if you're willing to let your teenage mistress have a baby, you're either stupid or in love."

"Both," I told him with a smile. "Look, man, the reason I needed to see you is that I need a favor."

"What's up? What d'you need?"

"I need to borrow three grand until I can sell my bike."

"Three grand? For what?" Kyle sat back and folded his arms.

"Ask me no questions, I'll tell you no lies." I looked at him, making sure we made eye contact. "I need the money, Kyle, and I'm asking for it on the strength of our friendship. Trust me, you don't wanna know what I need it for, but I swear I'm not gonna do anything illegal with it. I'm just in a jam."

"You sure that baby she's carrying is yours?"

"I need the money, Kyle," I pleaded in my most sincere voice.

He stared at me for a few seconds, smoothing his mustache like he was deep in thought. The suspense was killing me.

"Okay," he finally nodded, reaching into his suit jacket for his checkbook. "You can have the three grand on the strength of our friendship, but you're right, I don't wanna know what you're up to. And if Kenya asks, you did not get this money from me. I got enough women on my ass as it is right now. I really don't need *your* wife to join the club." He placed his checkbook on the table and wrote out a check. He handed it to me and I looked at it with a grateful smile. Kyle's cell phone started ringing before I could thank him.

"Hello? Hello?" Kyle checked the Caller ID then spoke again. "Hello . . . Hello? Dammit." He flipped the phone closed.

"Who was that?"

"I don't know. Somebody keeps calling me at home but they never say a damn thing. Now they're calling on my cell. I swear this shit is starting to piss me off."

"You checked your Caller ID, didn't you?"

"Hell, yeah. The number keeps coming up restricted."

"Well, anyway, thanks for the loan. I'll get it back to you as soon as I sell the bike." I hated the thought of selling my bike, but Tracy had to come first.

"Just be glad that Wil found a cheap apartment in my building or I wouldn't be able to loan you shit. I just loaned him three grand." Kyle shook his head.

"You loaned Wil money to get an apartment?"

"Yeah, I loaned him money. I had to. Have you seen him lately? The brother had to've lost twenty pounds in the last month. He looks like shit."

"What happened to him?" I felt bad that I hadn't seen Wil in so long.

"Diane's what happened to him. Wil thought that if he paid the bills and handled his business like he was still living there that she was gonna come around after a while. Well, guess what? She didn't. She's got him paying out the ass so much he came to me looking for a part-time job."

"Get the fuck outta here. Wil asked you for a part-time job?" I have to admit I was shocked. Wil was one of those brothers with a lot of pride.

"Yep. You know that fool signed an agreement to give her damn near eighty percent of his salary? And had the nerve to blame it on me."

"Blame it on you? Why?"

"Because Diane showed him my separation agreement. Somehow she convinced him that he would have to pay out as much as me. She just forgot to mention that I make ten times what Wil does."

"Damn! Eighty percent of his salary?" I made a face. "She wants his ass broke."

"That's what I been trying to tell him."

"Well, he needs to talk to her then."

"He did. She said if he breaks their agreement, he can't see his kids and she's gonna take his ass to court."

"Fuck it! Let her take him to court. Shit, I bet the judge reduces what he's gotta pay out and gives him visitation anyway."

"I told him that shit. Matter of fact, I told him I'd get my lawyer to represent him."

"Well, that's good. What he say?"

"He said ain't no white man gonna tell him how to take care of his family."

"I heard that, but that's not changing the fact that he's broke. Man, if Wil would let me do my thing, I could fix all this shit. Gimme a couple a days and he and Diane will be back together." Kyle didn't answer me because his phone went off again. It's probably a good thing, though. What I had planned was no joke and would never work without Wil's permission. I had to give it some more thought before I discussed it with anyone else.

"Hello?" He looked at the Caller ID again. "Dammit! I know this is you, Val. I can see the Roadhouse's number on my Caller ID. Stop playing fucking games." He hung up. "This shit is ridiculous. Look, Jay. I'm gonna head on home. I'll catch you later."

"Aw'ight, man, but be careful. You might wanna stay away from Val. Rumor has it she's hanging out with that crazy ass Terrance again."

"Don't worry. I ain't fucking with that big motherfucker."

"Hey, Kyle, thanks again." I waved the check at him and he nodded as he stood to leave.

34

Allen

It was a little after 6 P.M. when I walked up the steps to our apartment. I'd left work a little early so that I could get home and play with my son Jonathan. Let me tell you, he was only three weeks old, but that little boy was my life. I had so many plans for him. I just couldn't wait till he was old enough to play catch in the backyard or shoot hoops in the park. Not to mention what it was going to be like to take him to his first Knicks or Yankees game, or see his smile when I take him to Disney World. Yes sir, I was one of those fathers who planned on reliving my childhood through my son, and I couldn't wait. I honestly could not wait.

I placed my key in the door and I could hear Jonathan crying before I opened it. I'd be lying if I said it was the first time I'd come home to that. I just couldn't understand why the hell it was so hard for Rose to pick him up and give him the attention he needed. I'd always thought being maternal was built into a woman, but Rose had proven that theory wrong. The way she treated our son was more like he was her pet than her child. All she wanted to do was show him off to everyone. The minute there was no one around to impress, you'd think she'd never given birth to him. It's a damn shame, but any affection or nurturing he got came from me and Ma.

When I opened the door, I could hardly believe my eyes or ears. Rose was sitting on the living room sofa watching Ricki Lake and eating a box of chocolates like she didn't have a care in the world. She was fully made up and dressed like she was getting ready to go out on the town. I don't even think she realized that I walked in the door or that her son was crying at the top of his lungs she was so preoccupied with her television show. And that pissed me off.

"Can't you hear him? He's screaming!" I yelled. I gave her an angry look but she ignored me and continued to watch TV until a commercial came on.

"It's good for him to cry a little bit, Allen. You don't wanna spoil him, do you?" I rolled my eyes at her and quickly walked toward the nursery and my screaming child. I'm sorry, I love Rose, but there has to be something wrong with a woman who can just sit around and listen to her newborn child screaming at the top of his lungs in the next room.

"Hey there, little man. Don't cry. Daddy's here." I gently picked up my son and kissed him. His entire face was a beet red and he felt a little warm, but I figured it was because he was crying. I reached into his crib and picked up his bottle, placing the nipple in his mouth. He calmed down right away. He was just hungry. I walked back in the living room holding him. "Would this have been so hard to do?" I had sarcasm in my voice, which made Rose roll her eyes again.

"Please, Allen, ain't nobody holdin' no baby all damn day. Besides I got a headache." Rose's voice and body language showed all kinda attitude. "That little nigga cried all day long, and now he has the nerve to stop when you come home. You need to put his ass down. That's why he's so damn spoiled, 'cause you and your mama always picking him up." She sucked her teeth and both of us made evil eyes at each other. I didn't like this side of my wife. I didn't like it at all, and lately I was seeing more and more of it.

"You know what, Rose? You're . . ." I stopped myself and was about go back in the nursery to finish feeding my child when I spotted a small suitcase lying by the far end of the sofa. I saw Rose step in front of it, trying to conceal it from me. *Lord, please don't tell me she's going somewhere,* I thought. Especially since I had to go to work in the morning and she was supposed to take Jonathan to a pediatrician's appointment. He was only three weeks old and had already missed his first appointment. From the message the doctor had left, she'd better not miss this one.

"Going somewhere?" Rose looked down at the suitcase sheepishly as she answered.

"Well, yeah, a lot of the girls from the job are going to Philly to see the D'Angelo concert, and well, Tanya got me a ticket. So I figured I'd go too. It's only for a couple of days." She sounded nervous.

"A couple of days?" I yelled, looking at her like she was crazy. "What about Jonathan? Who's gonna watch him? And just when did you plan on telling me this? After you left?" I paced the floor as I held my son.

"I'm telling you now. And don't worry about Jonathan. He'll be all right. Get your mother to watch him. She's the one who wanted a grandbaby so bad, isn't she? Or can't she miss *Smackdown* one week?"

"*Smackdown?* You not coming back till after Thursday? I thought you said a couple of days."

"What I meant to say is I'm not coming back for a week."

"A week! Are you crazy, Rose? You gonna leave your newborn son for a week? What kind of mother are you?" I stopped pacing and stood staring at her. Yeah, that's right. I didn't like arguing, but we were about to have one hell of an argument.

"What do you mean what kind of mother am I? You act like I'm leavin' him alone. I'm not leaving him alone, Allen. I'm leavin' him with you! You are his daddy, aren't you?" She shook her finger in my face and rolled her head around with attitude. Then out of nowhere her stern face turned to a sweet smile, and that scared me. She was like Jekyll and Hyde.

"Look, Allen, I need a break. I've been putting up with this boy screaming every time I put him down for two weeks. Now you can be with the program or not, but I'm leaving." She smiled and kissed my cheek, then picked up her bag.

"You're really leaving? What about the baby? Doesn't he have a doctor's appointment tomorrow?"

"Oh, yeah, he does, doesn't he?" She looked at me and shrugged her shoulders. "Oh, well, I guess you better cancel it or call in sick tomorrow." I gave her a look of disbelief. Her response was to give me her best puppy-dog face. "Look, honey, I love you and I'll call you when I get to Philly, okay?" She walked out that door, and all I could do was watch in disbelief. She hadn't even kissed Jonathan.

The next morning I called in sick to work. Jonathan's doctor's appointment was at eleven o'clock, so I swung by Ma's for breakfast around eight. Jonathan had been acting a little cranky and I wasn't sure if he was sick or just missed Rose. I was hoping Ma might have one of those old-fashioned remedies for calming a baby, and of course she did. It was called a grandmother's love. Ma took Jonathan from me the minute I walked in the door. She rocked and kissed and fed that boy, then gave him a bath in the kitchen sink. By the time she got through with him it was ten o'clock, and he was dressed and ready to go to the doctor, cooing in her arms.

When we arrived at the doctor's office, I don't know why but I had this uneasy feeling, and the receptionist and nurse behind the counter didn't make me feel any better. They kept staring at Ma and me like they knew something we didn't. To be honest, I was afraid child welfare was gonna pop up on us at any minute and take Jonathan because he was three weeks old and hadn't had any of his shots or been to one doctor's appointment yet. I found out a few minutes later, though, that wasn't the case at all.

"Mr. Jackson, I'm Dr. Gerba. Why don't we talk in my office?" The doctor, an average-looking, clean-shaven white man with a receding hair line walked toward a door, gesturing for Ma and me to follow.

We did, and when he closed the door, first thing outta Ma's mouth was, "Why you got us in your office and not in the examination room?" Dr. Gerba walked behind his desk and sat down.

"Well to be honest with you, Miss . . ." Gerba glanced at Ma.

"Mrs. Jackson. Mrs. Audry Jackson. I'm Jonathan's Nana."

"Okay, well, Mrs. Jackson, we needed to talk about Jonathan before I examine him."

"Talk about him? What about him?" I asked sternly. If this fool doctor thought he was gonna get me to sit around his office while some nurse reported me and had someone take away my son, he had another thing coming.

"Mr. Jackson, your son has sickle cell anemia."

"Lawd have mercy. This can't be!" Ma shouted. I didn't say a word. I was still trying to comprehend what the doctor had just told me. How could Jonathan have sickle cell? He was a normal baby, a perfect baby.

"Where is this coming from? You haven't even examined him yet." I gave the doctor a suspicious gaze.

"When your son was born, the hospital ran different blood tests on him just like they do all newborns. We tried to explain to your wife that we really needed her to come in right away when she missed her first appointment, but she just kept saying we'd talk when she brought Jonathan in for his checkup in a week. Of course, you know she missed that appointment, too. I wish we could have told her over the phone but it's against hospital policy."

I glanced at Ma and tears were running down her face. I took a deep breath and tried to hold back my own tears.

"Is he gonna be all right? He's not gonna die, is he?" I looked the doctor directly in the eyes, terrified of what his answer might be.

"Chances are he will be fine. Matter of fact, I had two sickle cell patients who recently have become parents themselves. Things have changed a lot in the last twenty years and treatment has come a long way. Sickle cell's a painful disease, but it's no longer a death sentence for a child like it once was." The doctor smiled kindly. "Your son's going to be fine, Mr. Jackson, but his health will require some vigilance on your part. We'd like to start him on penicillin to keep infection down. Maybe have him come into the hospital a few days to run some tests."

"Okay, Doctor. I'm putting my trust and faith in you." I didn't know what else to do at this point. I had to believe that this man would help my son lead a normal life.

He nodded as he began to explain to us exactly what sickle cell was and how it could be treated. After about a forty-minute conversation and examination, Dr. Gerba suggested that we take Jonathan right over to the Long Island Jewish Hospital. Jonathan's low-grade fever and crankiness were telltale signs of infection, the doctor told us. Jonathan really needed to be placed on intravenous antibiotics to prevent any serious complications.

I watched those doctors and nurse at that hospital stick and probe my son for hours before they finally stopped around 8 P.M. They had poor Jonathan looking like something out of a *Star Trek* movie, he had so many different tubes and wires coming out of his arms and legs. It felt like they were sticking me every time they jabbed something into him. In my life I'd never imagined anything more painful than standing back helpless while your child is suffering.

Later that night I came home to pack up some clothes and a few toys for Jonathan. Ma was at the hospital with him, so I decided to stick around the house for a few hours hoping Rose would call. She'd called twice while we were gone but never left a number where she could be reached. I can't tell you how frustrating it was to have my son sitting in that fucking hospital with sickle cell anemia and not being able to contact his mother. For the first time since we'd been married I was starting to understand why people thought Rose was such a selfish bitch. I mean, what kinda woman would just disappear without leaving a number where she could be reached when she had a three-week-old baby at home?

I slammed my hand down on the coffee table. I couldn't take it anymore. What I really needed was someone to talk to, someone who would listen to me and not be judgmental. I wanted to call Kyle or Wil, but that wouldn't work. As much as I loved them, they wouldn't understand. Especially Kyle. Lately he couldn't stand to hear Rose's name. So I decided to call Cinnamon.

I went into the bedroom and placed my sock drawer on the bed. Then I bent down and reached into the space where the drawer had been. I pulled out the Express Mail envelope Cinnamon had sent, emptying the contents onto the bed. I stared at the two smaller envelopes that fell out. I was about to read Cinnamon's letter again, but the phone rang.

"Hello?"

"Allen, it's Rose. Where've you been, baby? I've been calling you all day." Would you believe she sounded sincere about that shit? "I even called you mother's house."

"Where have I been? Where have I been? I've been at the fucking hospital! That's where I've been!" I'd never been so upset in my life. "Where the hell have you been? Jonathan's sick. He needs his mother."

"Oh, please, Allen, don't start. I already have a headache, okay? You gonna tell me you can't handle a little cold for a few days?"

"He doesn't have a cold, Rose. He has sickle cell anemia." The line was silent and I expected her to cry or yell or something, but she didn't. I was floored by how nonchalant her response was.

"Don't worry, Allen. My cousin has sickle cell, and she's fine." Rose was actually taking the news like it really was just a temporary cold. "You didn't call my parents, did you?"

"No, I haven't called anyone. I just got home." She probably didn't want her parents to know her son was flawed.

"Good, why don't we wait till I get home in a few days? Then we'll call my folks. There's no need to get them upset over something like this."

"In a few days! Are you fucking crazy? You better bring you ass home tonight, Rose! Do you hear me? Tonight!"

"Look, Allen, the concert's not 'til tomorrow night and I've never seen D'Angelo. Jonathan's going to have sickle cell all his life, but I'm only going to have one chance to see D'Angelo. So I'll see you the day after tomorrow, okay?" Before I could reply, she hung up.

"Fuck!" I slammed down the phone.

She'd done it again. She'd left me without a way to get in touch with her. I slammed my hand down on the bed, jostling the envelopes that were still lying unopened.

Cinnamon would never do anything like this, I thought as I pulled out the photos. I looked through them until I found the one of her and her son. *That should be my family.* I was really feeling sorry for myself. Who would have thought that so soon after my marriage I'd be longing for a life other than the one I had? I loved Jonathan. I loved Rose, too, but this wasn't the family I'd envisioned when I got married.

I glanced at the clock. It was a little past eleven. Too late to call just anyone, but Cinnamon had said I could call her at any time. I dialed her number.

"Hello?" her voice was groggy.

"Cinnamon? This is Allen."

"I know your voice, Allen. How you doing?" I could tell she was happy to hear from me. Her voice was no longer groggy and it made me smile in spite of the hell my life was at that moment.

"Not so good," I replied.

"Allen, what's wrong?"

"What isn't wrong?" was my reply. "My wife gave birth to a little boy the same day I talked to you."

"Congratulations. But what could be wrong with that?" She paused, and then it must have dawned on her. "Oh, God. He's all right, isn't he?"

"No, he's not. I just found out today he's got sickle cell."

"Oh, Allen, I am so sorry."

"So am I, Cinnamon. So am I. But if you think that's something, listen to this. My wife's taken off to Philly for a week and I can't even get in touch with her."

"What? You've gotta be kiddin'."

"I wish I was." I explained everything that had gone on the past few days to Cinnamon and she was floored.

"So what you gonna do?"

"About what?"

"About your wife? About your son?"

"As far as Jonathan's concerned, I'm gonna do whatever it takes to help him lead a normal life. But as far as Rose is concerned, I don't even wanna think about it."

"I know the feeling. That's how I felt before I got divorced. Look, Allen, they have a great gene therapy study going on at the hospital here. They're really doing some great things. I can probably get you into it."

"I don't know. Long Island Jewish has a pretty good program too."

"I know that, but this is a research study. It's only for a few days each month and being a part of studies like this is gonna help find a cure. I know you wanna find a cure, don't you?"

"Hell, yeah. But what about LIJ? They're not going to be mad if we do this, are they?"

"No, most of the hospitals share information," she hesitated. "Plus I'm not gonna lie. It'll give me a chance to see you and meet your son . . . Oh, and your wife too."

"Okay. Why don't you set it up, and I'll give you a call tomorrow night to find out what's up."

"Sure," she agreed. We talked a little longer, then hung up. I had to get back to the hospital and she had to get some sleep for work in the morning. But I'm sure we could have talked all night long if given the chance. For some reason we just had chemistry like that.

* * *

It was five days later around midnight when I heard Rose's key turn the lock to the front door. So I said good night to Cinnamon and hung up the phone nervously. I don't know why, but all of a sudden I was feeling guilty about talking to Cinnamon the last few nights. All we'd done was talk about Jonathan and his treatment, but somehow it felt like I was cheating. Like I was doing something wrong, and I hated myself for feeling that way, especially since Rose was the one who'd been missing in action for six days while our son was in the hospital. The way she walked into the house, I don't think she felt a bit of remorse.

"Hey, baby, did you miss me?" She was standing in the bedroom doorway like everything was fine. Like she'd just gone to the grocery store and came home with dinner or something. Instead of taking off to who knows where for six days. She set her bags down before she walked over to kiss me.

"Where've you been, Rose? I thought you were coming home three days ago." I sat up on the bed and propped a pillow behind me. She kissed my cheek, then walked back over to her bags.

"I was coming home, but I was having such a good time I decided to stay a few more days." She reached into one of the bags and pulled out what looked like an expensive man's shirt.

"Look what I got you." I couldn't take it anymore. She's out shopping while I'm worried about what type of antibiotics Jonathan's going to be on.

"Rose, what is wrong with you?" I screamed, jumping out of the bed. She looked at me like she was amazed that I was angry. "Do you give a shit about your son? He was in the hospital for two days and you never even called to check on him."

She waved her hand like she was blowing me off.

"Please, Allen. Don't start with me, okay? I'm here now, and like I told you before, that baby's going to have sickle cell all his life. I'm not going to have many chances to party like that."

I couldn't believe her reasoning. I grabbed her arm, pulling her out of our bedroom into the nursery.

"Look at him. Look at him, Goddammit!" Rose peeked into the crib, very unenthusiastic. "That's your son. Do you see how perfect he is? How beautiful he is? His only flaw is that he has sickle cell anemia, and he can't help that. You know why?" I took hold of her face and made her look at me. "Because we gave that to him, you and me, Rose. We gave it to him. So as far as I am concerned, the party's over. You understand me? The party's over."

"I know that, Allen. I just needed to get away." She rolled her eyes and tried to pull out of my grasp, but I surprised her by tightening my grip on her face and not letting go.

"Well, the next time you need to get away, don't come home. You got it? Now, give your son a kiss." Rose's eyes widened with surprise as she nodded, reaching for the baby. I let go of her face with a wicked smile. We'd just come to an unspoken understanding. I may be weak in a lot of ways, but when it came to my son, she was not to fuck with me.

"We're going to Maryland in two weeks to be part of a sickle cell gene therapy study. Don't make any plans." I walked into the bedroom feeling pretty good about myself. That was the first time since Rose and I had started seeing each other that I walked out of a room feeling like I'd won the argument and had the upper hand.

35

Jay

"Jay?" Tracy whispered, her hand gently rubbing my back. I was sitting at the edge of the bed, about to put on my shirt. She was lying next to me, completely naked.

"What, baby?" I leaned back and kissed her full, soft lips. God, it was incredible how much I loved that woman.

"Can't you stay another hour? At least until I fall asleep." She batted her eyelashes and smiled. I smiled back and kissed her again.

"That's what you said an hour ago." I touched her naked flesh.

"I know, but then I wanted a quickie. Now I wanna be held." She wrapped her arms around me tightly, like she never wanted to let me go. Her request was tempting, but Kenya had called my cell phone three times in the last half hour. I hadn't answered the calls, but I knew she'd be calling again soon. I'd been with her long enough to know her patterns.

"Tracy, I gotta go. I'll see you in the morning, okay?" She frowned, and I felt like shit. I didn't wanna leave. It was getting hard to leave Tracy's warm bed every night. The more I stayed with her, the more I didn't wanna go home at all.

After I cashed Kyle's check, I rented a small, one-bedroom furnished apartment in Jersey City, about five minutes from my house. I know what you're thinking. Five minutes away is a little too close for comfort. But the section of town I moved Tracy into was so rundown that Kenya wouldn't have been caught dead around there. Still, it was affordable, and after I paid the first month's rent and gave the landlord two months' security, I'd spent half of what Kyle had given me. I wish I could've done better, but I was having a hard enough time running one household, and now I was running two.

But other than the money, it was a pretty nice situation for me. I could drive by every morning, have breakfast with Tracy, then drive her to summer school on my way to work. I'd pick her up on the way home, get in a quickie, and then go home to pacify Kenya for a few hours before slipping back over to Tracy's.

"This is getting really old," Tracy pouted, folding her arms as I pulled out of her grasp. "I've had my own place for almost a month and my man hasn't stayed past one A.M. once. I think I liked things the old way better. At least you'd spend the night when we stayed in a hotel."

"Come on, baby. You know I gotta go home."

"Yeah, go home to your wife and leave your pregnant girlfriend alone. I hate this shit, Jay." She looked like she was about to cry. Our little arrangement was getting on her nerves.

"I'll tell you what. It's your birthday Saturday, right?" She nodded eagerly as I told her my plan. "How'd you like me to spend the entire weekend with you? Matter of fact, why don't we go down to Atlantic City Friday night and celebrate?"

"Oh, Jay, for real?" She stopped pouting and was grinning from ear to ear.

"Yeah, for real." I buttoned my shirt and kissed her goodbye. Then I headed for the door.

"Jay?" Tracy stopped me.

"Yeah?"

"I love you." She rubbed her small belly. "And the baby does too."

"I love you, too. Both of you." I smiled back at her and realized that after two kids with Kenya I had never felt what I felt for Tracy right now.

I pulled into my driveway less than ten minutes after I walked out of Tracy's door. Suddenly I got a chill, but shook it off. It was probably because I knew I was gonna hear it for sure. Kenya had every light in the house on and I could see her peeking through the living room window. I checked my watch. It was twenty minutes after midnight. Not too late, but it was getting harder and harder to come up with alibis she would accept.

"Ahh shit," I mumbled to myself.

I'd fucked up big time. I'd just had sex with Tracy and hadn't taken a shower. Kenya was gonna be at the door waiting for me, and lately she was good for giving me the sniff test. I rubbed my hand over my face and took a deep breath. Fuck it, if she wanted to act stupid, I'd just leave. It wasn't like I didn't have a place to go. I wasn't gonna let anyone intimidate me in my own house, including my wife. I walked up to the door and put my key in the lock. I tensed up, surprised when Kenya didn't pop out of nowhere, trying to get all close to me to see if I smelled like sex.

"Jay?" She walked out of the living room with a smile. "I've been trying to call you for almost two hours. One of your college buddies is here to see you from Virginia."

"Get the fuck outta here," I grinned. "Who?" I walked toward the living room entrance past Kenya, wondering which one of my college buddies would have shown up at my house so late.

"I never met him before. His name is Jim Williams. He said he's a DC detective now." As I walked into the living room, Kenya's words finally registered what my eyes were seeing. My stomach lurched when I saw the man on my couch. Staring me in the face was Tracy's father.

"Hey, Jay, what's up, my brother?" He stood up, smiling as he grabbed my hand. "It's been a long time. How you been?" Now I'm a strong guy, but Tracy's pops had one hell of a grip. I felt like my hand was in a vise grip and he wouldn't let go.

"Nice little family you got here, Jay. Beautiful wife and two wonderful kids." He smiled at me. "Wait till I tell my wife that good old Jay has a wife and two kids. I tell ya, she's gonna flip." He raised his eyebrows and smirked.

I swear to God he was either the best actor I've ever met or a fucking psycho, because if I didn't know better, I would have sworn he was actually glad when he found out I was married. I glanced at Kenya, who was leaning against the living room entrance smiling. Can you believe she was absolutely oblivious to what was happening? But me, I was scared to death.

"Well, I'm gonna leave you boys to talk old times." Kenya yawned. "I'm going to bed. I've gotta go to work in the morning." She smiled at me, then waved at Tracy's father. "Nice to meet you, Jim. Good night."

"The pleasure was all mine, Kenya. And thanks so much for your hospitality and for letting me wait for Jay. Someday I'm going to have to bring my wife and daughter by to meet you."

Jim smiled at my wife. He was still holding on to my hand as he waved good night, but the second Kenya walked out of the room his smile became a sinister sneer and he tightened his grip on my hand so I couldn't get away. I'm not gonna lie. I hadn't been that scared of anyone since I got caught in bed with this married chick a few years back. The only difference was that instead of being a martial arts instructor like her husband, Tracy's pops was a cop, and at any moment I was expecting him to pull out his gun. Thank God he didn't, and that's when I made the decision that whether he was Tracy's father or not I wasn't gonna let anyone whip my ass in my house. I just wish someone woulda told him that, 'cause he definitely wasn't a believer.

He tightened his grip on my hand, faked like he was gonna punch me in the face with his free hand, then stomped down on my big toe like he was killing roaches. I jumped in the air, about to scream from the pain when he hit me between the legs so hard I couldn't do anything but buckle over in pain. I couldn't even fall to the floor until he let go of my hand. I was in so much pain I almost passed out. I couldn't scream, I couldn't yell, I couldn't even beg for my life, I was too preoccupied with trying to breathe.

When I finally got myself to the point where I was only grimacing on the floor, he looked down at me and laughed. "You probably thought you were gonna kick my ass, didn't you? Now, where the fuck is my daughter?"

"Look, Mr. Williams, I can explain everything," I whimpered through my agony.

"Shut up, nigger." He lifted his foot like he was going to stomp me. "I asked you a question. Where the fuck is my daughter?" When I didn't answer quick enough, his foot came down on my ribs.

"*Arrrhhh!*" I yelled, trying my best to protect myself from another attack.

"Shut the fuck up. You want your wife to hear? Then I'd have to tell her all about my pregnant daughter. You wouldn't want that, would you?"

I looked up at him and shook my head.

"Now I wanna know. Where is my daughter? It's been over a month since we came up here and she hasn't called home once since then. Her poor mother's worried sick."

Another fuck-up on my part. Tracy had asked me on several occasions to get her a phone in the apartment or at least a prepaid cell phone, but I had given her the runaround. I didn't want her with a phone. A phone meant bills. And since all her friends were out of state for the summer break, it meant high long-distance bills. I'd completely forgotten she'd also need that phone to call her parents.

"I'm not gonna ask again. Where's my daughter?" He lifted his foot.

"Tracy's in her apartment, not far from here."

"Get up. You're gonna take me there."

The five-minute ride to Tracy's place seemed like five hours. Tracy's pops had me drive his car while he sat in the passenger seat. He actually had his gun in his lap the whole time and I had no doubt in my mind that if I tried something stupid he would use it.

"What the hell kinda place you got my daughter living in?" he snapped, stepping out of the car. He was staring at the local drug dealers across the street and they were staring at him. It must be the kinda cologne he was wearing or somethin', 'cause drug dealers can always spot a cop. When he turned to me, that sinister look he had at my house had spread across his face again. He was not happy with where his daughter was staying. He followed me up the walkway and I knocked on the door. Tracy answered a few seconds later.

"Jay? Is that you?" She pulled back the curtain on the tiny window to the door and smiled when she saw me. She opened the door and exposed her naked body flirtatiously to me, not realizing that her father was lurking in the shadows. "Did you come back to spend the night with me?" Her voice was full of excitement. Until her father spoke.

"Put on some clothes," he demanded. I don't even think Tracy saw him, but his voice was enough to freeze her right where she stood. Her beautiful bronze skin went instantly pale, and I could see fear all over her face. "Did you hear me? I said put some clothes on!" He stepped out of the shadows, and when they made eye contact, she ran into the apartment. Tracy's father followed her, and reluctantly I followed him.

"Daddy? What're you doing here?" Tracy was no longer in shock, but she was definitely still very nervous as she put on a robe.

"Why do you think I'm here for? You haven't called home in over a month. Your mother's worried sick." Tracy looked like she was about to cry, so I tried to help.

"That's not her fault—"

"Shut up!" her father yelled. "You think that ass whuppin' you got at your house was somethin'? You get between me and my daughter again and I'm gonna do some permanent damage." I had no idea how to respond.

"Daddy, don't talk to him like that." Tracy came to stand by my side.

"What did you say? I know you're not talking to me. Along with messing with this idiot, you getting high too?" He walked over and flipped on the kitchen lights. Roaches started to run for cover, and so did he. He almost fell and busted his ass. I wanted to laugh until he started yelling.

"What the fuck was that?" His eyes darted back and forth across the room.

"Please, Daddy. It's just a few roaches."

"Roaches! Oh, hell no! Go get your things, Tracy. You're coming home with me, now!" Tracy looked at me like I was supposed to save her from her own father. So I tried.

"Mr. Williams, I don't think Tracy wants to come home with you."

"Did I ask Tracy what she wants? And what did I tell you about getting between me and my daughter?" He took a step closer and I eyeballed a lamp that would make a suitable defense weapon. Wasn't gonna be no more of that jujitsu shit he used on me at the house.

"No, Daddy, you didn't ask me what I want." Tracy took two steps to meet her father face-to-face. "I'm not going home with you, Daddy. Jay and I are gonna raise this baby together. We're a family now." Her father laughed.

"You're not gonna raise no baby with this man, sweetheart. He's got a family. He's married and has two kids."

"I know that already," Tracy said sternly. Tracy's words stopped her father in his tracks for a moment. I'm sure he never expected his little princess to stay with a married man by choice. But he regained his sense of command very quickly.

"Well, that just tells me that you really haven't matured at all. I'm sorry, Tracy, but I can't allow this. No daughter of mine is going to stay in this roach-infested, drug-dealers-across-the-street neighborhood, and that's final." He grabbed her arm.

"I'm not going anywhere, Daddy!" She raised her voice, pulling herself free. "Now you either deal with it, or get out. I'm gonna be twenty years old on Saturday. You can't tell me what to do." She folded her arms and sucked her teeth, and I could tell her old man wanted to slap her.

"You think you're grown, don't you?" He gave Tracy a disappointed look that only a father could give a daughter. "Okay, Ms. Grown. You wanna stay with him and fuck up your life . . ."

"It's my life," Tracy said sarcastically before he could finish.

"Well, let's see if you can live it without my credit cards or my ATM card. I'm canceling them in the morning." I could tell by his facial expression that he was as mad as you can get without screaming. "Oh and I hope your hot-shot boyfriend with the wife and two kids can afford to pay your tuition. 'Cause I ain't paying that no more, either. You think you're grown, Tracy? Well, I guess we're gonna find out how grown you really are." He stared at his daughter, hoping his threats would change her mind. He got his answer when Tracy grabbed my arm and pulled me close to her.

"We'll be just fine."

"Don't call my house." He turned toward the door. "Oh, I forgot you don't have a phone in this rat hole anyway." He shook his head as he walked out.

"You sure you wanted to do that?" I kissed Tracy as I heard his car door slam.

"I made my decision. Are you sure you can handle it?" She looked up at me.

"Sure, I can handle it," I told her nervously. At least I hoped I could, 'cause I had a feeling that what was left of that three thousand bucks Kyle lent me was gonna be going mighty fast.

36

Wil

I'd been in a meeting at work for the last two hours, but my mind was on Diane. I had this gut feeling that she was up to something. She'd called me three times on my cell phone this morning just to make sure I was going to work. Then she called my secretary Marge and asked if she knew where I was staying lately. I couldn't put my finger on it, but she'd been acting mighty funny since I'd canceled picking up the kids for church on Sunday. I hadn't told her, but I'd just signed a lease and was moving into my new apartment. Originally I hadn't planned on getting my own place. I'd figured that in time Diane would come around and ask me to come home. But it had been six weeks and she hadn't changed her mind one bit. She'd actually turned into that tiger lady everyone had warned me about before we got married. Don't get me wrong. I still loved her and wanted to go home, but now I had a better understanding of what everyone else was talking about. I just had to find a way to turn the Tiger Lady back into my pussycat.

I walked out of my meeting and was greeted at the door by my secretary Marge. She cut her eyes at a young woman sitting by her desk.

"Wil, this young woman would like to see you, but she won't give me her name or tell me what she wants," Marge whispered.

I glanced at the woman. She was a young, brown-skinned woman, probably in her midtwenties. She was a little skinny for my taste, but she had an attractive face and wore an expensive suit. I took another look at her. She didn't look like anyone I knew and I definitely had no idea what she was there for. Still, she looked harmless enough.

"Don't worry about it, Marge. I'll handle it."

Marge nodded, then returned to her desk. I approached the young woman.

"Hi, I'm Wil Duncan. My secretary said that you wanted to see me." I extended my hand. "And you are . . . ?"

She smiled as she stood. Then to my surprise, she didn't shake my hand but placed an envelope in it. "I'm Kimberly Taylor, and Mr. Duncan, you've been served." She flashed another smile, then quickly turned and walked to the elevator.

"Did she say that you'd been served?" Marge stared at me from behind her desk

"I think so," I muttered, in shock. I stared at the plain envelope with my name printed on it.

I walked past Marge and into my office, closing the door behind me. I was a little shaky, but I managed to get seated behind my desk to open the envelope. I let out a loud roar the second my mind registered what was happening. My worst nightmare had come true. With one swipe of my arm, I knocked everything from my desk to the floor.

"That fucking bitch!" I screamed as I collapsed back in my chair and reread the document.

Marge knocked on the door, and when I didn't answer, she opened it. "Wil, is everything all right?" I was holding the summons in one hand, staring at it. Marge's eyes surveyed the damage I had done so quickly to my office.

"It's Diane. She's taking me to court for more child support."

"Oh Wil, I'm so sorry."

I could feel myself getting choked up, and I wanted to scream again. I know my blood pressure was starting to rise, and if that wasn't enough, I had this knot in my chest that was making it hard to breathe.

"How could she do this to me, Marge? She's got everything. The house, the car, and the kids. Damn, all I ever wanted to do is love that woman. Why would she do this without talking to me?" I felt like I was about to cry when Marge walked over and placed her hand on my back. I'd never been so hurt in my entire life.

"I don't know, Wil. Maybe you should go over to the house and talk to her."

"Yeah, you're right. I gotta go talk to her. I gotta make this right." Somehow I got up out of my chair and walked to the door.

By the time I arrived at the house, all the hurt I had inside had become anger. I was angry with everyone. Diane, Kyle, Allen, hell I was angry with God for putting me through all this. I pulled in the driveway and didn't even close my car door. I just jumped out and started banging on the front door.

"Diane, open this damn door!" It didn't take her long to answer, and the second she did, I was in her face. "What the fuck is this all about?" I had the summons in my hand and I waved it an inch from her nose.

"What do you think it's about?" She shook her head from side to side. "I'm taking your ass to court to get more money. And keep the noise down. Katie's trying to take a nap." She musta known she had the upper hand, 'cause Di was awfully calm.

"You can't do this, Diane. We have an agreement."

"Oh yeah, we do. Don't we? Well, fuck the agreement." She lurched at me with attitude.

"Why? What did I do?" I was still angry, but I tried to keep myself under control.

"You didn't think I'd find out about your apartment, did you, motherfucker?"

"Is that what this is all about?" I shook my head. "Diane, I had to get an apartment. I was paying sixty-five dollars a night to stay in a motel the last two months. I was spending so much money I had to borrow against my 401K last month and I ain't got shit to show for it. Hell, I had to borrow money from Kyle."

"You expect me to believe that shit? Please. I know all you wanted to do is have somewhere to take your whores. You ain't shit, Wil Duncan. Every time I look at those pictures, I hate your ass more."

"Diane, don't start this. You know I love you."

"I ain't started shit. You came over here. I didn't come looking for you." She shook her head again.

"I came over here because you had me served with court papers. Why can't we discuss this instead of you dragging me to court? You act like I'm not paying enough."

"Let me tell you something, Wil Duncan. If you can pay an eighteen hundred a month mortgage, the car note, electric bill, give me six hundred a month, and still rent an apartment, then you ain't paying enough. So I'll see you in court." Her voice was dead serious and the look she gave me was ice cold.

"You really mean that, don't you?" I was in disbelief.

"You damn right I mean it. I hate you, Wil. I hate what you did to me and I hate what you did to our family *and* more than that, I hate the fact that I still love you." A few tears welled up in her eyes, but she quickly got herself back under control. "So yeah, I meant that shit. I'm gonna do whatever it takes to rid myself of you and my feelings for you." She took a deep breath. "Matter of fact, I'm goin' out Friday night and I'm gonna get drunk and I'm gonna get fucked."

I couldn't believe that she was talking to me this way. If she was tryin' to hurt me, she couldn't have done a better job reaching into my chest and ripping my heart right out. I knew I was going to explode if she said anything else.

"Don't do this, Diane. You just said you love me." Those words were the only glimmer of hope she had offered. "Don't do this. Let's work this out. I love you." I could tell by her expression that my pleading wasn't doing any good. "Come on, Diane. Let's do it for the kids' sake."

"I'm not gonna work out nothin' with you. I told you, I hate you. And if that means taking you to court and divorcing you to get you out of my heart, then that's what I'm gonna do. And yes I meant every word I said."

"You don't wanna do this, Diane. You couldn't possibly mean it."

"Oh, yes I do, Wil."

"I swear. You do this and you're gonna regret it," I offered as a weak threat.

"Not as much as I regret marrying your ass." She was not threatened at all.

"You know what, Diane? I've fuckin' had it." I exploded, taking two steps closer to her. I felt like I could kill her, but something inside of me stopped me before my hands went around her throat. She must have finally been scared because the tension in her body was visible. I backed up without another word and walked to my car. If she wanted to play hardball and make this ugly, then I could do it too. She'd never seen the nigger in me come out, but I guarantee she was about to.

"You know what, Di? You're gonna miss me when I'm gone," I shouted from my car.

"Don't count on it!" she screamed at me as she slammed the door.

It was late, almost ten-thirty on Sunday night, when Kyle and I walked into the elevator in our building. Who'd've thought a few years before that we'd end up two nearly divorced men living in the same lonely apartment building? We'd just returned from spending the weekend in Sag Harbor, Long Island, with a mutual friend, John Graves. Johnny had a huge house on the beach, a thirty-five-foot boat, and a membership in one of the local country clubs. Enough toys to make any brother forget his problems for a while. So we spent the weekend golfing, fishing, and drinking and not necessarily in that order. I had a chance to clear my head and relax for the first time since Diane and I split. I think it was good for Kyle, too. As bad a time as I was having with Diane, he was having an even worse time with his divorce with Lisa.

"Wil, I'll check you later." Kyle and I embraced and he stepped off the elevator onto the second floor. I hated to leave him alone because he looked so sad.

"Look, Kyle, if you change your mind and want me to call Lisa, just say the word. I mean, it can't hurt."

"Aw'ight, Wil, thanks." I watched the elevator doors close and rode alone to the third floor.

I stepped off the elevator and right in front of me was 3A, my studio apartment. Opening the door, I looked into what had become home for the past week and probably the next year. I didn't have much furniture. Just a table to eat on, two chairs, and a bed. The table doubled as a computer desk and the bed as a couch. I flicked on the lights and reached for my cell phone to check my voice messages. I'd left my phone behind this weekend on purpose because I knew Diane would be calling me every fifteen minutes when I didn't show up to pick up Teddy and Katie. Not that I cared. She'd started a war when she decided to take me to court, a war that I didn't want but was determined to win. I can't explain how much I hated not seeing my kids this weekend, but they were gonna have to suffer a little until we went in front of the judge in two weeks to settle the child support. Now that she was taking me to court, it was time for Diane to see how important it would be to work things out with me in a manner more friendly than she'd adopted.

I dialed my code into my phone and immediately shook my head when I heard the recording. *"Your mailbox is full. Please discard any unwanted messages. To hear your messages, please press one."* I knew most, if not all, of the messages were from my wife. I couldn't help but wonder what was more important to her, me not picking up the kids or me not bringing over the mortgage and child support checks.

I pressed one to hear the messages.

First message: "Wil, it's eight o'clock." Diane's voice was full of attitude. "Where are you? You were supposed to be here an hour ago." I pressed 3 to erase the message, but felt like shit doing so. I could hear Teddy calling my name in the background.

Message erased, next message: "Wil, dammit, it's eight thirty-eight. Where the hell are you? Lisa and Karen are sitting over here and we were supposed to go out to dinner at eight." I pressed 3, and laughed out loud, "Too bad."

Message erased, next message: "Wil! It's nine-fifteen and your ass better be in the hospital 'cause if you aren't, I'm gonna put you there." She sounded a little pissed off. I wonder if I ruined her Friday night. I laughed as I pressed 3.

There were five straight messages that were all hang-ups after that. I figured they were probably from Diane hanging up the phone in frustration. I erased each one until I heard a message from Allen.

"Hey, Wil, it's Allen. Diane called me three times lookin' for you. I haven't told her where you are, but she's talking about calling the police. I think she's really worried. Yo, give her a call, okay?" Damn, I didn't mean for her to bother Allen. I pressed 3.

Message erased, next message: "Wil, it's Diane and it's a little after two in the morning." Her voice was soft and sounded concerned. "It's not like you to not answer your cell phone. Please call me. I'm worried about you." I played the message back. Wow, she sounded like she actually *was* worried about me. I pushed 3 to get to the next message.

Message erased, next message: "Wil, it's six o'clock Saturday morning and I'm really worried about you. Please give me a call. Look, maybe you're right. We can work this out." I almost dropped the phone. She sounded even more sincere this time than the last message. Almost a little scared. God, would I love to work things out with her. I pressed 3. I was curious to see what else she might say.

Message erased, next message: "Yo, what up dawg? This is Jay. Listen, Diane called over here waking my ass up at six somethin' in the mornin' askin' a whole bunch of questions about if I knew where you were. I think she thinks you're gonna kill yourself or somethin'," he laughed. "Look, if you're out gettin' some, get some for me too. Otherwise, call your wife. She sounds like she's ready to let you come home," he laughed again.

I knew she really must have been worried if she picked up the phone and called Jay. I pushed 3 again, wondering about Jay's comment. Did she really think I would kill myself?

Message erased, next message: "Wil, this is Allen. I think I fucked up. Diane came by here a few minutes ago on her way to the police station. She said she was gonna file a missing persons report on you. I'm sorry, man, but I told her you were at Johnny's place in Sag Harbor. I mean the woman was crying, and she had my goddaughter in her arms. Man, I felt sorry for her. Look I tried to call you at Johnny's but his number in Sag Harbor is unlisted. I think you're gonna have to talk to her. To say she's pissed off is an understatement. Hey, I'm sorry, man. Call me." I pressed 3 and hung up the phone.

There were probably another ten messages to go, but I didn't wanna hear any more. I knew most of them would be from Diane and I had a good idea what she would be saying. I was sure it wouldn't be nice. I was about to call Allen when the phone rang.

"Hello?"

"Hi, Wil. How was your weekend? Did you have a nice trip?" It was Diane and her voice was a lot calmer than I expected.

"Yeah, it was nice. I had a good time. How was your weekend?" I decided to play along and not mention all the phone messages until she brought them up.

"It would have been fine if you came and got your fucking kids! *And* brought me my money!" she screamed. "Where the fuck is my money, Wil?" Her voice was so loud that it made the phone feel like it was vibrating. So much for her being calm.

"How are the kids, Diane?" I was being sarcastic, but I was hoping it might calm her down.

"Forget the kids! Where's my money?"

"You really want that money, don't you?"

"You damn right I want my money! I need that money to pay bills."

"Hey, what're you complaining about? You was getting your money like clockwork until now, weren't you?" I chuckled.

"Ain't a damn thing funny, Wil."

"Yes, there is something funny. What's funny is that you were getting child support money and I was paying all the bills and you still found it necessary to take my ass to court for more money."

"Don't play yourself, Wil. You know why I'm taking you to court."

"No, Diane, I don't know why. Why don't you tell me?"

" 'Cause I hate you, that's why." She said it like it was the most obvious fact on the planet.

"If you hate me so much, how come you said you wanted to work it out on those messages?" She was silent then she went back to her old routine.

"I want my money, Wil."

"Well, I don't wanna go to court, Diane, so we both want somethin'."

"Too bad. We're going to court. And you gonna give me my money too."

"You think so?"

"I know so, or you're not gonna see your kids."

"You know what, Diane? If you want your money so bad, then tell the judge to pay the mortgage, 'cause I ain't giving you *shit* until we go to court." The line was silent for about five seconds.

"Don't fuckin' play games with me, Wil."

"I ain't playin' games, Diane, you are. I was giving you more than I could afford because I wanted to do what's right. And you turn around and take me to court because I got a studio apartment. How petty can you get?"

"You better give me my money or—"

"Or what?" I cut her off. "You gonna keep my kids from me? I heard Teddy in the background when you called. He was screaming for his daddy. You really want that boy to grow up without his father, Diane? You know how close we are."

"Fuck you, Wil. I want my money." She hung up, but I was sure she'd call back tomorrow. She had to. The mortgage was due.

37

Allen

Beeep! Beeep! Beeep! Beeep! Beeep! Beeep! Beeep!
The alarm clock was screaming, but I was already in the bathroom taking a shower. I'd been up since five o'clock in the morning getting ready to take Jonathan to Johns Hopkins Hospital in Maryland. I'd already fed and dressed the baby, and now all I had to do was get myself dressed. Oh, and of course I still had to drag Rose out of bed. The last couple of weeks had been tough for Rose and me, but somehow we'd gotten through them. I was still pretty bitter about her whole disappearing act to Philly, but we'd had a few long talks and a couple of sessions with the pastor of the church, so lately I'd been giving her a pass. I found out from her doctor that she had been suffering some postpartum depression from her pregnancy and was actually jealous of the attention I was giving Jonathan. What she recommended was for us to spend more quality time together without our son. So I'd been taking Rose out at least once a week in addition to making quality time for her at home. So far it had been working out pretty well. She'd been acting more and more like a mother. Well, at least until this morning.

When I walked into the bedroom, Rose's arm was draped over the clock radio, which had been turned off.

"Rose, it's six-fifteen. Time to get up, baby." I removed some clothes from my dresser and sat down on the edge of the bed to put them on. When I had my pants and shirt on, I turned around to see her still snoozing.

"Rose, it's time to get up!" She didn't move so I shook her.

"Stop it!" she grumbled, rolling to the other side of the bed.

"Come on, Rose. It's time to get up. We've gotta drive all the way to Maryland."

"Please, Allen. I thought you were joking about that. I'm not goin' all the way to Maryland," she said in a raspy voice, trying to make herself comfortable on her pillow. I reached down and took hold of the covers, pulling them off the bed.

"Will you stop playin'?" She reached for the covers and pulled them back on her.

"Rose! Get up. We're supposed be there at ten-thirty." The only thing on my mind was getting my baby some medical attention. I was prepared to do anything possible to fight this disease.

"I changed my mind. I'm not goin'." She pulled the covers over her head.

"Oh, yes you are!" I grabbed the covers again, this time pulling them completely out of her reach. Rose turned over, obviously aggravated.

"I'm not going, Allen. I'm getting one of my migraines." I felt like smacking her. How many excuses was she gonna use?

"This is for the baby, Rose. You're always getting these so-called migraines when we've gotta do something for our son."

"Allen, I have a headache. So if you don't believe me, I really don't give a fuck. Now I told you I'm not goin'. My head hurts." She got out of bed, grabbed the covers, and got back into bed, turning her back to me.

"Aw'ight. Suit yourself, but this is fucked up and you know it." I reached down and grabbed my shoulder bag, leaving the room without a goodbye. If I ended up sleeping with Cinnamon this weekend, Rose didn't have anyone to blame but herself.

I pulled my car into the parking garage of Johns Hopkins hospital and found a spot right away. I sighed, looking back at my sleeping son in his car seat. He was about to be stuck and probed again and didn't even know it. We'd been driving for the past three and a half hours and he'd slept peacefully the whole way. I got out of the car and walked around to lift his car seat out as gently as I could. I fit it into the stroller without disturbing him at all. Whoever thought up the idea to have a stroller interchangeable with a car seat was a genius, because at that moment it really made my life easier. I was already feeling so guilty about bringing my son to this place where people would be hurting him in the name of helping him. At least I could let him sleep undisturbed for a few minutes longer. As I pushed the stroller toward the garage exit, my thoughts turned to Kyle.

Kyle had given us the stroller–car seat for a baby shower gift, even though he didn't show up at the shower. Now that I think about it, Jonathan was almost five weeks old and he hadn't stopped by the house to see him once. I kinda figured it had something to do with Rose, especially since both Kyle and Rose didn't want to have anything to do with each other since we'd been married. Matter of fact, I'd wanted to make Kyle Jonathan's godfather but Rose was completely against it. I don't know what was going on between those two, but their dislike for each other sure had become more intense. When I got home, it was one more problem I was going to have to address.

Five minutes later I was standing nervously in front of the receptionist. She'd just called up to the social work department and I was expecting to see Cinnamon for the first time in six years at any moment. We'd been talking on the phone every day for weeks, but just the thought of seeing her again had me pacing around like a teenager about to go on his first date.

"Mr. Jackson?" I couldn't see her, but I recognized Cinnamon's voice right away, calling me from behind. I took a deep breath before I turned around.

"Ms. Lindsey." I turned and there she was, looking as beautiful as ever. Neither one of us said a word. We just stared at each other until a young white woman standing next to Cinnamon snapped us out of our trance.

"Excuse me." She stuck her hand out in greeting. "I don't mean to interrupt this personal moment, but I'm Mary Peters. I'm the social worker for the blood clinic you and your son are going to today." Both Cinnamon and I blushed. At that point I couldn't help but be glad Rose had stayed home, because if Ms. Peters could sense the chemistry between us, Rose would've caught on right away.

"I'm sorry, Mary. This is Allen Jackson." Cinnamon's tone was all business now as she walked over to Jonathan's stroller. "And this is his son, Jonathan." I shook Mary Peters's hand as I watched Cinnamon lift Jonathan from his car seat. "Ohhh, Allen, he is so cute." She held him close and kissed him.

"Thank you," I smiled.

"Where's his mother?" Cinnamon looked around and I lowered my head. "No, she didn't have the nerve to not show up." Cinnamon sounded angry.

I glanced at Mary Peters. "I'll talk to you about that later." Ms. Peters decided that was her cue.

"Mr. Jackson, why don't you follow me? We've got a lot of tests to run," she told me. "You'll see Ms. Lindsey later."

"Aren't you coming with me?" I looked at Cinnamon, a little disappointed.

"No, I've got things to do here, and the blood clinic is Mary's baby. But don't worry. You're in good hands, and she'll bring you to me when you're done. I've got a pan of lasagna with your name on it at the house. Besides, you can't go back to New York without meeting my son."

Jonathan and I spent most of the morning with Ms. Peters. We both had blood drawn and I had to fill out a ton of paperwork on everything from my family's medical history to what kinds of food I ate and what formula he took. I felt pretty stupid with Rose not there. Especially since they really wanted to have both parents' information and blood. When I got home, I was gonna give her more than a headache.

I'd kicked off my shoes and had both my feet up on Cinnamon's coffee table, sipping a glass of wine. The smooth sounds of Al Jarreau were relaxing my frayed nerves. It had been a long, long day. I was waiting for Cinnamon to come back into the room. She had taken her son Evan into the bedroom to put him to bed. I'd put Jonathan down about an hour ago and he was already asleep in the portable crib in her guest room. I was pretty sure I wouldn't hear from him for another couple of hours when it was time for his bottle.

It took about twenty minutes before Cinnamon came back in the room, but when she came out, I saw that the wait had been well worth it. She looked more than stunning. She was wearing a red silk nightgown that draped down to her ankles and showed every curve of her body.

"I hope you weren't too bored while I was gone." She picked up the glass of wine she'd left behind and sat down next to me.

"No, not at all. Me and Al Jarreau go way back," I told her, sipping on my wine.

"I didn't have a chance to talk to Mary, but how did things go with the study?"

"As well as to be expected, I guess, considering they needed blood samples from my wife to complete half the tests." It felt strange saying "my wife" to the woman who I once thought I would marry.

"That's right. I forgot about that. What are they gonna do?"

"The doctor gave me a prescription for her to have blood drawn. I guess the lab will have the results sent down."

"Yeah, but is she going to be willing to give blood?"

"Oh, she's going to be willing," I said angrily. "Or she's gonna be looking for a new husband." Cinnamon smiled, then patted my knee to calm me down.

"You're a good father, Allen. You know that?"

"I try."

"No, you do more than try. I wish my ex-husband was like you." She reached her hand over and massaged one of my shoulders. "You're so tense. You're gonna have to learn how to relax."

"If you knew what I go through at home and at work, you'd know there's no such thing as relaxation. Just drama."

"Sit down on the floor," she ordered. I did as I was told without a second thought. I sat down in front of her, my back resting against her shins as she began to massage my shoulders. It felt so good, I closed my eyes for about twenty minutes before either of us spoke a word.

"Allen, can I ask you a question?"

"Sure. What's up?"

"When we were going out, did you ever cheat on me?" She stopped massaging me and I opened my eyes wide as I turned to look at her. I was hoping something in her face would tell me she was joking.

"No!"

"Come on. You don't have to lie to me. It was a long time ago."

"You're right, I don't have to lie. I did not cheat on you. What would make you think that?"

"What makes you any different than any other man? I figured you were like my husband and had some woman on the side." I turned my head and shoulders so that I could see her better.

"You don't understand how much I was in love with you, do you?"

"I guess not. Especially since you never came after me. Do you know how long I waited down here for you to come for me? A year, Allen. I was down here a year before I even looked at another man. Waiting for you." She was angry. I could hear it in her tone though she hadn't even raised her voice.

"Cinnamon, I wanted to come after you. I just . . ." She cut me off.

"You just what? You were just too afraid to leave your mother? That's why I left, Allen. I was hoping our love would be strong enough to make you cut those apron strings. But it wasn't. *Your mother* was the other woman in our relationship."

"You're right," was all I could say, and I think that's all she wanted to hear. She began to massage my shoulders again.

"One more question."

I was afraid to agree but I did. "Okay."

"If you had gotten my letter before your wedding, would you have called me?"

I'd thought about that question a lot over the past few weeks. I couldn't be sure if I would have, but I had no doubt that my feelings for this woman were still strong. "I think so, Cinnamon."

She didn't say a word but I could feel her smile behind me as her massage became tender, almost romantic.

"You're so tight," she whispered, gently kneading my muscles.

"I know. You were right before. I really do need to learn how to relax."

"I used to be good at making you relax." She laughed. Her voice was even softer now and sounded even sexier as I felt her face gently rub up against my hair. When she was close enough, she blew in my ear, sending goose bumps up my arms. I moaned when she did it again, her hands running down my chest. In one smooth motion she was opening the buttons on my shirt.

I turned my head toward her and her soft lips met mine. Memories of our once-tender lovemaking flashed through my mind. My desire for her was even more intense now. I slid my tongue into her mouth and she sucked on it gently. When we broke the kiss, she lay on her back and I slid on top of her. My stiff manhood rubbed against her crotch as she gently kissed my earlobe.

"I never stopped loving you, Allen," she whispered.

"And I never stopped loving you," I whispered back, kissing her again. She slowly lifted her nightgown above her hips and I felt the smooth skin of her buttocks and thighs with my hand. Without missing a beat, she unhooked my pants and slid her hands into my boxers, sliding my pants and underwear below my knees.

I could hear Jonathan crying in the background and I tried to ignore him as Cinnamon took hold of my manhood, making me moan.

"I want you, Allen." She positioned me to enter her and I could feel the warmth and heat she was offering. But just as I was about to push myself into her, I heard Jonathan cry once more. This time it jolted me back to reality.

"I want you too, Cinnamon, but I can't do this." I pushed myself off of her and stood up to pull up my pants.

"What's wrong? I thought you said you want me too. You loved me." She pulled her nightgown down as if she was embarrassed to be exposed.

"I do love you, and I want you so bad I can taste it. But you hear that little boy in there? I'm married to his mother, and although it's dwindling, I do have love for her. I can't do this to my son. Not until I'm sure it's over with his mother. I love you with all my heart, but I can't do this until I'm sure. I hope you understand."

"Yeah, I understand, Allen. That Rose is a lucky woman to have a husband like you. I hope she realizes that."

"Somehow I doubt it, Cinnamon. Somehow I doubt it." I turned around and walked back to her guest room where Jonathan was crying. Once I closed the door, I didn't open it until morning when it was time to leave.

38

Wil

My heart was beating fast and I was nervous as hell as the elevator doors opened. I peered out onto the busy second-floor corridor and couldn't believe that life had come to this. I took a deep breath, then stepped off the elevator. Allen, Jay, and Greg Thomas were following behind me. We were in the family court building on Parsons Boulevard and in about ten minutes I would be standing in front of a judge to temporarily settle the child support and custody battle I was having with Diane. To say I was antsy and nervous was an understatement. I was scared to death. I'd wanted to have all my boys there, especially Kyle, but he insisted that it'd be a bad move for him to be there since Diane hated him almost more than she hated me.

"Yo dawg, there she is." Jay nonchalantly motioned to his left, and there was Diane, sitting on a bench about twenty feet away. I was surprised when I didn't see Lisa sitting next to her but she was probably expecting Kyle to be there and wanted to avoid seeing him. Instead of Lisa, Diane was surrounded by her three ghettofied girlfriends, Sonya, Michelle, and Desiree. They must've noticed us right away because immediately they began whispering like there was some type of conspiracy going on.

"You guys wait here. I'm gonna go talk to her." I took a step forward, but before I could take another, Greg grabbed my arm.

"As your lawyer, I don't think this is wise, Wil." I grabbed his hand and removed it from my arm.

"You're my lawyer, Greg. Not my daddy. It's your job to give me advice. I heard your advice. Now I'm gonna go talk to my wife. So move!" I gave him a cold look and he stepped aside, but I could tell he wasn't happy about it.

Diane was less than twenty steps away, but I swear it felt like a mile. I could see her and her friends whispering and pointing as I walked over. It was enough to make a brother paranoid.

"Can I help you?" Diane looked up from the bench and rolled her eyes.

"Yeah, can we help you?" her fake-blue-eyes, bad-weave-wearin' friend Desiree added with attitude as the rest of her friends laughed.

I glanced at each of the women, then at Diane. "Can we talk? In private?"

"The only thing I have to say to you is *show me the money*." Diane clapped her hands and laughed, and her friends joined in like it was the funniest joke she'd ever told. Personally I didn't see a damn thing funny, so I scowled at each of them, which only made them roll their eyes more.

"Okay, Di, you had your laugh. Can we talk now?" I glanced at my watch, then back at Diane. It was almost time to go in the courtroom. If I was going to talk her out of this silliness, it had to be quick.

"Y'know, you are really aggravating me." She sounded annoyed, but that didn't stop her from getting up and walking away from her friends. I followed her down the hall, and when we were out of listening range, she turned around.

"What do you want, Wil?" She placed her hand on her hip.

"I want you to stop this, Diane. I want you to let me come home so I can take care of you and the kids like I always have. We don't need these people to tell us how to take care of our family," I sighed.

"What's wrong, Wil? Scared you're gonna lose everything?" She smirked.

"No, Diane, I'm scared I'm gonna lose you." I gave her my most sincere look. "I love you, Di, and I'm going crazy without you."

"I love you too, Wil. And that's why I hate you so fucking much for doing what you did to me. You fucking, no-good dog!" She tried to slap me but I grabbed her arm. "Let go of me before I scream," she demanded.

"Last chance, Di. I love you. Always will. And you just admitted you still love me, but if we walk in that courtroom today, I become the enemy." She forced herself to laugh, trying to get free.

"You still don't get it, do you, Wil? You've been the enemy ever since I found those pictures of you and those hoochies." She pulled her arm free and walked toward her friends. I shook my head as I walked back over to mine.

"What'd she say?" Jay asked as he watched them walk into the courtroom.

"She said that I'm the enemy." I glanced at Greg. "You sure we can win this?"

"Well, like I told you before, there's never a winner when children are involved. But yeah, I can't see her getting anywhere near what she's asking. And you've got a real good shot at joint custody. I'd take your case before I'd take hers."

"Good. Maybe if I win, it'll make her see the error of her ways and she'll let me come home."

The courtroom was small and looked more like someone's office than the courtrooms you see on TV. There was an expensive-looking desk, which was supposed to be the judge's bench, with about ten chairs in front of it, along with a small table for the stenographer. The judge, a white woman in her late fifties, looked more like someone's grandma than a judge, but her demeanor was very official. She wanted the hearing to start as soon as we sat down.

The child support hearing itself was short, and except for Diane and me, there was no testimony. Greg had explained to me earlier that because it was only a hearing to determine child support and visitation, not a divorce proceeding, the judge was the only one who would ask any questions of us. Both Diane's lawyer and Greg had a chance to state their cases. Diane's lawyer, a forty-something white yuppie, did her best to portray me as a sex-crazed degenerate who hadn't given his wife money or come to see his children in almost a month. She'd done everything from show those pictures of the naked girls and me, to dumping a bag of sex toys Diane and I had accumulated to spice things up on the judge's bench. I couldn't believe my ears when she had the nerve to tell the judge that I forced Diane to use them. What a crock of shit that was.

Greg, on the other hand, portrayed Diane as a money-hungry bitch who had no love or concern for her children's welfare. I wasn't too happy about this strategy, but he had assured me Diane's lawyer would portray me much worse, which she did. He showed the judge the agreement and canceled checks I'd written during our separation along with pay stubs to validate our claim that I could not afford that or any increase. He also presented my 401K loan and loan papers I had Kyle draw up when he loaned me money for my apartment. He tried his best to explain the pictures as a practical joke, but I don't think the judge bought it at all. Despite that I was comfortable with the job he'd done. The rest was up to the Lord.

"Mr. Thomas, you and Ms. Lewis have both presented persuasive arguments. Why don't we adjourn for lunch till two o'clock, and when we return, I'll give you my decision."

When we returned from lunch, it took the judge about ten minutes before she came back into the courtroom carrying a file. She sat in her chair silently as she shuffled through the papers, finally taking off her glasses before speaking.

"As you all know, this is a custody and support hearing, not a divorce proceeding. So this court is only concerned with the welfare of the children involved, and not the parents." The judge placed her glasses back on her head and began to read the papers in front of her.

"Okay, in the case of custody of the two minor children Katherine and Teddy Duncan, the court awards custody to the mother Diane Duncan."

What? My eyes went wild with surprise. I couldn't believe what I was hearing. My God, she was taking my kids away from me. I turned toward Greg with a bewildered look, hoping he was going to object or something, but he was face front staring at the judge like everything was going according to plan. I couldn't believe it. I didn't want to take the kids away from Diane, but I did want to be a part of their lives. Now with this crazy-ass judge giving her custody, it meant that she had all the power when it came to my kids. It meant I had nothing.

As every second went by, it was getting harder and harder to breathe, and I could feel my stomach knotting as the judge's words became painfully real. I glanced at Greg again, and he was still staring at the judge. That son of a bitch had practically promised me I'd get joint custody. How the hell he could sit there without saying a word was beyond me. I was about to give him a piece of my mind, but he got lucky and the judge started to speak again.

"Mr. Duncan, since your wife is presently living in your house and you are living in a studio apartment, the court has decided that it is in the best interest of the children not to award you joint custody. If in the future you find more suitable arrangements to house your children, we will gladly reconsider. Now as far as visitation, Mr. Duncan, you will have every other weekend, holidays, and two weeks during the summer."

I exhaled slowly. At least I'd be able to see my kids. I glanced over at Diane, who was grinning from ear to ear. Things were working out just the way she had planned. All she had to do was get my child support raised and she'd have all the power and all the money. Damn, would you believe after all this I still had love for that woman? But just once I'd love to smack that grin off her face. Especially now that this psycho judge was probably gonna make me pay her out the ass.

"Mrs. Duncan, it says here that you made almost fifty thousand dollars last year. Is that correct?"

"Yes, your honor." Diane nodded with a smile.

"And Mr. Duncan, you made sixty thousand dollars last year?"

"Yes, ma'am," I replied, though I felt like I could barely breathe. My knees were wobbling.

"All right, in the matter of child support, the court awards Mrs. Duncan one thousand dollars a month, plus half the cost of child care." I almost lost my lunch. I held on to the desk in front of me so I wouldn't fall flat on my face. I couldn't believe it. That bitch of a judge had just raised my child support four hundred dollars. How the hell did she expect me to pay an extra four hundred dollars a month, half the day care, and all the rest of the bills at the house? I glanced at Greg, and he had the nerve to smile.

"What are you frowning for? We won," he whispered.

"How do you see that?" I raised my eyebrows in confusion. Diane's loud voice made me turn toward her before Greg answered.

"What the fuck do you mean, that's all I get?" she yelled at her lawyer. "You got Lisa ten times this!" Her face was beet red. The only time I'd ever seen her that angry was the day she kicked me out. I watched in amazement when she turned to the judge, who was about to leave. I could tell by her facial expression that she was about to do something stupid. I think her lawyer sensed it too, because she tried to stop her from speaking. But it was too late.

"Is that all I get?" Diane yelled at the judge. The judge stopped where she was and sat back down in her chair, placing her glasses back on her head.

"Yes, Mrs. Duncan, that's all you get. I don't know what your lawyer told you, but we have very strict laws when it comes to child support in this state. And the law in this state says that you get twenty-five percent of Mr. Duncan's income for two children, and that's what I awarded you." Diane stared at the judge in amazement.

"To be honest, I can't believe Ms. Lewis didn't advise you to keep your previous agreement with Mr. Duncan." It might have been my imagination, but it almost looked like the judge smirked as she said this.

"I did, your honor," Lewis interjected. Diane looked at her lawyer and sucked her teeth.

"But, but . . . what about the electric and the car note? Who's gonna pay the mortgage or the other bills?" The helpless look Diane gave the judge even made me feel sorry for her. She'd been so arrogant and determined to get me that she hadn't even listened to her lawyer.

"Mrs. Duncan, you make fifty thousand dollars a year. I think you'll be able to manage." The judge stood up, ready to leave again.

"You gotta be fucking kidding me. You can't do this!" Diane was out of control, and took a step toward the judge with balled-up fists, like she was about to kick her ass. Lucky for her, her friends grabbed her before a court officer did.

"Yes, Mrs. Duncan, I can do this. Now one more outburst from you and I'll have you locked up for contempt." She took off her glasses and pointed at Diane's lawyer. "Ms. Lewis, if I were you, I would get your client out of my courtroom right now." The judge and Diane exchanged angry stares as her lawyer and friends escorted her out the door.

Once Diane was out of the courtroom, I had a short conversation with Greg, who explained everything that had just happened, then quickly left, saying he had to see another client. I'd won. I'd beaten Diane in the courtroom. But even though I had supposedly won, the only thing on my mind was the look she gave me as I left the courtroom. Her friends were trying to console her, but she looked like something out of *The Exorcist*.

"What the fuck are you looking at, Wil?" she screamed. "You think you won something? You ain't won shit, Wil!" I tried to ignore her and kept walking down the hallway, but she was right on my heels. I could hear her pumps stomping behind me. "Did you hear me, Wil? You ain't won shit! And don't think you gonna see the kids!" I stopped dead in my tracks as I turned to face her.

"What do you mean, I can't see my kids?" I roared. I think I scared her friends more than I scared her, because they all took a few steps backward. "Didn't you hear what the judge said in there? She said I get the kids every other weekend." Diane twisted her lips and sucked her teeth.

"Please, you get the kids when I say you get the kids. And you ain't gettin' shit till I get my money. Now, you can think I'm playin' if you want to."

I stepped closer. "Look, Di. You took me to court. I didn't ask for this. All I wanted to do was come home. But I won, and if you wanna play games, we can be right back here in court next week. Then you can explain yourself to the judge. 'Cause I'm gonna see my kids and all I'm gonna give you is a thousand dollars. The law on my side."

"We'll see," she said threateningly. "It's Monday, Wil. You've got until next Monday to get me my money. There's an opening in the Atlanta distribution center, and they've offered me the job. If I don't get my money by Monday, I'm putting in for a transfer." Diane turned and strutted with her friends to the elevator.

"Don't do this, Di. I don't wanna fight with you," I pleaded as she stepped on the elevator.

"I want my money, Wil. And you won't see those kids if I don't get it. 'Cause we'll be in Atlanta at my mother's place, and that's a mighty long drive every other weekend." I watched the elevator doors close.

"Shit!" She was right. I hadn't won a damn thing.

"Yo, dawg." Jay grabbed my arm. "I told you before, I can get you and Diane back together. All you gotta do is say the word."

"I don't need your help, so stay out of this! I've had enough help from my friends. That's how I got into this mess, remember?" I gave Allen an evil look.

"But you haven't even heard my idea." I turned to Jay with a menacing glare. I knew he was trying to help, but his kind of help I didn't need.

"I said stay out of it! I'll just have to pay her if she's gonna be this way." I had no other choice.

39

Allen

If it weren't for bad luck, I wouldn't have any luck at all. It was Thursday morning, and I was having a bad day. On my desk was a stack of files a foot high, and I was clueless as to where they came from. To top that off, the only person who would know where they came from, my assistant Jill, called in sick. So I was going to be clueless at least one more day. And if that wasn't bad enough, at the last minute Rose had one of her mysterious headaches and I had to get Jonathan dressed and take him over to Ma's house before work. That made me twenty minutes late, and I missed a meeting with my boss. So she chewed my ass out for a good twenty minutes. Then the minute she left my office the phone started ringing.

"This is Allen in Benefits. How can I help you?"

"Hi, Allen, this is Cinnamon." I smiled. I'd been thinking about her a lot since I left Maryland last week. Truth is, I missed her, and although it was the right thing to do, I still regretted not making love to her the other night.

"What's up, Cin?"

"Nothing. How are you?" She sounded so serious, so professional, and the only thing I could think of was how upset she was when I told her I couldn't make love to her. God, I had hoped she'd understand by now. The last thing I wanted was for her to be upset with me. I decided to avoid the subject and try to lighten the mood.

"How's everything goin' down there in Maryland? Evan all right?"

"He's fine, Allen. Look, I need to—" She still sounded like this was business, not personal, so I cut her off.

"Look, Cin. I hope you're not mad about last week. I would never try to hurt you. I swear. I was just trying to do the right thing by you and my son."

"I know that, Allen, and that's not why I called."

"It isn't?" I was confused and worried. Cinnamon had called my office a dozen times since I'd found her letter at Ma's, but she never sounded so serious before. "What's going on, Cinnamon?"

"Allen, Dr. Stone, the head of the hemoglobin department, just called me. He wants you to come down to the hospital and take another blood test as soon as possible."

"Why? What's wrong?" Now I was really worried.

"I'm not really sure. Probably nothing. I just know they wanna do some more blood work." I took a deep breath.

"Okay, let me talk to my boss and see if I can get the rest of the day off. Then I'll stop by Ma's and get Jonathan. That kid's gonna hate me for lettin' y'all stick him again."

"Why don't you leave Jonathan with your mother? I'm sure the doctors can get what they need from you."

"Don't they need his blood?" Now I was even more confused.

"No, the doctors just need to see you."

"What's going on, Cin? Is there something wrong with my boy?"

"No, Allen, they just musta spilled your blood or misplaced it. It happens sometimes. No big deal." She was trying to sound nonchalant, but she wasn't fooling me.

"Look, don't bullshit me, okay? I know you. What's wrong with my boy?" She hesitated, took a breath before speaking again. Whatever was going on, she didn't wanna be the one to tell me.

"Allen, I honestly don't know what's going on, and they're not going to tell me because of how close we are."

"Aw'ight, I'll buy that for now. But when I get down there, I want some answers, and I want you to have them. I'll see you around one o'clock."

"Good. Mary Peters will be waiting for you. Just have them page her when you get here." She hung up, and I had to wonder why I was paging Mary Peters instead of her.

I could tell something was up the second Cinnamon and Dr. Stone, the head of the hemoglobin department, walked into his office. I'd just given blood about an hour ago and was waiting patiently in the doctor's office to find out why they needed the additional blood in the first place. Up to this point, no one had given me any answers. This was the first I'd even seen Cinnamon since I'd arrived. Dr. Stone's face looked as if he were getting ready to deliver some bad news, while Cinnamon looked like she was about to cry. I just knew they were about to tell me I had cancer or something. Especially since my friend JB from work was diagnosed with prostate cancer after a blood test last year. Suddenly I felt a wave of depression take over me. I could deal with the fact that I might die. Everyone has to die one day, but what was going to happen to Jonathan if I wasn't around?

Cinnamon sat down next to me, and the doctor sat down behind his desk. Both of them were staring at me, but neither of them said a word. The silence was driving me crazy, and I couldn't take it anymore. I had to know what was going on.

"Will somebody tell me what's going on?" I stared back and forth between the two of them, holding on to the arms of the chair so my hands wouldn't shake. I hoped they could sense I was not in the mood for games. Cinnamon looked at the doctor, and the doctor looked at me.

"Mr. Jackson, I don't know how to tell you this, but we found something very disturbing with the blood sample we took last week. That's why we requested the second."

"I kind've figured that, Dr. Stone, especially since Ms. Lindsey here"—I cut my eyes at Cinnamon, then back to the doctor—"has been avoiding me ever since I got down here." I sighed. "I want you to be honest with me, Doc. How long do I have to live?"

The doctor exchanged a glance with Cinnamon, then looked at me quizzically. I'm sure they never expected me to figure out that I was dying.

"Oh, no, Allen," Cinnamon said sadly, "you've got this all wrong." She patted my knee, trying to comfort me.

"Mr. Jackson, you do have this all wrong. You're not going to die." The doctor tried to give me a reassuring smile.

"I'm not? Then who?" My eyes went wide with fear. "Oh, God. Not Jonathan. Not my boy." I could feel tears welling in my eyes. I felt like I was about to pass out.

"Allen, no one is going to die," Cinnamon whispered, gently rubbing my back.

"Then what's going on, Cin? Tell me what's going on. I know you guys didn't have me come down here for nothing." My eyes never left hers. She tried to look at the doctor, but I grabbed her wrist. "No! Don't look at him. Look at me. Tell me what's going on." She took a deep breath and exhaled before she spoke.

"When they ran your blood through the tests last week, they couldn't find the trait." She looked like she was about to cry, but I didn't understand what she was talking about.

"What d'ya mean they couldn't find the trait?" I turned to the doctor for clarification.

"What she means, Mr. Jackson, is we could not find the trait for sickle cell anemia in your blood."

"What?"

My stomach started churning. I felt like I was about to lose my lunch. This man could not be saying what I thought he was saying. *Please God, make him wrong.*

"Are you crazy? Do you know what you're saying? Do you?" I leaned forward in my chair and was about to get in the doctor's face. "You're trying to tell me that Jonathan's not my son?" I was yelling at the doctor, but even as I said the words, I knew inside that it was possible. I didn't wanna admit it, but I knew my wife well enough by now to know there might be a chance the lab was right. Especially with Rose swearing Jonathan was premature and the doctor saying he was full-term. Now it was starting to make sense. I should've known something was up when Rose was so eager to try to get pregnant *before* the wedding. I slammed my hand on the doctor's desk.

"Mr. Jackson, please, please calm down," the doctor pleaded. Cinnamon reached up and grabbed my hand as the doctor continued. "We're not sure of anything right now. It was quite possible that we had mixed up your blood with someone else's or that there was some type of error. That's why we asked you to come down and give us another blood sample." The doctor tried to smile, but I think the way I looked at him killed that idea.

"Allen, please sit down." Cinnamon guided me back in my chair.

"So what did the other test say?" Maybe there was still a shred of hope that the new test would uncover a mistake on the part of the hospital, so I could get the hell out of there and go home to my son. I didn't know what I would do if Jonathan wasn't my child. I could barely process the thought.

"We haven't gotten the results yet. We're waiting for them now." The doctor looked at his watch. "It's going to be another ten minutes or so."

So we sat in the doctor's office and waited in uncomfortable silence for almost half an hour till the phone rang. I could tell by the doctor's expression as he spoke that the news on the other end wasn't any better than what they told me the first time.

"Jonathan's not my son, is he, Doctor?" I was sitting at the edge of the chair, holding my breath.

"I'm afraid it doesn't look that way, Mr. Jackson, but there are still some tests we should run."

I wanted to jump up in the air and scream, throw things at him, tip over his desk for giving me such bad news, but everything I wanted to do I couldn't. I was too numb. I felt like I'd been given a huge shot of novocaine that had spread throughout my entire body. I'd never been so overcome with grief in my entire life. I'll never forget the pain I felt sitting in the hospital when my dad died of cancer, and it was devastating to learn that Jonathan had sickle cell. But nothing I'd ever experienced could compare to the way I felt when this doctor confirmed that Jonathan was not my biological son.

"Allen, are you okay?" Cinnamon placed one hand on my lap and the other on my back, rubbing it gently.

"No, Cinnamon, I'm not okay," I growled. Somehow I pulled my shoulder from her. I didn't wanna be touched or consoled. I just wanted to get my hands around Rose's neck and choke the life outta her. "I gotta get back to New York."

"Why don't you stay down here with me a few days? I'll take the rest of the week off. I'll show you DC. Maybe we'll go to Virginia Beach."

"No!" I shook my head. "She's not gonna get away with this, Cinnamon. You don't understand. You don't do shit like this to people. Especially not people you're supposed to love." I stood to leave, but she grabbed my arm. I gave her an evil look, but it didn't matter. She still didn't let go.

"I know what she did was wrong, Allen, but you don't need to see her. Not yet, anyway. You might do something you'll regret."

She was right. Anger had taken over my emotions. I was no longer feeling sorry for myself. I just wanted to put my foot in Rose's ass.

"I've got to go home. That bitch ruined my life." Tears rolled down my face.

"Please Allen, just stay with me a few days. I don't wanna see you in jail." The way she pleaded confirmed how much she still cared for me, and for a split second the thought actually comforted me.

"I'm sorry, but I've gotta go home and handle my business." I pulled myself away from her and walked out of the office.

I'd been sitting in my car for the better part of an hour staring at the front door. I wanted to go inside, but I was scared. Scared of what might happen if I went in. Scared of how I might react if I walked through that door and saw Rose. I wasn't a violent person, but I was so hurt inside that I would've done anything to make the pain go away. And killing Rose was at the top of my list. I reached over to the passenger seat and took hold of the claw hammer I'd bought at Home Depot about an hour ago.

I could do a hell of a lot of damage with this, I thought as I slammed the hammer into the passenger seat. Yep, a couple of hard swings and it would be all over. Rose would be dead as a doorknob. Funny thing is, I was mad enough to do it. The only problem was Rose wouldn't have to suffer that way. I opened the car door, then slammed it shut without getting out. Goddammit! I wanted her to suffer just like I was suffering. Killing her was just too damn easy. So I decided not to take her life, but to make it the most miserable existence in the world. I glanced at my watch. It was a little after midnight. I opened the car door and walked to the front door. Rose opened the door before I could even take out my key.

"Where the hell have you been? Your mother dropped off your son three hours ago. He's been crying for two damn hours."

"My son?" I raised both eyebrows. You know, I had to laugh. Here I am sitting out in my car for an hour thinking about killing her ass because Jonathan's not my son and she's upset because I haven't been home to take care of him. She's got some fucking nerve. It's a good thing I left that hammer in the car, 'cause I might've been smashing it up side her head right about now.

"What the hell's so funny?" she demanded.

"You are, Rose! You're what's so damn funny. Did you give Jonathan his medicine?"

"No. That's not my job. It's your job." She gave me this superior little smirk, and I felt like smacking her.

"You stupid idiot. That's probably why he's crying. Get the fuck outta my way." Somehow, instead of smacking her I contained myself to giving her a dirty look, then pushed my way past her. She was so shocked by my actions and comments that she just stood there with her mouth open. When I got in the apartment, the first thing I heard was Jonathan wailing. My mind told me to ignore him and go pack up my shit, get the hell outta there before I did get violent. But my heart told me to go check on my boy. I followed my heart.

"What's up, little man?" He was lying in his crib, crying his eyes out, but he stopped the second he heard my voice. I smiled when I saw that he was wearing the New York Yankees pajamas I'd bought him the other day. God, I loved that kid so much. I took his medicine off the changing table and gave him a dropper full. "There you go, buddy. That should make you feel better."

I picked him up and held him against my chest. Tears began to well in my eyes and I could feel myself getting all choked up when he started to coo. I wasn't sure if the medicine kicked in or if he was just glad to see me, but that's when I realized that he was my son. I didn't need no blood test to validate that. He had my name, and I'd taken care of him since he was born, so it didn't matter whether we shared blood or not. He was my son. I loved him, and I would continue to take care of him.

"Damn, that baby sure loves his daddy." I could hear Rose in the doorway behind me, but I never turned around. How the hell she could just let him lay there without giving him his medicine was beyond me. I shook my head and bit my lip. I felt like packing up all our shit and running away with him. Maybe then she couldn't ruin his life like she'd done mine.

"That damn baby has a name, Rose. It's Jonathan. Why don't you use it sometime? After all, he is named after your father." I kissed Jonathan, then placed him in his crib, making sure that his pacifier was in his mouth before I turned to face Rose. "You hate him, don't you?"

"No, I don't hate him. He's just an inconvenience sometime," she answered so nonchalantly.

"Inconvenience! That's your baby. How can you call him an inconvenience?" I ran up to her and gave her a hearty shove, pushing her out of Jonathan's room and onto the living room floor.

"What the fuck is your problem?" she shouted as she struggled to her feet.

"You wanna know what my problem is? You! You're my fucking problem!" I shoved her again.

"I'm calling the police!"

"Go head! Call 'em!" I pointed to the phone. "I don't give a shit. You've already ruined my life. What else can you do? You fucking whore!" I raised my hand to scare her, but Rose didn't move.

"What did you call me?" Her voice was weak, and shock was all over her face. The whole time we'd been together, I'd never, ever called her anything but her name.

"I called you a fucking whore! And that's what you are! A whore!"

"I'm not a whore, Allen. And don't you ever call me that again." She said it like it was a label she'd been trying to rid herself of a long time.

"Yes, you are! You fucked Jay. You fucked Kyle. For Christ's sake, you even fucked Wil. You're a fucking whore, Rose, and I hate you!" I'm not gonna lie, I was taking pleasure in the fact that Rose's eyes were starting to tear, and she was now shaking with fear. I'd never seen this woman humbled in all the time I'd known her.

"That was a long time ago, Allen. I'm not like that anymore. I swear to God I'm not like that anymore." She was pleading with a trembling voice as she choked on her tears. "And anything Kyle told you is a lie." She sniffled.

"Yeah, right. Once a ho, always a ho. I feel like I should run to the doctor for an AIDS test."

"Allen, I'm not a whore. Please, you've got to believe me. I stopped acting like that the day I met you." She actually said that shit with sincerity, which pissed me off even more. So I lifted my hand in the air like I was gonna smack the shit outta her. I wasn't gonna do it—I just wanted to see fear on her face. I was about to tell her that I was leaving her ass, and more importantly that I was taking Jonathan with me, but that's when I heard a knock on the door.

"Don't you fucking move!" I ordered, and she didn't.

I peeked through the peephole. *Fuck!* One of my neighbors must've heard us fighting and called the cops, because two police officers were standing at my door. I took a deep breath, gesturing for Rose to get up, then opened the door.

"Can I help you?" I smiled at the two cops, praying that Rose wasn't going to run over and tell them I'd attacked her. Thank God she had some sense and just sat on the couch.

"Mr. Jackson?" the white cop asked.

"Yes."

"My name's Officer Monroe, and this is my partner, Officer Rollins. Are you related to an Audrey Jackson?"

"Yes, she's my mother. Is everything all right, Officer?" I swallowed hard. *Please God, don't let anything be wrong with my ma.*

"Mr. Jackson, there's been an incident. We need for you to come with us." I was trying to breathe but it was hard.

"Why? Is something wrong with my mother? What type of incident?" I was starting to hyperventilate as I waited for an answer. Both cops looked at each other, then the black cop spoke.

"Your mother was robbed and shot in front of her house a few hours ago. She's in critical condition," he said somberly.

"Oh God, no! Not my ma. Not my ma!" I started to pace around in a circle, imagining my mother lying in a pool of blood. I could feel Rose's arms wrap around me, and for that brief instant I didn't care about the things she'd done. I needed someone to hold on to me before I collapsed.

40

Jay

I'd just taken a shower and packed a small overnight bag. I was headed out the door, my arms filled with birthday presents for Tracy, when the phone rang. Tracy and I were going to spend the weekend in Atlantic City together to celebrate her birthday, and as usual I was running about an hour late. When the phone rang, I actually considered letting the machine answer it, but decided against it at the last second. I'd sent Kenya and the girls down to her parents' place in Baltimore for the weekend and I didn't wanna take a chance that her car had broken down or that she mighta had an accident and turned around. So I placed my bag on the floor and answered it.

"Hello?" The line was silent, so I spoke again. There was still no answer, and it reminded me of the trouble Kyle was having with Val. Only I hadn't given my home number to anyone, not even Tracy. Finally I heard a very deep male voice.

"Your ass is dead, nigga."

"Who the hell is this?" I reached over and pushed the button to the Caller ID. The number came up unknown. *Fuck!* I hung up the phone. That's when I got a sudden chill. What if Tracy's pops was playing games?

Nah, it couldn't be him, I reasoned, staring at the phone. *Or could it?*

It wouldn't be hard for him or his cop friends to get my home number after they found out where I lived so easily. I felt myself break out in a cold sweat. Damn, that guy was really becoming a pain in my ass. As soon as I picked up my bag, the phone rang again. I dropped the bag and snatched the receiver, yelling this time.

"Hello!"

"Jay?" A male voice spoke so quickly, there was no chance for me to recognize it.

"Who this?"

"It's Wil. Why you answering the phone like that?"

"Somebody just called here talkin' shit and hung up. That wasn't you, was it?"

"No, it wasn't me. Like I got time to play games on your phone."

"What's up, Wil?" His voice sounded troubled, not to mention that this was the first time he'd called my house in months. Something had to be up for him to call me at home.

"I've got some bad news." His voice was so low.

"What's up?" I braced myself.

"It's Ma Jackson. Somebody shot her."

"What?" I screamed.

"She's in critical condition, Jay." Wil's voice cracked like he was about to cry. We were both silent, and a good thirty seconds passed before he spoke again. Me, I was tongue-tied and couldn't speak at all. I could feel the tears, but they wouldn't fall. My stomach knotted up and I felt nauseous as I thought about all the things Ma Jackson had done for us as kids. She'd really been there for us. When our moms had to work, Ma Jackson was the only one who was home after school. Wil, Kyle, and I spent most of our time with her during our teenage years. She'd been our den mother in Cub Scouts, taken us all to Disney World. Hell, she'd given me my first condom. She'd always been hard on Allen, I'll be the first to admit that, but she sure as hell had been good to me.

"Jay? You there?"

"Wha-wha-what happened, Wil?" I finally calmed myself enough to speak.

"I don't know, man. Rose called me about ten minutes ago and told me Ma got shot. She said they'd taken her to Jamaica Hospital. I called the hospital pretending to be her son and the nurse said she was in critical condition, about to be operated on. Then out of the blue she tells me it doesn't look good and that her family better get down there. I'm in the car headed over to the hospital now. Kyle's already on his way, too. You need to meet us there, man."

"Okay, I'll be there in thirty minutes. Did anyone talk to Allen? Is he all right?"

"Nah, I didn't get to talk to him, but Rose said they're treating him for shock."

"Damn." I exhaled.

"Jay?"

"Yeah?"

"Don't fuck around and make a whole bunch of stops like you usually do. This is important. Not only is this possibly the last time we get to see Ma Jackson alive, but we need to be there for Allen. He's really gonna need us."

Wil was right. Allen had lost his pops back in high school and it really devastated him. If he lost his mom, he'd be ready to kill himself.

"Did you hear me, Jay?"

"I'm leaving right now, Wil. The only thing I've gotta do is get gas."

"Aw'ight, man. I'm counting on you to be there." I hung up the phone and walked straight out the door to my truck.

Without thinking, I'd left behind the suitcase, flowers, all Tracy's birthday presents, and my cell phone. For the first time since Tracy moved into the apartment, I wished I had gotten her a phone. She was gonna be pissed that I didn't at least stop by and tell her what was going on, but her place and the highway were in totally opposite directions. And like Wil said, this was not a time to fuck around and be late.

It took me about twenty minutes to get from Jersey to Jamaica Hospital. Probably a new speed record, but by the time I got there, it was all over. Ma Jackson was dead. I knew it the second I walked into the hospital and saw Wil and Kyle's faces. Neither one spoke, but Kyle's eyes were bloodshot like he'd been crying.

"She's dead, isn't she?" I tried to stand up straight and take the news like a man, but I knew when I heard it out of their mouths, I would break down.

"Yeah, she's gone," Kyle nodded.

"Fuck!" I turned toward the wall and pounded my fist into it repeatedly. "This shit ain't fair!"

"Life's not fair, Jay. That's why you have to make the best of it while you're here. Ma Jackson did that, bro. She made the most of her life while she was here. That's all we could ask." I felt Wil reach out and pat me on the back.

"I know, but it's still not fair," I sniffled, wiping my face. "Where's Allen?"

"He's in the operating room saying goodbye to Ma," Kyle sighed.

"Damn, how the fuck does something like this happen to a sixty-year-old woman?" I turned around to face my friends, my moment of weakness gone for now.

"You know how it is around the way. Some young boy probably shot her 'cause she wouldn't give up her pocketbook fast enough. You know how Ma is. I mean was. She probably fought him," Kyle said sadly.

"Yeah, Ma Jackson ain't take no shit from no one. Knowing her, she probably laughed at the gun." I tried to smile, but that's when I saw Allen walk around the corner headed for the door.

"Allen," I called out, but he ignored me and kept walking. I was about to run after him, but Kyle grabbed my arm.

"Jay, he's having a really hard time with this. When we arrived, he fought with Wil and me when we tried to calm him down. Let him have his space. He needs to be alone. I told him we were all gonna spend the night at my place, so when he's ready he'll come over there. Okay?"

"Okay," I shook my head. "Think they'll let me see Ma Jackson?"

"I don't know. Let's find out."

Life's not fair, Jay. That's why you have to make the most of it while you're here. I kept thinking about what Wil had said, and he was right. It was time to make the most of my life. As of today, I was going to make a lot of changes in my life. Most of those changes weren't gonna be popular with my friends and family, but that was their problem, not mine. I was tired of living my life for other people. It was time to live my life for me and make me happy. And what was going to make me happy was being with Tracy.

Speaking of Tracy, I knew she was gonna be pissed at me. Not that I could blame her. Hell, I'd stood her up on her birthday without explanation. But when I told her everything about Ma's death and that I was leaving Kenya and moving in with her, I was sure she would forgive me for everything. That's just how she was. God, I loved that woman so much.

"Yo, black! She ain't there," Tyrell, one of the drug dealers across the street, yelled. I'd just pulled in front of Tracy's place and was stepping out of the car. It was Saturday night, almost twenty-four hours after I was supposed to pick her up, but better late than never. I walked across the street and touched knuckles with Tyrell and his boys. For young brothers they seemed all right. At least they kept an eye on things when I wasn't around. I didn't like the fact that they were selling drugs across the street from my lady, but all I could do was talk to them about it. And the truth is, they were making so much money they weren't really listening to me, just giving me that respect. Besides, they were there way before we arrived.

"Where'd she go? To the store?" I looked down the block to see if I could spot her.

"Nah, she left in a cab a few hours ago. Had a little suitcase and a knapsack on her shoulder like she was goin' on a trip or somethin'," Tyrell told me.

"You sure she didn't come back?" Tyrell turned to his boys, and they all shook their heads.

"Nope, don't nothin' go down on this block without us knowin' it. We out here twenty-four seven."

"Yeah, I know that. Look, y'all hold your heads. Aw'ight?"

"No doubt," I heard them say as I crossed the street, heading to Tracy's apartment. Tyrell ran up next to me as I walked.

"Yo, black, that your wifey or your shorty on the side? 'Cause she is *finnnnne*."

"That's my wifey," I growled. "I'll kill a nigga over her. Know what I mean?" I gave Tyrell my most threatening look.

"No doubt. Keep it real, kid. But if that's your wifey, why you treating her like she your shorty on the side?"

"What you mean by that?"

"If that's your wifey, why you got her livin' in a place like this? She a queen, not a chickenhead. You don't even come by that much to check on her. 'Cept at night for a few hours. If that was my wifey, I'd be with her twenty-four seven." I glanced at Tyrell. For a young boy he was pretty smart, and too damn observant for his age. But he was right about one thing. She was my queen, and I had to get Tracy out of this dump.

"Yeah, well, we movin' out next week."

"I heard that." Tyrell and I knocked knuckles and he ran back to his partners. I let myself into the apartment and found a note that Tracy had left for me.

Dear Jay,

It's Saturday afternoon and I'm about to leave. I'm going over to my roommate Mia's house in the Bronx, if you even care. I can't believe you stood me up on my birthday. I swear I've never felt so alone in my entire life. I think we both need to think about where this relationship is going. Especially me. I'm starting to think my parents were right about you and me. I'll see you on Sunday. Hopefully we'll talk then, if you're there.

Luv you????
Tracy

What the hell did she mean by those question marks? Damn. All of a sudden things weren't working out the way I planned. Well, when she got back, I was just going to have to talk to her and explain to her how much I love her. After I read the letter again, I moped around the apartment for a while, then I wrote Tracy a little note letting her know why I stood her up, then got in the car and headed back to my house. There was no need for me to stick around, especially since she wouldn't be back home for another day. Besides, I wanted to spend the day with my kids before dropping the bomb on Kenya that I was leaving her.

They'd come home early after I called her parents' place and told her about Ma Jackson's death. I had a feeling that once I told her I was leaving, she wasn't gonna let me see the kids at all.

When I pulled into the driveway, I got a little chill as I got out of the car. The last time that happened, Tracy's pops was sitting around my house, talking to *my* wife, drinking *my* liquor, waiting to kick *my* ass. I wasn't about to go against my intuition again, so I decided to go in through the back door. That way I could sneak up on any unwanted surprises that might be waiting for me. But the only thing I found was Kenya and the girls sitting at the dinner table. I still felt uneasy, though, especially when I made eye contact with Kenya. She had this cold look about her like she was up to something.

"Daddy!" my daughter Tiffany yelled, jumping out of her seat and into my arms. She kissed me, and I hugged her tightly. I was going to miss her running into my arms every day after work. I was gonna miss it a lot.

"How's Allen?" Kenya asked. She started to make me a plate.

"I don't know. He took off before I even got to speak to him. Rose called Kyle's and said he showed up at the house sometime this morning. We're gonna go see him tomorrow morning."

I sat down and ate dinner with my family for what would probably be the last time. It was awkward, and I dreaded talking to Kenya about family issues like who was going to take the girls to Sunday school and was there enough money in the checking account to fix the gutters. Somehow I would get through it after dinner. When we finished eating, Kenya did the dishes while I put the girls to bed.

I'd already put LaShawn in her crib and had read Tiffany a story. I was about to turn out the light when Tiffany said, "I love you, Daddy."

"I love you too, Tiffany." I turned out the light sadly, thinking this was the last time I was going to do this. I was about to walk out of the room when Kenya scared the shit out of me.

"You love me, too?" she challenged. She was right in my face. "Well, do you?"

Instinctively I said, "Of course I do."

"Then kiss me like you do." She pulled me out into the hallway and shut the door to the girls' room. She wrapped her hands around my waist and looked up at me, waiting. I knew exactly what she was up to. She wanted me to make love to her, something I hadn't done in almost two months and wasn't about to do now. Unfortunately, there was no way around giving her a kiss. I lowered my head and gave her a quick peck on the lips.

"A real kiss, Jay," she ordered, pulling me in closer. I sighed, but this time I gave her what she wanted. She smiled when I finished. "I want some Jay, I want some right now."

"Not now, Kenya. I've gotta call Allen. Why don't we wait till later?" I tried to walk away but she held on to my waist.

"What's your excuse gonna be then?" She rolled her eyes.

"What's that supposed to mean?" I knew what she was talking about but I tried to play dumb.

"What do you think it means, Jay? What, you gonna have a headache later? Not gonna be feeling well? Too depressed over what happened to Ma Jackson? Too tired? What's it gonna be this time?" Damn, she had all my excuses down pat.

"Why you trippin', Kenya? I told you I'd give you some later."

"Why'm I trippin'?" She threw her hands in the air. "I'm trippin' because I think my husband's a homosexual, that's why. What's up, Jay? You like dick or what? 'Cause you damn sure don't like pussy no more." She placed her hand on her hip and I stared at her with wide eyes.

"Now you know damn well I don't like dick." She'd hit a nerve, probably exactly what she intended to do. If there was one thing I hated more than anything in the world, it was when someone challenged my manhood.

"I don't know shit 'cept you don't seem to like pussy no more. And if you don't like pussy, you must like dick. Right, faggot?" She tilted her head sister-girl style, then smirked. I was breathing hard and trying to keep my emotions under control. I knew what she was trying to do. She was trying to get me to prove I was a man. The thing I hated most was that it was working. I was about two seconds away from ripping all her clothes off and showing her exactly what kinda faggot I was.

"I can't believe I married a fuckin' fruitcake! So you the pitcher or the catcher, Jay?" She shook her head like she was disgusted.

That was it. I'd had it. I reached over and grabbed her by her blouse, pulling her to me and pushing my lips against hers roughly.

"Get in the room and get your fucking clothes off! I'm gonna show just how much of a faggot I am!"

"Promises, promises," she smirked at me as I let go of her blouse. She was purposely swaying her round hips as I followed her into our bedroom. When we got in the bedroom, she reached in her purse and pulled out an unopened box of condoms and threw them at me.

"What are these for?" I looked at her strangely. In the seven years we'd known each other, she'd never asked me to wear a condom before.

"I left my pills home when I went down to my folks' house so we have to use these until after my period." She took off her clothes as she explained.

"Oh." I removed my shirt.

It was always better to go raw dog, but I was willing to use condoms. Until I found out Tracy was pregnant, we used them all the time. So condoms were no big deal. Plus the last thing I wanted was for Kenya to get pregnant again, especially with me about to leave her. When I walked out that door, I wanted to make a clean break.

When we were both naked, we crawled into the middle of the bed and started kissing passionately like when we first started dating. I decided that if this was going to be the last time we made love, then she was never gonna be able to tell anyone I was gay with a good conscience. As the night went on, things between us got pretty steamy, and to tell the truth, I was more than a little impressed. She wasn't Tracy, but I have to give credit where credit is due. Kenya was doing her thing. She was throwing moves on me I didn't even know she had, and by the time it was all over, I was exhausted and fell asleep right away.

The next morning I didn't get up until the sun beamed into my room and woke me. My body was still tired and I was still feeling the effects from the night of passion I had with Kenya. Believe it or not, I had no regrets. The sex had been some of the best I'd ever had with her. Might as well go out in style, I guess.

When I opened my eyes, Kenya was standing in the doorway. I glanced over to the clock. It was a little after nine and instinctively I panicked, thinking I was going to be late for work. But then I remembered it was Sunday.

"Hey, what are you doing in jeans? Aren't you supposed to be taking the girls to Sunday school this morning?" I sat up and stretched, trying to wake up.

"Diane came over and got the girls about an hour ago." Just the mention of Diane's name woke me.

"Diane? What was she doing over here?" Anytime Diane came around, I got a little worried. She'd always been a good friend to Kenya, but ever since her and Wil split up, she'd been around way too much for me.

"She took the kids over to her house because I had to help somebody move."

"Oh, yeah?" I yawned. "Who's moving?" Kenya hadn't mentioned anyone moving last night. Then again she had other things on her mind last night. The thought of us making love brought a smile to my face and my manhood to attention. *What the fuck,* with the kids gone and Tracy not coming home till this evening, one more for the road wouldn't hurt. Unfortunately Kenya had other ideas and killed mine with a quickness.

"You wanna know who's moving, Jay?" she smirked. "You are. You're moving." I was about to laugh but her facial expression was so serious I couldn't. If I didn't know better, I'd think she knew I was leaving her for Tracy.

"What'ya mean I'm movin'? I'm not movin'." I looked at her like she was crazy. "What's going on, Kenya? Why you actin' like this?"

"You wanna know why I'm acting like this, Jay? 'Cause you ain't shit, that's why." Her demeanor was calm—not at all what you would expect from a woman who sounded like she was kicking me out my own house. She walked over to my dresser and picked up a neatly folded pair of pants and shirt, handing them to me. I stared at the clothes, then at her. "It took me half the night, but I packed up all your shit, and it's waiting for you on the front porch."

"You're not serious. You can't be." I chuckled, trying to lighten her mood, but it didn't help.

"Oh yes I am, and I don't see a damn thing funny." She folded her arms over her chest with an attitude. "Now get dressed and get out."

"Wh-what about last night? You trying to say that last night wasn't shit?"

"No, Jay, I can't say that." She took her finger and scratched her chin. "Last night was actually pretty good. But I'll tell you a secret." She smiled, looking kinda distant. "I've had better, much better." Her smile widened.

What the hell did she mean? *She'd had better.* I'd been the only one she'd been with in seven years. My eyes opened wide as I thought, *or was I?* Her words hit my ego like a ton of bricks and I got a knot in my stomach as I tried to comprehend what she was saying.

"You been fuckin' somebody on the side, haven't you?" I shouted angrily, throwing the clothes to the floor and taking a step off the bed. I expected her to take a step back, but she wasn't even fazed.

"Actually I haven't been fucking anyone on the side, Jay." She smiled. "He's been on top most of the time, but that's not the issue. Considering how many women you've been with, it's gonna take me twenty years to catch up." I don't know why I was upset. Especially since I was leaving her anyway, but a wave of jealousy took over me.

"Who is he, Kenya? Tell me who he is, 'cause I'm gonna kill the son of a bitch. I swear to God I'm gonna kill 'im."

She laughed at me. Not just a regular old laugh, but a hearty laugh. Like she thought what I said was the best joke she'd ever heard.

"I guess that means I get to kick Tracy's ass, huh?" She placed her hand on her hip, and her laugh transformed into an evil grin. I was so shocked I almost peed on myself. "Who is Tracy, Jay?" She hesitated for a second, waiting for an answer. Of course I didn't give her one. "I asked you a question, Jay. Who is Tracy?"

I didn't say anything. I just looked at her in stunned disbelief, trying my best to read her thoughts. The anger I had toward her was gone, and now I was standing in front of her trying to think of a lie. How the hell did she find out about Tracy? I watched her reach inside her pocket and pull out a yellow envelope. When she pulled a card out of the envelope, all my questions were answered. In my haste to get to the hospital Friday night, I left behind my cell phone, my overnight bag, and Tracy's presents. Kenya must have seen the flowers and presents the second she walked through the door. My ass was caught. But for the life of me, I couldn't understand why she was being so calm. Shit, I can't believe she didn't go off last night. Hell, I can't believe she made love to me last night. But then again, she mighta been getting one for the road, just like me.

"Who is she, Jay? Who is Tracy?"

"She's just a friend."

"Oh, yeah." It was obvious from her expression she saw right through my lie. She looked down at the card and read out loud the inscription I wrote on the back. I never realized how mushy and melodramatic I was until I heard Kenya read my words. I was embarrassed and proud at the same time. That note took me three hours to write, and it sounded good.

"That's one hell of a friend you got there, Jay. I can't remember the last time you wrote me a note like this." She started to cry, and I felt like shit. "You expect me to believe this woman is just a friend?" She lifted her head and waited for an answer.

Like a fool, I nodded. She balled both her fists up and hit me on the side of the head repeatedly. "Don't fuckin' play with me, Jay! Don't you fuckin' play! Goddammit!" She wasn't calm anymore. She was hysterical, and kept hitting me.

Finally I grabbed her by the wrists and screamed. "Okay, okay, you want the truth? She's my lover! Is that what you wanna hear?" She stopped her attack and just stood, sobbing and staring. I felt like I was shrinking in front of her.

"Do you love her?" I looked away from her, trying my best not to make eye contact. But she was right in front of me. I couldn't avoid her. "I asked you a question, Jay. Do you love her?" Our marriage was over, and it was confession time. I swallowed hard and answered her question.

"Yeah, Kenya, I love her." I tightened my jaw, still trying to avoid eye contact.

She nodded her head slowly, like she'd already known my answer.

"H-how long?" Her voice was choked up. "How long has this been going on?"

"About six months." I looked down, and she was wiping her tears away with her sleeve.

"Is she pretty?"

I nodded my head, answering her in a whisper. "I think so."

"She's young, isn't she?" She stared at me as if the answer was of vital importance. "How old is she, Jay?" I thought about lying, but she'd find out the truth sooner or later.

"She just turned twenty."

"My God, she's just a kid. She's the same age as my niece. What is wrong with you?" Kenya twisted her face up and stepped away. Tracy's age must have just added insult to injury. I dressed as fast as I could and walked out of the room. It was obviously time for me to go. I didn't wanna answer any more questions. I just wanted to get out of there. But by the time I got to the bottom of the stairs to walk out the door, she called my name. Like a fool, I turned around.

"I hate you, Jay. Do you understand me? I hate your child-molesting ass."

"You don't hate me, Kenya. You can't hate me." She threw a vase from the top of the stairs to convince me that she really did. I stumbled backward as the vase hit me.

"Something to remember me by," she yelled. I wasn't bleeding, but I was gonna have a hell of a knot on my head. I walked out the door and retrieved my belongings, which were packed up neatly in suitcases. It was finally over, and all of a sudden I wasn't sure I was ready to let go.

41

Kyle

I'd never seen Allen A.M.E. Church so packed, and there wasn't a dry eye in the place, including mine. It was Monday, three days after the tragic shooting of Ma Jackson, and the funeral service had been standing room only as the pastor and different members of the community made testimony after testimony about how great a woman Ma had been. I hated funerals, but I had to admit as funerals go, Ma Jackson's had to be the best I'd ever attended. As much as I disliked Rose, she had done one hell of a job putting together all the arrangements. She'd really done right by her mother-in-law, and it's a good thing too, 'cause Allen was in no shape to handle anything. Not that I blamed him. They'd have shipped me off to Creedmoor Psychiatric Hospital in a straightjacket if my mom had been gunned down in front of her house.

"Yo, dawg, you ready to get up outta this place?" I looked up at Jay, who was standing over me with his coat over his arm. I don't know why he was so eager to leave. We'd only been at Ma Jackson's house about a half an hour and we hadn't even eaten yet. Like the rest of Allen's friends and family, we'd gathered over there after the funeral for the traditional potluck dinner and chance to pay our final condolences to the family. Jay had been bugging me ever since we left the church to leave because I'd promised to introduce him to my landlord, Mr. Sanford.

"Nah, not yet, Jay. I think we need to stick around here awhile 'til the crowd thins out. We can help Allen and Rose with the cleanup." I hadn't talked to Allen since he stormed out of the hospital the other night, and I wanted to make sure he was all right. I looked up at Jay, who tried to hide a frown. He was standing next to his new woman, Tracy, and by the way she sucked her teeth, I'm sure she was ready to leave too. Not that I cared if they wanted to get into my building. She was gonna have to wait 'til I was ready.

"You sure you wanna stay?" Jay sounded a little desperate this time, and kept glancing over at Tracy.

"Yeah, I'm sure. But if you two wanna leave, go 'head. We'll just have to meet with Mr. Sanford on another day."

"Come on, Kyle." He sounded like a baby.

"Sorry, Jay, I'm not leaving here until I see Allen and make sure he's okay." I watched him sigh. "You do wanna make sure he's all right. Don't you?"

"No, you're right," he agreed. "We gotta make sure he's aw'ight first." Jay reached out and wrapped his arm around Tracy kinda cautiously. "You don't mind if we stay until I see Allen, do you, boo?" He smiled liked a little boy, but it didn't work.

"I wanna go, Jay," she pouted, pulling herself away from him.

"Come on, boo. You want this apartment don't you?" I'd never seen him plead with a woman before, not even Kenya. It was pretty pathetic, especially for him to be cowering in front of this young girl who was sounding like such a selfish bitch right about now. She should've known Allen would need us at a time like this. She should've cut Jay some slack.

"Okay," she sighed, "we can stay. But I swear to God if that bitch points at me one more time I'm gonna smack her." Tracy glared evilly at two women standing in a corner, whispering back and forth. They were trying to be nonchalant, but they were nothing but obvious.

"Be cool, aw'ight? We're at a funeral," Jay pleaded.

I lowered my head and let out a chuckle. I don't know why I hadn't figured it out earlier. The reason the two of them were in such a rush to leave wasn't because they wanted to see my landlord at all, but because of all the dirty looks they'd been getting. No offense to Ma Jackson, but Jay and Tracy were the main topic of conversation both at the church and here in the house. Not that Jay should've expected anything less. When you're thirty-six years old and show up to a funeral with a woman damn near half your age and she's wearing maternity clothes two days after you and your wife split, you gotta expect people to talk. Especially when half the women there are your wife's friends and the other half are her enemies because you was fucking with them at one time or another.

"Hey, baby. Why don't you go get us a couple of plates to take home? Hopefully by the time you're done, Kyle and me will have found Allen and we can leave." Tracy nodded and Jay kissed her lips before pointing to the dining room where the food was being served. "And ignore those dumb bitches. They're just jealous 'cause you so damn fine." Jay winked at her with a smile, then patted her on the ass.

"Okay, baby, but don't you be talking to none of these old ass bitches while I'm gone. I don't wanna have to turn this place out." She smiled, and the two of us watched her disappear into the crowded dining room. When she was out of sight, I gave Jay a curious look.

"She's a little jealous," he said timidly. I could tell he was embarrassed. He wouldn't make eye contact.

"I can see that," I grinned.

"So what do you think, man? She's *fine*, isn't she?"

"*Ohhh* yeah, she's *fine* all right. As *fine* as you are *stupid!*" My voice was so serious Jay did a double take.

"Huh? What the hell's that supposed to mean?"

"You tell me, Jay. What the hell were you thinking about bringing her to Ma Jackson's funeral?"

"Please, Kyle. Ain't nobody question you when you was hanging out with Val at the Roadhouse."

"Duh!" I said sarcastically, rolling my eyes. "Lisa's friends don't hang out at the Roadhouse Bar, Jay. But *everybody* here knows Kenya. I wouldn't be surprised if she hasn't gotten five calls by now, and by tomorrow she'll get fifty." I shook my head. "Besides, you didn't see me taking Val to Allen's wedding, did you?"

"No."

"All right, then. Don't let that good-ass pussy you been gettin' get in the way of common sense." I looked at him seriously, then softened my tone. "Besides, Tracy shouldn't have to put up with this shit. Everybody in here's whispering behind her back like she's the hunchback or something. Isn't that why you was about to leave?"

"Yeah, I guess so, but I had to bring her, Kyle. You don't know what I went through last night. She had her shit packed up and was gonna leave when I got home. She's sick of being left alone."

"That's still no excuse for bringing her here." I was about to read him the riot act but I spotted Wil heading our way, and this was not a conversation he needed to be a part of. "Hey, let's talk about this later. Here comes Wil."

"Aw'ight," Jay replied as Wil walked right up to him.

"Yo, Jay, I need to talk to you, man." Wil looked agitated. I was praying he wasn't gonna start with Jay about bringing Tracy to the funeral.

"What's up?" Jay exhaled, and I'm sure he was thinking the same thing.

"I just got a call on my cell from Marcus Stetson. He's the head of shipping at the job." Wil wiped his face. It looked like he was trying to hold back tears. "He just told me Diane took the job at the Atlanta distribution center. She's gonna take my kids to Atlanta."

"What? *Awww,* shit." I shook my head. "Wil, I'm so sorry, man."

"So am I, but I'm not gonna let her get away with this." Wil sighed.

"Jay, I need your help to stop her." You could hear the desperation in his voice.

"You need my help?" Jay raised an eyebrow and his tone revealed his amazement. Hell, I was pretty damn amazed myself. After all they'd been through in the last year, I never thought Wil would ask Jay for help with his marriage.

"Yeah," Wil nodded. "I need your help. You said you could get me and Diane back together."

"I thought you didn't want me to get involved."

"Yeah, well, I changed my mind. Desperate times call for desperate measures," Wil said sternly.

"Okay man, if that's what you want. All we gotta do is—" Wil raised his hand, cutting Jay off.

"I don't wanna know what you're gonna do. Just do it, okay?" Wil wiped away a tear. "Get my family back for me, Jay. I'm begging you. I don't care what you gotta do. Just get them back." Wil grabbed Jay's arm and started to squeeze until Jay nodded his head.

"Hey, Wil, relax. I'll take care of it. Trust me on that. But it's not gonna be pretty."

"I don't care if it's pretty. I just want my family back."

"Okay, you got it." Jay patted Wil on the back confidently.

"Thanks, Jay. I don't know what I'd do without you guys." Wil finally sounded at ease as he wrapped his arm around Jay and smiled at me. The two of them embraced in a brotherly hug that reminded me just how much we all meant to each other.

"Come on, dawg, what are friends for?" Jay said.

"Speaking of friends? Y'all seen Allen?" I decided it was time to change the subject before our male bonding session had us all in tears. There'd been way too many tears lately.

"No, but I been looking for him," Wil replied. "I haven't seen him since I left the church."

"Me neither." I was a little worried now.

"You know they still haven't caught those boys who shot Ma Jackson?" Wil blurted out.

"Well, when they do, they don't need to send them to jail. Just let me have about fifteen minutes with 'em. I'll save the city a whole bunch of money on a trial." Jay slammed a fist against his palm.

"Yeah, just make sure you save some for me," Wil added. His face was red with anger. "You know they shot her for ten fuckin' dollars? She went to the ATM, took out twenty, and spent ten on groceries. All she had was ten fucking bucks in her purse." Wil's voice was shaking.

"I'll tell you what. The cops better find 'em before I do," Jay stated flatly.

"What we need to do is find Allen," I interrupted.

"I'll find him. Hold up." Wil walked over to a group of people and grabbed Rose, who was accepting their condolences.

"Rose, where's Allen?"

"He's in the den with the baby." She pointed to the den. "Do me a favor, Wil. Go in there and make him come out here. All he's doing is sitting in there talkin' to himself. I know he's upset, but the least he can do is come out here and say thank you to these people for bringing all this food. Some of them came all the way from down South." Wil looked at me, then at Jay. Without saying it, we all knew what we had to do. We had to go in there and show Allen he wasn't alone. That it was possible to go on with his life now that his mother was gone.

"Yeah, we'll talk to him," Wil nodded, then headed for the den. When we opened the door, poor Allen never said a word. He just sat there in his mother's recliner holding a framed picture of her in one hand and a manila envelope in the other. I felt sorry for 'him. He looked like the world was about to come to an end, and I guess for him it had.

"Hey, Al, sorry about your mom, bro." I grabbed hold of him then let him go, and Jay took my place, squeezing him tight.

"You know I really loved her, right?" Jay sniffled, and Allen nodded.

"She was like a mom to all of us, Al." Wil wrapped his arms around Allen when Jay stepped away.

"Yeah, I know," Allen said sadly. He tried to smile, but it just wasn't working. "She loved you guys, too. She even left you in her will." He lifted the envelope as the three of us sat down.

"She did?" Jay's eyes widened.

"Yeah, she did. Three grand each." I suppose we were all surprised by the news, because none of us said a word until Allen finally spoke.

"I tried to be a good son to her, y'all, but all I ever did was fuck up. She only asked me for one thing before she left this earth and I couldn't even do that right. Dammit!" He slammed the picture down on the table next to him and the frame broke. Jay and I looked at each other, then at him. As far as we were concerned, he was talking crazy. He'd been a better son to his mom than any of us had been to ours, and Wil made sure he knew it.

"You're being kinda hard on yourself, aren't you? You were a good son to your mom. Better than I could ever be."

"I wish you was right, Wil." Allen stood up, throwing the envelope on Wil's lap. He walked over to the portable crib and gently picked up his sleeping son. It was amazing he hadn't woken up when his father slammed that picture down. "What's the only thing my ma ever asked me for, Wil?"

He kissed Jonathan then stared at Wil, who shrugged his answer. Wil never even looked up because he was reading whatever was in that envelope.

"What about you, Jay? You remember?"

"I don't know." Jay gave him a puzzled look.

"Kyle?" He looked at me and I ran my finger over my mustache. Truth is, I didn't know what he was talking about, but after watching the way he held on to his son, I decided to take a stab at it.

"She always told me she wanted a grandchild of her own." I had to chuckle as I thought about how Ma Jackson used to always bitch and moan about not having grandchildren. "Y'know, I think she was jealous that we all had kids and you didn't." I looked at his boy and smiled. "Thank God she had a chance to spend time with Jonathan before she passed."

"Yeah, too bad he's not her grandchild." He let out a pathetic laugh and my smile became a frown. I couldn't believe he'd just let that shit come out his mouth. If I didn't know he was grieving, I swear I would've smacked the shit outta him right there. 'Cause there was no need for him to talk about his mother or his son that way.

"Look, Al, I know you've had a rough couple of days, but that shit ain't funny." I tried to control my attitude, but it wasn't easy.

"Do I look like I'm laughing, Kyle? I love this boy." The sarcasm was gone and his voice was dead serious now. He kissed the baby again then looked at us solemnly. I'm sure he was seconds away from tears. "I love him, but he's not my son."

"Yeah, right. Then whose kid is he?" Jay laughed sarcastically. I shot him a dirty look, hoping to shut him up, but there was no need. Allen took care of him with a sharp tongue.

"He's got a better chance of being your son than mine, Jay. Didn't you have a cousin that died of sickle cell?" I still didn't have a clue about what he was talking about. I watched him place the baby back in the crib then wipe away tears.

"Allen, what makes you think he's not your son?" I sat back in my chair, confused but willing to listen.

"I don't think, Kyle, I know." He swallowed hard and took a deep breath before he explained the events that had unfolded at Johns Hopkins Hospital the day of his mother's death. The way he told the story there was no doubt in my mind he was telling the truth. But even so, I couldn't help but peek in the crib and look at the baby to search for some resemblance to Allen. I mean damn, shit like this didn't really happen, did it? Besides, how the hell did Rose think she was gonna get away with something like this? Sooner or later the truth would have to come out.

"Wait a minute, let me get this straight. You don't have the sickle cell trait at all?" I could hear the frustration in Wil's voice as he looked at Allen, then back to the papers he was holding.

"Nope, and they must've tested my blood five times." Remarkably, Allen looked like he felt better now that he'd gotten this off his chest. I guess that was his first step toward healing, 'cause all of a sudden he looked much closer to his old self.

"This is unbelievable," Wil groaned. He lifted his head from whatever he was reading, and I'm not sure if he was talking about what Allen said or about the papers in his hand. "Okay, so he's not your biological son. What are you gonna do now?"

"He's gonna kick that bitch Rose to the curb, that's what he's gonna do!" Jay jumped up out of his seat.

"No, Jay, he's not gonna kick her to the curb." Wil shook his head at Jay. "He's going to think this whole thing through like an adult. That's what he's gonna do."

Jay twisted his face. "What the fuck is there to think about, Wil? The baby's not his!"

"Kyle, will you please talk some sense into this guy?" Wil looked at me for support, but this time he was on his own, 'cause I agreed with Jay. No way in hell would I stay with a woman after she did some shit like this.

"Sorry, Wil, but he's right."

"No, he's not, Kyle! You need to read this." Wil slapped the papers he'd been reading across my chest then walked over to Allen, who was trying to settle down the baby. He'd started hollering when Jay screamed. "You really love him, don't you, Al."

"Yeah, I do. That's what makes this whole thing so fucked up. She don't give a shit about him."

"Don't worry, man, we're gonna get through this. We just gotta be there for each other."

"Holy shit!" I screamed. "Is this shit for real?" I waved the papers in the air.

"Yep," Wil frowned. "Now you see why I said we have to think this through."

"Damn, what the hell was she thinking about?" I sighed.

"What are y'all talkin' 'bout?" Jay demanded.

"Ma Jackson. She left Rose a two-hundred-thousand-dollar life insurance policy."

"Get the fuck outta here. Ma Jackson wouldn't do that." Jay snatched the policy out my hand.

"Yes, she would. I was there when she signed it." All six of our eyes were on Allen as he began to pace the room, holding the baby.

"Why would you let her do a dumb thing like that?" I was pissed. No wonder Rose was so eager to put on a first-class funeral for Ma. Once it was over, she was gonna get paid 200 gees and maybe more if the double indemnity clause kicked in.

"At first I thought it was a bad idea too, and I fought Ma on it. I swear I did, but then she gave me this speech about the baby needing security in case something happened to me. And about how she would have never made it if it wasn't for the life insurance policy she had out on my dad. Then she started to go into this whole thing about cancer running in my family and about how my dad died so young, and his father died young. After a while, the more I thought about it, the more it made sense. Rose was about to be my wife. Why shouldn't she have security?" He continued to pace, then laughed out loud. "Funny thing is, after we found out Jonathan had sickle cell, me and Ma had a long talk at the hospital. Ma was real pissed off that Rose had gone outta town and wouldn't come home to be with Jonathan. She swore up and down that she was gonna have that policy changed to my name first thing Monday morning." Allen stopped pacing, then looked at us sadly. "I guess she never got around to it."

"Damn, Al, what you gonna do now?"

Allen smiled evilly.

"First I'm gonna make sure she spends every dime of that insurance money before I divorce her ass." He kissed the baby. "Then I'm going to figure out a way to get her to sign away her parental rights. I'm not gonna let her get Jonathan. She doesn't deserve him."

"Amen to that," I whispered, my eyes opening wide as a thought came to mind. "Hey, Allen, you sure Ma was robbed?"

"Yeah, that's what the cops told me."

"Why?" Wil folded his arms, studying my face as if he was trying to read my mind.

"No reason," I sighed, shaking my head. I tried my best not to make eye contact, but he wasn't going for it.

"No, Kyle, why?" He wouldn't stop staring at me.

"It's nothing, Wil. Look, I don't wanna start no shit. We just buried Ma." I gave him a look to end the conversation, but he didn't take the hint. Now Allen and Jay were staring at me too.

"No, it's not okay," Wil insisted.

"Look, Kyle, if you know something, I wanna know what it is," Allen demanded.

"Look, man, it's probably nothing, but did you ever think of the possibility that Rose might've had something to do with your ma's death? I mean, two hundred thousand is a lot of money."

"To be honest with you, Kyle, I did. I even went to the police and told them about the policy."

"You did? What'd they say?" Jay was all up in it now.

"They said they appreciated the information but they were sure that this was a robbery-related shooting and that there had been at least three other killings or robberies of elderly women in Ma's neighborhood in the last few weeks."

"Then how come they haven't found them yet?" Wil demanded.

"Well, I guess that takes Rose off the hook—" A loud crash interrupted what I was about to say.

"What the fuck was that?" Jay shouted. A few seconds later, Allen's cousin Malcolm popped his head in the door.

"Yo, Jay, that girl you came here with is out here fighting," Malcolm laughed, and I could see the embarrassment on Jay's face.

"Shit!" Jay ran out of the room, followed by Wil. I was about to follow them myself when Allen grabbed my arm.

"I need to talk to you about something."

"Sure, Al. What's up?"

"That night me and Ma talked at the hospital."

"Yeah, what about it?"

"Ma told me about you and Rose being together the night before my wedding, Kyle."

"She did?" I think my heart stopped.

"Yeah," Allen nodded.

I'm sure my jaw had dropped down to my knees. I'd never been so humbled in my entire life, and to be honest I would have done anything if I could have just disappeared. Surprisingly, Allen never even looked my way. He just kept pacing back and forth as he held the baby.

"Allen, I swear nothing happened." He finally looked at me with a half smile.

"Hey, don't worry, Kyle. I believe you. I know you wouldn't do me like that. Ma wasn't sure about what happened, but she told me you wanted to call off the wedding and she had to talk you out of it."

"Yeah, I was pretty mad that day. That's why I played sick at your reception."

"That's also why you asked me if I was settling. Wasn't it?"

"Uh-huh," I shrugged as I nodded. "Look, you want me to tell you what happened?"

"Nah, man. You don't have to prove yourself to me. You've been doing that all your life. I know you're a true friend, and I love you for that."

"Thanks, man. I love you too." I stood up and wrapped my arm around him, praying that all the drama in our lives was gonna end.

42

Jay

"Lemme go! Lemme go! I'm gonna kick your ass, bitch! Y'all better lemme go!"

When I made my way through the crowd, I spotted Tracy kicking and screaming hysterically as two brothers tried their best to hold her back. She was trying to get to Crystal, the sister who had been pointing at us earlier. It's a good thing those brothers were there before things got too physical. What Tracy didn't know, or at least didn't care, was that Crystal was Allen's cousin and half the people in the room were her relatives. If Tracy got one good shot in on Crystal, her relatives would be on her like white on rice. Pregnant or not.

"Let her go!" All eyes were on me as I walked over and stood in front of Tracy. I stared the two brothers down and they wisely let go of my lady. Right away Tracy tried her best to get at Crystal, but I grabbed her.

"Calm down, boo," I whispered.

"Lemme go, Jay!" She tried to squirm free.

"Stop it. We're at a funeral," I insisted, louder this time. She didn't pay me no mind and lunged at Crystal again. "Goddammit, Kenya! Did you hear me? I said stop it!" I shook her and she stopped right away. I could hear a gasp from the crowd and then a whole bunch of whispering.

"Ohhh, no you didn't." Tracy tried to twist away, but she wasn't lunging at Crystal anymore, she was just trying to get away from me. "You motherfucker!" She tried to kick me in between the legs.

"Will you stop it, Kenya? What's wrong with you?" I looked at her evilly.

"I can't believe you just called me her name again." She swung at me.

"Whose name?"

"Your wife's! You just called me by your wife's name! Twice!"

"No I didn't!"

"Yes, you did. You called me Kenya!"

"He sure did, honey," some woman from the crowd yelled. "You lucky he didn't call you by some other woman's name. Many women as he mess with." I didn't bother to look for the culprit. I just figured it was some sister hating player.

"I did not call you Kenya," I told her sincerely. "Did I, Wil?" I looked back at him. His expression was clear. He did not want to be in this one, which basically meant I had fucked up and he couldn't help.

"Look at you. Your own fucking friend even heard it! Let go of me!" Tracy pulled herself free and headed for the door. "I wanna go home."

I finished my Heineken, thinking about my situation with Tracy. We'd been fighting for a week and she'd threatened to move out about ten times. Hell, she'd even packed her bags a few times. She'd really taken my slip of the tongue personally. Every time I turned around she was in my face, bringing up Kenya, Kenya, Kenya. Not that I could blame her. If she'd called me by some other guy's name, I'd be pretty pissed too.

But what Tracy didn't know was she was better off not mentioning Kenya at all. The more she brought up Kenya's name, the more I started thinking about my wife. Things had gotten so bad that on at least five occasions I had to catch myself from calling her Kenya again. I guess deep down I had a little more love for Kenya than I had realized. Still, it didn't compare to the love I had for Tracy. All I really wanted was for her to forgive me and put this Kenya stuff behind us.

Things had calmed down a little last night when Kyle's landlord finally offered us a one-bedroom apartment in his building. The thought of moving out of that rat hole, not to mention the dozen roses I brought home, loosened up her mood, because she made dinner for the first time since the funeral and afterward she initiated our lovemaking. She even told me she was sorry and that she loved me when I left the house this morning.

"Hey, Judy, what d'ya think of this?"

Judy, a short, pudgy waitress at the Roadhouse Bar, placed another Heineken on a napkin. She watched as I opened up the small jewelry box I'd been holding.

"Damn, who you givin' this to?" She took the box out of my hands and admired the contents.

I smiled. Even in the dim light of the bar the half-carat diamond engagement ring sparkled. I'd spent half the afternoon looking for a jewelry store that would give me enough credit to buy Tracy a nice ring. It wasn't easy, but I found one in the Coliseum Mall in Jamaica. Now all I had to do was make sixty payments and the ring would be paid off.

"It's for my girl, Tracy. I'm gonna ask her to marry me tonight." I tried not to, but I couldn't help it. I was grinning from ear to ear, at least until Judy spoke her mind.

"Get the fuck outta here! You? Married? Now that's a laugh." Judy slapped her hand against her hip and cracked up. She probably woulda bust a gut if she knew I'd been married the whole five years I'd known her and that I was actually still legally married.

"So where is this mystery woman? How come I've never seen her?"

"Oh, you're gonna meet her real soon." *As soon as she turns twenty-one and can come into the bar,* I thought, just as I spotted Diane walking in the door. Like I'd planned, she couldn't see me sitting in the dimly lit, back half of the bar. I watched as she checked her watch then scanned the bar. She probably thought I late or going to be a no-show.

"Hey, Judy, do me a favor." I pointed toward the bar. "See that heavyset woman standing at the bar?" Judy turned to look at Diane.

"Yeah, what about her?"

"Tell her I'm back here." Judy's eyes widened.

"Is that the woman you gonna marry?"

"Nah, she's just a friend."

"Yeah, right, Jay. Everyone's just your friend." She shook her head and walked toward Diane. When she was out of listening range, I started punching a few numbers on my cell phone.

"Yeah?" a male voice said.

"Biggie, you ready?"

"Yeah," the voice replied.

"Okay. She's here. We'll see you in a bit." I clicked my phone off just as Diane approached. I smiled. She didn't.

"Hey, Diane, how are you?" I pointed at the chair across from me and she sat down with a nasty look on her face.

"You got my money?" she snapped.

"I'm fine, Di. Thanks for asking," I said sarcastically. "Would you like a drink?"

"Fuck the pleasantries, Jay. You know I don't like you. I just want my money so I can go home. Now did Wil give you my money or what?"

"Yeah, he gave me your money, but there's a few things we have to straighten out before I give it to you." I paused, and when she didn't bother to respond, I let her know what was on my mind. "Why you moving the kids to Atlanta? You know you're wrong for that shit."

"Huh," she snarled, sitting back in her chair. "What the fuck gives you the right to tell me what to do with my kids?"

"You wanna know what gives me the right, Diane?" I reached inside my coat pocket and pulled out a folded check. "This gives me the right. Your money. Three thousand big ones. So if you want it, why don't you relax and have a drink so we can get down to business? I mean, you do want your money, don't you?" I folded my hands over my chest to let her know I intended to wait all night if that's how she wanted to play it. "Now what are you drinkin'?"

"Long Island iced tea," she sighed.

"You sure about that? They make the drinks pretty strong in here."

"Will you just get me the damn drink?" She sucked her teeth impatiently.

"No problem. I'll be right back." I got up and walked to the bar.

When I returned to the table and handed Diane her drink, she had obviously given some thought to my question and decided she didn't care. She was her usual cheery self, insulting me the second I sat down.

"So how are Kenya and girls?" She sipped her drink, and I wanted to smack the smug little grin off her face.

"Why you always playin', Diane? You know Kenya and I aren't together. You was probably the first person she called when I left her."

"When *you* left *her?*" Diane laughed. "From what I saw on your porch, she kicked your ass out, Mr. My-bags-were-packed-for-me. Oh, by the way, what's this I hear you got some teeny-bopper pregnant and took her to Ma Jackson's funeral?" She laughed again, and took a long swig of her drink. Any second thoughts I had about my plans for the evening were instantly forgotten. This bitch needed someone to put her in her place, and I would gladly be the one to do it.

"I'm sorry, Jay." Diane stopped laughing and reached across the table to pat my hand. "From what I hear, Kenya still loves your sorry ass. If you were smart, you'd take your black ass home tonight."

"You think so?" I raised my eyebrows and leaned forward to the edge of my chair. "You think she still wants me back?" I don't know why I asked her that, or at least why I sounded so eager. Maybe it was out of curiosity and maybe a little bit of ego, but I really wanted to know what Kenya was thinking. Like I said before, with Tracy's constant reminder, I did kinda miss Kenya. Diane's cackle brought me back to reality.

"Hell fucking no, she don't want you back! Who the hell would want your two-timing ass?"

"Oh, you're funny as hell, Diane," I frowned. "Is that how you kept Wil so happy all these years? Cracking jokes?" The laughter stopped and Diane shot daggers with her eyes.

"No, Wil's just like you. He can't be happy with just one woman. He needs three or four whores to keep him happy."

"Y'know what, Diane? I been a player all my life. I can't help it. My daddy was a player. My granddaddy was one. Shit, it's just who we Crawford men are. But Wil, he's only loved one woman his entire life, and that's you. Kyle and them fucked up when they took those pictures, but you fucked up by being so damn stubborn and not believing in your husband. One day you're gonna find out what really happened that night and then you're gonna want him back. I just hope it's not too late."

"Oh, please!" She waved her hand at me. "Can we get on with this? I don't need to hear no more sob stories for Wil Duncan. The way people been talkin' you'd think he was a saint."

"Yeah, we can get on with it. I'm just gonna get another beer." I polished off what was left of the one I had and stood up. "You want another drink?" She picked up her drink, which was almost empty, and drained the glass.

"No, you was right. These drinks are strong. I can feel this one already." She took her napkin and wiped her forehead. "Hurry up so I can leave."

"Sure, I'll be right back." I smiled as I went to the bar.

When I returned, Diane's head was down on the table. I shook her to see if she was awake. "Diane," I whispered, shaking her again. She didn't move. I looked around the room to see if anyone had noticed what had happened. Nope, most of the early-afternoon crowd was up front at the bar and none of them were paying attention to us. The only people nearby were the two brothers in the booth in front of me, and they were my frat brothers, Walter and Jeff.

"Yo, y'all, she's out," I whispered.

Like clockwork they stood, grabbed Diane under the arms and carried her the ten feet out the side door of the bar. Within seconds we were all in my car, headed down Jamaica Avenue on our way to the Budget Motor Inn on Rockaway Boulevard.

"Think anybody saw us?" Jeffrey, the larger of my two frat brothers, asked. He looked back to see if we were being followed.

"Nah, ain't nobody see us. I was watching the whole time." I grinned.

"Good, I love it when a plan comes together," he laughed.

"Hey, Walter, how's our guest doing?" I turned my head quickly to see if Diane was all right.

"I don't know, man. She looks awfully quiet if you ask me. You sure she's breathing?" Walter, the more paranoid of my frat brothers, leaned over and pressed his head against Diane's chest, cupping his hand over his ear. I'm sure he wasn't doing anything raunchy, but I didn't like the idea that he was so close to copping a feel from my best friend's wife. Besides, Diane was just the type of woman Walter liked.

"What the fuck are you doing, Walter?"

"I'm trying to see if she's breathing, Goddammit!" He sounded nervous as he placed his head back on her chest.

"Well, is she?" It took him a few seconds to answer, and that made me a little nervous too.

"Yeah, she's breathing," he sighed.

"Good, now get your hand off her titty." Walter snapped his head back, sitting up straight.

"What did you give her anyway?" Jeff asked.

"It's called *night-night*. The white boys in the clubs call it the date rape drug."

"Isn't that shit dangerous?" Walter's voice was all concern.

"Nah, it's safe. I went on the Internet and checked it out."

We pulled in front of Room 103 of the Budget Motor Inn less then ten minutes after we left the bar. I jumped out of the car and knocked on the door while Walter and Jeff quickly carried Diane from the car. My other frat brother, Biggie, opened the door with a big smile.

"Man, this is gonna be funny as shit." Biggie stepped aside so that Jeff and Walter could carry Diane into the room.

"Look, don't be gettin' no weird ideas. We just gonna do what I told y'all and get the hell outta here." I gave Biggie the eye and he smiled. "I mean it, man," I warned.

"Yeah, well, let's just pray she don't wake up. We could all go to jail behind this shit," Walter reminded us.

"Will you calm down, Walt? She ain't gonna wake up, and we ain't gonna get in trouble. Now prop her up on the bed so we can get started." Walter walked over to the bed and sat Diane up straight.

"Should I take her clothes off?" Jeff asked, smiling.

"No! Hell, no! We can do exactly what we need with her clothes on. Damn, y'all some perverted mothafuckers!" I shook my head. I knew these brothers were gonna have to be kept in check.

"You calling us perverted? Who came up with this idea?" Jeff laughed. I ignored him and turned to Biggie.

"Come on, Biggie, let's get the show on the road."

I reached down into my little duffle bag and found the Polaroid camera I'd brought. By the time I read the directions and looked over at Diane, Biggie was standing next to her with his johnson hard as a rock about six inches from her open mouth. If you didn't know she was passed out, you'd swear she was about to deep-throat him. And that would be one hell of a feat considering they didn't call him Biggie because of his height. The man had a johnson the size of a baseball bat.

"Yo, Jay, you gonna take the picture or what?" I watched the way Biggie held Diane's head and suddenly I was starting to think this wasn't such a good idea. Just looking at Diane knocked out, with her mouth open and Biggie's thing so close, made me a little uneasy. But then I started thinking about all the shit she was talkin' about Kenya and me at the bar and I thought, *Fuck that bitch.*

"Yeah, I'm'a take it." I snapped two shots then waited for Jeff to pose himself on the other side of Diane. I snapped two more. By the time we were done, we'd taken some of the freakiest pictures you'd ever wanna see. Phase one of my plan was complete. Diane was about to learn firsthand what happened to Wil could happen to anyone. Now all I had to do was get her back to her car safely and figure out the best way to get these pictures into her hands so that she'd stop torturing Wil.

43

Kyle

That was it. With one swing of the judge's gavel, I went from being a married man to a divorcé. I glanced over at Lisa, and when we made eye contact, both of us looked away quickly. I rubbed my hands over my face, trying to stop the tears from welling up in my eyes, but it was useless. I'd had more than my share of bad days in the past year, but this was by far the worst.

I could barely remember how this rift between Lisa and me had started in the first place. I watched Lisa walk toward the courtroom door, followed by an entourage of family and friends. Diane turned around and gave me the finger with a smirk. It took all I had not to flip her the bird myself. Thank God Lisa had enough class to grab her hand and chastise her. I couldn't tell what she was saying to Diane, but I'm sure Lisa put her in her place. Damn, even after what we had just been through, Lisa still showed me respect. That was one classy lady. I had really fucked up. Seven fucking years down the drain and I had no real explanation for my failure.

"You okay, Kyle?" My friend and lawyer, Greg, patted my shoulder and handed me a tissue.

"No, Greg, I'm not okay." I was still staring at Lisa as she disappeared behind the door. "I just watched my life walk out that door."

"You mean your wife?"

"No, I mean my life. Lisa was my life, Greg. And like an idiot I wasn't smart enough to realize it until it was too late."

"Yeah, I know, buddy. I know." He patted me on the back as we left the courtroom. "Come on. Let's go get a drink. I have some news that might cheer you up."

Greg and I sat down in a booth in a small Irish pub called Dwyer's, about two blocks from the courthouse on Hillside Avenue. He ordered a beer and a burger. I wasn't hungry, so I just ordered a Dewars.

"Okay. What's this big surprise that's going to cheer me up?" I doubted seriously that any news would help at this point unless he was about to tell me this was all a bad dream and it was time to wake up.

Greg looked at me and smiled. "The city finally made an offer to settle your false arrest lawsuit." I stared at him. He didn't realize it, but he had just reminded me what had set into motion the destruction of my marriage.

"What's the offer?" I asked, but interrupted before he could answer. My cell phone was vibrating. "Hold on a minute." I flipped open my cell phone. "Hello? Hello? Goddammit, Val! I know this is you." I was really starting to get annoyed by all the bullshit phone calls I'd been getting. I didn't have any concrete proof, but I was sure it was Val.

"You all right, Kyle? Anything I need to help you with?" Greg looked a little concerned.

"Nah, man. Just someone I know acting stupid. Nothing I can't handle." I didn't want to explain what Val had been doing lately. Especially since Greg had warned me about dating before the divorce was final. "So what kind of offer did the city make?" I tried to sound enthusiastic.

"Believe it or not, three hundred thousand," he smiled.

"I thought you said their initial offer would be about a hundred thou?" I asked incredulously.

"I did. Somebody big must think they really fucked up."

"Take the offer, Greg." Greg flinched, and looked at me like I had three heads.

"What d'you mean, take the offer? It's their first offer. We might be able to squeeze seven figures out of them and still not go to court."

"Take the offer, Greg," I repeated seriously. He stared at me with confusion, and I could tell he was disappointed. But I was not in the mood to explain myself to anybody today. Not even my old college roommate.

"Any particular reason why?" he pressed.

"Yeah, because I said so." I'm sure I surprised him with my attitude.

"Kyle, do you realize that after I get my third, you're only gonna get two hundred thousand dollars out of this?" He spoke like I was mentally deficient.

"Yeah, Greg, I do. Matter of fact, take out a pen and write this down." Greg did as he was told but he still looked disappointed. Without my interference he probably woulda cleared over three hundred grand for himself. That's a lot of dough to take out of a lawyer's pocket, especially a lawyer you call a friend.

"Outta the two hundred grand, I want you to put forty-five into each of my daughters' trust funds. Then—" Greg interrupted.

"You sure you want me to do it that way? Maybe we should set up new trust funds for your kids. The way your divorce decree reads now, Lisa's the administrator of all existing trust accounts for your kids. Besides, maybe you should use this money to buy a house."

"Trust me on this one, Greg. I'd mess up the money for the girls before Lisa would. And as far as me buying a house, I'm not ready for that yet. I'm comfortable right where I'm at. " Greg was silent, but his expression told me he thought I was making a big mistake. I continued my instructions. "I want you to open college trust accounts for ten grand for each of Jay, Wil, and Allen's kids. Make sure the mothers can't get to the accounts, especially in Allen's case." Greg shook his head a few times but continued writing. I know he was too through with me.

"What should I do with the remaining money?" he asked flatly.

"Put it in a blind trust for now with me and Jay as the administrators. Just between you, me, and the wall, Jay got some girl pregnant. I'm just trying to look out for the baby like I would do his other kids."

"Very honorable of you," Greg sneered. He obviously thought I was a complete fool.

I left Greg and his attitude about a half hour later. Once he wrote down my instructions, there wasn't any need for me to stick around listening to him tell me how stupid I was. Hell, friend or not, he was working for me. I headed over to my Jamaica Avenue store, and when I arrived, I didn't say a word to anyone. I just went into my office and shut the door behind me. I poured myself a drink and gulped it down, hoping to rid myself of the pain that had become my life. I was drained, and I felt like I was gonna collapse at any moment. I lay down on the office couch, squirming around until I was comfortable. The stress of the divorce, Ma Jackson's death, and the lack of sleep I'd had lately were really starting to catch up with me. Within minutes I dozed off and probably would have stayed that way till morning if it wasn't for a knock at the door.

"Kyle, I'm getting ready to leave. You okay?" It was Sharon, my store manager.

"Yeah, I'm okay. Go ahead. I'll lock up." I glanced at the clock. Damn, it was almost 7:15 P.M. I'd been asleep for nearly six hours. I sat up and rubbed my face with both hands. When I looked up, I was staring at one of my wedding pictures. I felt like I needed to cry, but I couldn't.

The phone rang and I picked it up.

"Hello?"

Whoever it was didn't answer, but I could hear Luther Vandross playing in the background. I spoke one more time, then hung up when I got no response. I picked up my briefcase and keys and locked up the store. I headed over to my Highland Avenue apartment and was glad to see Wil's truck parked out front. At least with him home I'd have someone to talk to. I figured once I took a shower and changed, I'd head on upstairs to his place to see if he wanted to go to the Ponderosa in Green Acres Mall for something to eat. They had one hell of a buffet over there, and the big man loved to eat. I was pretty hungry myself. Plus I really needed somebody to talk to. Wil's about the best listener I know and this was a subject I know he'd wanna talk about. Especially since he and Diane were headed down that divorce court road.

When I stepped off the elevator, I was immediately hit with the wonderful aroma of Caribbean ox tails coming from down the hall. *Mmm, mmm, mmm,* that shit smelled so good I could almost taste it. And the farther I walked down the hall, the better it smelled. When I finally reached my apartment, it took me about two seconds to realize the smell was coming from underneath my door. As bad a day as I was having, I had to take a deep whiff and smile. Only one person I knew could make ox tails like that, and that was my mom.

I'd told her and my friends that I didn't need or want any of them to come down to the courthouse. In my mind the divorce was something between Lisa and me. At least that's the way I felt before I saw the entourage Lisa walked in with. That's when I realized I'd made a big mistake and could have used some moral support.

I guess my mom decided that if she couldn't come to the courthouse, she'd show up at my house and cook me dinner. Even though I was a thirty-six-year-old man, it felt good knowing that Mom would fly all the way up to support me. My mom lived in Florida with her new husband Joe, who I couldn't stand. It wasn't that Joe was such a bad guy. It's just that he was a bad guy for my mom and I hated the thought that he was always trying to replace my dad. But that's another story.

I opened my door expecting to see good old Mom stirring a pot, watching *Who Wants to Be a Millionaire?* on the TV. Instead I was greeted by dozens of white glimmering candles and Luther Vandross on the stereo. The small kitchen table was set with two long white candles illuminating the very elegant table setting, highlighted by a dozen white roses in a white vase. Speaking of roses, on the floor was a trail of rose petals that led down the hall to the bedroom. I walked over to the stove and lifted the lid off one of the smaller pots. I was tempted to reach in and take a taste when I saw that it was spicy cabbage, my favorite vegetable. Spicy cabbage and ox tails? Someone was going to a lot of trouble to impress me, and by now I was pretty sure it wasn't my mom. The rose petals and the candles were a pretty sure tipoff to that, and the Luther Vandross on the stereo was a dead giveaway.

"Val! I know you're here." When I didn't get a reply, I put my briefcase down and angrily headed for my bedroom. It had been quite a while since I'd seen Val in person. But what I saw next made me put aside my anger and take a deep breath. Some women look nice in candlelight. Others look good in lingerie. But Val? Let's just say Val had it *goin' on* as she lay on my bed wearing a sheer white baby doll nightie with feathers around the edges and a matching thong. To say she looked breathtaking in that candlelight was an understatement.

"Hi," she purred. "I was starting to think you weren't going to come home." She reached over to the ice bucket and poured a glass of champagne.

"What are you doing here, Val? This is breaking and entering." I folded my arms across my chest to show my displeasure, but I must admit it was getting mighty hard to be angry with a woman who looked so damn fine. She got up off the bed and walked over to me. The sway of her hips and breasts was even more enticing than ever and she knew it.

"I'm here to apologize, Kyle," she said in a sincere voice, handing me the glass of champagne. I smiled. As much as we'd been through, I had to admit it was good to see her. I thought she hated me, and for her to take the high road and apologize was truly honorable. Hell, I could totally understand her wanting an apology from me.

"Apologize about what? You don't have to apolo . . ." She took her finger and placed it on my lips to quiet me.

"I want to apologize for the way I've been acting lately. Especially the phone calls. It's just that I missed you and I needed to hear your voice. I'm sorry." She took a step closer and kissed me. I didn't resist, so she did it again, this time parting my lips with her tongue.

"Come on. I wanna show you something." She grabbed my hand and led me into the kitchen where she lifted the lid of the big pot. The smell that came out of it was to die for.

"About a month ago I called your mother and asked her for the recipe to those ox tails you're always talking about. It took me a while, but I finally got all the ingredients to make some. You'd be surprised how hard it is to find freshly slaughtered ox tails. So when I found them I figured I'd come over and make you your favorite dinner. Kinda make up for all the trouble I've been causing you. Oh, and just so you know, I didn't break in. I used my key." She took a spoon and dipped it into the pot, offering me a taste, which I gladly accepted.

"Damn, that's almost as good as Mom's." I took the spoon out of her hand and dipped it in for another taste.

"Well, thank you. I'll take that as a compliment. Why don't we sit down and eat? I've got a long, exciting night planned for you." She licked her lips then lifted her head for a kiss. I gave her exactly what she wanted with no regrets. After the day I'd had, what she was offering was like a breath of fresh air, and as long as she didn't mention Lisa or the divorce, we were straight. At least for tonight anyway.

We'd been eating, drinking, and talking for the better part of two hours, and both of us had a little buzz. She'd even managed to make me laugh a few times, which was no small feat considering my mood lately. I was on my third plate of ox tails and about ready for a little dessert in the bedroom, especially since Val had been teasing me by massaging my inner thigh with her bare feet all night.

"Hey, how about we go in the room and I give you one of my patented massages?"

"Sure," she smiled, raising her eyebrows a few times. "But first I'd like to propose a toast." She filled our glasses with champagne.

"So, what are we toasting?" I lifted my glass. So did she.

"Your divorce. We're toasting your divorce. Thank God it's finally over." She sounded as if this was the happiest moment of her life. She even tried to clink glasses, but I pulled mine back. She didn't realize it, but she'd offended me. And all of a sudden her presumptuousness reminded me that Lisa and I might still be together if she hadn't busted in that night, talkin' about how she was pregnant.

"What the hell do you mean, we're toasting my divorce?" I rolled my eyes and sucked my teeth. The entire day's misery began to creep back into my mind again. "Do you actually think I wanted to get divorced?" I took my napkin off my lap and threw it on the table. I don't think she liked my attitude or my tone because her smile became a frown right away.

"Look, don't act all stink with me because she divorced your ass. Not after I spent all day cooking your ass ox tails and spending all my money on this outfit and candles. You would want to act grateful." She was heated, and so was I. We were definitely not on the same page.

"You know what, Val? I think you should leave." I got up and walked into the bedroom with her hot on my tail.

"What the fuck is wrong with you, Kyle? I would think you'd be relieved to finally get rid of that bitch." I turned around in a fury.

"I love that bitch, Val! Okay? Do you understand? I love her!" I picked up her clothes and handed them to her.

"Yeah, I understand perfectly. You go to the black bitch when you want some pussy, but it's the white bitch you wanna go home to. That's fucked up, Kyle!"

"You got it all wrong, Val. It's not about what color she is. It's about the woman I love. The woman who had my three kids. If you can't understand that, I don't know what to tell you. Now can I have my key back?" She threw the key at me.

"You're going to regret this, Kyle." She slid into her jeans. "I swear on my dead grandmother you're gonna regret this!"

"You know what? I already have, Val." I started to blow out the candles around the room.

"You think I'm playin', don't you? Aw'ight, mothafucker. When I get finished, you're gonna regret ever fucking with me." She slipped on her shoes and stomped out.

When I finished blowing out all the candles and straightened up my place a bit, I sat on the couch trying to relax. All the weight of the divorce and the shit that just went down with Val was torturing me. I'm not gonna lie. I felt bad about how I had treated Val. She was the kind of woman any man would want. It wasn't her fault that I was still in love with Lisa. I should have been man enough to ask her to leave when I first got home, instead of letting my stomach and my hormones get in the way. I was about to pick up the phone and call her with an apology when I heard a car alarm go off. A car alarm that sounded just like mine. I jumped up from the sofa and looked out the window. Yep, it was my car all right. The horn was beeping and the lights were flashing, but more importantly Val was standing next to it and she was holding something shiny in her hand. Whatever it was, she used it to stab my front tire. I watched that tire die right before my eyes and my anger erupted. I almost ripped the window off the track trying to open it.

"Get the fuck away from my car before I kill your ass!" I couldn't believe what she was doing. And would you believe she had the nerve to look at me and smile as she made her way to the rear tire? I closed my eyes when I saw her hand go up in the air.

"Fuck this shit," I yelled, as I grabbed my keys and ran out the door. I decided against the elevator and bolted down the staircase, hoping to stop her before she killed my remaining tires. If she was smart, she'd be gone before I got down there. I wasn't the type to hit a woman, but if I got outside and she was there, I was not gonna be responsible for my actions. When I raced outside and saw my car, I couldn't see Val but I could hear the loud hiss of one of my tires being punctured.

"I swear to God! I'm gonna kill you, Val!"

She must not have thought I'd get downstairs so fast 'cause she popped her head around the side of the truck and let out a scream before taking off down the street. About two seconds later I was on her tail. We must've run down Highland Avenue two or three blocks before I was close enough to catch her. And she must've sensed I was right on her heels because she put on a burst of speed as she zigzagged across the street without looking. Unfortunately for her she was headed right into the middle of the street and a car.

"Val, Goddammit! Look where you're going!" I screamed.

She wasn't paying me no mind, and I realized her only chance was for me to stop her. Thank God I was able to grab hold of her blouse and throw her to the ground before she entered the street again. But her blessing was my curse as my momentum took me right into the middle of the street and into the path of the car. I slipped and fell and only had a few seconds to get out of the way. I was scared like shit as I tried to scramble to my feet. Unfortunately, when I finally got up, there was loose gravel on the road and I slipped and fell to the ground again. This time I knew I wasn't going to make it and braced myself for the impact as I heard Val's scream. I don't remember being hit, but I do remember Lisa and the girls flashing through my mind right before everything went dark . . .

44

Tracy

I was in the rest room of the Lobster Inn on City Island admiring my new engagement ring. I was so happy, my smile stretched from ear to ear. Jay had just proposed over dinner and I'd slipped into the rest room when we finished eating to fix my makeup. I must have cried a river of tears I was so overjoyed at his proposal. Not just because he asked me to marry him but also because this finally proved that he loved me. I'd really been having my doubts about us lately, especially since he kept calling me by his wife's name. I hadn't pointed it out to him but he'd been doing it more and more lately. My friend Tia practically had me convinced I should leave him and move in with her, but I was trying to stick it out for the baby's sake. Besides, I was in love with the guy.

"*Mmm, mmm, mmm. Girrrrrl,* who was he?" a pretty brown-skinned woman sighed as she walked into the rest room. She went into a stall and closed the door while her friend, a supercurvy light-skinned woman with a cheap weave stood in front of the mirror next to me. "Girl, that man was so fine he looked like a chocolate god. And the way he smiled at us with those dimples. Lord, he made me wanna feel his rhythm in my thighs. Why ain't you introduce me, Keyshawn?"

The woman beside me sucked her teeth and her words made me drop my purse. "Please, Renee. Trust me, you do not want no introduction to Jay Crawford." She barely glanced at me as the contents of my purse scattered across the tile floor.

"Jay? That's the brother you used to talk to when I was livin' in Atlanta? The one who used to send you flowers all the time and took you to that fancy hotel on the beach?"

"*Mmm-hmm,* that's him." She twisted her lips as she teased her weave in the mirror.

I felt a little queasy all of a sudden. She had to be talking about the Beach Comber Hotel in Bayville, the one Jay had sworn up and down he'd only been to with me. I picked up my purse and rushed to put everything back in it. Jay was about to get a piece of my mind. I can't believe he would lie about something like that.

"I thought you said he was ugly." Her friend flushed the toilet and came out of the stall to wash her hands. "Girl, he is not ugly. That man is *fine*."

"He may be cute, but he sure as hell is a dog. And when was the last time you saw a pretty dog?" They both laughed. "Besides, Renee, that fool's married."

"I don't know, Keyshawn. Fine as he is, I think I could deal with him being married." I lifted an eyebrow and glanced at her out the corner of my eye. *Not if he's married to me, bitch,* I thought. But I kept my mouth shut and my ears opened.

"Hmmph, think I wasn't dealing with it? As good as that dick was, I didn't give a shit about his marriage. It was the VD I had a problem with. That fool gave me gonorrhea." She faced her girlfriend, head bobbing as she spoke.

I gasped and dropped my purse again. They both turned to me with evil glares. I smiled like a fool as I picked up my belongings for the second time.

"Forget her." Renee waved her hand and got back to the subject. "You mean to tell me that fine-ass nigga out there burnt you?"

"Like a Yule log," Keyshawn said matter-of-factly as she applied her lip gloss.

"Damn, now that's fucked up." Renee shook her head.

"No, I'll tell you what's fucked up. That bastard had the nerve to accuse me of givin' the shit to him."

"Well, did you?" I couldn't help it. I had to interrupt their conversation. They were talking about my man and I know he ain't give no one VD.

"Hell no! I ain't give him shit."

"Well, how can you be sure how many guys was you fuckin'?" She was about to answer me, until I guess she came to her senses. Her long, red fingernail was waving in my face.

"Who the hell are you, and why are you all up in my business?"

"Come on, Keyshawn. Let's go. She's pregnant." Her friend pulled her a few steps away from me.

"I know. But she needs to mind her business. She don't even know me like that. What's up with you, anyway? You mess with Jay or somethin'?"

"No, I don't mess with him. I'm engaged to him." I flashed my ring and she examined me from head to toe, shaking her head.

"Damn, girl. He gave you one of those cheap-ass rings too? I guess some things never change." She shook her head again. "Do yourself a favor. Before you go runnin' around tellin' people you're engaged to

Jay Crawford, make sure that he's divorced. 'Cause believe me, his wife ain't never gonna let him go."

"Come on, Keyshawn, leave her alone. The girl's pregnant. You gonna mess around and make her go into labor." Renee tried to pull her to the door.

"Let me go, Renee." She pulled herself free and took a step toward me. "All I'm tryin' to do is give her the same advice I wish someone had given me."

"Oh yeah, and what's that?" I asked sarcastically. This sister was obviously just jealous because I was with Jay now. All that shit about VD was probably just to cover up the fact that my man dumped her ass.

"Stay as far away from Jay Crawford as you can get. If you don't, you're the one who's gonna need an AIDS test. With me he was just passing on clap, but as many women as he messes with, I'm sure he's moved on to bigger and better things. Take it from me, honey. Every time you sleep with him, you're taking your life in your hands."

Her words hit me like a ton of bricks. Could she really be talking about the same man who had just proposed to me thirty minutes ago? What if Jay really had given her gonorrhea? And what if he was really sleeping with other women? Nah, this bitch was lying. It couldn't be true. Jay wouldn't do that to me.

"He's not like that." I glared at her. "And I don't appreciate you talking 'bout him like that. He probably never even messed with your stupid ass."

"You calling me a liar?" She took a step forward and I took a step back. Damn, if I wasn't pregnant, I'd be putting my foot right in her ass.

"Come on, Keyshawn, don't do this. I keep tellin' you she's pregnant." Renee was pleading now.

"I ain't gonna touch her, but I don't like no one calling me a liar, 'specially some young, stupid bitch."

"Well, I don't like no one lying on my man, so we even." Pregnant or not, I had a real attitude now. This wench was getting on my last nerve.

"Oh, yeah?" she laughed. "Why don't we go ask him if I'm lying?"

"Why don't we?" I headed for the door, eager for Jay to put this bitch in her place. By the time I got to where Jay was sitting in the lobby, I was about three strides ahead of Keyshawn and Renee.

"Ready to go?" he smiled.

"Do you know her?" I pointed at Keyshawn and his smile disappeared.

"Yeah, Jay. Do you know me?" She stood right next to me with hands on her hips, a wicked grin on her face. Jay didn't say a word. He just glared.

"Jay, I asked you a question. Do you—"

"Yeah, I know her," he stopped me. "Why? What'd she say?" His eyes never left hers.

"I told her you ain't shit, nigga. That's what I told her." Keyshawn poked her finger in Jay's chest.

"Yeah, well, it takes a nigga to know a nigga, Keyshawn." He stood up and reached for my hand. "Come on, baby, let's go. It's starting to smell around here."

I pulled my hand back.

"No, Jay. I wanna know if you gave her gonorrhea." Jay's eyes got huge. He looked at me, then Keyshawn, then back at me.

"She told you that shit?" he asked slowly.

I nodded.

"And you believed her?"

"Just answer my question, Jay," I demanded. I was still hoping he was gonna put this bitch in her place when the truth about them came out. He gave me this stupid look, then exploded.

"Hell, no! I ain't give her shit. I told you there were gonna be girls like her trying to fuck our shit up. She's just another player hater, mad that she can't get none."

"Can't get none? What the fuck would I want from you? The last time you gave me something, it took two shots to get rid of it!" Keyshawn was screaming, out of control, and the entire restaurant lobby was now staring at us.

"I ain't give you shit, you fuckin' project ho!" Jay took a step toward her. I could see the muscles in his neck start to bulge and I was afraid he was going to hit her. I reached out and grabbed his hand.

"Come on, baby. Fuck her. I believe you."

"You one stupid bitch. Can't you see I'm trying to help you? He's gonna dog you just like he done everyone else." She was breathing heavy, and she had this wild look in her eyes. Damn, she was really tryin' to convince me of her story. She musta really wanted Jay back or something.

"No, I can't see shit you trying to do for me but break up my engagement. You jealous heifer." I smiled and flashed my ring near her face. "And I swear if you call me a stupid bitch again, pregnant or not, I'ma kick your fuckin' ass. Come on, baby, let's get the hell out of here." I strode toward the exit, pulling Jay's hand.

We spent most of the ride home holding hands in total silence, me staring at my engagement ring, Jay entranced in his own thoughts. After that scene, I guess neither one of us had the strength to even deal with it. Truth is, I was grateful for the chance to sort out some of my emotions.

"You like it?" He pointed to my ring as he parked in front of our apartment.

"I love it."

"I love you." He smiled and then just as quickly changed the subject. "Look, I'm gonna go get some beer. When I get back, we can celebrate our engagement the right way." He winked and let his eyes roam over my body.

"We got beer in the house," I pouted. I was still a little shook up, and I just wanted him to come inside and hold me.

"I know, but I want a Heineken. Kyle, Wil, and Allen can have that Budweiser tomorrow when we move."

"Oh, all right," I sighed. "But can you go to Carvel for me? I been craving Carvel." I figured if he was gonna be out, I might as well take advantage of it. He'd be back soon enough to take care of me.

"Sure. What you want?"

"Get me a strawberry sundae with extra hot fudge. And don't forget the nuts and whipped cream."

He looked at me and made a face. "Okay. If that's what you want."

"And can you leave me your cell phone? I wanna call my mom."

"You gonna tell her we're engaged?"

"Uh-huh, that's why I'm callin' her."

"Good," he smiled, handing me the phone as I stepped out of the car. "You make sure you tell your ma how big that rock is." I nodded and he pulled off.

I watched his car drive away wondering about his sudden need to go out to buy beer. What a time for him to be so eager to leave, and why didn't he just drive there before coming home? I'd never had any doubts about him messing with anyone other than Kenya, but now I wasn't so sure. I'd have to be blind not to notice how women seemed to always be looking at him. Some of them looked like they wanted to eat him for dessert. God, what if I was just one of his many girls? Keyshawn sure made it sound that way, and so had that woman at the funeral. I looked at the ring on my finger and tried to smile. Jay wouldn't give me a diamond like that unless he really meant it, would he? I wished I really believed that.

I wasn't going to get any answers standing outside in the night air so I headed into the house to call my mom. I hadn't talked to her in so long, and I was feeling like I really needed her now. We'd been more like sisters than mother and daughter until Jay moved me to this roach motel out here in Jersey. I hadn't spoken to her since the day me, her, Jay, and Daddy went to brunch and she announced that I was pregnant. I was so mad at her, I didn't think I would ever forgive her for that. But now she was the only person I wanted to talk to.

I maneuvered through all the boxes we'd packed up to move. They were scattered all over the living room. Somehow I found some empty space and sat down on the sofa. I closed my eyes and inhaled deeply before I dialed the number to my parents' house. I was praying my father wouldn't answer.

"Hello?" My eyes filled with tears when I heard my mom's voice.

"Mom?" I whispered.

"Tracy? Is that you, baby?" She sounded like she was going to cry, too.

"Yeah, Mom, it's me." I took a breath. "How you been, Mom?"

"I'm all right, Tracy. But I been worried about you. Is everything all right with the baby? You're going to the doctor like you're supposed to, aren't you?" It felt good to hear my mother's concern. I hadn't realized just how much I missed that feeling of security I always had with my parents. Why hadn't I noticed that it was missing with Jay?

"Yeah, Mom, I been goin' to the doctor and the baby's fine. I had a sonogram the other day." I smiled as I remembered seeing my baby moving on the screen. "They told me you're gonna have a grandson."

"Oh, Tracy. You for real? I'm going to have a grandson? Wait 'til I tell the girls in the office. You decide what you gonna name him?"

"No, not yet. Any ideas?" We talked about names and I could hear the excitement in her voice as the two of us prattled on just like the old times. I hadn't even brought up what happened at the restaurant or that Jay and I were engaged yet. Suddenly that didn't seem important. It just felt so good to be connecting with my mom again.

"When you coming home, Tracy?" Her voice was so soft, and her question sounded more like a plea. "I'm not asking you to come home for good, but just to visit for a week or two. I miss you, baby."

"I miss you too, Mom. But Daddy said—"

"I don't care what your father said, Tracy. You're my only child and you're always welcome in this house. Do you understand me? Besides, he might not admit it, but that big lug misses you just as much as I do."

"You think so?" I grinned at the thought of my big, tough daddy with the soft heart.

"I know so. He's just worried about you, Tracy. And so am I."

"Well, that makes three of us." There was silence on the other end as my mom processed what I had just told her. She finally cleared her throat.

"What's wrong, Tracy? Everything all right with you and Jay? Is he treating you all right?"

"I guess. We got engaged today." I tried to sound excited, but I don't think it worked.

"You don't sound too happy about it, baby."

"I am. I'm just a little confused."

"About what, baby?"

"I don't know. I'm just thinking maybe I don't really know Jay well enough yet. Everything just happened so fast with us, with the baby and all. And now we're talking about marriage. We can't even afford for me to go back to school."

"Tracy, I wasn't gonna tell you this . . ." Mom hesitated. "But there's something your father told me about Jay that maybe you should know."

"Mom, I already know he's married. He's going to see a lawyer tomorrow about a divorce."

"That's not it, Tracy." She hesitated again before she dropped the bomb. "Your father found out that Jay was arrested five months ago."

"Arrested! For what?" I closed my eyes and prayed it was nothing too bad. Something Jay would be able to explain. When Mom told me, I didn't think I'd wanna hear Jay's explanation, even if he did have one.

"He pleaded guilty to soliciting a prostitute."

"Are you serious? Mom, that's not possible." I didn't want to believe it, but after everything else I'd been learning about the man, I guess anything was possible.

"Yes, baby I'm serious. Your father showed me the printout."

"Oh, Mom. What am I gonna do?" I started crying as I gave her the news about everything else I'd heard about Jay. "I just found out he gave another woman gonorrhea."

I explained everything to my mom about my relationship with Jay. From the day he left me at his house, to the fight at the funeral, to him calling me Kenya, to the scene in the restaurant bathroom. Mom was a great listener. She didn't say a word 'til I finished the entire saga. Then she asked me something I didn't expect to hear, but something that made me so glad. She asked me if I wanted to come home.

When Jay walked in the door, he must have sensed something was wrong. Then again, I would hope that after taking two hours to get some beer he'd know he was in some trouble. He put down the six-pack of Heineken and took slow, apprehensive steps toward me.

"What's wrong? Why you looking at me like that?"

"Where's my ice cream?"

"Oh, shit." He hit himself in the head with his fist. "I knew I forgot something. I'm sorry, baby. I got a flat tire and completely forgot about your ice cream." He gave me this innocent look.

"It took you two hours to change a flat? What do I look like, a fool?" I looked at him from head to toe, and there wasn't a speck of dirt on him. That was the cleanest tire change I ever heard of. Jay must have known what I was thinking, 'cause he had an excuse prepared before I even opened my mouth.

"My jack was broke so I had to call Triple-A."

"Yeah, right. Tell me anything." I rolled my eyes and used my coldest voice.

"Look, you're not still mad about that Keyshawn shit, are you?"

"Yeah, believe it or not, after waiting for you for two hours, I'm still not over it," I said sarcastically.

"I told you she's a liar." He was starting to sound worried. "And you're playin' right into her hands. She just wants to mess up what we have." He tried to reach out for me, but I pulled back. I couldn't let him touch me.

"So was my father lying when he told my mother about you being arrested for soliciting a prostitute?" Jay's bottom lip started trembling and he didn't answer. Which could only mean there was some truth to what Daddy told Mom.

"Goddammit! Answer me, Jay!"

His phone went off and I picked it up from the sofa. My parents were on their way to pick me up, so I figured it was Mom calling to check on me.

"Hello?"

"Hi Tracy, this is Wil. Can I speak to Jay, please?"

"Yeah, hold on a sec." I tried to disguise the annoyance in my voice. I shoved the phone at Jay.

"Hello?" After he answered, Jay didn't speak again. He just listened, his eyes growing wider by the second.

"I'll be right there." He hung up and stared at me with a blank expression. "Look, Kyle's been hit by a car and they don't think he's gonna make it. Can we talk about this when I get back?"

"I won't be here when you get back, Jay." I felt bad if the news about Kyle was true, but for all I knew, Wil's call was part of some scheme Jay had cooked up to get out of the house again. It wouldn't be the first time those boys had hooked each other up with excuses for their ladies. Jay had done it a few times to Kenya so that he could spend more time with me. And right now I wasn't about trusting Jay. I took off the engagement ring and placed it on the coffee table.

"Come on, Tracy. Don't act this way. Not with Kyle in the hospital. I can explain all of this to you when I get back. It's not what you think."

"It's not what I think?" I looked at him, mystified. "Then what is it? When I hear the words 'prostitute' and 'arrest' in the same sentence with your name, the only thing that comes to mind is I better get an AIDS test. Now I'm sorry about your friend, Jay. He's a nice man and I'll be praying for him." I hesitated and swallowed. "But I mean what I say. I won't be here when you get back. My parents are on their way here right now."

"Please, Tracy. Don't do this. I love you." His eyes were actually glistening with tears.

"Go see your friend, Jay. He needs you. Just like I need to go home."

45

Diane

I brushed the hair out of my eyes with an aggravated look on my face. I'd been thumbing through the proofs of my son Teddy's pictures from Sears, trying to decide which ones to purchase, and was getting more and more upset with each one. I was sick and tired of how much that boy looked like his father. It was hard enough trying to forget Wil Duncan and move on with my life. Now every time I looked at Teddy, there was a reminder of his father staring me in the face.

"Diane, did you hear me?" Lisa startled me out of my daze.

"Huh? What'd you say?"

"I asked if you wanted some more tea. Your cup is empty." She held up the teapot.

"Oh, tea. Yeah, I'll take some more." I put down the pictures and lifted my cup for Lisa to fill. "Thanks." Lisa poured herself a cup then sat across from me at the table.

"You were thinking about Wil, weren't you?" She smiled at me suspiciously.

"No, why would I think about that no-good dog?" I rolled my eyes. Lisa didn't say a word. She just picked up her tea and smiled as she sipped. I knew she knew I was lying, but I didn't care. I just didn't wanna get into another long conversation about Wil.

"What about you? Did you think about Kyle a lot before the divorce?" I decided to change the subject. It was easier to talk about *her* failed marriage than mine.

"Well, I've only been divorced one day, but yeah, I used to think about him all the time. Who am I fooling? I still think about him a lot." She took a deep breath, looking rather distant. "As stupid as this may sound, Diane, I love Kyle. He was a good father, a good provider, and a great husband. I just don't believe he loves me anymore." She sipped her tea before continuing. "But I'll tell you what. If I could have things back the way they were a year ago, I'd take them in a minute." I nodded my head slowly. I totally understood. Seemed like Lisa was always able to express how I was feeling.

The phone rang and I stopped breathing for a second. It was Wil. It had to be him. It better be him or I was gonna be pissed. I hadn't spoken to him in over a week. Not since I cursed his ass out when that no-good Jay got me drunk and slipped me a thousand-dollar check instead of the three thousand dollars he'd promised. I'd been expecting Wil's call all day. Especially since I made sure each and every one of his friends at work were informed that the movers were coming today and that the kids and I were leaving in the morning. I figured it was just a matter of time before he'd come by to try to talk me into staying in New York. Not that he could change my mind, but I still wanted to see him one more time before I left. When I hadn't heard from him by now, I was actually disappointed. Maybe even a little hurt. I don't know, I guess I figured he'd fight for his family a little more than this.

I answered the phone, making sure I had a twinge of attitude to my voice, but my tone was wasted. It wasn't Wil, it was the driver from the moving company, calling to let me know they were going to be a little late. I placed the phone back on the cradle a little harder than necessary. Where the hell was that no-good Wil Duncan anyway?

"You all right, Diane?" Lisa patted my hand.

"Yes. No. I don't know." I bit my lip in frustration.

Truth is, I felt so alone and unwanted I wanted to cry. And looking at my son's pictures didn't help things at all, 'cause all that did was remind me of his father. Lisa was right—why the hell couldn't things be the way they were a year ago? I walked to the kitchen window and peered out to the backyard. It had taken Wil and me six years, but that yard had been the final touch to fixing up our dream house. I was gonna miss this house. Here it was a day before I was supposed to leave, and all of a sudden I was having second thoughts about moving. Lord, what was I gonna do?

"Lisa, can I ask you a question?"

"Sure."

"Do you think I'm doing the right thing moving to Atlanta?" She was silent for a second.

"That's up to you, Diane. I'm your friend. I'm going to support you in whatever you do."

"I didn't ask you all that," I snapped. "I wanna know if *you* think I'm doing the right thing." I wasn't trying to be mean, but I was frustrated. Lisa always found a way to be supportive, but I wasn't looking for support. I was looking for an honest opinion. In twenty-four hours I would be in the car, driving my kids to Atlanta. I needed to know if what I was doing was right. Lisa held her teacup in her hands and looked up at me.

"You really want the truth?" Her expression made it clear I wasn't gonna like what she had to say.

"Hey, like the kids say, 'Keep it real.' We're friends, right?" I braced myself for whatever it was I was about to hear.

"Okay," she exhaled. "I think you're being selfish, Diane. I think the only person you're thinking about is yourself and I think you're hurting your children by moving to Atlanta." She was right. I didn't like what she said.

"How am I hurting my children?" I took offense to that especially. I loved my kids.

" 'Cause you're only moving to Atlanta to deprive Wil of his kids, and that's wrong. Those are his kids too, and they love him despite the problems you two may have. You're forgetting that when you punish Wil, you're also hurting those kids."

"What am I supposed to do, Lisa? Let him see his kids when he won't give me enough money to support them? Please," I sucked my teeth. "Wil has a responsibility to take care of his family and he didn't do it. Now he's got to deal with the consequences." Lisa shook her head. It was obvious she didn't agree. I think she was about to drop the whole thing out of frustration, but changed her mind.

"Come on, Diane. You can lie to me, but you can't lie to yourself. You know Wil was taking care of his kids, and you know he was giving you more than enough money to get by. You just got greedy. That's why you lost in court."

"You know what, Lisa?" I pointed my finger in her face.

"What, Diane?" She cut her eyes at me. I wanted to curse her out but I knew she was right. If I really thought about it, she was the only one of my friends who was woman enough to stand up to me and tell the truth. With everything that happened between her and Kyle, she knew her fair share about being hurt. Yet through it all she managed to keep her kids' relationship with their father separate.

"Maybe you're right, Lisa. Maybe I am being selfish. But aren't I entitled? Don't six years of my life mean something? You don't know what those pictures did to me." I started to cry as once again the image of Wil and those women flashed in my memory. I still couldn't understand how he could dishonor our marriage like that.

"I can only imagine what it felt like to see those photos," Lisa said softly. "But I do know what it's like to be hurt. I don't think I'll ever get over how sick I felt when that bitch told me she was having Kyle's baby. But for what it's worth, I don't think Wil had anything to do with those pictures. I really don't. That Saturday I spent with Kyle and the girls a few weeks back, when I found out Val was pregnant . . ."

She paused and grimaced at her own painful memories. "Kyle told me the whole story about how those pictures came about. He swore on his daughters that it was his doing. Wil was passed out."

"Please, Lisa." I waved my hand at her. "I can't even believe you would fall for that. You know those men will do anything to protect each other. I saw those pictures, and no one is gonna make me believe that Wil was not a willing participant in that shit." I was pissed off now. Could she really be defending their lying, cheating asses? Thank God someone knocked on the front door before I really gave her a piece of my mind.

"Expecting company?" I think Lisa was happy for the interruption too.

"No, but I've got an idea who it is. Can you do me a favor and get that?" I tried to compose myself. I knew it couldn't be the movers yet, since they'd just called to say they'd be late. It had to be Wil. I wiped my tears away, but I was sure my mascara was smudged.

Lisa got up to answer the door while I tried to do something with my hair and face. When she returned, she was alone. I couldn't conceal my disappointment.

"Who was it at the door?"

"Mailman." She handed me a priority mail envelope, and the two of us sat down.

I checked the label before opening the envelope. The return address only read *A friend of the family*. I pulled a white paper out of the envelope and placed it on the table. Lisa picked up the envelope.

Dear Diane,
    A few months ago you found some pictures of Wil and some naked women at a bachelor party. Although we agree those pictures should have never been taken, you need to understand something. What happened to Wil could happen to anybody. Even you. It's time to put a halt to all the nonsense. Call your husband. He still loves you.

                        A friend of the family

Yeah, right. Some friend of the family. I wonder who Wil asked to send this. Too bad it wouldn't work. This letter just reminded me once again of those goddamn pictures and made me madder than ever. Call your husband, my ass. They must be fucking kidding me. I was about to show the letter to Lisa when I noticed her nervously hiding something in her lap.

"What you got?" I gave her a suspicious look.

"Nothing," she said nervously. Which obviously meant something. I picked up the envelope and peeked in it.

"What was in this envelope?" I demanded.

"Nothing," she repeated. She was even more nervous now than at first.

"Stop lying, Lisa. I could feel something else in the envelope when I opened it."

"Diane, trust me. You don't wanna see this." I had been sorry when I told her I wanted the truth before, and I'd probably be sorry now, but I was not about to let her keep hiding whatever it was in her hands.

"Give it to me, dammit!" I reached my hand out, palm up, and waited with a frown.

She hesitantly lifted her hand so I could see that she was holding some pictures. Probably more pictures of Wil and his whores, I figured as I snatched them. But I was in for quite a rude awakening when I looked at what I was holding.

"Oh my God! That's me!" I dropped the pictures like they were on fire, and looked at Lisa in disbelief. My mind could not process what I had just seen. There was no way those pictures were really me. No way in the world.

"Diane, you all right?" Lisa got up and stood behind me, her hands on my shoulders.

"That's not me, Lisa. That's not me," I kept repeating. I closed my eyes tight but the image of two of the biggest penises I've ever seen rubbing up against my lips like they were trying to apply lip gloss was burned into my mind. Somehow I managed to open my eyes again and look at the rest of those pictures. Each one made me sicker than the last. By the time I got to the last one, my stomach did a flip and it took everything I had to stop myself from throwing up.

"Why? Why would someone do this to me?" I was crying hysterically now and looked up at Lisa for the answer.

She rubbed my shoulders and spoke softly. "I don't know, Diane. Are you sure they weren't taken before you met Wil? We've all done things we're not proud of." I shrugged her hands off my shoulders and turned around to face her.

"No you didn't! No you didn't just ask me that! You think I would take pictures like this? I wouldn't even do that with my husband. I thought you were my friend, Lisa." I reached down and threw the pictures across the room in anger. "Get outta my house."

"I am your friend, Diane, but there has to be a reasonable explanation for these pictures. They didn't just appear out of nowhere."

"Well, I don't know what it is." How the hell did she expect me to be reasonable after what I just saw?

"Maybe they're computer enhanced?" Lisa bent over, picked up one of the pictures from the floor, and studied it. I wasn't too happy about her looking so closely at me with that monster penis in my face.

"Well?" I held my breath, waiting for her answer.

"No, I doubt they're computer enhanced. It would be pretty hard to do with a Polaroid. So that's out. What'd that letter say?" I handed her the letter and then reached for a picture from the floor. There had to be a way that somebody faked these pictures.

"Oh my God!" I screamed.

"What?" Lisa looked up from the letter.

"I'm wearing my new blouse in this picture. I've only worn it once. You remember last week when I asked you to watch the kids and I came back drunk?"

"Oh, yeah. You and the kids slept over that night." Lisa still didn't know where the pictures came from, but I sure as hell did.

"Hand me the phone," I growled.

"Who you calling?"

"The police. I'm gonna have that son of a bitch Jay arrested." Lisa looked shocked.

"Why?"

"Because he got me drunk and took these pictures of me." Lisa placed her finger over the phone and hung it up.

"What are you doing?"

"I think he was trying to teach you a lesson, Diane."

"Who the hell is he to teach me a lesson? He's running around with some damn girl half his age."

"Think about it, Diane. It's right in front of your face." Lisa waved the letter in the air. "Wil told you those pictures weren't of him, but you didn't believe him. Now there are pictures of you, and you swore that it wasn't really you. What does that say about the pictures taken of Wil? Read the letter again."

I read the letter again, this time out loud. The words hit me like a ton of bricks now that I had seen the photos. What had happened to Wil could obviously happen to anyone.

"So maybe Wil wasn't lying?" I asked sadly.

"I don't think he was, Diane."

I felt like such a fool. I'd taken that man through the wringer over this shit. Made him sleep in a hotel, took away his kids, took him to court. And suddenly I had second thoughts about it all. God, he must have hated me.

"What do you think I should do?"

"Why don't you call him? Tell him how you feel. Tell him you love him. If that's how you feel."

"I don't know if I can do that. I mean, there's so much shit that's happened since then. Why should I think he'd even want to talk to me now?"

"Maybe because he loves you."

The phone rang before I could answer her.

"Hello?"

"Diane, this is Wil."

"Uh, hi, Wil." I didn't know what to say. I was still confused, and although I wanted to believe he was innocent, I wasn't totally convinced. This was one big mess to be sorted through.

"Look, I didn't call to fight, okay?" He sounded so defensive and I knew I'd driven him to it. He was getting used to a fight every time he phoned me. I was about to tell him I didn't want to fight either, but he never gave me a chance. "Is Lisa there? It's an emergency."

"Emergency? Yeah, she's here. Hold on a moment." I handed Lisa the phone. "It's Wil. He said it's an emergency."

"Hey, Wil." I watched Lisa's face go from a smile to a frown as she nodded her head. She muttered "yes" and "all right" a few times, but I wondered what Wil could be telling her that had her looking so pale. By the time she handed me the phone, she was in tears. I put the phone to my ear to ask Wil what happened, but there was a dial tone. I hung up and faced my crying friend.

"What happened?"

"It's Kyle," she sniffled. "He's at North Shore Hospital in Forrest Hills. They said it's critical."

"Oh, God! Come on. Let's get to the hospital." I grabbed Lisa's hand and pulled her to the door. She was too stunned to move on her own, but somehow I managed to get her into my car and sped toward the hospital.

"Where's Kyle Richmond's room?" Lisa demanded. We were standing in front of the nurses' station and she was staring down the nurse like a drill sergeant. She'd regained her senses during the drive and was a woman on a mission. The nurse nonchalantly looked at a chart and pointed down the hall.

"He's in Room 302, but he already has three visitors. Hospital policy says only three visitors per patient in the intensive care unit at a time."

"Well, then somebody's going to leave." Lisa ran down the hall without another word. I glanced at the nurse and shrugged my shoulders.

"Where's the waiting room?"

"Last door on your right." She pointed to the opposite end of the hallway.

"Thanks. If she comes back looking for me, tell her I'm in the waiting room." The nurse nodded and I went to sit and wait.

I didn't follow Lisa because I figured Wil was probably in the room with Kyle, and I wasn't ready to see him yet. Unfortunately I guessed wrong, because he was sitting in the waiting room by himself when I walked in. He had his eyes closed and his head resting against the wall. He was probably asleep and I was glad. I wouldn't have known what to say to him yet.

The big lug still looked good, even in his sleep. He'd grown a mustache and looked like he'd lost a little weight, too. I'd always thought he was a good-looking man, even when he gained a few pounds over the years, but now he was looking like he did when we first met. A sea of emotion washed over me when I realized how much I still loved Wil Duncan. I turned around and headed for the door, bumping a chair on my way out.

"Diane!" I froze when I heard his voice, and turned toward him hesitantly. I tried my best not to make eye contact.

"I'm sorry I didn't mean to wake you," I said timidly.

"It's all right," he stretched, yawning. "I wasn't asleep. I was just thinking about you and the kids."

I gave him a half smile, then turned, hoping to make a quick escape.

"Diane, can we talk? Please." I took a deep breath and turned to face him. He was standing now, looking better than ever.

"Yes, Wil," I nodded humbly. "We can talk. I think we need to." I walked over to where he was standing and the two of us sat down across from each other. Neither of us smiled. We both looked nervous. I didn't know where to start, so he did.

"Look, Diane, I don't know how things got to this point, but I'm sorry."

"Wil, you don't have—" He raised his hand to stop me.

"Please, Di. Can you just let me finish?" He gave me a pleading glance. "I promise you can curse me out all you want when I'm finished. I just wanna say my peace."

I nodded. I had so much I wanted to say to him all of a sudden, but the least I could do was let him say what was on his mind.

"It took me a while to accept it, but now I realize that it's . . ." He hesitated for a second like the words wouldn't come out. "That it's over between me and you." He looked so sad when he said those words. "If you don't move to Atlanta, I'll give up my apartment and move in with my mom. I'll also pay all the bills at the house like I did before. I just wanna see my kids, Diane. I don't want my son and daughter growing up without their father. We may be over, but I don't want my life with them to be over." He reached into his coat pocket and pulled out his checkbook, exhaling a long breath.

"You finished?"

"Yes." He lowered his head.

"Look me in the face, Wil, and tell me you had nothing to do with those pictures." Wil sat at the edge of his chair. I'm sure he was skeptical, since we'd had this same discussion a million times, but he tried once more.

"Diane, I was drunk that night. I don't even remember being there." He sighed. "I can't tell you how many times I've racked my brain trying to figure out how I could let them do that to me without my knowledge. And the only thing I could come up with is that I'm just stupid."

You and me both, I thought.

"Okay, Wil. I'll tell you what. I won't move to Atlanta and you can see the kids anytime you want, but you've gotta pay the bills like you used to."

He nodded, trying to conceal a grin. I'm sure that's not the response he expected after all the grief I'd been giving him.

"Don't get all happy yet. That's not all." His grin flattened. "You're not moving in with your mother either. She's not calling me every other night to tell me how you're driving her crazy."

"So I can keep my apartment?" He looked surprised.

"Hell no!" I sat back in my chair. "Are you crazy?"

"Diane, be reasonable. I can't afford to stay in a hotel."

"You said you wanna be a father to your kids, didn't you?"

"Yes."

"Well, you can stay in the guest room until we figure this out." It took a while before what I said registered, and I think he still wasn't sure he heard me right.

"You serious? You want me to come home?" He studied my face.

"Yes, Wil, I'm serious. We've both made a lot of mistakes. Me probably more than you for not believing in our marriage. But I realize my mistakes now, and I want you to come home. Not in my bed yet, but home." I took his hand and moved from the chair across from him to the seat next to him.

"What made you change your mind?" It's strange. This should have been a happy time, but neither of us was smiling. I guess we were still feeling each other out.

"Something Lisa said, something I was feeling, but mostly a friend of the family."

"A friend of the family?" He had this puzzled look, but then all of a sudden he smiled. "Jay, huh?"

"You knew what he was up to?" I didn't think he would do something like that, but I was gonna be pissed if Wil was in on that shit.

"No, but I knew he was going to do something. What did he do?"

"That's not important, but you tell him I didn't appreciate it. You also tell him he's not welcome in my house."

"Whatever you want, Di. I just want to come home." He had tears in his eyes.

"This isn't going to be easy, Wil. We need counseling. We still have a lot of issues. You know that, don't you?"

"Yeah," he nodded and squeezed my hand a little tighter.

"I love you, Wil Duncan, and I'm sorry." I stroked his face.

"I love you too, Diane," he whispered. I kissed my husband for the first time in months. It's amazing, I finally felt whole again.

46

Lisa

I ran up to Kyle's room and almost fainted when I saw him in that hospital bed. I couldn't help it. I didn't even recognize him with all those bandages wrapped around his head. And he was hooked up to so many machines. I swear if Allen wasn't standing next to him, I might have thought I was in the wrong room.

"You aw'ight, Lisa?"

Allen walked over and wrapped his arms around me. But I didn't answer him, I just buried my head into his shoulder and burst into tears. He rubbed my back softly, trying to control his own tears, but it was useless. I looked over his shoulder at Jay, who was sitting on the other side of Kyle's bed, staring at his best friend. I'd never seen him look so solemn and that scared me.

"Is he going to be all right?" I held my breath, waiting for one of them to give me an answer, but neither of them reacted as if they'd heard me. "Oh, my God, he's going to die, isn't he?" They didn't answer that either, and I panicked. "Will somebody please tell me if he's going to die?" I yelled frantically.

"We don't know if he's going to die, Lisa." Allen finally snapped out of his trance. "The doctor said he's stable, but he's got some pretty bad internal injuries. Not to mention a few broken bones."

"He's lucky, he could have just as easily been killed," Jay added quietly.

I closed my eyes when he said that. It took all my strength not to completely break down in Allen's arms as my mind repeated their words. God, what was I gonna tell my girls? I walked to the bedside and sat in the empty chair, taking Kyle's hand in mine.

"Don't you do this to me, Kyle Richmond. Don't you die on me. You understand me? I want you to wake up," I sobbed. "We've got three little girls at home who need you. And they love you more than anything in this world." I hesitated. "And so do I. So wake up baby. I can't live without you." I covered my tear-stained face because I couldn't look at him like that anymore. God, I wish I had told him how much I loved him before this happened.

"How? How could something like this happen?" I lifted my head to stare across the bed at Jay.

"Something went down between him and Val and he got hit by a car," Jay said abruptly. "We don't know the rest."

"Val? The one he got pregnant?" Just the sound of her name made my blood boil. "What does she have to do with this?" I looked to Jay for an answer but he never even glanced my way. "What does Val have to do with this?" I asked again, this time more sternly.

"I've got everything to do with it. This whole thing is my fault." We all turned toward the door, and there she was. Val, the home wrecker. The bitch that took my man, and like she said, the reason he was in that hospital bed. She was standing at the door with a bouquet of flowers like she was part of the family, and my first instinct was to get up and smack the shit outta her. She had some fucking nerve coming to the hospital.

"What are you doing here? Haven't you done enough? Or have you come to finish what you already started?" I yelled.

"I just came by to see how he was doing. They wouldn't tell me over the phone." I kept looking her way, but she wouldn't make eye contact.

"Yeah, well, he might die. Is that what you wanted to hear?"

"No," she said weakly, tears running down her face.

"So, what happened? How the fuck did he get hit by a car?" She looked at me then at Kyle before speaking. I got up to take a step toward her, but Allen stopped me.

"That car wasn't supposed to hit him," she said quietly.

"No shit, Val. Tell me what happened," I demanded.

"I was in the street. It almost hit me, but Kyle pushed me out of the way." Tears were streaking down her face now. I almost felt sorry for her—at least until she told me the rest of her story.

"We got in a fight about your divorce and he kicked me out of his apartment. I was so mad at him I wanted to teach him a lesson. So I brought an ice pick and slashed his tires. I never thought he would come downstairs as fast as he did to stop me, but when he did, I panicked. I ran into the street. I'd be the one lying in that bed if it wasn't for him. He saved my life."

She began to cry uncontrollably. She must have felt like the entire world had come crashing down on her shoulders and it was all her fault. She looked like it, too. Not only were her eyes red and swollen from crying but her weave was all over the place and it looked like she hadn't combed it in days. Her pants and blouse were all wrinkled and stained with brown spots that looked like mud. I swear she looked like she'd been sleeping in them last night. Matter of fact, the more I looked at those spots, the more I think she did sleep in those clothes, 'cause those stains weren't mud at all. They looked like dried-up blood. Probably Kyle's blood.

"I didn't mean for this to happen. I swear to God, I didn't want this to happen. I love him," she sobbed, glancing over at Kyle's motionless body.

"You said you were fighting about our divorce? Why would you fight about us? Weren't you two supposed to be getting married?"

"I wanted to get back together with him, but he got upset when I brought up your divorce. I wanted to celebrate us, but he was still mourning you," she managed to explain through her tears.

"What do you mean, get back together? I didn't know you weren't together." I gave her a puzzled look.

"We broke up that night I told you I was pregnant. He told me to lose his number and that he didn't wanna be with any woman who could lie about that."

"Wait a minute," I demanded. "Lie about what?" She glanced at Kyle instead of me. "Hey, don't look at him. He didn't ask you the question. I did."

"I know," she replied meekly. "I'm just ashamed of the answer." I didn't feel sorry for her anymore. I wanted to kill her.

"You're not pregnant, are you?" I asked slowly.

She shook her head silently. I suddenly understood how Diane must have felt when she got those pictures and realized Wil wasn't lying. I felt like shit.

"You fucking bitch! I would have never divorced him if I knew that! You did that shit on purpose."

"Calm down, Lisa. We're in the hospital," Allen warned.

"I'm not gonna calm down!" Allen's words made me even angrier. He should have been yelling at her, not at me. I don't know where it came from, but I reached out and grabbed Val by the neck, trying to choke the hell out of her.

"Oh shit, Allen. Get her!" Jay jumped out of his seat.

I squeezed Val's neck tighter, pleased that she was gasping for breath. "This is all your fault, you fucking liar! He'd be home with his kids if it wasn't for you!"

"Stop it! Stop it right now!" I heard a man's voice yelling but paid it no mind. I wasn't about to let go of her until she was dead. "I said stop it! This is a hospital, not a wrestling ring! I'm not going to let you jeopardize my patient."

"Let go of her, Lisa! The doctor's right. This is not good for Kyle."

Allen tugged my arm until I finally let go of Val's neck. It wasn't until then that I realized what I was doing. My rage subsided and I broke down. I succumbed to a fury of emotions and the reality that we might lose Kyle. I was blaming Val, but I still couldn't shake the feeling that it was my fault for not believing him in the first place. Tears streamed uncontrollably down my face. My knees got weak and I lost all the strength in my body as Jay grabbed hold of me. Allen pulled Val out of the room, and I could hear him in the hall convincing her it was time for her to go.

"I want you all out of here," the doctor demanded. Jay tried to guide me toward the door, and I followed as best as I could on my weak legs.

"Lisa, Lisa, don't go." We all froze when we heard the raspy voice. Jay was the first to speak as we all turned to face the bed where Kyle lay.

"Look! He's awake." Jay was ecstatic, and I could feel the joy spreading in the room. After all the tension, it was like we were witnessing a miracle.

"Please, don't go," Kyle gasped again.

"Oh baby. I'm not going anywhere." Tears ran down my face as I went to his side.

"I'm . . . sorry . . . about everything," he whispered as I leaned as close to his face as I could.

"Oh Kyle, you don't have to be sorry," I sobbed. "I'm the one who should be sorry. I love you." I stroked his face to wipe away the tears that had fallen on him.

"I love you, too."

47

Rose

"Waaaaaaaa! Waaaaaaaa! Waaaaaaaa! Waaaaaaaa!"

"Damn! Where the hell is he?" I ignored the baby's crying and peeked out the window. I'd been pacing back and forth to the front window for the past hour, waiting for the mailman. It was a little after four and he should have been here by now. He always came around three.

"Waaaaaaaa! Waaaaaaaa! Waaaaaaaa!"

"Jesus, Jonathan, will you shut up?" I yelled as I walked into the nursery. As I suspected, the little pain in the ass had spit out his pacifier for the tenth time today. God, I couldn't wait until he was old enough to go to day care, 'cause that's exactly where he was going. I swear I never realized how much I hated kids until I had one of my own. I stuck the pacifier in his mouth and breathed a sigh of relief when it shut him up. What the hell was I thinking about when I decided to have a baby? He spit out the pacifier again and I had to stuff it back in his mouth again.

"Y'know, I can't wait till your father gets home," I muttered. The phone rang and I ran to the living room, thankful for a distraction from that screaming baby.

"Hello?"

"Rose, it's Allen. I'll be home in about ten minutes."

"Okay, baby, how's Kyle?" I made sure I asked about his friend 'cause the night before I hadn't bothered and he cussed me out. I couldn't believe it. Allen almost never even raised his voice. But lately every time I opened my mouth, he had something smart to say.

"He's good. Although the damn guy won't shut up now that he's awake." Allen's voice sounded dull, like he was drained. He'd been at that hospital for almost two straight days. When he got home, I was going to have to pamper him a little. "What's Jonathan up to?"

"Oh, he's been asleep most of the afternoon," I lied, praying the little brat wouldn't start hollering. "You still at the hospital?"

"Nah, Jay, Wil, and I are at Margarita's Pizza Parlor on Jamaica Avenue."

"Oh, that's the place with the really good pizza everybody talks about, right? Get me two slices."

"You got two slice money?" I jerked my head away from the phone. Why was he being so cheap all of a sudden? It wasn't too long ago that I could ask for a Coach bag and it would be home before he was. I guess it was time to remind him who was boss.

"I got something better than money, and you ain't had none in a long time," I told him in my sexiest voice. Allen and I hadn't made love since the baby was born, and I know he had to be fiending. Besides, I missed being intimate with him. Truth be told, I really loved the guy. "What d'ya think of that?" I giggled.

"No thanks. I'd rather have the money." His voice was dead serious, and I held that phone in my hand with my mouth open wide. Allen had never declined my advances before, so I figured it had to be a joke.

"Very funny, Allen." I could hear Jay's laughter in the background.

"Did I say something funny?" He was playing with my emotions and I didn't like it. I never thought Allen could hurt my feelings, but ever since his mother died, he'd been doing a lot of that.

"Look, just bring me a slice. I got another call coming in," I clicked over without saying goodbye. He'd better not be messing with nobody.

"Hello?"

"Rose?" I almost peed on myself when I heard Ray Johnson's voice. Where Allen was everything good in my life, Ray was everything bad. Ray was a small-time con man who was trying to make it big. Regretfully I used to mess with him every once in a while when Allen couldn't afford something I wanted. I'd given him the boot a few months after Allen and I got engaged, but he still called every so often since we had a little business to finish. Thank God that would be over soon, 'cause he was getting on my last nerve.

"What're you doing?" I asked, talking real fast. "I told you not to call me at home, Ray. My husband could've answered the phone."

"Well, he didn't, so what's the problem? How's my son?"

"He's not your son. And I wish you'd stop saying that." He laughed and I felt like hanging up. "What do you want, anyway?"

"You know what I want. I want the same thing I wanted yesterday and the day before. I want my share of the insurance money," Ray growled. "I did my part, now give me my money."

"Look, Ray, you'll get your money when I get the check. I haven't got the check yet, okay?" I tried to make my voice sound calm, reasonable, but it was getting hard.

"When my pops died, they paid my mom two days after they got the death certificate. It's been two weeks and I want my money, Rose. Or am I gonna have to tell your husband why his little boy doesn't look like him?"

"Goddammit, Ray! Don't you dare threaten me!"

"You call that a threat?" he laughed. "That's not a threat. A threat would be me going down to the cops and telling them you hired me to kill your mother-in-law. Now that's a threat."

"Who you think you're foolin'?" I hoped my voice sounded more confident than I felt. "You wouldn't do that 'cause you got just as much to lose as I do."

"You think so? I've been to jail before, Rose. I know what to expect. Do you?" That thought gave me a chill.

"Hold on. I think I see the mailman. I'll call you back later." I was grateful to end the conversation. I hated talking about what we had done. I just wanted the act to be erased from my memory so I could live happily ever after with my riches. I hung up and ran to the door impatiently. The mailman handed me my mail like he'd been expecting me. He should have been, considering the way I'd been hounding him lately. I thanked him and went back in the house.

"Damn! Where the hell is it?" I threw the envelopes on the sofa. "Where the hell is my fucking check?" I sat down, trying to calm my nerves, but of course the baby started crying. I ignored him and picked up the phone.

"New York Life Insurance," a female voice answered.

"Can I speak to Mr. Murphy?"

"Please hold." I waited nervously until I heard the insurance agent's deep voice come on the line.

"This is Mr. Murphy. Can I help you?"

"Mr. Murphy, this is Rose Jackson. I still haven't received my check." I didn't have time to exchange pleasantries with this man. I just wanted my money.

"Oh, Ms. Jackson." He sounded like he was surprised to hear from me. I don't know why, as many times as I'd called him over the last two weeks. Maybe even he thought my check should've arrived by now. "I was told that your situation would have been taken care of by today."

"Well, it hasn't," I snapped.

"Okay . . ." He paused. "Why don't you hold on a minute? I'm gonna see if I can straighten this out."

"You do that."

I listened to the elevator music in one ear and the baby crying in the other as I waited. I needed this man to tell me some good news because Ray was starting to be a pain in the ass. He wouldn't implicate himself in a murder, but I'm sure he'd make good on his threat to talk to Allen about the baby if he didn't get his money soon.

"Ms. Jackson? You still there?"

"Yes, I'm here."

"Good. Let's give this one more day. If it's not settled, you can come down to our office and we'll cut you a check. Okay?"

"Yeah, I can live with that." *But after that, I'm gonna have somebody's job if I don't get this damn money,* I thought. "I'll call you tomorrow if my check doesn't arrive." I hung up the phone and was about to go deal with the baby. That's when Allen walked in with Wil and Jay, who were carrying pizza boxes.

"Waaaaaaaa! Waaaaaaaa! Waaaaaaaa! Waaaaaaaa!"

I closed my eyes and held my breath, 'cause I knew what the first words out of Allen's mouth would be.

"Why is he crying? I told you about that shit." He shook his head and walked straight to the nursery. I followed behind him.

"I was just hanging up the phone. I was gonna get him. I swear," I hurried to explain.

"Yeah, right. I could hear him when I got out of the car." He bent over and picked up Jonathan, kissing his forehead. "What's up, little man? You miss me?" The baby stopped crying and grinned at Allen.

Damn! I hated that shit. Here I am busting my ass all day to take care of his spoiled ass and he won't even give me a smile. But the minute Allen walks in the door he's grinning from ear to ear like he hit the Lotto. Sometimes I can't believe I gave birth to him.

"Yo, dawg. Y'all eating or what? Pizza's gettin' cold," Jay called from the kitchen.

"Yeah, we're coming." Allen carried the baby out of the room and I followed. We all sat down at the kitchen table. I could tell Jay and Wil were whipped.

"You guys look tired," I said sympathetically.

"Yeah, it's been a pretty hectic few days." Wil took a slice of pizza and bit into it. "Thank God Kyle's gonna be all right."

"Yeah, between him being in the hospital and getting you and Diane back together I haven't gotten any sleep in three days." Jay sat back in his chair, chewing pizza with an arrogant grin. If Diane and Wil did get back together, he must've had something to do with it. He was just too full of himself.

"Jay got you and Diane back together?" I asked Wil.

"Yep, he sure did." Wil smiled humbly then turned to Jay. "Hey man, I know I haven't told you, but I appreciate what you did. I owe you big-time." He wrapped one arm around Jay's shoulders.

"You don't owe me shit. Ain't nothin' you wouldn't have done for me, dawg." Jay grinned.

"That's great. I'm really happy for you Wil." I set my pizza down. "For a while there I thought Allen and I were going to be the only married couple around here." I laughed, but stopped when I noticed I was laughing alone. They were all staring at me, and the tension in the air was thick. Allen finally broke the awkward silence.

"They're not the only ones. Kyle and Lisa are getting back together too."

"Hmm, it looks like everyone's getting back together. Except you, Jay? When you gonna leave that young girl and get back with Kenya?"

"Will you shut up?" Allen poked me with his elbow.

"What? I was just asking a question." I sucked my teeth.

"No, it's aw'ight, Al. Better she hear it from me than out on the street." Jay took a deep breath and picked up another slice. "Me and Tracy broke up for good a couple days ago."

"I'm not gonna pretend like I'm surprised. She seemed real immature. Did you see the way she acted at the funeral? She had to be five or six months pregnant and had the nerve to wanna fight somebody . . ." Allen elbowed me again so I stopped. Damn, I really wanted to know if that was Jay's baby.

"Yeah, well. A lot of that was my fault," Jay mumbled.

"So what about Kenya? You getting back with her?"

"I wish. The biggest mistake I ever made in my life was walking out that door. I should've never left her in the first place. At least not until I was really sure." He dropped his pizza on his plate. Guess the conversation made him lose his appetite. "Y'know I was miserable most of the time I was married, but now that it's over, I'd do anything to have my wife and kids back," he laughed. "Go figure."

"I guess it's true. You don't know what you have till it's gone." Allen kissed the baby.

"You got that right. You don't know what I'd do to go home and make love to my wife tonight," Jay laughed sadly.

"Yeah, I do," Wil said sadly. "That's why I'm telling you to go over there and ask her to take you back. What you got to lose?" Wil thought for a moment, then smiled. "If you want, I'll talk to her for you. It's the least I can do."

"You don't understand, Wil. Kenya hates me. You didn't see how she acted when I left. Trust me. She don't want me back." This was something new. Who would've thought there'd ever be a day when Jay sounded so humble?

"Please, Jay. You was at the child support hearing. Diane didn't want my ass back either, but she'll be over here in fifteen minutes to pick me up. You never know what's gonna happen 'til it happens, bro."

"Yeah, but it's been three weeks and she hasn't tried to call me either."

"Absence makes the heart grow fonder, Jay. Trust me, that's what happened with me when Cinnamon left." I swear I detected a sigh in Allen's voice.

I cut my eyes at Allen and he had the nerve to smirk. Talkin' about that bitch in my house? He was about to get cussed out. Lucky for him Jay and Wil were there.

"So Rose, what d'ya think? Think she'll take me back?" Jay interrupted my thoughts.

"I don't really know Kenya that well, but it can't hurt to ask. I mean, you guys got two kids together. That's gotta mean something. I don't care what anyone says. You don't just fall out of love with someone you been married to for six years. And believe me, if she loves you, she is probably lying awake at night thinking about you. Wondering where you are. Wishing you were there."

"Well, she sure don't act like she's missing me."

"Of course she don't," I laughed. "She's still gotta have some pride, don't she? When was the last time you called her?" He didn't say anything. "Look, you owe it to yourself to ask her the question."

"What question?" they all asked in unison.

"What question? Isn't that obvious? Ask her if she still loves you. If she can look you in the face and say no, you haven't got a shot. But if she looks away or doesn't answer you, you've got a chance. You gotta read a woman's body language."

The doorbell rang and Wil got up immediately.

"I'll get it. It's probably Diane." He grabbed a slice and walked to the living room. He returned quickly, but not with his wife. Two white men dressed in cheap suits followed behind him. I knew they were police right away. I started to sweat.

"Sorry to disturb your dinner, Mr. Jackson. My name's Detective Thompson. I don't know if you remember, but we met at the station house the day of your mother's death. This is my partner, Detective Royce. We've got some good news about your mother's homicide."

"Just tell me you found my mother's killer."

"Actually, we have." The detective gave a strange smile. "We'd like to talk to you and your wife about it in private if you don't mind." It had to be paranoia, but I swear it felt like both those detectives were staring at me when they said that.

"Look, we're eating dinner, and the people in this room are the only family I got left. Anything you can say to me and my wife can be said around them."

"Okay, suit yourself. Do either of you know this man?" He handed Allen a Polaroid.

"Nah, never seen him before." Allen handed the picture to me. I looked at it, then passed it to Jay. I probably would have peed on myself if Ray had been in that picture.

"What about you, ma'am? You ever see this man?"

"No, I've never seen him before either," I smiled truthfully.

"Is this the son of a bitch that killed my mother?" Allen demanded.

"That's him. His name is Eugene Watson. He's a small-time armed robber and member of the Bloods. A uniformed unit picked him up on a traffic violation and found the gun in his car. When we ran it for ballistics, it came up a match for your mother's homicide, among others."

"Thank God. Now my ma can finally rest in peace," Allen sighed.

"Well, almost."

"What do you mean, almost?" Allen stared at the detective. "Don't tell me he's gonna get off."

"No, but Eugene had some accomplices."

Oh, shit. Ray was supposed to get rid of that gun. What the hell was he thinking about? And why did this kid have it in the first place? Dammit, I don't even know who this Eugene is. I wiped the perspiration from my face and tried to conceal the way my hands were shaking. I was terrified of what else this detective knew.

"Have you ever seen this man?" The other detective handed me a second Polaroid. I handed it quickly to Allen, wondering if everyone else in the room could hear my heart beat like I could. It felt like it was about to pound right out of my chest.

"No, never seen him before either," I mumbled. I didn't take my eyes off the table as I spoke.

"You sure? You looked at it pretty fast. Why don't you take another look?"

"I said I never seen him before," I replied.

"Wait a minute, Rose. Isn't this your cousin?" Allen studied the picture.

"No, Allen, I've never seen that man before," I insisted. Wil and Jay seemed to be shifting uncomfortably in their seats.

"Yeah, you have. That's the guy who ate my steak! I'm positive! I'll never forget that smug-ass smile he gave me." Allen waved the picture under my nose. "Look again, Rose." Everyone was staring at me. Oh God, this could not be happening. Ray promised me they'd never be able to trace anything back to us.

"Are you sure you don't know him, ma'am?" the detective repeated.

"Look! How many times I gotta tell you I don't know him?"

"Well, his name is Ray Johnson. We took him into custody this morning and he seems to know you pretty well." The detective's tone was much harsher now. "He said that you hired him to kill your mother-in-law."

"That's not true." I tried to sound angry. "I never hired anyone to kill anyone."

"Oh, shit! Kyle was right!" Jay yelled from across the table.

"What the hell's going on, Rose? Did you kill my ma?" Allen demanded.

"No, Allen. I don't know what they're talking about." I was on the verge of tears by now. This wasn't supposed to happen this way.

"Before you continue, Mrs. Jackson, I have to inform you that you are under arrest for the murder of Audrey Jackson. Stand up, please."

"What for? I didn't do anything! Allen, tell 'em I didn't do anything!" He wouldn't even look my way.

"Mrs. Jackson, please. Don't make me have to use force." I did as the officer said, and he handcuffed me while his partner read me my rights. I barely heard a word he said because I was too busy trying to will Allen to look at me. He hated me, that much I could tell. "Do you understand your rights?" The cop nudged me.

"Yes, I understand."

"So Mrs. Jackson, did—" Allen interrupted the detective.

"Don't call her that! She doesn't deserve that name. My mother's name is Mrs. Jackson."

"Rose, did you speak to a Ray Johnson on the phone today?"

"No, I told you. I don't know a Ray Johnson." I had to play this cool and deny everything. The way the court process goes, I could probably beat a murder charge with a good lawyer. They didn't have any evidence against me except Ray's word. Who the hell would believe an ex-con?

"So you're saying you didn't speak to Mr. Johnson today?" the detective asked slowly as he produced a small tape recorder from his pocket. He pressed Play, and I knew my fate was sealed.

"Goddammit, Ray! Don't you dare threaten me!"

"You call that a threat? That's not a threat. A threat would be me

going down to the cops and telling them you hired me to kill your mother-in-law. Now that's a threat."

"Who you think you're foolin'? You wouldn't do that, 'cause you have just as much to lose as I do."

"That's you speaking with Ray Johnson, isn't it? He was down at the station when he made the call." I didn't look at the detective. I was too busy hoping that Allen would look my way. I needed him to understand one thing.

"Allen, I love you."

He finally looked me in the eye.

"You fucking bitch. You don't love me. You killed my ma."

"Come on, Bill, let's get her out of here." The officer turned me toward the door. I turned back to look at Allen one last time.

"I love you, Allen."

"Get the fuck out of my house."

48

Kenya

I walked to the front door with an attitude. Someone was knocking on my door, and whoever it was, was about to get a piece of my mind. The knocking had become an obnoxious banging, and it was giving me a headache. Not to mention the fact that it was two in the morning and I really didn't appreciate that I had to get up out of my warm bed to answer the door in the first place.

"Who is it?" I yawned.

"It's me."

I froze, trying to catch my breath. I recognized that voice right away, and my heart started racing. I flipped on the porch light and looked through the peephole. I was hoping my ears were playing tricks on me, but they weren't. Jay was standing outside the door, looking like there was nothing wrong with him being there in the middle of the night. What the hell was he doing here? I hadn't heard from him since the day I kicked him out three weeks ago. I knew I was going to have to deal with him sooner or later, but I would have much preferred that it be *later,* much later.

"Me, who?" I played dumb. I was trying to buy myself some time to think of a good excuse to get rid of him. When I kicked him out three weeks ago, almost everything I said was scripted. Diane and I had gone over every single scenario that might come up that morning and I was prepared for anything he might say. But now he had caught me off guard. He was the one who would probably have things prepared, and that made me nervous. Jay had a way of manipulating me that I can't even explain. I could have my mind made up about something, but after listening to his bullshit, I'd end up doing a complete flip-flop. So the last thing I wanted was for him to come in my house trying to smooth-talk me. I might not be able to get rid of him. Shit, I might not wanna get rid of him. Truth is, even though I kicked him out, I hadn't totally gotten over Jay. I probably never would. I'd accepted a long time ago that part of my heart would always belong to him. So getting rid of him was not going to be easy. Besides, I had other reasons for not wanting him in the house.

"It's me. Jay! Your *husband*."

"What do you want, Jay?" My knees were shaking. I was wishing this was a dream.

"Open the door so I can come in." He sounded so calm, so nonchalant, like he had no doubt I would do as he said. And instinctively I reached for the door. It was like he had this power over me and I had to obey him. Thank God I found the inner strength to stop myself before I opened the door.

"I'm not opening this door till you tell me what you want." I tried to sound like I was in charge, but I knew I wasn't.

"I wanna talk to you."

"Talk to me about what?"

"About the kids and us." The word "kids" hit a nerve and I got pissed. He hadn't even called to see how they were since he'd left.

"You wanna talk to me about the kids? At two in the morning? I don't think so." I turned off the porch light, feeling stronger all of a sudden. "Oh, by the way. Maybe you don't remember, but there is no *us*." I was back in charge.

"Look, I know I shouldn't have come by so late, but you're up now. Can't we talk?" I couldn't believe he was actually groveling. It was so unlike him. Still, it didn't move me.

"Good night, Jay. I'm going to bed."

"Come on, Kenya. I got some money for you, too. I know you could use some money, right?" He was right. I could use some money. After paying the bills, I was broke. I turned the light back on and looked at him through the peephole. He was actually holding some money in his hand. I didn't wanna let him in but I could sure use that money.

"Just leave the money in the mailbox, Jay. I'm not feeling well. I've got a headache. Why don't you come back some other time?"

"Stop playin' and open the door, Kenya. I know you ain't got no headache." I could hear the frustration in his voice as I watched him put the money back in his pocket. It was now or never. I had to put my foot down and get rid of him or we'd be doing this all night.

"No, Jay. I'm not going to open the door. You should have called before coming. Now I'd appreciate it if you'd leave." There. I'd done it. I'd finally put my foot down. But instead of ending the discussion, I think I pissed him off even more.

"What! I gotta call to come see you? Why? You got a man over here or something?" I could hear him fiddling with the doorknob. "Open this fucking door, Kenya!" He slammed his hand against the door, scaring the shit out of me.

"No, you didn't! No, you didn't just accuse me of having a man over here when you're strolling around town with some young-ass girl. Y'know what, Jay? Fuck you! And good night." I turned off the porch light and checked the deadbolt to make sure it was secure.

"Don't do this, Kenya. Please don't do this. I need to talk to you."

"Go home, Jay. Wherever that is," I laughed, walking toward the stairs.

"I'm not gonna leave 'til you tell me to my to face that it's over." He started banging on the door loud enough for the entire neighborhood to hear. Thank God the kids were at my mother's. I walked back to the door and flicked on the light.

"Will you stop it?" He was getting on my damn nerves now.

"No, not until you tell me to my face that it's over. Open this door. Or would you rather I use my key?" My heart went in my mouth when I heard his keys jingling. Shit, Diane had warned me to change the locks but I never got around to it. Lord have mercy. How did I ever get myself into this? I glanced up the stairs.

"Okay, Jay. I'll open the door." I said a silent prayer. *Dear Lord, if I open this door, please don't let this man get violent.*

"I don't want you in my house, Jay. Do you hear me?" I opened the door and stepped onto the porch. I was trying my best not to look nervous, but I was scared to death about what might happen.

"That's fine with me. We can talk out here." He was leaning against the porch railing using this smooth, sexy voice. The way he was smiling you woulda thought we were getting ready to go out on a date. "You're looking good, Kenya. Real good." He smiled flirtatiously. I'm sure he wanted me to see his dimples. He knew I'd always loved his dimples.

"Please, how good could I look? I just woke up and I'm wearing this beat-up old housecoat."

"You see, that's where you're wrong." He gave me the eye from head to toe stopping to grin in a few obvious places. "That old housecoat of yours shows off all those fine curves you got. Baby, you might not see it, but with a body like that, you'll always look good to me. Real good." I knew he was full of shit but I couldn't help it. I was blushing. Jay knew just how to get to me.

"Here. These are for you." He was holding a bouquet of roses and tried to hand them to me. I loved roses and I wanted to take them so badly, but my conscience kept reminding me that he was in love with another woman. So I pulled my hands back.

"Give them to your girlfriend, Jay," I said sadly. "I don't want them." I wanted to go back in the house, but I had to get that key from him.

"Come on, baby. Why you gonna be like that? Me and her aren't even together no more. How could I be with her when you and I are meant to be together?" He was flashing those dimples again, using that same sexy voice along with his charming bullshit. Deep down I wanted to jump up into his arms, tell him how much I still loved him. How much I missed him. But instead I forced myself to remember how I felt when I came home that night and found those flowers and that card he wrote for his little mistress. And I got mad.

"Look! You said you wanted me to tell you to your face it's over. So listen to my words very carefully. We are over, Jay. Finished. Through. Done. No more . . ." I looked at the floor.

He grabbed me and pressed his lips against mine. Instead of fighting, I let him do what he did better than any man I'd ever met. I closed my eyes and let him kiss me. I let him tongue me down like there was no tomorrow. And when he finished, I sighed deeply. Being with Jay was like pregnancy. No matter how painful it was the first time, you could always be talked into doing it again.

"Well? What do you think of that?" He smiled as our lips parted.

"*Mmmmm*," I sighed, stretching my arms. "I think I'm ready for bed."

"Well, aw'ight. Now that's what I'm talkin' 'bout." He took a step toward his car, grinning. "Let me get my bag."

"Wait a minute, Jay," I stopped him. "I didn't mean you were going to bed with me. You're not coming in my house." His grin faded.

"You're joking, right?"

"No, I'm not joking," I said seriously. "Did you really think a little kiss was going to make everything better? I loved you, Jay. Do you understand what that means? I gave you everything I had and you gave me shit. I deserve better than that. No, I demand better than that."

"If you're so against us being together, why'd you let me kiss me in the first place?" He folded his arms across his chest smugly.

"I don't know. I guess I just wanted to make sure I wasn't making a mistake letting you go. Deep down, I love you, and I wanted to see if the sparks were still there."

"Well? Were they?" He flashed those dimples at me.

I hesitated. Smiled as I thought about all the good times we'd shared.

"Yeah, there were definitely sparks there, but you know what?"

"What?" He moved in close like he was about to kiss me again.

"A spark don't mean there's a fire, Jay. I'm sorry but I can't forget all the shit you've done. We can never be together, 'cause I'll always have regrets and I'll always have suspicions. So no matter how many sparks there are, they'll always be doused out by my doubts. I've moved on, Jay. I think you should, too." I was about to go back in the house but he grabbed me by the arm.

"What do you want from me, Kenya? I told you I love you." He was upset, real upset, and his grip was starting to hurt me.

"What do I want?" I pulled myself free. "I want an apology. I want a husband that can admit when he's wrong. I want someone who's going to be there for me and not have women all over the world. I want someone who's gonna say he's sorry. You been here for fifteen fucking minutes and you still haven't apologized for being with that Terry, or Tracy, or whatever the fuck her name is. So what I want is for you to get out of my life." I folded my arms across my chest, figuring that I might just get the first apology of our seven-year relationship. But I'd never been so wrong in my life.

"What do I have to apologize for? You cheated on me, too."

"You know what, Jay? Just give me my money so I can go to bed, 'cause you just don't get it. I only cheated on you because you weren't around and I needed to be held." He actually looked at me as if he didn't understand.

"I love you, Kenya. Doesn't that mean anything to you?"

"No Jay, those words are not enough anymore." He reached out and grabbed me, trying to kiss me again. I resisted this time with a scream.

"Get your fucking hands off of her!" I felt myself being pulled toward the door.

"Huh? Wh-What the fuck? What's he doing here?" Jay let me go right away as he stared at his worst nightmare come true. Standing in the doorway, wearing the robe he'd left behind, was my new lover and Jay's worst enemy, Malcolm. Jay glared at him for a second, then turned his attention back to me.

"Oh, hell no! Not him. You're not fucking him, are you?" His wide-eyed look of confusion was now replaced by a solemn frown. He actually looked hurt, and would probably erupt at any second. The look of betrayal he gave me made me feel like shit, and I wished I could have buried my head in the sand. Malcolm placed his hand on my shoulder and pulled me toward him.

"How could you? How could you do this to me?" Jay murmured, his eyes filling with tears.

"I'm, I'm, I'm . . . s-sorry. I'm so sorry. I didn't want you to find out this way," I pleaded.

"You ain't got to explain nothing to him, baby. We talked about this before. He doesn't deserve you." Malcolm wrapped his arm around me and I swear I wished I could have made him disappear. I didn't want this type of confrontation. Damn, why couldn't Malcolm have stayed upstairs?

"Get over here, Kenya," Jay ordered, and I obeyed, pulling myself free of Malcolm. I took two steps and stopped right between the two of them. Thank God Malcolm didn't demand for me to come back to him 'cause I wouldn't have known what to do. "So that's why you wouldn't let me in the house. 'Cause this nigga was in my bed." Jay shook his head in disgust.

"Not entirely," I answered meekly. I thought about taking a step back when the muscles in his neck started to bulge.

"Why, Kenya? Just tell me why. Why him? Was it revenge?" Jay looked mystified.

"I don't know, Jay. Maybe at first but . . ." I turned toward Malcolm, who was probably not happy about the truth of the situation.

"You ain't got to explain nothing to him, baby." Malcolm gestured for me to come to him, his eyes practically begging.

"Shut up nigga! I'ma deal with you in a minute," Jay threatened. Malcolm took a step closer, throwing his hands up in the air like he was ready to fight.

"No time like the present!"

"Please, Malcolm. Go back in the house." I raised my hand to stop him.

"I ain't going back in the house without you. I'm not leaving you out here with him."

"Why not? She's my wife." Jay tormented him with that fact.

"I don't see no rings on her fingers except the one I gave her," Malcolm shot back. Jay looked at my hand and his face went pale.

"Wh-where's my ring?" Jay glared at me evilly, but I wasn't about to tell him I'd pawned it to pay bills. "I asked you a question. Where's my ring?"

"I told you. She ain't got to explain shit to you. You got two eyes. Figure it out for yourself. Come on, baby, let's go inside." Malcolm wrapped his arm around me.

"Mothafucker, if you don't get your fucking hands off my wife, I swear to God I'll kill you!" I didn't know about Malcolm, but Jay's tone scared the shit out of me. I wasn't afraid for my own safety. He'd never hit me in seven years, but I was definitely afraid for Malcolm.

"Malcolm, go in the house," I pleaded.

"I told you. I'm not going in the house without you." I turned around with an attitude, ready to curse him out. I hated what I was about to do to his ego, but if he didn't realize it was for his own good, too bad. It was better than a beat-down by Jay.

"Look, Malcolm, go in the house or go home! I've got to talk to my husband alone for a minute." My eyes locked on his and I guess he knew I was serious, 'cause he turned and went back in the house without another word.

"I'm telling you right now! I'm not standing out here if you can't act civilized," I warned Jay.

"Aw'ight, I'll be cool." He took a deep breath and wiped his eyes. "Do you love him?"

"I'm not sure I know what love is anymore. But I like him. I like him a lot."

"What about me? You love me?"

"Yeah, Jay, I love you." I wasn't sure I should be admitting that, but I'd already said it, so I continued. "I'll always love you. But that don't mean we should be together. It's time to move on."

"Why? If you love me and I love you, why can't we just get rid of him so we can have our family back?"

"You know why."

"No, I don't."

"Do you remember what I asked you before you left?"

"No, all I remember is you hitting me in the head with that vase."

"Well, I do. I remember it like it was yesterday. I think I'll always remember it." I let out a pathetic laugh. "I asked you if you loved her. And you said yes." The memory still hurt. "Now I wanna know again. Do you love her?"

He looked like I had caught him off guard with that question. Guess he wasn't as scripted as I expected. He didn't even have an answer. He just stared at the ground. Which was an answer in itself, as far as I was concerned. But I still wanted to hear him admit it.

"Come on, Jay. It's not that hard. It's a simple yes-or-no question. Either you love her or you don't."

"Yes, I love her," he finally said.

"That's what I thought . . ."

"But I love you too," he added quickly, though his tone was a little less convincing than before.

"No you don't. You don't love me. You never have." I took a few steps closer and stared him dead in the eyes so he would know I was serious. "I don't know what happened between you and that girl, Jay. But I do know you came over here more out of loneliness than love. I'm falling in love with Malcolm, Jay. I might not be in love with him yet, but he's a good man and I'm gonna give him a chance. You're still in love with that girl. I won't take you back out of pity just because you broke up. Now if you ever cared about me, you'll give me a chance to fall in love." I turned my back on him and went in the house. Thank God he didn't try and stop me.

Epilogue

Wil, Allen, and I walked into the Roadhouse Bar together for the first time in six months and we were all greeted with handshakes and smiles. I must have heard "where've you been," or "I thought you were dead," twenty times as we made our way to a table in the back where Jay was waiting for us.

I have to admit, it felt good to be back in our old haunt. Since my release from the hospital, I'd spent most of my time with Lisa and the girls trying to make up for lost time. What time I had left, I'd talked the fellas into spending most of our free time at Benny's bar instead of the Roadhouse. I'd been avoiding the Roadhouse like a plague because I didn't wanna run into Val. But word had leaked back to me that she and her ex, Terrance, had gotten back together and moved to her hometown in Virginia.

"Damn, just like old times isn't it?" Wil smiled.

"Yeah, I guess," I glanced over at the bar where Val used to work. Deep down I was gonna miss her. We'd had a lot of good times. It was just too bad things had gone so wrong between us. Truth is I had no one but myself to blame for that whole fiasco anyway. I shouldn't have messed with her at all 'til I was sure things were over between Lisa and me.

"What's wrong, Jay? You look like shit." Wil sat down next to Jay.

"Nothin'," Jay sighed sadly. Wil was right. He did look like shit.

"What's up bro? You okay?" I leaned my cane against the table and took my seat. I'd just about fully recovered from the accident, though I did have a noticeable limp that the doctors said would probably never go away.

Jay sighed again as he showed us an envelope. "I got this from Tracy today. She had the baby last week."

"She did?" I raised an eyebrow, studying his face. I didn't know whether to congratulate him or keep my mouth shut. "What'd she have?"

"A boy. She named him Jason." Jay tried to smile, but I knew he was hurting inside. He'd always wanted a son. Now don't get me wrong, I'm sure he loved both his daughters, but there's something special about a man and his son.

"So? You happy about this or what?"

"Of course I'm happy, Kyle. I've got a son, man. How can I not be happy? Do you know how long I've waited for this?" He waved the letter in the air. "What's tearing me up is that Tracy won't let me see him."

"What? Why not?" I asked angrily.

"Some shit about she's not ready for that. She can't see me 'til she knows she's over me." Jay shook his head. "He's my son, Kyle, I should be able to see him."

"You're right, man. Maybe we should talk to Greg about it. He could . . ." Jay raised his hand.

"No, no lawyers." He shook his head. "I'm not gonna take her to court."

"Why not?" Wil asked.

" 'Cause I love her. That's why."

"Yeah, but Jay, you love Kenya, too. And you're taking her to court for visitation." Wil looked confused.

"This is different, Wil."

"How so?"

"I know I've acted like I was in love with Kenya, but I never really loved her. Not the way I love Tracy." Jay hesitated, looking up at the ceiling misty-eyed. "I never knew what love really was 'til I met Tracy. She's changed me. I'm not the same ol' player I used to be. Taking her to court would just send her the message that it's over between us. And it ain't." Our conversation was interrupted by the obnoxious laughter of Judy, the waitress.

"Damn, y'all out on parole or what? I ain't seen y'all together in months." She kept talking without taking a breath. "And Kyle, I heard you were dead."

"No, I'm still alive and kicking, Judy," I smiled at her.

"Well, I'm glad to hear it. What are you boys drinkin'? The usual?"

"Nah, let us have a bottle of Möet," Allen grinned. "Matter of fact, make it two bottles. Oh, and is the grill still open?"

Judy glanced at her watch. "Yeah, it's open for another hour."

"Good, tell Lou to cook us up four of those twenty-dollar steaks he keeps hidden in the back. I want mine medium rare. How do y'all want your steaks?" He looked around the table at each of us.

"It depends on who's paying for it," Wil laughed. "I'm broke. Diane's got me on a budget."

"Don't worry about that, Wil. I got you. Everything's on me tonight, guys." Mister Moneybags gave us all a broad smile and puffed out his chest.

"Well, in that case, make mine well done, and I want two baked potatoes instead of one. With lots of sour cream and butter," Wil ordered without hesitation.

"I'll have mine medium. And can I have some fried onions and mushrooms with that, Judy?"

"Sure, Kyle. And what about you, Jay?"

"Make mine like his." Jay pointed at me.

"Aw'ight. I'll be back with your champagne in a minute." Judy walked away.

"What's up, Al? You hit the lotto or what? I ain't never seen you spend money like this." I sat back in my chair.

"I got the insurance check from Ma's death today." He paused, and we all remained quiet. Finally Allen grinned and continued. "But that's not why I'm picking up the tab. I asked Cinnamon to marry me today and she said yes."

"Get the fuck outta here. Congratulations, Allen!" I grabbed his hand and pulled him in close. "I'm happy for you, man. Damn, I'm happy for you."

"Me, too, bro," Wil smiled.

"I'm happy for you, too, dawg." Jay still sounded depressed.

"So, when's the big day?" I slapped Allen on the back again.

"Hopefully, about four months from now. That's about how long it's gonna take for my divorce to be final from Rose."

"Damn, I keep forgetting you're still married to her. I'm surprised Rose isn't trying to contest the divorce."

"So am I. I was prepared to have to pay her off for my freedom, but she agreed to the divorce and to giving up her parental rights. The only thing she wants is to keep her engagement ring." Allen laughed, and we joined him.

"I just wanna be there ten years from now, when she gets out of jail expecting to cash in that ring and they tell her it's a worthless piece of shit," Allen said seriously.

Judy brought over the champagne and handed Jay a folded-up napkin.

"What's this?" Jay asked.

"Lady over there asked me to give it to you." She pointed at the bar and we all turned. A beautiful, dark-skinned woman with long, shoulder-length hair waved.

"Now, she's fine," I thought out loud.

"Sure is," Wil agreed.

I turned to Jay.

"What's that?" I pointed at the napkin and he handed it to me. I looked down and read the short note.

Hi, handsome. My name's Tammy and I'd like to buy you a drink.

"Well? What you gonna do?" I turned toward Jay and he smiled for the first time since we arrived.

"I'm gonna go over there and let her help me forget my problems with Tracy. That's what I'm gonna do." He reached over and picked up one of the bottles of Möet and two champagne glasses. "If you gentlemen will excuse me." He winked as he left to meet the dark-chocolate beauty.

"I thought he said he'd changed?" Allen laughed. I watched Jay sit down at the bar and place his arm around the woman. He looked back and grinned at us.

"Don't let him front. He might be acting like he's back to his old ways, all right, but that don't mean he ain't learned some lessons along the way. Hell, we've all learned some lessons in the last year. Six months ago Wil and I had our own apartments and were headed for divorce. You were happily married to Rose. Now look at us. Wil and I are back with our wives and you're getting ready to divorce Rose and marry Cinnamon." I glanced over at Jay and his new friend. "The way I see it the more things change, the more things stay the same. That's the way it is when you're married men."

MARRIED MEN

CARL WEBER

ABOUT THIS GUIDE

The suggested questions are intended to enhance your
group's reading of Carl Weber's MARRIED MEN.
We hope you have enjoyed reading about the power of
friendship and what happens when the grass looks greener
on the other side.

DISCUSSION QUESTIONS

1. Kyle's arrest was tragic and should have never happened. How did it affect his marriage and what did you think of the end result?
2. Jay made no secret that he was a womanizer and had no intention of stopping. So why did he decide to marry Kenya in the first place?
3. After five years of dating, Allen finally asked Rose to marry him. What pushed him to pop the question and why did Rose reject the ring he offered?
4. Who were the other women in Kyle's, Allen's, and Jay's life and what did you think of them?
5. What would you have done in Diane's situation? Would you have kicked Wil out? Would you have taken things to that extreme? Did Diane get what she deserved when she finally went to court?
6. Do you think Tracy's father overreacted? Or was he right for cutting his daughter off?
7. Kyle had the chance to tell Allen the truth about Rose before he walked down the aisle but he didn't. Why didn't he and do you think he should have?
8. Who was Keyshawn and what was her significance in Jay's and Tracy's life?
9. Allen was caught between a rock and a hard place when he found out Jonathan wasn't his son. Should he have told Rose he knew the truth or left things the way they were?
10. If you could choose one of the characters in this book to be your mate, who would it be and why?

The following is a sample chapter from Carl Weber's upcoming novel, BABY MAMA DRAMA.

BABY MAMA DRAMA will be available in January 2003 wherever hardcover books are sold.

ENJOY!

1

VALERIE

My neck was stiff from sleeping the wrong way most of the bus ride, but I didn't let that bother me. The only thing I was really concerned about was that my hair was going to look like shit from leaning against the fogged-up window. Lord, please don't let my hair be messed up. My hair was my strength, kinda like Samson's. When my hair was a wreck, I was a wreck. But as much as I hated what these long trips did to my hair, the thought of seeing Derrick every weekend was the only thing keeping me together. Yes, I hated the fact that it was Thanksgiving Day and that I'd be missing my mom's smoked turkey dinner. And the Lord knew I didn't wanna hear my sister Stephanie or my grandmother, Big-Momma's mouth, about me missing all my family from out of town for the second year in a row. But Derrick was my man, and he had to come first no matter what.

I met Derrick about four and half years ago. At the time I was working in the downtown Richmond, Virginia, branch of the Post Office as a clerk. When he walked into the lobby my tongue fell out of my mouth. He was so fine in that designer suit that I wanted to jump across the counter and tongue him down. Six-foot-one inches tall with an olive complexion highlighted by blue-green, bedroom eyes, and hair black as coal, with big, soft curls. His face was narrow, with two of the cutest dimples I'd ever seen. He wasn't just fine. He was *fine!* And I wasn't the only one licking my lips. Every woman in the lobby was staring him down, even the stuck-up old woman who always complained about our service. When he walked up to the front of the line he must have known I was looking, 'cause he gave me a smile that could have melted Mr. Freeze's heart.

"Can I help you?" I blushed, practically begging him to come over to my counter.

"I'd like to mail this priority." He leaned over the counter with a seductive stare. I looked down at the package and noticed that it had a large white label with a James Center law office as a return address.

Damn, fine and a lawyer! I think I've died and gone to heaven, were the only thoughts I could muster at the time.

"I'm a lawyer," he said, showing me those gorgeous teeth as if he was reading my mind. "My name's Derrick Winter."

"Nice to meet you, Mr. Winter. My name's Valerie. Valerie Johnson." I couldn't help but blush again.

"Well, Valerie Johnson, you taking time off your modeling job or what? 'Cause baby, I've never seen a post office clerk look as good as you."

I know it was just a line but the way he said it made me turn three different shades of red. Not only was he gorgeous, he had a way with words that made me weak. He eased me into small talk so smoothly that I ended up talking to him for five minutes at my counter. Somehow small talk became an invitation to dinner and a Post Office line full of angry customers. When I saw my supervisor walk into the building, I jotted down my address and phone number so he could pick me up later that night, and watched the man of my dreams walk away.

It took me almost two hours to get ready for dinner that night, and Derrick, unlike most brothers I'd dated, was on time. There I was, standing in front of the bathroom mirror with a curling iron in my hair, trying to decide if I should open the door or just let him wait until my hair was done. I decided on the latter and ran to the front door, shouting.

"Just a minute, I'm still getting dressed!" I ran back to the bathroom and my curling iron, praying he would understand.

I don't know how long I left him outside, but he was the perfect gentleman when I let him in. He just smiled at me with those pearly white teeth while I admired his dimples.

"Damn baby, if I'd known you were going to look this good I could have waited outside all night." He smiled seductively, looking me up and down.

I spun around so he could see all the curves that my tight-fitting mini-dress would reveal. Taking my hand, he led me out the door to his Porsche and whisked me away to the James River Café, Richmond's fanciest restaurant for dinner and atmosphere.

Derrick treated me like such a lady that night. When we arrived at the restaurant, he wouldn't even let me order. It was as if he knew exactly what was right for me from that point on. We ate shrimp scampi and drank Möet till I was silly drunk, then we walked over to the Riverside nightclub and danced until they were ready to close. Derrick was having such a good time he bribed the owner and DJ into staying open a half-hour longer. It was the most perfect evening I've ever had, and quite honestly, the most fun I've had in my adult life. It was as if that perfect date would never end. By the time I awoke from my fairy tale, it was two weeks later and we were a couple. A month later he'd moved in.

Derrick had shown me romance in ways I'd never dreamed of, showering me with diamonds and furs. He even bought me a new car. There is no question that those were the happiest six months of my life, and if you knew my life, you'd know happiness was rare. Yeah, those were happy times, all right. That is until my grandmother, Big-Momma, got involved. I remember it like it was yesterday. Big-Momma was at the house eating dinner when Derrick looked at his watch.

"I've got to go to court," he said, kissing me as he got up and put on his sports coat.

"What kind of lawyer did you say you were?" Big-Momma asked him with that look she used to give us kids when she thought we were lying.

"I'm a defense attorney. I do mostly legal aid work through the night courts," he answered, no doubt expecting Big-Momma to shut up. But he didn't know Big-Momma at all. Big-Momma never said anything unless she was going to make a point.

"Ohhhh, so that's why you leave my grandbaby every night and don't come home until the wee hours of the morning?"

She lit a cigarette, and that scared the hell outta me. 'Cause when Big-Momma lit a cigarette one thing was for certain, trouble was about to raise its ugly head.

"Big-Momma why you askin' Derrick all these questions?" I interrupted.

"Hush child. Let the boy answer for himself. He's a grown man." Big-Momma smirked at Derrick. "Well Derrick, is that why you leave my grandbaby all alone at night?" I could see Derrick sensed trouble, but he still played it pretty cool.

"Yes ma'am, night court doesn't close until four o'clock in the morning."

I sighed with relief. Big-Momma was up to something, but Derrick seemed up to the task.

"So I guess you know Judge Jackson and Judge Jones?"

"Yes ma'am. I've had a chance to be in both their courtrooms quite a few times." Derrick answered with confidence, although he did look a little agitated.

"Then how come neither of them seem to know you? They both belong to my club, and I asked about you." Big Momma tilted her head as she released the smoke from her lungs.

"Well, there's a lot of lawyers in Richmond, especially in night court. You know the night court judges are pretty busy men." Derrick was visibly nervous as he glanced back and forth from Big-Momma to me. "They probably don't pay attention to a young lawyer like me."

"That's not what Judge Jones said. He told me that night court was actually a very small world and he made it his business to know every lawyer that came into his courtroom." Big-Momma took a long drag on her cigarette then blew the smoke in Derrick's face. "How old are you, young man?"

"Twenty-four," he answered meekly.

"And how old were you when you finished college?" I could see Derrick doing the math in his head.

"Twenty-two." It sounded almost like a question rather than a statement.

"Lord have mercy. Either you're the smartest man in the world or the dumbest! 'Cause in addition to college, law school takes three years to complete, and your math don't add up." Big-Momma shook her head and stared Derrick in the face. "Now, young man, what do you really do for a living?"

Derrick was so embarrassed that he walked straight out the door without saying a word. I got up from my chair to chase him, but Big-Momma grabbed my arm.

"Child if I told you and your sister once, I told you a thousand times. A good man is hard to find, and that is not a good man." I sat down reluctantly and listened to her lecture.

Derrick didn't return home for three days, and I was sick to my stomach with worry. It didn't matter what Big-Momma said, it didn't matter what anyone said. Derrick was a good man. He was probably just a night watchman or factory worker who got caught up in a lie he couldn't get himself out of. I promised myself right then and there that if God sent him home to me, I would forgive all his lies and be supportive in whatever he really did for a living. But I must admit I never expected what he would finally tell me.

"Hey baby," he mumbled, walking past me into the bedroom. I followed behind him and sat on the bed as he opened the closet and pulled out his suitcase.

"What's that for?" I asked, taking the suitcase out of his hands.

He looked at me like I'd just asked the most obvious question.

"You're not leaving me, Derrick. I love you too much to let you leave me."

"Look Val, I'm not a lawyer. I'm the farthest thing from a lawyer." I could see he was embarrassed.

"I know, and I don't care if you're not a lawyer. You lied to impress me? Well baby, I'm impressed. Not with you being a lawyer, but with you as a man. I love you Derrick. I just want to be with you." I walked over and placed my arms around him.

"Valerie, I love you, too." He hesitated before continuing. "But baby, I'm a hustler, a drug dealer. When you first met me I was leaving my lawyer's office trying to beat a possession charge. My lawyer asked me to do him a favor and mail a package."

I'd be lying if I said I wasn't shocked. For some stupid reason I never even imagined that he could possibly be a drug dealer. I suppose the tons of cash he always carried should have tipped me off, but I was blinded by my love for this man. He always seemed so mature, nothing like those roughneck gangbangers whose pants hung halfway down their backsides. I looked up at him. Nothing about him said drug dealer.

"Our whole relationship is built on a lie, Valerie." He reached for the suitcase.

"That's not true. Our relationship is built on love." I felt compelled to reassure him of my love. So without thinking or caring I said, "If you're a drug dealer, Derrick, then so be it. Just make sure you're the boss and not some unimportant street corner gangbanger. Be the best drug dealer you can be, 'cause I don't want my man being anything but the best." I could see the shock on his face as I pulled him onto the bed. We made love right there, sealing a relationship that would end up with Derrick spending three years of his life behind bars and me traveling up every weekend to see him.

I was stunned out of my thoughts when the P.A. system on the bus blared, the driver's voice announcing that we had arrived at Roanoke Regional Prison. As usual, I got the chills when I looked at the tall, castlelike structure of the jail. This place gave me the creeps. Thank God Derrick only had six months to go.

It took almost an hour before I finally reached the visiting room. By then I was dying to see him. I smiled, eagerly telling the captain I was signing in to visit Derrick Winter. A brief look of jealousy came across his face, disappearing just as quickly. I bet he was wondering why a five-foot-eight-inch tall, caramel-colored, Tyra Banks look-alike would be visiting a convicted drug dealer. Well, it was none of his fucking business. I hated black correction officers more than any law enforcement officers, mostly because of the stories of abuse Derrick had told me. They always seemed to be harder on the black inmates because they needed to prove to the white officers that they weren't cut from the same cloth. I wanted them all to know that someone like me was out of their class.

The captain flipped through his book, managing to keep one eye on my chest at all times before he found Derrick's sign-in page. He smirked as he handed me a pen. I almost cursed out loud right then and there when I looked down at the sheet. There on the sign-in sheet for the previous day was Wendy Wood's name. She was Derrick's baby's mama, and I couldn't stand that bitch. She'd been trying to take Derrick away from me ever since we got together. I sighed heavily, tempted to turn around and not visit him at all, though I quickly changed my mind. I had traveled three hours to see him, so I was going to stick around to have the satisfaction of cursing his ass out. I stalked into the visiting room and found Derrick sitting at a table, waiting for me.

Even in those orange prison overalls he was so damn fine. I almost wanted to forgive him for Wendy's little visit. But I couldn't let him get away with that. I had made too many trips to see him and brought too many pairs of tennis shoes, not to mention the two and a half years of celibacy I was going through. He wasn't gonna play me, especially not for that big-ass, weave-wearing bitch he had a baby with. Hell no!

"Damn baby, you think you could look any better? Every week you seem to get finer and finer. Mmm, mmm, mmm, come 'ere and give your man a kiss." He smiled flirtatiously, and I almost melted at the sight of his gorgeous dimples.

He was doing it to me. He was making me blush even though I was mad at him. God, I hated the power he had over me. I was mad. He had done me wrong. Nonetheless, a smile was creeping over my face and I was about to give in as I felt his hands wrap around my waist.

"What the fuck was Wendy doing here?" I pushed him away as I regained my resolve. I could have plenty of attitude when I wanted, and I needed it then. I had to, because he was going to kiss me and then it would have been over. "I asked you a question, Derrick! What the fuck was Wendy doing here?" He raised his eyebrows in surprise then looked around to see who was watching.

"Sit down and I'll tell you," he ordered me through gritted teeth. "What are you trying to do, make me look like a punk?" He guided me into a chair.

"This had better be good, Derrick, or this is the last time I bring my black ass to visit you." I sat down but wouldn't let him touch me. My hands were trembling with anger.

Derrick was silent for a minute. I was tempted to slap him across that pretty face of his, but I waited for his explanation. Finally he spoke in a whisper.

"A couple'a fellas and I started a little business selling weed to the other inmates. Part of our agreement was that each of us would recruit someone to bring weed up to us each month. Now baby, you're my woman, so there was no way I was gonna ask you. I don't want you gettin' into no trouble." He smiled and I felt like I would melt.

"But Derrick, why did you have to ask her? You know I can't stand that bitch." I was indignant.

"Because she's stupid enough to do it. Wendy's not smart like you, baby. She's nothing but a ho from the street. You're a college-educated woman."

He covered his face up with his hands. I wasn't sure, but I think he was trying to hide some tears. I hated times like this. The last thing I wanted was for my man to feel like he was less than a man.

"Val, I love you baby. It brings tears to my eyes just thinking about you coming up here to see me." He reached over and touched my hand. "Look, I'm just using Wendy so I can do business. She brought me two ounces yesterday. Do you know how much that's worth in here?"

I didn't care how much it was worth, I didn't like it. Derrick only had six months left to see the parole board. If he got caught, they'd give him another two years as sure as I was looking at him.

"Derrick this is stupid. You have more than enough money in your commissary. Why do you have to do this?"

"Baby, I can make ten grand easy in the next six months. I'll be able to start up a legit business with that kind of cash." His eyes lit up.

"I thought you were going to college. We don't need any money. I'm making good money now that they made me supervisor at the Post Office."

"Hey, lemme decide what's right for us. I *am* supposed to be the man in this relationship, right?" He waited for an answer. "Right, Valerie?"

I nodded my head weakly and he kissed me.

"Now that's my girl." His voice brightened as he changed the subject. "Hey, did you bring my comic books?"

We made small talk during the rest of the visit, but deep in my heart I was worried about the drugs and about Wendy Wood.